Twinkle, Twinkle

The Sand Maiden
Book Four

L. R. W. LEE

LRW Lee

ISBN: 978-1705822302
Woodgate Publishing

Table of Contents

Map of Wake Realm

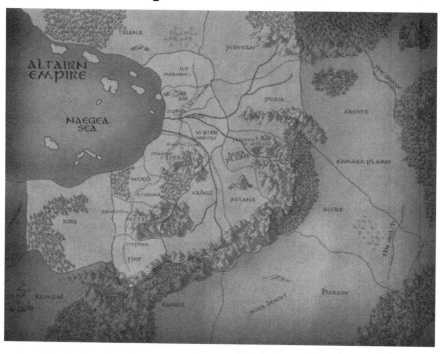

Map of Dream Realm

Map of Lemnos Island

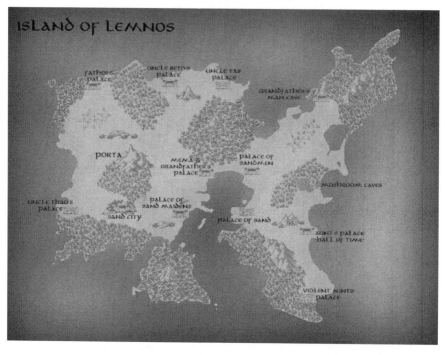

Part I: REM

Twinkle, Twinkle, Little Star

By Jane Taylor
Essex Wake Realm

Twinkle, twinkle, little star,
How I wonder what you are.
Up above the world so high,
Like a diamond in the sky.
Twinkle, twinkle, little star,
How I wonder what you are!

When the blazing sun is gone,
When he nothing shines upon,
Then you show your little light,
Twinkle, twinkle, all the night.
Twinkle, twinkle, little star,
How I wonder what you are!

Then the traveler in the dark,
Thanks you for your tiny spark;
He could not see which way to go,
If you did not twinkle so.
Twinkle, twinkle, little star,
How I wonder what you are!

Chapter One

I tried desperately to beat back the dread that longed to overwhelm me as I followed Empress Rasa.

It had been three suns since she surprised me—shocked me more like—by calling me "sister" and publicly welcoming me into her open arms on the winter solstice. She'd hugged me with a fierceness I could never have imagined her possessing, and I'd relaxed, hugging her back with equal intensity. Sister. I'd spotted silver lining her eyes when she stepped back.

"I think I'm going to enjoy having a sister," she'd added. Her voice had wavered.

I'd nodded. It was all I could do as I brought a hand to my mouth. Rasa sought the closeness of a sister. With me.

She'd gone on to introduce me as Princess Alissandra even though I wasn't yet a princess of the Empire, but of Dream. She'd recognized my nobility all the same.

I would never forget that night.

But she'd been under the inebriating influence of The Canyon's powers, and I didn't know if I should trust this new Rasa to be all I enjoyed with my blood sisters in Dream.

That's why, when I'd received a summons from her steward as the sun rose with instructions to meet her outside the stables in my leathers, dread had instinctively risen in me.

When I probed, Kovis had just chuckled and said to go with it. Sure, go with it. I hardly knew her.

"Good morning, Empress. Would you like me to saddle Arion for you?" a groom asked as Rasa strode into the stables.

"No need, Louvel. I'll do it myself," she replied. I knew from weaving Kovis's dreams that she had started riding when she was five, so she knew her way around the task with no problem.

"Princess?" Louvel asked.

I caught Rasa's glance out of the corner of my eye. I had no choice but to accept his offer. No one had yet taught me how to saddle a horse, not to mention that I was height challenged and probably would have dropped the saddle on my head. I scrunched up my face and nodded.

The groom was kind and gave nothing away concerning my failing. He simply turned and led us down a long row of wooden box stalls. Most of the equines were busy at their feed boxes. Only their twitching ears peeked over the walls on either side.

Rasa stopped at a half door above which a royal-blue sign with the insignia of a swooping altairn, talons extended, declared, "Arion, mount of Empress Rasa Altairn."

She greeted her bay, "Hey boy, ready to go for a ride?"

She talked to her horse as if he was a friend. Did she have a relationship with her mount similar to what Kovis felt for his? Was it even possible? Rasa was always so stiff, so royal.

I heard the stallion nicker in response. I wished I could have stayed to listen in to anything more she might have said to the horse, but the steward continued on, and I followed him past Kovis's charcoal destrier, Alshain, and Kennan's raven-colored stallion, Onyx.

Louvel stopped at the next box stall. "If you'll wait here, I'll have Fiona saddled in no time." With that, he opened the half door and disappeared inside.

The stables smelled of leather tack, fresh forage, and clean horses. Motes danced in the light that streamed through windows near the roofline that spanned the length of one side. I toed the few blades of straw that had fallen on the stone path between the stalls and breathed deeply, trying to calm myself.

When I'd met Rasa outside the stables several heartbeats before, she'd simply said she wanted to show me something. I hadn't dared probe. What could she possibly want to show me?

Not long after, both Rasa and I rode under the portcullis, out of the gatehouse, and followed the path to the left. Only the sound of snow crunching under the horses' hooves filled the air. It was sunny despite the chill, but my mind was too full to contemplate any of nature's beauty that surrounded me. I was too busy glancing at my companion from the corner of my eye.

At the fork, she motioned, then moved ahead directing Arion right, up a steep hill. Fiona plodded behind, along with Rasa's personal guards who kept a respectful, yet protective, distance behind us. I recognized the path as the one Kovis took every annum on his birthday when he paid a visit to their late mother.

Rasa sat rod straight in her saddle as she picked up the pace, trotting up and around a handful of switchbacks until the steepness of the incline forced us to let our mounts set the speed. And Arion did, racing hard up the remainder of the hill. The crisp air made my breath fog in front of me and a chill run up my back.

The snow proved deeper once we crested the hill, and the horses had to plow through drifts that rose to their knees until Rasa stopped Arion and motioned me forward. The horses snorted, catching their breath as she said, "Isn't this just the most magnificent view?"

The view? That's what she'd wanted to show me? I resisted shaking my head. Why not. She was empress. She could show me anything she wanted.

Before us stretched the capital city of Veritas. With the sun just above the horizon, sounds of a city waking and getting on with the tasks at hand rose to meet us. The landscape looked as if a fluffy white blanket had been thrown wide and allowed to settle where it willed.

"It's beautiful," I agreed.

"Seeing the city from here helps me regain perspective at times. From here, I don't see the imperfections. Put another way, I don't see those who make ruling a challenge. From here, I can believe we all get along and that we can build a lasting empire where everyone prospers."

I swiveled my head and looked her up and down as she continued drinking in the view.

Her admission begged for a response. I wondered if it's why she'd said it, but I didn't know what to say. I finally offered, "I want that, too."

"Am I the right one to bring that to this empire?" Again, she didn't move, just looked out over the city.

My heart caught in my throat. She was being vulnerable and more transparent than ever. "Rasa."

She finally turned and caught my gaze.

"We all doubt ourselves at times," I said. "But I believe you have a heart that wants only the best for the people of this empire. I believe if you are steadfast in that pursuit, you will accomplish that desire."

The crisp air fogged as she exhaled sharply. "That perspective is what gave you the strength to leave your family and come here. I admire that." I sucked in a breath, but she went on. "Kovis said you knew about his, about our, past from weaving his dreams."

I nodded.

She looked down. "I've never had anyone I felt like I could tell things and they wouldn't take them the wrong way."

I didn't know if she felt it, but I couldn't miss hearing her longing for connection, for unconditional acceptance. Though unspoken, it was as if she shouted it, and in this heartbeat, I knew I could be that for her. No doubt, she'd never had any close girlfriends; she'd only had her brothers to confide in, and probably hadn't even told them everything. She'd been alone her whole life, through all the horrors she'd endured... I couldn't begin to imagine how she'd coped. I could be a listening ear and an accepting heart for her if she'd let me, no different than for my sisters in Dream.

I pushed down worry that I might be too forward, and said, "Sister,"—she caught my eyes again—"I love you."

Silver rose to line the corners of her eyes. "Thank you." She reached her hand out and squeezed mine, then forced a smile.

She was more like Kovis than I'd ever realized. Her heart had been shut down, and she desperately longed to have it thaw, no doubt so she could experience what it truly meant to live. Kovis had probably told her about that, too.

Rasa swiped a quick finger under her eyes and cleared her throat. "Didn't mean to get all emotional. Shall we continue on to what I planned to show you?"

"This wasn't it?"

"Hardly," she chuckled, then made a clicking sound and spurred Arion forward through the drifted snow.

We passed the ornate but rusted gate to the royal burial grounds and followed the rock wall that spanned the space until it ended. Not long after, Rasa pulled back on the reins and I stopped Fiona beside her. She threw a leg over her mount, and her boots found footing with ease despite the snow.

I, on the other hand, would be unable to repeat her graceful dismount without assistance, and I felt uncomfortable asking her, the empress, for help.

When I hadn't moved, she looked over.

"I'm too short." I shrugged.

She smiled, then trudged between the horses.

A heartbeat later, my boots disappeared in the snow, too. "Thank you."

"We all have our challenges," she said. "Now, come on."

Turning to her guard, she called out, "Please give us privacy. We won't be far."

We dropped the reins in the snow and left the horses to forage what little they could. They wouldn't wander off.

I followed in the knee-deep path Rasa plowed until she stopped, seemingly in the middle of nowhere. The snow smoothed all the rough edges of the trees, shrubs, and other vegetation that surrounded us, and it reminded me of the sandcastles we used to build at the shores of Lemnos Island after the waves had gotten hold of them.

I came up beside her, and she asked, "So, what do you think?"

I glanced about. "The snow is beautiful?"

She laughed. "You're refreshing. You'll always find the best in things."

"My family says I'm all sunshine and rainbows."

"Well, I appreciate your positive outlook." She looked out across the snowy landscape. "I've never shown anyone what I'm about to show you, not even my brothers."

My eyes jetted to her as she raised her hands, palms out and directed my gaze with a nod.

Not far away, the branches of a bush about my height, shook loose their blanket of snow to reveal brown, bare limbs. But they didn't stay bare for long because little green buds erupted. The buds continued growing and became stems with leaves.

I knew Rasa had trained as a healer, and like every healer she would possess both Wood and Terra affinities. So the fact that she could use her Wood affinity to accomplish this didn't surprise me. I'd made seeds sprout and become the vine that Kovis found and followed to find me in that snowstorm mere moons before. But what was she doing?

I kept watching. The stems kept growing and soon tangled with other fast-growing stalks to form… what? What was I seeing take shape?

Wait, part of it started looking like a horse's head? Were my eyes playing tricks on me? The form grew taller and… I swore I could make out the beginning of two front legs.

"Is it a horse?" Awe filled my words.

Rasa shook her head. I furrowed my brow.

I looked again. Was that a fin sprouting from its back?

"It's a hippocampus!" I clapped, as a tail took shape. "That's amazing!"

A corner of Rasa's mouth turned up as she put the finishing touches on the creature—a mane, ears, and flippers for its feet. "Do you really like it?"

"Do I like it? I love it. You're so creative. I'd no idea."

Her eyes danced. "I've been building a collection of figures over the annums. Once I shape a bush or tree, I've gotten it to retain that shape; so all I need to do is direct some of my power to it, and it reforms into the way I left it."

My mouth dropped open. "That's incredible. How did you figure out how to do that?"

"A little trial and error." She beamed and couldn't hold back a giggle. She actually giggled. "Do you want to see the rest of my collection, or at least a part of it?"

"Yes! Absolutely!"

She didn't hesitate to direct life into the menagerie of forms that hid under this cover of snow. She brought to life a sheep, a ram with enormous horns, a sea serpent with its body arching out of the ground six separate times, giant frogs around a pond, a horse-drawn carriage, and even an entire maze. I was speechless. She was a regular topiary artist.

"You said no one else knows about these. How do they stay hidden without the snow?"

"I withdraw my magic and they blend into the foliage of the hill."

"This is just amazing, Rasa. I feel honored that you would trust me enough to let me see your art. I promise I won't breathe a word of it to anyone."

As she'd worked and thrilled with each exclamation I made, joy replaced worry in her, lightness replaced heaviness, and she seemed younger than I ever remembered. She needed more of this. I could definitely be comfortable with this Rasa.

She glanced skyward. "We best be getting back."

The sun had crested in the sky and duties, no doubt, beckoned her. Her smile faded as we retraced our steps, mounted, and headed back to reality and those who were making her life difficult.

What would they do to her next?

Chapter Two

I was enjoying spending time with Rasa, but guilt from knowing I'd killed Velma continually plagued me.

Regret, remorse, culpability, whatever you want to call it, hadn't stopped nagging me since we'd returned from Dream a fortnight ago, and I didn't appreciate Kovis's jocularity as I strode through the door to our rooms.

"Guess what I'm writing?" Kovis asked, grinning.

"Why must I always guess what part of our adventures you're writing about? Why can't you just tell me?" I snapped at Kovis's playful question as Allard closed the door behind me. I regretted it in the blink of an eye.

Kovis furrowed his brow as he looked up from where he wrote at the large, wooden desk. A good size stack of pages lay face up. He'd been laboring on his latest novel for some time by the looks of his ink-stained fingers. He put the quill down.

"I apologize." I stopped, let my shoulders slump, and bowed my head. My emotions had been running high, and I was exhausted.

I'd enjoyed spending more time with Rasa since our return, but I still held aspirations of becoming a healer and had a lot of catching up to do—at least that's what I told myself. In reality, it was the busyness that distracted my angst, which I craved—and so, this sun, I'd been down in the healers' suites with my fellow apprentices, Haylan, Hulda, Svete, and Arabella honing my skill to sense where disease infected a patient.

But when busyness left and I was alone with my thoughts, guilt threatened to swallow me whole. I'd killed my big sister, my most ardent defender, the one who had helped me escape Father's clutches at her own peril. She'd suffered plenty because of me—my back muscles twitched instinctively, my body ever aware that she'd sacrificed her wings because of me.

Velma was alive, thanks to Selova, but I couldn't dismiss the part I'd played in her demise and in her pain. She'd had to give up immortality and come to Wake to escape Father, all because of me. I knew she didn't hold it against me. She'd reiterated that time and again and kept reminding me that she was the one who had urged me to slay her rather than Kovis when Father demanded one of them perish. But facts couldn't ease my guilt. It had gotten to the point that I avoided her, which made me feel even worse. What kind of a sister was I? A horrible one.

Kovis rose and approached. His hair looked like he'd run his hands through it several times. His jaw bore a sun's worth of stubble. His gray shirt and black pants looked a bit rumpled but still showed off his trim form. I usually sent a sensual message—hot, hot, hot.—through our bond as he approached, because it was true, but I didn't even have energy for that tonight.

He drew his arms around me and hugged me tight. I didn't deserve to feel better, but my body surrendered despite what my mind told me. He didn't say a word or demand I stop thinking these self-defeating thoughts, just loved me, as he had since the weight of all that had happened crashed down on me not long after we

• • •

18

returned. It was too much. I was numb, and wondered if I would ever feel again.

At length, he took my hand and led me into our bathroom. A warm bath usually warmed my spirits and chased away the gloom.

I slumped down on the edge of the tub as he turned on the water. Steam began to rise as he removed the decorative clasps adorning my green healer's robe. Rasa had awarded the fasteners bearing two gold altairns to me as champion of The Ninety-Eight along with a money bag. Kovis insisted I wear the jewelry to remind myself as well as everyone else of my accomplishment—for dignity's sake he said.

Next he took my hand and eased his mother's teardrop sapphire ring from my finger. After setting it on the counter, he reached up and loosed the top button of my robe. Despite the intimacy, my fatigue silenced any sensual thoughts. He continued undoing each and every button with care I didn't deserve.

I needed to stop, I told myself, catching my mind's negative monologue. I needed to let go of self-loathing at least for now. It would be unfair to him to hold it so tightly when all he wanted to do was show me love.

He eased my robe off, then started work on my dress and undergarments. Every closure he loosed, he did so with great gentleness until I sat naked before him. He'd started this practice when we first returned from Dream, and it was fast becoming a ritual. Every time he removed my clothes, it felt as if he removed my covering of shame.

"I wish I could truly unburden you, my love." He kissed the tip of my nose. "Now sit up."

I looked into his eyes, silently pleading. Sitting up was the last thing I wanted to do—it took energy—but he wasn't swayed.

"Up straight. That's it. Hands at your sides."

I'd ceased feeling embarrassed when naked before Kovis, but he didn't usually stare at me. Sure he *appreciated* my body when we had sex, but my eyes were usually closed, enjoying all the wonderful sensations he stoked in me. Sitting up made me bare every part of my body to him, leaving no place to hide anything.

Clearly he'd been listening in to my thoughts through our bond because he said, "That's right, my love. I just removed all your guilt, and now there's no place for it to hide or fester. I want you to hold on to this image when your mind starts to throw blame. Banish it. Leave no room for it."

"Is this more of what you learned from your time with Aunt Dite?" I let a corner of my mouth curl up for a heartbeat.

"The specifics were my idea, but it's based on what she said, yes."

Kovis worried that I'd fall into the same trap he had, that he'd been unable to extricate himself from for annums without help from the gods. He wasn't wrong to worry. It had become a real possibility.

I sat up, picturing my naked body, every part of me on display, every part of me laid bare. I drew my shoulders back further to exaggerate the point in my mind. Yes, my breasts were completely exposed, vulnerable. No guilt, no shame, no blame covered me.

That's right, Ali. No shame, no guilt, no blame. Believe that.

I fixed the image in my mind.

"Promise me you'll try this."

I nodded. "I'll try. I really will."

"That's all I ask." He leaned forward and kissed the top of my head. "Shall we get you cleaned and warmed up?"

"Please." Goose flesh had risen as I'd worked his exercise.

"Then in you go." He placed me in the near-scalding water, and while it shocked initially, I soon treasured the warmth.

Kovis removed his shirt as he drew a stool to the head of the tub. His tattoo shown azure—contentment. "Lie back."

I felt my body float upward as it always did when he bathed me. Water began swirling about my prone form. It leapt up, flowed over one arm, across my chest, wet my other arm, and fell back into the tub. It expanded down to my legs and feet and rose up to my head, a water cocoon, just as it had when he'd eased my tired muscles as I'd trained for the Ninety-Eight. He lathered and washed every part of me and hummed lullabies that I'd sung to him as a child.

As he ministered to my body, he stirred life and warmth back into my soul. He loved me unconditionally, as I loved him. Shame and guilt sucked life from me, but he was beating it back. Yes, this was living, and living to the fullest just as Aunt Dite had extolled. I would try, I just hoped I could hold on to it.

Too soon he finished and drained the water, but I felt warm to my very core. He helped me out, then wrapped me in a large, warm, fluffy towel.

"Can we cuddle?" I asked.

"Your wish is my command. Let me clean up. I won't be long."

I changed into my white robe and situated myself on the couch before the roaring fire, tucking my feet under me, and stared into the flames as I waited.

He emerged from the bathroom shortly after, in his white robe and slippers. His dark chocolate hair was wet but combed and his chiseled jaw shaved clean. The part of his tattoo that shown above the vee in his robe shown magenta—emotional balance. I looked twice at the color. I could count on one hand the number of times it had shown magenta.

After sticking his head out of our rooms and asking Bryce, one of his personal guards, to arrange with the kitchens to send up dinner, he nestled beside me on the sofa and pulled me close with an arm around my shoulders. I snuggled into his chest. He was my home and my comfort, and he smelled good—fresh air just after a rainstorm with a hint of evergreen. Masculine. I breathed him in, bringing a smile to his lips.

I reached up and with the tip of my finger, traced the top of the funnel cloud of his tattoo. He looked down and watched me draw.

I loved the artistry that Kennan had used when he'd drawn it— water sprayed from the whirlwind from which altair wings sprouted, and where the funnel touched the ground, it left a trail of

·

cracked ice. It perfectly embodied Kovis's three affinities, Water, Air, and Ice.

"I haven't seen it that color much," I said.

"I haven't been emotionally stable in quite some time, but it seems my body thinks I'm getting there. Hopefully, we'll see it that color more often." He covered my hand with his, then picked it up and kissed my palm. He added another kiss on the top of my head.

Silence reigned for some time until I asked, "How was your sun?"

"Good. I was helping finalize plans for the annual meeting of ministers and nomarchs that starts in a moon. The empire's leaders will start to arrive soon."

"What's that?"

"Every annum all of the province leaders—ministers from magical provinces and nomarchs from insorcelled regions—gather together and discuss concerns and opportunities for the various areas."

"But I thought the Council did that."

"It does, but the ministers and nomarchs are closest to what is happening, so they can report the current state of things. Besides, it gives them opportunity to strut about and act important."

I chuckled.

"They all stay here." He said it matter-of-factly.

"Here, what do you mean, here?"

"In this palace."

I locked eyes with him. "All those leaders stay…"

"Downstairs."

I raised my eyebrows.

Kovis bobbed his head. I sat back.

If they were anything like their representatives on the Council… My stomach tensed. I hadn't thought about the nasty politics Kovis and Rasa had to deal with, in moons. I hadn't missed it, at all.

I'd had a taste of the Council. It had been sour to say the least. They'd been the ones who'd sent me to The Ninety-Eight because they saw me as a playing piece in their game to grab political power from the monarchy. They hadn't cared that it would probably end me; I was expendable to them. Except it hadn't ended me. I'd won, much to their collective dismay. Their scheme hadn't worked. In fact, as the crown's champion, I'd strengthened the monarchy.

And Kovis had strengthened it further when he'd proposed to me. I grinned. Council of little weasels.

Kovis smiled. "It's not at all why I asked you to marry me, but yes it did, my love." He'd obviously been listening in through our bond.

"How long does this meeting last?" I asked, afraid of the answer.

"A fortnight."

There were fourteen provinces of the empire, and their leaders along with their contingent would be staying downstairs. They'd be everywhere. It would be a tense half moon. I'd have a lot to distract me from my guilt over Velma, that was for sure.

Kovis shook his head. "You need to overcome it, not bury it, trust me."

I sighed. "You're not going to let this go are you?"

"No." There was no humor in his eyes.

My shoulders sagged and I barely held back a whine.

Chapter Three
Auden

"Stop!" I cried. "Get away from Rasa! Stop!"

The mare ignored my plea and bit into my charge, as it always did. I despised my powerlessness and fisted my hands. How I wished I could pummel it, give it a dose of a potion it wouldn't forget, but no.

My charge, Empress Rasa Altairn, had always been a challenge to weave dreams for. The cause early on had been her father's doing. The things he'd—I sucked in a breath—even now it filled me with rage. He was gone, I reminded myself. The gods had shown mercy in ending him.

The mare kept tearing into Rasa, emitting greedy, savage sounds. Her terrorized screams filled my ears, and I pulled at my hair and rustled my wings. "Stop, please stop." I hated begging, but I would if it ended this. It never did, but I pleaded anyway.

I tried to block out the gut-wrenching sounds and took to pacing. I'd thought I could weave narratives to help her heal from the emotional trauma that—I refused to call him a father—had caused her, but this damn Council was proving an equal challenge in the upset they caused her. Rogues. Damn scoundrels.

Of late, several members were using her stance on The Ninety-Eight to drive a wedge between her and its civilized members. Emotionally, she felt like she walked on eggshells, but she had to maintain a strong presence so they wouldn't sense weakness. It caused her no end of angst. I did my best, but some nights my best wasn't good enough to suppress her scent of fear, and there was nothing like fear to attract mares.

More of Rasa's screams rose, and I punched a plaster and lath wall. My fist came away bloodied, but I didn't care.

It had to leave her alone soon. My wishful thinking had no effect. At all. And her terror filled my head.

I cursed.

The attack lasted for what felt like eons. Crying, screaming, shrieking, on and on and on it went.

I yanked at my hair, but still her anguish persisted.

I panted as Rasa's shrieks finally abated, becoming cries, then whimpers. That mangy beast slobbered saliva all over her before turning its squalid self around and lumbering away. Good riddance.

I blew out an exhausted breath and ran a hand through my hair. I had work to do.

I hadn't gotten far when pounding on the front door interrupted me. I was at home alone tonight, so I'd have to answer it—Mama and Papa had taken Lizzie, my little sister, to the tavern to hear the traveling minstrel perform. It was a highlight and they tried not to miss it.

Papa was a cobbler and Mama helped run the shop along with Lizzie. I was the only one in my family who wove dreams. They'd been surprised when I'd chosen to become a dream weaver rather than follow father in his work, but they supported my ambition to help humans.

I moved the curtain aside and peered out the front window, down to the street below. In the torchlight, I saw three uniformed troops standing on the doorstep. Odd.

I looked either way, up and down our street of two-story waddle and daub homes, but only lit torches beside front doors populated the street. They'd scared off our neighbors—this time of night folks usually abounded on our street.

Troops had a way of doing that. We lived in a humble village not far from Satirev—above Wake's capital, Veritas—and authority made everyone nervous. Most were simple folk who just wanted to live simple lives. Few held ambitions as I did, and authority was everything simplicity was not. Our friends and neighbors paid their taxes and tried to avoid those with power. For the most part, life turned out fine.

So why would troops be at our front door?

Rumors of citizens disappearing with no trace had surfaced of late, and everyone was justifiably anxious. Mama had said one of their customer's had been questioned. It was all supposed to be hush, hush, so naturally everyone talked about it.

Were they here because people talked in the shop? Did they want to question Papa and Mama about what they might have overheard?

I glanced back at my bed where I'd been working. I hated to leave Rasa in her present state. I'd let them know my elders weren't at home and get right back to work.

"Good evening," I said with a smile as I opened the wooden door.

"Are you Auden?" the tallest, the one in the middle, asked.

I furrowed my brow, confused. "Ye... Yes, why?"

The troop to his right, the one with wrinkles in his blue uniform, rustled his wings as if in a hurry. The shortest, to his left, stared intently at me and fingered the top of the sword that hung at his side.

"King Ambien has need of you, you will come with us."

"King Ambien?"

"Yes, your sovereign. He has need of you."

I ran my eyes over the three of them, not understanding. Finally I blurted, "I am honored, but what could I possibly do for him? I'm just a dream weaver."

"We were not told details, only to bring you."

Out of the corner of an eye, I saw the troop with the wrinkled uniform look up and down the street, and I realized I was alone with them. The bark of a dog down the street ricocheted off the fronts of the houses lining the way.

My stomach tightened. No one knew how those who had gone missing had disappeared, but I could hardly suspect the king's troops. Still they were making me uneasy. Surely one of our neighbors would appear. The street couldn't stay deserted. I'd stall. "Very well. Let me just say goodbye to—"

"There's no time. You must come with us, now."

"I couldn't possibly. I'm working, weaving dreams for my charge." I started to close the door. "You'll have to come back—"

The male to the left shoved a boot in the door's path and all three males lunged for me. It happened so suddenly that I had no time to react. I struggled to wrench my arms free.

"Calm yourself or we'll have to—"

I opened my mouth to cry out and pain shot through my head. Then everything went black.

Chapter Four

"This could be a very *interesting* evening." An empty feeling filled the pit of my stomach.

"Perhaps," Kovis agreed, stopping before me. "Kennan may be upset. Tough. He's going to have to deal with it. You're mine." He planted a claiming kiss on my lips before heading to the bath to clean up.

Such a male. If only it were that simple.

I couldn't get past Kennan's behavior, fury more like, over my engagement. He'd believed I loved him more than Kovis and claimed it had been the only thing that kept him sane throughout his wilderness wanderings. When I'd womaned up and confessed the truth, he hadn't taken the news well, at all. He'd accused me, along with the gods, saying we'd both misled him.

As a result, I hadn't seen, much less spoken with Kennan in quite some time, despite Alfreda's maintaining that I should, but dodging him would end this night whether I wanted it to or not because Rasa had decided our families should get to know each other better since we would soon be related. She'd called for a family night. As far as I knew, she wasn't aware of my strained relationship with her brother, and this evening could well prove awkward.

"You doing okay?" Kovis asked as he reappeared from the bath not long after, buttoning his royal-blue tunic. I loved that color on him because it made his blue and hazel eyes stand out all the more. My heart picked up its pace, making him grin.

Arrogant bastard.

I thought we'd established that I'm not a bastard.

I chuckled, trying to settle my nerves.

"Have a good evening my prince, princess," Ulric, another of our guards, bid as we headed for Rasa's suites. As empress, her rooms were double the size of ours at the other end of the palace's sixth floor.

I squeezed Kovis's arm and took a deep breath as one of her guards opened the ornately crafted door for us and we stepped into the receiving room. It was tastefully decorated in royal blues and golds. Golden sconces, from which a host of candles burned, adorned the walls between the windows on one side, through which I spotted the lights rippling over the Canyon. It was clearly the room of a monarch.

We were the last to arrive, and Velma enveloped me in a warm embrace just inside the doors. I forced myself to return it in full despite the guilt that still plagued me—I was working on it, beating it back, I reminded myself. Jathan switched his champagne to his left hand and gave me an awkward, one-arm hug. It was odd having my master as my sister's beau, but we'd make it work.

Alfreda left Kennan on the other side of the room in Kovis's rough but brotherly greeting and headed my way, gently squeezing my arm when she reached me. She seemed to be healing from the trauma she'd endured at Father's hands a moon before, but it would take time for her to fully return to her former joyful self.

I excused myself and approached Rasa who stood with the windows to her back, sipping champagne. Her ivory dress hugged her curves perfectly, falling to just below her knee. She'd pulled her dark ash hair up in a simple but elegant twisted topknot. She rewarded me with a smile and open arms—she was a pretty good hugger when you got to know her.

I felt Kennan's eyes on me, but he didn't approach. I was okay with that. I wouldn't start something that I didn't know how to finish.

A liveried steward stepped into the room, drew his hands behind his back, and announced, "If you would all proceed to the dining room, dinner is ready."

"Thank you, Rynald," Rasa said, and motioned me forward with an outstretched hand. Stepping through the archway into Rasa's private dining room whose adornments mimicked the receiving room with its royal blue and golds, I took in the gold place settings on the more modest table that graced the middle of the space. A crystal chandelier watched over all the goings on from above the middle of the table. No doubt it had witnessed a plethora of family dynamics, and not just from Rasa's reign but from well before. It would witness the events of this night, too, and I was glad chandeliers couldn't talk.

"No coupling up tonight," Rasa declared. "I'd like everyone to sit next to someone who is not your significant other."

Alfreda bit her lip and wrinkled her brow. Her eyes moved to Kennan, but he didn't react.

I didn't know what was going on between the two of them, but I wouldn't ponder it further in this heartbeat. I had enough of my own to worry about.

I swallowed and waited for several to commit to a place to sit. I figured if I delayed, waiting for Kennan to commit, I could grab a position as far away from him as possible, not that the table for ten granted much leeway.

Ali, you'll eventually have to talk to him. Kovis's tone was light. He was laughing at me.

I know, but...

Kovis's distraction cost me, for by the time I surveyed the table, the only spot unspoken for was beside Kennan. I rolled my eyes. Kovis chuckled through our bond.

Velma sat on my right with Kovis beside her. Kennan was on my left. Jathan, then Rasa, then Alfreda lined the other side of the table. This would be a long evening. At least I had my big sister to chat with.

I turned to Velma as the first course was served, but she and Kovis were already engaged in conversation along with Alfreda. Kovis had apparently asked them about their first impressions of Wake.

Across the table, Jathan was oozing about experiments he and Velma wanted to try with their bond, to Rasa who listened with rapt attention.

I ran my hands down my thighs as I turned to Kennan and forced a smile.

"Guess you'll have to talk to me," Kennan said with a jest that didn't reach his eyes.

I forced the corners of my mouth to rise.

"Seems you've been avoiding me. Alfreda denies it, but—"

I cut him off. "My studies have kept me busy. I missed a lot while I was gone. I've got quite a bit to catch up on."

Kennan raised a brow.

"I was glad to hear they finally let you off bed rest." I hoped he'd run with the topic.

He huffed. I wrung my hands in my lap.

I thanked the gods when the second course interrupted our uncomfortable silence. I busied myself with the soup. "Mmm, this is delicious," I said, trying to avoid more conversation.

"Bed rest gave me time to think." Kennan waited until I looked at him to continue. He smiled and relaxed further in his chair, then found my hand beneath the table and started stroking the back with a thumb. He took a sip of his champagne and in a whisper said, "And I think you nearly pulled off a very funny joke. You almost had me believing your story that you love Kovis more, and I understand why. You felt you needed to uphold his dignity. It's okay, I understand. In fact, I find that not only honorable, but also—" He glanced about. "—very seductive."

I only barely stifled a snort. His thumb kept caressing slowly, stroking gently, circling. It took everything in me not to pull away. He thought I'd been joking? What was going on in that head of his? How deluded had he become because of what Father had done to him? How sick was he still?

"Kennan—"

"It's okay. Nothing you say can stop me loving you. You are the one who completes me, I know that."

My mouth opened and closed. I'd no idea where to even begin talking sense into him. I hadn't sought him out in a moon. Did that not communicate something?"

"All the time I wandered about, our kiss was the only thing that brought me joy, so I dwelt on it, pondering every aspect of it."

Gods help me.

"Despite it being only one kiss, you revealed so much about yourself. You're warm and caring and *passionate*..." His chuckle held heat and left no doubt he'd enjoy going further. He pulled my hand into his lap and continued stroking my palm.

How I wanted to rip it away—his damn caresses nearly pushed me beyond the limits of my endurance—but would I send him over the edge of sanity if I did? As much as every fiber of my being begged me to pull away, I needed to let him down gently.

His eyes danced. "You've probably envisioned me when you're, you know, with Kovis."

I looked down and studied my plate. He was completely delusional. How many times had he undressed me, in his mind? I barely suppressed a shudder.

"What astounds me is that despite what I allowed to happen to you, you trusted me. I saw it in your eyes. There was no hesitation or holding back. Gods, for you to love me like that, I couldn't deny we were made for each other."

"Kennan—" I eased my hand away, or tried to, but he held firm.

Servers set our main course before us, but he paid them no mind, just continued on, smiling. "We both know it, that's the beauty of it. Of course, we'll need to figure out how to let my brother down gently but—"

"Kennan, stop," I said with firmness. I couldn't let this continue. I had to set him straight no matter where it left him. I yanked my hand away, setting it atop the table, in full view. Especially my ring. I made the blue sapphire and diamonds sparkle in the chandelier's light.

He furrowed his brow. "I don't understand." His voice rose.

I whispered, "Kennan, you're mistaken. I wasn't joking or lying to you when I told you I love Kovis with all my heart."

Kennan cleared his throat and his posture stiffened as he took another sip of champagne. I sensed rage rippling off him, and we finished the course in uncomfortable silence.

How bad would this night get before it was over?

Chapter Five

"Our family has a game we love to play called 'dare to bare.'" Rasa drew out her enunciation as dessert was served, leaving no doubt as to the direction things might go.

I had my answer. That's how bad this evening could get. While Kovis and I had played the game several times, things could get downright embarrassing in a mixed setting like this. And with Kennan in the mood he was... my stomach clenched.

Velma wiggled her eyebrows at Jathan, succeeding in pinking his cheeks.

Rasa continued, "It's a perfect way to get to know each other better. Nothing is off limits, just finish the sentence that the questioner poses. We withhold judgment about the response."

"Would you show us how to play?" Velma asked, eyes sparkling.

A corner of Rasa's mouth turned up as she nodded, then turned toward Kovis. I peered down the table to see him grin. Gods, how I loved seeing him smile.

"Let's show them how it's done, brother. Finish this sentence. My strangest proclivity is…"

Kovis dropped his jaw in mock offense. "I have no strange proclivities."

"Finish the sentence," I heckled from two seats down. We'd see if it lined up with my experiences.

His eyes twinkled as he turned to me.

"Very well. My strangest proclivity is that… I *love* running my hands over…" Kovis let the beginning of his answer dangle for effect. Jathan's eyes went large for a heartbeat before he reined in his thoughts. Velma mouthed something to him bringing a smile to his lips—an inside joke no doubt. Rasa was eating it up, grinning like a cat who'd eaten a particularly tasty mouse. Alfreda was clearly at a loss as to how to react. I didn't check Kennan's reaction.

Only once everyone was whispering suggestive possibilities to their neighbor or clearly thinking them, did Kovis finish, "I *love* running my hands over my forest fresh soap."

I locked eyes with him and furrowed my brow. Laughter exploded around the table.

He grinned as he shook his head. "You all need to get your minds out from where you let them roam because it's anything but dirty. I love lathering my soap until the bubbles get so full they fall from my hands. The scent it releases—" He inhaled as if reliving the experience. "—is just amazing. I've never found another soap that smells that fresh."

Soap was his proclivity? I never would have guessed. What other oddities was he hiding?

Because Kovis had responded to the last question, he got to pose the next. I felt relatively sure he wouldn't pick me because I'd probably end up divulging something about us. He peered around the table and finally stopped at Jathan. Beside him, Rasa's eyes danced.

Yes, welcome to the family.

The healer's shoulders stiffened. This would be interesting. I'd never known anything personal about my master. I'd be getting to know him *a lot* better if Kovis's answer was any indication.

"Jathan, old friend," Kovis began. The healer forced a smile and Velma bit her lip. "Finish this sentence if you would. I most enjoyed intimacy with Velma when..."

I couldn't contain a yip. No beating around any bushes. Velma drew a hand to her chest and crossed her legs.

Jathan cleared his throat. "Well now... there are so many possibilities to choose from." Velma pinked as he rubbed a finger back and forth across his lips several times. "I most enjoyed intimacy with Velma when she tunneled through our bond and—" He gave Velma a wink. "—planted several *suggestive* thoughts in my mind."

Had he acted on them? Details, we needed details.

Velma's hand jetted up to cover her mouth. She turned redder than I'd ever seen.

I barely squelched a snort. It seemed he had. No follow up required. I nudged Velma's shoulder. My big sister, the seductress.

Alfreda, who sat across from Velma, bowed her head, but I caught her body shaking in laughter.

Kennan shifted beside me. I didn't turn to see what it meant.

"So then, it's my turn it seems," Jathan said, sitting up straight. He scanned the table much as Kovis had searching for his victim, and stopped at Rasa.

She brushed a lock of hair behind an ear and beamed.

Go, Jathan. It took guts to ask a question of the sort that had been bandied about, to his empress. Even though I'd been getting to know Rasa better, I wasn't sure I'd have had the courage.

"One of my secret fantasies is..." Jathan posed.

"Oh!" I exclaimed.

Jathan's eyes lit with mischief.

From the titters about the table, he'd succeeded in getting minds to go where Kovis had.

• • •

Well played. I didn't know he had it in him. Kovis's tone was full of mirth.

Rasa held up a hand. "I must remind everyone that there is to be no judgment."

Oh boy. It would be a doozy. I wasn't sure I wanted to know Rasa's most secret sexual fantasy.

She dipped her chin down. "Okay, one of my secret fantasies is chasing after and mounting a Pegasus."

Mounting? "What?" I begged.

"Spicy enough for you?" Kennan suggested. His tone held no whimsy.

I ignored him as my mind galloped.

Rasa held up her hands. "I've always wanted to fly a Pegasus. To be unfettered, soaring above the land, experiencing freedom like never before. Of course, I'd make friends with it so we could do it often." She pulled her hands together, drew them against her heart, and sighed. "It would be amazing."

Ah, my mind was a funny place. Not mounting, but mounting. I giggled to myself. Her fantasy was sweet. We had more in common than I'd thought although I'd never envisioned Rasa as a Pegasus kind of gal.

Questions bounced about the table for some time, and we all learned more about each other than ever before. Boy, did we ever. My stomach hurt from laughing so hard. I wasn't alone, judging by the number who held their stomachs.

At length, it was Kennan's turn to pose a question. I braced as he scanned the table and stopped at me. I tried not to stiffen, but failed.

"Okay, Ali, finish this..." His voice lacked all joviality. "I've never felt betrayed like I did when..."

The rawness and hurt that flashed in his eyes, pierced me at my core. Betrayal. That's how he saw the situation? I hadn't... or had I?

Like a burst balloon, levity vanished. Everyone looked on in shocked silence.

"Kennan, that's enough," Kovis warned. "Ali, don't answer that."

Alfreda shifted in her seat and fingered the neckline of her dress. Clearly she and Kennan hadn't been intimate, not with him holding onto the crazy notion that I loved him more than Kovis.

I didn't know if I should be glad he finally understood or worried that I'd sent him over the edge of sanity. Maybe I'd freed him up to take more of an interest in Alfreda; I could always hope. But my optimism sounded hallow, even to me.

Rasa stood. "Oh goodness, it's gotten late. I think it's time to call our evening to a close."

"I agree, sister," Kovis said, also standing. "Thank you all for an evening of levity. I've learned much." He forced a grin in an attempt to lighten the mood, but it fell flat.

Kennan bolted for the exit, leaving Alfreda behind, probably for the best considering the mood he was in. Velma gave me a long look—it was a question only my big sister could pose in that way. I replied with a single nod—yes, Kovis and I would walk Alfreda back, and while we did, I'd get a full measure of their relationship.

I'd told Kennan the truth, but this situation was far from over.

Chapter Six

Alfreda was still bearing the brunt of the aftermath with Kennan a fortnight later, and I felt horrible.

She exhaled heavily, holding up her hands in surrender to my probing. "Fine. Fine. I'll tell you. Kennan has been virtually shut down. He's been unwilling to engage in much of any conversation since that family dinner."

In other words, since I'd set Kennan straight two sennights ago, and she hadn't been willing to talk. It's why I'd been pestering her about it since.

My shoulders slumped. Kennan was behaving exactly as I'd feared.

"I'm sorry, Alfreda."

She bobbed her head, but her empty stare told me everything I needed to know. His moodiness was beginning to make her doubt her worth, no different than how I'd felt when Kovis had behaved similarly with me.

Who knew where Kennan might be in the process of getting over me, but Alfreda needed cheering up. The only question was how?

A possible answer presented itself the next morning when Hulda announced, "Haylan, Arabella, Swete, Myla, and I are headed into Veritas to do some shopping. Want to come?"

"Maybe next time, I was going to spend the sun with my sisters. Alfreda's been feeling sad." I didn't add, no thanks to me. "Between Velma and me, I was hoping we could cheer her up."

"There's nothing like dress shopping at Madame Catherine's to lift the spirits." Hulda wagged her eyebrows.

Madame Catherine's. I tilted my head as I considered. The seamstress had helped boost my self-confidence, no doubt about it. "You know, that's actually a great idea. Are you okay if my sisters come too?"

"Absolutely," Haylan replied. "The more the merrier."

The others echoed her sentiment, so I headed for Jathan's rooms.

"Want to come with the girls into Veritas?" I asked when Velma opened the door.

She smiled and gave me a hug. "Thank you for the invitation. Any other time I'd love to join you, but Jathan's taking me into the city for brunch at a café."

"Things coming along, are they?" I didn't try to hide a smile.

Velma chuckled. "I suppose you could say that."

"Well, I'm happy for you, big sister. Have a good time."

"Thank you."

I grinned as I turned and headed for Kennan's rooms to find Alfreda.

Not long after, Alfreda, my girlfriends, and I strode under the gatehouse's portcullis and emerged into the chill air. Green buds swelled on the branches of the army of almond trees lining the gently sloping path from the castle. It wouldn't be long before they blossomed and broadcast their wonderful scents.

The mountains surrounding Veritas came into view as we cleared the trees. I'd seen plenty of mountains in our travels, but these surrounding the capital never ceased to amaze me. They brought to mind the image of hands cupping a priceless treasure. Having my sisters here with me made it feel as if Dream had gifted me with treasures all its own, and I reached over and squeezed Alfreda's hand as we continued.

"It's selfish of me, but I'm glad you and Velma decided to come."

"I'm glad I came, too." She returned the squeeze.

"Alfreda, have you been into Veritas before?" Hulda asked from behind.

"Just once. It was wonderful."

Hulda moved beside us and wagged her eyebrows. "Did Ali tell you about the time Madame Catherine made her some dresses and… negligee?"

My cheeks warmed.

My sister drew a hand over her mouth and giggled.

Hulda went on to explain with exaggerated mannerisms about the seamstress. At every turn, my sister's eyes grew wider.

"And that's where you're taking me?" Alfreda asked, her pitch rising.

The other girls beamed as I said, "You're a beautiful maiden. Seems to me a little self-doting will do you good."

She looked down, but not before I caught her lips turn up.

Indeed, she was beautiful as well as shy.

We passed wealthy council members' homes off to the right and the spherical-shaped building where the Council met, further on— the outside shifted in appearance, in tribute to the seven affinities, but it didn't affect the inside. I leashed a growl. We'd soon have leaders from every province running about the capital, and I wasn't looking forward to it.

My musings fled when fire, representing Fire magic, leapt up and surrounded the building as we passed—even after all this time, it never ceased to startle me. Alfreda shrieked.

"It's okay," Arabella reassured. "My father is a councilman. I've been inside many times. It doesn't harm anyone. All's well."

Alfreda exhaled and squeezed my hand as we continued on.

At the base of the hill, we reached a tree-lined walking path running along both sides of a watery street and hailed a water taxi.

"Food district, please," Haylan said to the Water mage captaining the craft. He dipped his head, and we pulled away from shore.

We had agreed we'd grab brunch first before shopping, and it wasn't long before the sorcerer was pulling into a dock.

A host of sidewalk cafes with full tables spilling out into the pathway greeted us. Many citizens enjoyed a late breakfast. Others chatted over coffee.

Cinnamon, nutmeg, and pastries—the aromas from one café we approached wafted across our path and grabbed me. There was no way I was passing this place.

"Let's eat here," I said.

No one objected, so we joined the line to be seated. While we waited, I surveyed those already enjoying their food, looking for those who oohed and aahed at the tastes that enraptured them so I'd know what to order.

"Lady Cedany!" Arabella waved, and the woman approached with a warm smile. She was one of two representatives from Water province to the Council.

"Well hello, Arabella. How are you? Fine sun, isn't it?" As always, she was overdressed. A peacock feather that thrust from her broad-brimmed, blue hat fluttered as she stopped beside my friend.

I'd never liked the woman. It was mutual. She'd teamed up with Lord Beecham, and together they'd spearheaded sending me to The Ninety-Eight. Well, them and several of the other representatives. I'd been a convenient playing piece in their political games.

"Me and my friends are going to eat brunch," Arabella said.

Lady Cedany smiled, then raised her chin and sniffed as she looked Hulda and Haylan over. When her eyes fell on me, she wrinkled her nose. "You've picked a fine place to brunch, Arabella, but I won't keep you." And with that she strutted away.

I only barely stifled a sneer. Good riddance. I didn't doubt but what with my engagement to Kovis, she no longer saw me as a convenient game piece to be used, but an extension of the monarchy and part of a bigger challenge she was intent on overcoming.

"She was rude," Alfreda whispered.

"You don't know the half of it," I replied. "I'll tell you later."

"Hey, isn't that your sister and Jathan," Myla said, indicating with a nod.

I grinned. Jathan held Velma's hand across the small, round table for two on the other side of the outdoor patio—they were situated beside the waist-high stone wall that separated this restaurant from its neighbor and hadn't spotted us. It seemed they were deep in conversation, well, conversation and ogley eyes.

Had Kovis and I behaved that way? No, I didn't want to know.

Swete folded her hands against her chest.

Arabella rolled her eyes.

"They're so cute," Hulda oozed.

"Shhh, keep it down," Haylan warned.

A corner of Alfreda's mouth rose.

"Right this way, ladies," a server said, interrupting my thoughts.

She led us the few steps to a table near the walk, and we seated ourselves. I knew what I wanted after having seen two different patrons gush over a stack of flatcakes smothered in sauce and berries, and it wasn't long until our orders arrived.

While I dug into my food, I stole glances at Jathan and Velma. They still chatted, but the looks they exchanged were now pregnant with passion. Several patrons seated nearby them looked away. I stifled a laugh.

We were halfway through our meals when yips and excited cries drew my attention. What looked like black smoke had begun wafting across tables near Jathan and Velma, and it grew thicker.

Patrons cried out, then rose, bumping chairs as they hurried between tables.

I threw down my utensils. "Velma! Master Jathan!" I called, standing and waving my arms about. My friends mimicked, trying to get their attention.

Jathan hustled a wide-eyed Velma toward us with a hand to her back as the black continued to expand.

Was there no fire-bearing mage near who could extinguish it?

We hurried out onto the pathway. People stared, unable to take their eyes off the spectacle as the thick blackness kept expanding. It engulfed most of the now-empty seating area and billowed after us, growing in height as well as breadth.

I stared into the black. "Look at that! It's so dark, everything it touches disappears from sight!"

"Damn!" Hulda exclaimed.

I yipped despite our continued retreat when streaks of the blackness shot up and splintered off, turning at sharp angles as if driven by an invisible force. This wasn't smoke. Smoke didn't move this way.

Passing river taxis slowed, and their passengers pointed and marveled.

"What is it?" Swete's voice waivered.

"Where's it coming from?" Arabella asked.

Alfreda and Myla cowered, and Haylan threw her arms around them as we scurried on, the utter darkness continuing its creep.

As a pack, we stopped in front of the neighboring café, two doors down, but the blackness kept growing. I couldn't see if it expanded in the other direction, but it didn't waft out, over the canal like smoke would, rather it trailed us on the path. At the back of our group, Jathan pulled Velma close.

Blackness continued billowing up. More and more and more of it. I looked hard and traced the newest, blackest part of the cloud, then sucked in a breath. Shit! All this darkness... it was spilling off of *Velma*.

Her face was buried in Jathan's chest, and he was too absorbed in comforting her to notice.

What was happening to her?

My heart raced as more and more black poured off her. I'd never seen anything like it, but it couldn't be good. I had to do something.

I extended my senses to the blackness, and magic slammed into me. Velma was manifesting! It had to be. I'd no clue what affinity this was, but I couldn't deny the feel of raw magic. My powers weren't from the Canyon, neither were hers, it seemed.

My breathing labored. This blackness was nothing but pure, raw power. I sprinted toward her. "Jathan, back away! I think she's manifesting. She'll burn herself out if I don't help stop it."

He furrowed his brow, doubt ghosting across his face.

"My powers aren't from Wake, why should hers be?" I said, quietly. Recognition dawned in his eyes, and he stepped away, leaving Velma trembling, her eyes locked on me.

I'd stripped magic from sorcerers more times than I could count. I hoped I could handle this. Was magic just magic, no matter the manifestation? I'd soon find out.

I planted my feet and braced, then lifted my hands, palms out. *Come to me*, I commanded. I didn't know how much of her power to draw. I didn't want to strip her of all of it and cause other problems, so I took it slow. I singled out one thread of magic from the chaotic bundle and coaxed it loose, then repeated with another, then another, and another. I pulled and tugged and nudged the threads apart. Despite the magnitude of her raw power, it was untrained and submitted to my demands, and I brought it into myself.

I panted and felt dizzy by the time blackness stopped rolling off her. Jathan rushed back and had Velma in his arms in a heartbeat. She would be a force once her powers fully matured and she learned to control them.

I'd saved my big sister. The thought made me grin. Yes, I'd saved her.

"What happened to me?" Velma's voice quaked. I'd never seen her unhinged like this.

Jathan pulled back and grinned. "I believe your magic manifested."

"My... my magic?"

"I've never seen anything like it," he added. "Thank you, Ali. I'm glad you were here. You're the only one who could have saved her."

"Little sister to the rescue," I joked, trying to lighten the mood.

"Are you okay?" Jathan asked me. "You drew in quite a bit of magic, judging by the time it took."

My legs twitched as I bobbed my head. "I went slow so it took longer. I didn't want to hurt her."

"I'd suggest you head back and have Prince Kovis draw some of it off."

Jathan referred to the time during The Ninety-Eight when I'd ripped so much power from fellow competitors that I'd collapsed from the glut of it. I'd convulsed until Kovis bled some of it off through our bond. That had been Water and Ice magic, both affinities he possessed. I just hoped we could do the same with this foreign magic.

"That's a great idea," I agreed, hoping it would work as tremors raced up both my arms. At least I didn't hear buzzing this time. That had to be a good sign.

Alfreda stopped abruptly at my side. "Thank the gods you're okay, Velma."

My shopping companions gathered around. As healers, they'd accompanied us to The Ninety-Eight, so they'd seen me compete, but watching what I'd just done no doubt put my abilities in a wholly different light.

Arabella said, "That was seriously impressive, Ali."

"What caused it?" Velma asked, her voice still quaking.

Having experienced it myself, I knew intense emotions could cause magic to manifest, but Jathan confirmed it when his mouth turned up. "Perhaps we should head back to our suites and find a few *creative ways* to work off some of your passion."

Velma turned bright red. "You mean...?"

Everyone burst out laughing.

I'd saved Velma from overexerting herself with whatever power this was, and it felt good. I had to admit it, and a tiny bit of my guilt over killing her eased.

But what if it happened again and I wasn't around?

Chapter Seven

Ambien

A lightness filled me as I soared over Ramloc, the capital of Abuj, the most remote of the fourteen provinces. Not only was my ability to control humans improving, but my troops had done a commendable job with the tasks I'd assigned, for they'd harvested nearly enough remorrigan—creatures given life by nightmares, as mares fed—to begin my campaign.

Ah, remorrigan, such beauties. The fear dripping off them seduced me, and I couldn't help marvel at my creations. Plain and simple, they enraptured me. My heart raced just thinking of them as I flew on.

Dyeus still had his emissaries searching for me, but traveling alone made finding me similar to finding Aphrodite without a lover. Dyeus was the chief of gods, but he wasn't omniscient nor omnipresent, and on the off chance I was spotted, I'd trained several of my mares to become doppelgangers. The situation wasn't ideal, but it would do until I completed the mission I'd set.

I squinted as I approached my destination.

I knew I was close, but it was never easy to spot the scrim that camouflaged the opening to the underground cave amongst the trees—you'd never find it if you didn't know to look. Dusk made it even harder, but I persevered and several downbeats later, I spotted it and set down.

"All bow for King Ambien," Aamon, the leader of this outpost, cried over the din and laughter as I strode into the low-ceilinged common room. As with every one of my testing outposts, this room was a welcoming space, adorned with a plethora of tapestries hanging about the rough-hewn walls, the finest in stone floors, fresh flowers, abundant torchlight, and more.

Sequestering my subjects in one place, in each province, had accelerated my research in simultaneously controlling the thought threads of multitudes of humans. I'd selected citizens whose dream charges had complaints against their monarchy—humans referred to them as 'rebels'—and extended personal invitations. To a one, they had been eager to participate. I hoped this willingness persisted as more and more of them joined us.

Of course, I'd incentivized them to stay the course with the posh accommodations and superb cuisine I offered. No cutting corners. I needed the utmost in cooperation, and while how I spoke of our objective was important, what they thought about my treatment of them was critical. I could get them to try virtually anything as long as they perceived I valued them and their service.

A hush blanketed the room in a heartbeat and was replaced by the scraping of chairs and the brushing of fine silk robes against the stone floor as they bowed.

"Rise," I commanded, rustling my wings and throwing my black cape over a shoulder.

I scanned their midst, making eye contact with each. Most looked away. A handful held my gaze—these I could work with beyond these experiments. They weren't afraid of me, and I would reward them handsomely.

I nodded to Aamon, and he stepped forward. "Your king would like to continue the experiments he started. Form a circle and grasp your charge's thought thread."

"Majesty." Aamon invited me to the center of the circle.

Several heartbeats passed as each subject connected with their dream charge, but they all looked up in eagerness once they completed the task.

"Thank you, Aamon. As you know, we have been working toward harnessing humans' collective power to rid them of mares. It is why I've been experimenting with directing greater and greater numbers of your charges to perform a specific task."

Heads bobbed.

"Tonight we will attempt a task bigger than any we've yet tried. Together, I will undertake to have your humans rise and gather at a location I specify."

My subjects sent me wide eyes as well as grins, and I nodded Aamon to continue.

"Hand your king your threads."

Without a word, each subject stepped forward and relinquished their charge's thought thread to me, then stepped back. The number of threads were hard to hold, but I managed; and once I had a firm grip, I scanned their midst. Not one had a concerned expression, rather they beamed with pride. They trusted me completely.

My heart panged. If only my children were as they. I beat the thought back and refocused.

While the task was a simple enough ambition, it would take all my focus. I opened my mouth to affect the command when a shriek rose from one of the threads. Judging by the urgency and hysteria of the cry, a mare in Wake had begun feasting.

My subjects fidgeted and looked to me with hopeful eyes.

But it gave me an idea. There were nearly enough remorrigan to begin my campaign, but I'd never had the opportunity to harvest one while controlling a host of humans. What would happen if I was able to create a super creature by harnessing their collective fears? Might I speed my plans?

My subjects became more restless the longer I pondered with the human continuing to shriek, and I held up a hand to still them. I would accomplish my ends, while positioning myself as their hero while doing so.

"I hadn't planned to try this, but I'm going to see if I can combine the power of your charges threads to drive it off," I said. It didn't matter that I misrepresented my true ambition. They might not appreciate it if they discovered it in the near term, but they would love me for it in the end, just as my children would.

I didn't wait to see their reactions because more shrieks rose from the thread. I closed my eyes and followed the scent of terror down the one thread. I glimpsed a sea serpent attacking a boy. I couldn't help but smile. Humans, especially females, created the most frightening remorrigans when they feared for the survival of their young.

I melded all of the threads as the green-scaled snake circled, then lunged at the boy. The female shrieked again. It had to have been an incident that had actually happened because the detail was too vivid for imagination. Even better. This would be an amazing creature. My excitement grew. I just needed to enlarge it and then harvest this beauty. If I could accomplish that... My heart fluttered.

Blood clouded the waters, and the long-fanged beast swished its feathery tail as it came around for another attack. It opened its maw, and I seized my opportunity. I funneled all of the combined energies of these humans into it, and it morphed. Bigger and bigger and bigger. It was working. I was doing it. This remorrigan would be enormous.

The female screamed again and again. I hated to prolong her terror, humans were frail enough as it was, but I would for the greater good. Her next shriek nearly shattered my concentration, and I barely managed to hang on, but I did, clinging to the threads until the mare had gorged itself and released the female, before slinking away.

A creature of immense beauty was left in its wake as I cut the flow of energy. It roared and thrashed, such a wonder and enormous. She'd slither on land and would be a handsome addition to the host. Our enemies would tremble when they saw her. But enough fantasizing.

I refocused and directed the humans' power, sending the creature to the compound for this region, which wasn't far off. I just hoped my troops there would be able to handle her. I'd never sent them such a magnificent beast. I'd find out soon enough. It was my next stop.

"I sent it away!" I boomed as I opened my eyes once more.

Some of my subjects exhaled, others grabbed a neighbor's hand.

I forced the corners of my mouth to rise in an effort to reassure them. "It was a wily one, but I was able to harness the combined power of all of your charges."

I'd stretched the truth, but it had worked.

"What a breakthrough we've experienced," I praised. "This is the first time I've performed such a feat. We've more work to do to expand this on a wider scale, but it's a very good start."

Shaky laughter gave way to renewed pride, and smiles soon abounded as I handed them back their charges' threads.

Aamon and I needed to talk, but as had become my habit, I lingered with my subjects a bit longer.

A female approached. She bowed and kissed my ring. "My liege, thank you so much for this opportunity to serve you in this way. I cannot express how grateful I am to be assisting you in ridding humans of mares."

Another added, "They're vile and despicable and evil, and they've done unspeakable damage to my charges. You've no idea how happy I will be once you complete this important work."

I nodded. "Thank you for your kind words and for your selfless service. Together we will see this accomplished."

They beamed, genuflected, then backed away.

These subjects made me truly happy.

And if my plans received the benefit of more surprise breakthroughs like these, they would come to fruition sooner than I'd hoped.

Chapter Eight

Velma was quiet this evening.

We'd waited until the pits were empty—unwilling to repeat the mistake of revealing unknown powers to unfriendly eyes—before Velma and I headed upstairs to change into practice garb.

I hung up my green healer's robe on a hook and picked up the blue-gray drawstring pants the attendant downstairs had given me, given both of us. "You should see the practice outfit I had to wear in warmer weather." I told her about the skimpy sleeveless top with plunging V-neck that stopped just below the bust line that left my stomach completely bare. "Only a male could have designed it," I added.

She forced a laugh.

I put on the matching long-sleeved, V-neck pullover, as did Velma.

"Definitely female by design." I wagged my eyebrows.

She rubbed the back of her neck.

"I'm here, Velma. Your power won't hurt you, I won't let it."

She only nodded.

After her powers had awoken in such a dramatic fashion, Jathan, Kovis, Velma, and I had researched whether others had experienced anything similar, and if so, how they had harnessed it. Our search had turned up nothing, and I knew that terrified her.

She stood unmoving as I engulfed her in a hug. I wanted to tell her everything would be okay, tell her I understood, tell her she'd master her powers, but I knew from experience, words alone wouldn't help. My heart hurt. She felt out of control and alone, and I felt powerless to help.

We headed back downstairs and found Kovis in the smallest of the four practice pits.

From where she sat looking down into the pit, Alfreda waved as we passed. As had become her habit, she held a sketchpad and charcoal. She was still healing, and I presumed it would be a while before her powers manifested. In the meantime, she'd taken to artistic pursuits. Drawing wasn't among the maidenly arts Mema advocated so I'd never seen her draw, but it was giving her an outlet to release her pain—for some of her sketches were dark. Kennan had given her a few pointers, and she'd taken it from there. She was pretty good.

Velma's afraid. You need to reassure her before we start, I told Kovis.

"This is a controlled area," Kovis said as we reached him in the center of the oval. Then putting on a charming smile, he added, "And you have the most powerful sorceress *and* sorcerer this empire has ever known to aide you."

Velma looked between us, her expression even. Her fears would not be so easily assuaged.

Kovis frowned, then stepped forward and placed his hands on her shoulders. "Velma, you're not alone. Every newly manifesting sorcerer feels out of control. They fear their power can lash out and hurt them as well as others." He let his words linger. "*I* understand.

My powers were particularly difficult to make reveal themselves, but when they finally did, they were immense. No one before had ever had three affinities. I felt completely alone, like a freak of nature, and I had no idea how to control so much power. I felt like it would carry me away."

Velma looked up, into his eyes.

"I have confidence that you can learn how to control your power despite it being something unknown until now. Most of Ali's powers are not of the Canyon either, but she has learned to control them."

Velma glanced to me. She was considering his words; I could see it in her eyes.

"You can do it, Velma." I encouraged her from where I stood a man's height away.

She pondered several more heartbeats. At length, she took a deep breath and let it out slowly, then bobbed her head. "I'll try."

"Trust yourself," Kovis said, before stepping back.

She gave him a long look. I knew that look. She wasn't about to trust herself.

"If you are to learn how to control your power, we need to get it to manifest again. I want you to close your eyes, hold out your hands, and focus on something that makes you not just happy, but giddy. Ali said thoughts of a particular chief healer accomplished it the first time." Kovis wagged his eyebrows. I snickered. Sexual suggestions had definitely worked for me.

Velma smirked, then shut her eyes and held her hands out.

Scratching sounds rose from above. Alfreda was at work capturing us.

"Do you have an image in mind?" Kovis asked. His eyes danced.

Velma nodded, smiling.

"Good. When I use Air magic, I focus on the air moving around me. I picture it moving between my fingers. I want you to imagine pushing your shadows out of you, directing them between your fingers."

She nodded.

We waited several heartbeats, but nothing happened.

Velma opened her eyes again. "I can't keep both images in mind."

"There's no hurry. Take your time, just keep trying," I encouraged.

She took a deep breath and closed her eyes again.

The sky had darkened and the torches ringing the perimeter of our pit lit up without warning, and I yelped.

Kovis glanced over and winked. *I'm imagining a little something between you and me that'll make you yelp. Interested?*

A corner of my mouth rose. *I might be.*

"I... I can't do it." Velma interrupted our banter.

I really hated thinking about my big sister's love life, with my master no less, but if it helped her... "Try imagining your shadows erupting *from certain of Jathan's parts* as he... you know." I drew out the words trying to make them sound seductive.

Kovis's mouth dropped open, and he barely stifled a laugh. *Is that how you mastered it, for me?*

I'll never tell. I grinned.

Velma's cheeks pinked, and she furrowed her brow, but she shut her eyes again and raised her arms.

In the blink of an eye, a wisp of black issued from her outstretched hands.

Kovis grinned.

I suppressed a giggle. What a passionate minx she was.

The smile fell away from Kovis's face as he watched more of the darkness erupt. I'd tried to describe what had happened at the restaurant, but I hadn't done it justice. I'd never seen anything like it.

He looked to me. *This is what I drained off you?*

It had been a challenge to bleed me of the excess magic surging through my veins, especially when Kovis hadn't known what we were dealing with and he didn't possess the affinity. It had been experimentation at its finest, but it had worked.

More blackness leaked from Velma and rose into the night.

She's doing it!

The darkness, as thick as it had been at the restaurant, floated aimlessly as more and more of it rose. It obscured the moon as well as the stars and blotted out the lights dancing above the Canyon.

The torchlight ringing the pit vanished next, and we stood in near darkness, blackness swirling around us. I could barely make out Kovis and Velma.

Alfreda's scratching ceased.

"Ease up. You've done well," Kovis instructed.

But Velma's breathing accelerated, and she began whimpering. More inky blackness shot from her hands, obscuring both of them.

"Velma," Kovis said with firmness.

But in the blink of an eye, the blackness coalesced into a column above us. Velma was shaking uncontrollably as the darkness surged straight up into the night sky, then took a sharp turn and shot back for us.

Alfreda shrieked.

"Velma!" I yelled as I dove out of the way.

Kovis tackled her, covering her with his body.

The column of darkness slammed into the sand on the floor of the pit, then surged around the curved wall, swallowing all light.

Velma moaned, and the darkness again shot skyward. "No! Don't! Please don't hurt me!"

The torches reappeared and Kovis rolled off her.

"Velma, focus on Jathan," I told her. It seemed her mind had strayed and relived how she'd gained Jathan to begin with, chased from Dream to Wake as it were.

"Please… No! Not my wings…" Velma mewled as blackness continued pouring from her hands.

"Velma, refocus," Kovis commanded.

Alfreda flew down the steps and threw her arms around Velma's fetal form as darkness consumed us again.

"I'm here, Velma. I'm here," Alfreda's voice punctured the void.

Velma loosed an anguished cry and began sobbing. "He cut off..."

Blackness shot skyward again, but crashed back down upon us in heartbeats.

Velma's sobs turned agonized. "I tried to protect..."

Over and over and over again the blackness swallowed us. Faster and faster as Velma shattered. It rippled off her in waves, more and more and more of it.

I scrambled over to Kovis. "Help me stop it before she burns herself out!"

I'd grown accustomed to and stopped noticing Kovis's thrum, but in this heartbeat it intensified. "Tell me how."

Velma cried out, "Stop! Stop!" Her voice was rough, desperate.

She'd bottled up all that pain and abuse, no doubt because she thought she needed to be strong for us. But all pain, especially as traumatic as Father had dished out, eventually showed itself. Kovis and I knew that all too well.

"It's okay, Velma," Alfreda soothed.

The growing mass of blackness swooped down upon us again, then shot back into the sky.

I'd never tried to harness free-flowing power; I'd only drawn raw magic from a sorcerer before they released it. How could I grab hold?

I stood and assumed a fighting stance, arms extended, as Velma continued sobbing. Kovis stood beside me, bracing.

I held up my hands. *I'm going to try and draw it in like I usually do. It just won't be from a sorcerer.*

It's too strong, there's too much of it. It'll overpower you, Ali. Worry laced his words. *Water dilutes lots of things. Let me try to dilute it with Water magic first. I've no idea if it'll work, but it's worth a try.*

I nodded and Kovis extended his hands as the darkness shot for us. Water magic exploded from his palms wetting every surface of the pit, but the dark column didn't slow or thin. He tried again as it returned. Still nothing.

Let me try freezing it, he said.

Kovis directed Ice into the void as it shot for us. Water vapor must have remained from his first attempts, because a vein of ice formed in the midst of the black and its pace slowed.

It's working! I said.

I grabbed threads of Ice magic from sorcerers in the castle and joined with his, enhancing his Ice for the thing's next pass, and it slowed further.

Velma had calmed some, crying softly.

More pummeling with Ice slowed the darkness further, and it began to drift about the pit.

Kovis looked over at me. *I've never seen anything like it.*

Guess it's not from here. I grinned.

Kovis rolled his eyes. *More powers from an unknown origin. What is this world coming to? I'm curious to know if she got any of the Canyon's gifts.*

Another time.

Velma eased up to sitting, wiped her eyes, and took a deep breath. "I'm sorry..."

Alfreda sent her a watery smile.

"You've nothing to be sorry for, Velma."

The black floated between us, and she and Alfreda again winked from sight.

"Are you okay?" I asked once it passed.

She didn't say, only explained. "I tried focusing on Jathan, but whatever this magic is, it brought horrific images to my mind. I felt as if I was drowning in evil. I couldn't stop it. It overwhelmed me."

I shivered at the horrifying thought. So her episode hadn't been brought on by her mind tracing the events that drew her to Wake; no, it had been a feeling of being overwhelmed by evil. I didn't know which was worse. "Oh Velma, I'm sorry you had to experience that."

"We will have to find another way of accessing your powers," Kovis said.

"Thank you," Velma whispered.

Alfreda wrinkled her nose and waved at the odious black that continued drifting about. "Ali, can you get rid of the rest of that?"

I looked to Velma. What was the saying "If you get thrown by a horse, you have to get back on."?

Alfreda gave me a long look.

"It's greatly diminished. If you can harness this, you can control it," I said.

Velma bit her lip and shifted, considering for several heartbeats. At length she said, "I'll try."

"Think about drawing it into yourself and burying it," Kovis coached.

Velma glared at him, the idea repugnant, but she held out her hands, then closed her eyes and said, "Return to me." Nothing happened at first, but the longer she tried, the shadows finally drifted toward her. She winked from sight as they condensed, and Alfreda gasped.

But the black obeyed, disappearing into her outstretched hands. More and more and more of it until no shadows were left, and she let out a long breath. "It's a start."

"And a good one at that," Kovis agreed.

Her gift, if that's what you called it, was darkness and shadows. I wondered how much of the same dwelt in her. Would it ever be something Velma treasured, or would it always cause her pain?

Chapter Nine

"I have a surprise for you," Kovis said as I returned to our rooms sometime later, after a long sun spent with the healers. His eyes danced and brought a smile to my face. "Go pretty yourself up."

I did as he bid and headed for the bath.

I emerged after cleaning up. I'd donned my favorite black evening dress, another of Madame Catherine's exclusive designs. "Kovis, can you help me with this choker?" I looked around. "Kovis?"

Where was he? Where could he have gone?

I set the necklace aside and popped my head out the door. "Bryce, did Prince Kovis leave?"

One of our personal guards, Bryce smiled, then extended a white primrose bouquet. Markett, who stood guarding Kennan's rooms across the hall, straightened.

Bryce went on, "He asked me to give these to you. You are to follow the trail." He pointed at a host of white petals scattered in a line that began at our door and extended down the hallway toward the vestibule.

I laughed as I accepted the flowers and sniffed—they smelled sweet like honey. *What are you up to, my Dreambeam?*

Come and see. He gave a smoky-sounding chuckle.

Oh boy.

"Do you know where this leads?" I asked Bryce.

"I'm sorry, I do not. Would you like me to escort you to find him?"

Judging by Kovis's inflections, the guard's assistance would only lead to one or both of us being embarrassed. "No, that's okay."

I stepped back inside, grabbed my cloak, then headed back into the hall. Sniffing Kovis's gift again, I set out to find him, joy filling my heart. It seemed my Dreambeam was continuing to take Dite's admonitions to heart. It's what I'd always wanted for him, and I would help him succeed.

Curiosity and Kovis's deep, seductive chuckle had my heart skipping a few beats before long as well as heat igniting between my legs.

The trail turned right at the first-floor landing, and I furrowed my brow. I'd never gone this direction. The only things down here were storage rooms as far as I knew. It's where those rebels had hauled those boxes when I'd happened upon them in the dark that time.

A clandestine meeting in a storage closet? Trying to up the excitement of having someone happen upon us as we... you know...

Kovis laughed. *You're giving me some excellent ideas, love.* I could picture his depthless blue eyes with those luscious hazel centers sparkling as he said it.

I continued past and the trail came to an abrupt halt at a heavy, reinforced wooden door. *What?*

Put your shoulder into it, Kovis coached.

I strained and the barrier finally gave way. I stepped through and stopped as the door thudded close behind me. I drew a hand to my chest. *Is this your mother's garden?*

It is.

It's beautiful. No doubt awe filled my words.

I'd known of its existence but had never considered where it might be.

I scanned the space. A wall stretched around the garden a good ways off. A greenhouse stood to my left. Torches lit a stone-bordered, pebble walking path that meandered through and between colorful and fragrant trees and flower beds. It was a horticultural masterpiece.

Come find your surprise, Kovis said in his sexy bedroom voice, breaking the trance the garden's beauty had cast over me. My face warmed.

I was practically jogging, still following that damn petal path as I emerged from the manicured beds.

A large pond stretched out before me with a quaint little island in the middle. A sandy beach marked the shoreline along with glowing torches. Two birds exchanged calls as dusk swallowed the last vestiges of light. I just wished I could fully enjoy it, but the heat growing between my legs was slowly stirring me into a frenzy. I threw the bouquet of flowers down.

I had to find him. Soon. Sooner. Now.

Kovis cleared his throat, drawing my attention left, and oh my ever-loving heart did race.

Torches surrounded a blue and white striped blanket he'd spread out on the sloping bank, and I could see nearly every fingerbreadth of his sculptured, naked body. He grinned, in all his glory where he lay, propped up on an elbow, his muscled legs crossed at the ankles. His manhood stood at attention as he patted the blanket. "Come join me."

I beamed like a stupid fool in love as I joined him on the blanket. "There's a lot of sand. You're not worried I'll put you to sleep?" It seemed every time he pleasured me, I unknowingly used my magic. Who knew what might happen with all this sand.

"It's a risk I'm willing to take."

• • •

He reached over and pushed my open cloak from my shoulders, and I found that the air was warm. I furrowed my brow.

I couldn't very well expect you to disrobe and freeze.

I looked about as I felt the heat turn to liquid and pool between my legs.

"No one else is allowed in Mother's garden save my siblings and I."

Might they stumble upon us? Somehow the idea turned me on all the more.

Kovis made it worse when he rippled his chest muscles, making his altairn tattoo move. No surprise, the ink was bright red.

I inhaled sharply.

"You're so beautiful," he said, running a thumb down my jaw. "Let's make your fantasies, reality, my love."

My cheeks burned right along with my center.

He rose to his haunches and took my hands in his, spreading them wide on his chest. He leaned forward and his lips met mine. The kiss was slow, tender, gentle, that of a lover seeking to know the depths of his beloved.

"You shaved." It spilled out as my fervor grew.

I felt his lips turn up. "Anything for you, love."

I moaned as I squeezed his muscled chest. He was so sexy, so strong. My fingers brushed his nipples, and he exhaled sharply. He was ticklish, but I wanted to caress them as he did mine.

His tongue asked permission, but I broke the kiss and bent forward to find one of his swollen buds. I licked it, and a tremor raced through him.

"You excite me," he whispered.

I didn't voice that he was doing the same to me as my hands continued stroking his chest. I couldn't get enough of him. He was sensuous, seductive, and sexy. He was my lover. And he was my home.

I moved to his other nipple, and he reached behind me and began unbuttoning my gown.

I was burning up, and my hands reached for his manhood.

He sucked in a breath. "Oh, Ali, I don't know how much I can take." It came out choked.

I tittered. I was making him fumble with my buttons.

"You make it very difficult to..." a moan finished the thought as I eagerly stroked every glorious fingerbreadth of his generous length.

Every button he succeeded in loosing, he groaned as I ran a finger over the tip, spreading his moisture. I wanted him, needed him.

He exhaled when he finished and rose up on his knees to lift the dress over my head, but I had other ideas. I grabbed his erection in my mouth and began sucking on it. I barely stifled a groan.

"Oh, Ali..." He dropped the dress and grabbed my hair to steady himself as I continued my assault. I'd never been so bold, but in this heartbeat, I didn't deny myself. I wanted every bit of him.

I licked and sucked, drawing him deeper and deeper. He was massive. His manhood hit the back of my throat and I started to gag, so I eased him forward, but I would have all of him. My tongue guided him into my cheek, and I continued sucking.

He couldn't speak. His whole body trembled as he grasped my hair tighter. Somehow the pain stimulated me more, and I drew him in to his hilt, then started massaging his firm balls.

He groaned and I smiled, then sucked harder.

"Oh, Ali, I'm going to..." he gasped.

He tried pulling out, but I threw my arms around his hips and pulled him closer.

"Ali!" he bellowed, and his body bucked as he climaxed. My mouth filled with his salty seed, and I swallowed. My core still burned, but this was damn seductive.

"Oh, Ali...," he panted, collapsing beside me.

"I love hearing you say my name when you come," I whispered as I brushed wet hair away from his brow, then planted soft kisses.

He gave me a lazy smile. "That is not how I envisioned this night going. You've never done that before. You were so sexy. Where did you learn that?"

My cheeks burned from my boldness, and I whispered, "I couldn't help myself. I saw your manhood and wanted you."

Laughter rumbled in his chest, and he rolled up onto his elbow. "Nothing to be embarrassed about. I'd love you to do it again if you feel so moved." He grinned and stroked my jaw. "How did I ever deserve you?"

As I leaned in to kiss him, he rose to his knees and grabbed my gown again, but just as I raised my arms, I heard the sound of footsteps on the gravel path. My heart raced, and I yanked my arms back down and tight to my chest.

Kovis grinned. "Ali, it's only a coypu."

"A what?" My heart slowed.

"A coypu. Several live in the garden. They're large, fuzzy, brown, herbivorous rodents that like water. You'd think they're cute if you saw one."

I exhaled.

"Now can we please continue?" He didn't wait for my reply. He drew my arms up and yanked at the fabric that was hopelessly twisted beneath me. It was clear from his force that he would allow nothing to come between us, which was fine by me. I couldn't wait to bare myself to him.

He tossed my gown to the sand, then laid me back onto the soft blanket. The stars had awoken and the lights rippled above the Canyon, adding their spray of colors to the dark sky. I could have wished for no other backdrop to realize my fantasies.

He stretched out beside me and rose up on his elbow. "I was going to make you bare, but you look so sexy in this that I've changed my mind." His eyes devoured me in the pink, lacy shift I'd purchased from Madame Catherine a while back. The sheer pink material was just that, very sheer. Even in the torchlight, he could easily make out my form and the pink tones of my skin.

He grinned, no doubt hearing my heart accelerate through our bond as I gazed into his fathomless blue and hazel depths, and he began tracing my shift's generous scooped neckline with a finger. My nipples rose to meet his touch, and his eyes began to dance. "Your ladies are excited for my attentions."

My core burned. "What can I say? You have quite an effect on me."

His tongue followed his finger investigating my cleavage and every contour of my chest. More and more heat built between my legs, and my hips began to squirm. I was in trouble. He hadn't even touched my straining nipples much less freed my ladies from my shift.

So impatient, my love.

He'd no idea.

He slowly, torturously pulled one breast free from the confines of its sheer prison, and I arched my back, straining for his touch. He just smiled as his eyes roamed every fingerbreadth of it.

"Touch me," I breathed out.

"As you wish, my love." He began tracing circles, first large, then smaller with his finger, but he never brushed the tip. I would lose my mind.

"Please..." I begged.

"What would give you pleasure?"

"Ravish me..."

Passion smoldered in his eyes, and his seductive digit finally crossed a pebbled tip. I couldn't hold in a moan. The torturous buildup had made his touch all that more intense, and a shiver rocked me.

He freed my other lady in short order, then rose and straddled me, rubbing my nipples with his thumbs. Up and down. Up and down. Over and over and over again. I arched my back further. It felt *so* good. I couldn't get enough.

"Oh...," I groaned loudly, as the swell of sensations obliterated all sense of propriety.

His mouth crashed down on one breast, and he moaned as he began sucking hungrily. His teeth and his tongue and his lips ravaged my lady while his thumb continued its ministrations on the other. His hunger only fueled my fervor.

How long would I last?

The heartbeat the thought tickled my mind, I screamed as a wave of ecstasy broke over me, then swept me away. I was plunging, falling, awash in indescribable pleasure. I flipped and tumbled in its boundless power and hoped it would never end. Kovis enhanced and extended the chaos, biting one and pinching my other nipple. On and on and on it carried me.

I panted as reason finally began nibbling at my mind, and I cracked open one eye. Our sex was usually good, but this had taken it to beyond great.

Kovis grinned, then kissed me.

I opened and closed my mouth, but words wouldn't come.

"We've only just begun, love." And with that, he moved off me, but his fingers began migrating ever so slowly down my stomach making light swirls as they went.

It was sweet torture before he finally reached the hem of my shift and slid it up.

"I..." My back arched. How could my body respond so soon after? But it did.

He eased my legs apart with his hands and made his way to my center where his fingers did the most amazing things, circling, rubbing, right where I'd desperately needed it.

"Oh..." Pleasure made me draw it out as heat again built.

Reason fled, and my mind blanked. There was no past, no future, only the present. Nothing else existed, only the inferno Kovis coaxed to life between my legs. It was growing, stronger and stronger and stronger. It would not be quelled and would overwhelm me if I didn't... A second wave of rapture, as monstrous as the first, ripped me away from reality. I didn't fight as it tore through me and was replaced by sweet, sweet ecstasy that went on and on and on.

My chest heaved as sense eventually reasserted itself. I felt like a ragdoll.

"Did you enjoy that, love?"

I could only nod.

"This time we're going to come together."

Again? How?

Kovis rose, pulled my shift up to my chest, then over my head and tossed it aside.

I arched my back. Despite the thrall, I was thrilled to finally bare myself completely.

"Mmm, you're so wet for me," he groaned as his knees eased my legs further apart and his manhood entered me.

His hands started kneading my ladies, his lips found mine, and our tongues began dancing. In, out, in, out. His strokes were slow, and while I'd felt drained, his fervor reenergized me.

I blocked out the sounds of another coypu not far away.

"Faster," I whispered, feeling my climax building.

He picked up his pace, thrusting faster and faster.

"Oh... oh, gods." Kennan stopped short, then turned away.

"Kennan? Shit!" Anger surged through Kovis's words. "What are you doing?"

I froze, then locked eyes with Kovis's twin. A cacophony of emotions raced past, in his gaze: shock gave way to disbelief, gave way to horror, gave way to fury.

"What am I doing? What are *you* doing? Can I not even take a walk to clear my mind without...?" Kennan shouted. He shook his head and waved his arms. "Never mind."

He turned on his heels and strode back to the path, fists clenched. I watched him go, but before he reached the path, he shot me a long, pained look.

My lungs constricted, making it hard to breathe. I waited until the sound of his footsteps faded before I exhaled.

Kovis dropped to his back, drew an arm over his brow, and laughed.

"I'm glad you think that was funny," I said.

"So he knows the truth. We're crazy in love and enjoying each other body, mind, and soul."

I laughed. "Well, the body part for sure."

Kovis chuckled. "No doubt about it. Now, can we pick up where we were before we were so rudely interrupted?"

"Fine, but if I hear one more coypu—"

Kovis didn't let me finish, for he rose up and ravished my mouth with his, and it wasn't long until we yelled together plummeting over the cliff of euphoria.

I still panted, utterly spent. Kovis lay beside me, chest heaving. Despite the interruption, tonight had been the most mind-blowing sex of my entire life, no matter which realm.

When Kovis and Aunt Dite had talked, she'd told him she longed to bless us, but he had held her back. No obstacles remained it seemed. Was I up to this god's blessed sex?

Before I could ponder more, a wail rent the night. Had it been heartbeats before, I might have accused Kovis of making it. As it was, he grabbed my hand as the high-pitched, inarticulate cry, went on and on just beyond the garden wall.

Our eyes locked.

My charges had screamed when mares ravaged them, but this wail was nothing like that. Never had I heard something so pained. It sounded not of this world.

Chapter Ten

Ambien

Roars and snarls echoed up the stone-lined sloping corridor and mingled with the sounds of hammers striking anvils, trowels scraping stone, and pickaxes chiseling rock as I strode down it. The notes joined together and told me this compound was adhering to my edicts.

Didacus, the commander of Abuj's remorrigan compound, walked beside me. "We've nearly mined enough rock for the next section of cells, but I decided to get the troops started on the bars. No sense in waiting, we're nearly out of capacity."

"I agree. How many remorrigans have arrived since my last visit?" I asked as we continued following the line of torches past one of several corridor fireplaces that attempted to warm this subterranean world.

"Five, including that beauty you sent us three suns ago, bringing our census to three hundred forty-seven."

I'd set my goal at four hundred for this compound. We were nearly there.

The stench of straw and feces hit me as we reached the cells.

Angry bellows filled the corridor ahead as two troops stuck prods through the bars of a cell. Metal hinges protested as another troop opened the door, thrust rank carrion in, then slammed it shut again.

"It's feeding time," Didacus said. "This is our newest addition."

I slowed as we reached the ghoul-size creature. Straw and bones littered the edges of its cell. Its color shifted from yellow to brown to black as it devoured its meal, but sensing us watching, it raised its misshapen head and glared. It was truly a thing of nightmares with its long, pointed teeth and razor-sharp claws. The human it had been harvested from had an irrational fear of being attacked by wild beasts, no mistaking it. I didn't even have to try to sense it. The pungent fear rippled off of it.

When we didn't flinch, the creature shifted its head, adding rounded horns and shaggy black hair to its hideous features. Then it began rocking and growling as saliva dripped from its maw.

"Very nice." I couldn't help but smile. It would do nicely, but I had work to do and nodded my commander onward.

The sounds of digging and hammering grew louder, then receded before we reached our destination. I unbuckled my black cape and tossed it onto a bench, striding into the large-domed, circular, torch-lined arena. This was not an arena for spectators but one for work.

A beastly howl followed a roar, then an outcry of voices echoed through the metal bars of the gate on the other side of the oval.

A troop scurried from behind us over to my commander.

"She's ready, in the tunnel, my liege," Didacus said, as the soldier saluted and left us.

Gravel crunched beneath my boots as I strode to the center. I would meet this wonder head on and control her before I was done. "Release her."

The sound of the metal door slamming behind me, echoed about the arena until it was replaced by the shrieking hinges of the door ahead along with shouts, as my beauty slithered in.

My heart raced with excitement, and my wings quivered. I'd formed her from the terror of one human, enhanced by nearly thirty others, and I'd never seen anything so alluring, even in this dim light.

The heartbeat she cleared the door, metal clanged, sealing me in with her.

Her body was that of a thick, emerald-scaled serpent. She rose up, equaling my height, but paused to take in the space with those cunning ebony eyes. Her tail flicked and her tongue tasted the air.

My breathing labored as wave after wave of terror curled off her. It took no effort to sense her composition: self-doubts, fears of death, overestimations of catastrophes, certainty of dire calamities, they hit me like a wall. My heart pumped like an anxious squirrel, and my mouth went dry. What was happening to me?

I shifted my shoulders as the barrage of perturbations continued pelting me, but an edgy feeling I couldn't escape, settled on me.

Her scales hissed against the floor as her body wended like a whip about to crack as she advanced, never taking her eyes off me. She knew she affected me and was teasing. Cruel beauty.

I clutched my chest as it constricted. I was not afraid. I was powerful, immune to fear. Fear was a malady reserved for mortals. Still the sensations refused to ease, unrelenting like a brutal taskmaster.

I *needed* to control her, I reminded myself, and loathing erupted within me. I *needed* to? How had my narrative shifted? How had doubts begun to fill me? I shook my head, trying to get a grip.

More hissing, scales against gravel, filled my ears as she took to a circular path, winding and slithering sideways, taunting yet more.

I pivoted in place, following her movements. The corners of her eyes crinkled as if enjoying my wariness. I was her toy, at least she seemed to think so.

I was not. I would control her.

After reaching the door through which I'd entered, she altered her path, gliding directly toward me.

She'd blocked any escape. There was no flight from the fetid fear that poured off her, repugnant and vile as it was. My knees began to feel weak, my stomach turned rock hard, and my bowels threatened to spill.

I nearly retched as I realized I was afraid... like mortals... *because* of her. Their pitiful, wretched terrors were making me weak. Contempt, disgust, and revulsion welled up inside. I was better than this, damn it! I was a god!

This unabashed creature eased to a lackadaisical pace as she closed the distance between us. Ten men's height away, then nine, and my anxiety spiked making it hard to draw breath.

I wagged my head. I would not be taunted. I thrust my arms out in disgust. I'd had enough.

She'd closed to eight men's height as I straightened, threw my shoulders back, and forced myself to take a deep breath. Fear was an emotion, nothing more. Humans wished their fears away. It never worked.

"I will control you," I boomed, then loosed a deafening laugh that reverberated around the oval.

The remorrigan didn't break our gaze, challenging me. She advanced to seven men's height.

Agitation rose in me. She was becoming irksome, vexing me no different than my children, but I could deal out consequences differently. No bonds of relationship held me to her.

"You will sleep... soundly." My tone left no room to argue, and she recoiled.

Tenacity lit her eyes, and she slithered, albeit more slowly, to six men's height away and rose up, to above me.

A mixture of pride and apprehension swelled in me at her petulant display. She was my creation, so she would not be easily controlled. It seemed she was brash enough to try even me.

She set her jaw, straining under the full power of my command as it continued punishing her, but she managed to crawl to five men's height away and, faster than I'd guessed, launched her towering frame at me.

I caught only the heartbeat her emerald body left the ground before I dove to one side. My wings unfurled as my body skidded across rough stone.

She'd expected her strike to impale me; so when I surged up and whirled around, she was just rising. The power of my command, to sleep, made her slow.

I drew my hands to my hips and furled my wings. Her stubbornness brought a smile to my lips for a heartbeat, but that cowardly, anxious feeling erased it just as quickly, incensing me. "You know I'll best you. You're nothing but a damn pest," I spit.

She reared back as my words dealt another blow, but mortal terror still trickled off her, and my body begged to shudder.

I tamped it down, striking again before she recovered. "I will *not* submit." Rage laced my protest.

Her eyes grew large, and her tongue tasted the air.

"That's right," I said, squinting.

She would no longer taste fear, not from me; I'd pushed it aside.

"*You* will submit." It came out a growl.

Her head jolted back, but her mouth opened as if to strike again. I stared her down.

She wavered for several heartbeats, tongue flicking, watching as I bared my teeth and flared my nostrils. She bobbed her head, forward and back, forward and back, but her movements lacked energy.

She was tiring. She could not endure.

She froze, locking herself in place as if that would preserve some perceived advantage. I knew differently. She wavered just a heartbeat longer before she toppled forward and her head met the gravel.

I closed the gap in two strides and patted her green-scaled head. "Never again."

Her eyes narrowed, but when I raised my hand to strike, she looked away.

"That's right, my lady. I am your master, and you will obey me."

I'd bested her, and she would do my bidding, henceforth. She would no longer affect me—a remorrigan would never be that bold—but I would leverage her talents in my quest just as I'd set out to do.

The sound of creaking hinges erupted, and I nodded my troops forward to return this beauty to her cell. They moved swiftly, even skittishly around her, but I narrowed my eyes and locked my gaze with her, making her cower.

Several heartbeats later, left in solitude, self-loathing erupted within me despite my victory. I scowled. I'd been pitiful, allowing myself to succumb to the mortal plague of fear. Me. A god.

Never. Ever. Again. Whatever it took.

Chapter Eleven
Auden

A cell door slamming woke me.

"Uncooperative peasant." The grumble trickled through the metal bars followed by the shuffling of one, two, three sets of boots. A thud and then a moan were the only replies.

The sounds were all too familiar. My stomach clenched, and I fisted a hand. I didn't bother rising from the cot that hung by two chains from the stone wall. I pulled the blanket up over my ears trying to warm myself.

I'd woken up here. How long I'd been out, I'd no idea; but it had been three suns since, if I'd deduced the routine correctly—although with no sunlight I couldn't be sure, but I wasn't stupid enough to ask my fellow prisoners again.

I opened and closed my mouth, then moved my arm up and down, trying to work out the stiffness those brutes had left when they'd roughed me up for talking.

I glanced at the pot, the only other adornment of my cell. It stood near the front corner a man's height away, not far enough to avoid the stench of my own feces and those of others before me. How long could I ignore my bowels?

Tap, tap, tap-tap.

The other prisoners had worked out a way to communicate, but all I'd understood thus far were simple yes and no answers. Not that there was much time to exchange information with the guards constantly surveilling us.

Speaking of which, in the dim torchlight, the shadow of a soldier moved toward me, a beefy male this time. I closed my eyes, pretending to still sleep until the scraping of leather boots on stone faded again.

Tap-tap, tap, tap-tap. The conversation picked up.

Despite the exchanges, I'd learned more from watching the other prisoners. The three cells across from me all held dream weavers. I knew because they all retreated to their cots and sat, hands in their laps, eyes closed for extended periods. Like me, they'd continued weaving dreams for their charges despite their circumstances. And rightly so, our charges shouldn't have to suffer—human lives were hard enough as it was.

My stomach grumbled half-heartedly, not that it would be getting anything close to what Mother made. They'd soon toss a meager half-loaf of hard bread into the cell along with a skin of water. I'd dubbed it "barely breakfast." For "damned dinner," they added a ration of dried meat.

The guards' treatment had quelled much of my appetite. I hadn't deduced the purpose of taking and returning prisoners and was in no hurry to find out—they roughed up their target when taking him and returned him worse off.

I feared when they'd come for me, although I did my best to hide it. I kept my expression neutral and stared ahead when they forced us to stand, hands behind our backs, at the front of the cell each time they came for one of us.

I only prayed no harm had come to my family. I pushed the thought away. I couldn't worry about them, or I'd have no courage when my time came.

"Rise and be seen!" The call sounded, and my stomach clenched as I stumbled to the metal bars and assumed the required position.

Don't be me. Please don't pick me, I pleaded with the gods.

They'd answered my pleas before. Would they again?

The pair of brutes stopped before my cell and the larger of the two locked eyes with me. "You will not move." He ran his thumb back and forth across the pommel of the club that hung at his side.

I froze, knowing they'd beat me if I so much as twitched. My eyes migrated to the prisoner across from me. His clenched jaw and barely perceptible nod gave me courage. These brutes controlled our bodies but not our spirits.

One soldier unlocked my door, and despite obeying, the other grabbed my arm and yanked me into the corridor, but not before my ear slammed into the doorframe. Despite its throbbing, I refused to grab for it. I wouldn't give them the satisfaction.

"Move." A meaty hand thrust me forward, and I stumbled, barely catching myself.

The pair guffawed.

"Seems he's had a bit too much to drink," one said.

I heard the wood of a club sing behind me as it was drawn from its holster, and I braced.

Seeing me tense must have given them the thrill they sought, for they snorted, and the end of the club struck the top of my back, right between my wings a heartbeat later. I gasped for air but managed to keep my feet under me, putting one foot in front of the other as we made our way toward the solid metal door at the end.

I didn't dare look directly at my fellow prisoners, but I snuck glances as I stumbled past. I shouldn't have been surprised that most wore bruises on their faces. Several sported black, swollen eyes and cuts across their cheeks. Who knew what abuse their soiled and torn clothing hid? My breathing labored.

The only positive, I would finally find out who was behind my capture and imprisonment. The three troops who'd abducted me had said King Ambien needed my service. I'd hoped they'd lied. I hadn't wanted to believe my sovereign treated people this way. I'd only ever been a loyal subject.

The door swung open, and I staggered through as another blow to my upper back propelled me forward. They directed me across a small area, bare save for two torches, past a set of old wooden stairs.

One of my captors pushed ahead of me as we neared the last of three doors on the right and knocked.

"Enter."

"My liege." The guard bowed.

Liege? My heart picked up pace. I hesitated, and that's all it took to feel yet another blow that came with such force that I sprawled across the floor, back screaming, wings splaying.

"Rise." The tone came out bored.

It wasn't easy with pain searing my back, but I managed to stand and furl my wings, hiding a grimace.

I'd seen King Ambien only a handful of times. He'd stood regally in fine black robes with a golden sash crossing his barrel chest. That image had drawn my respect as well as allegiance. At present, his wings draped lazily over the back of the gilded, dragon-inspired chaise lounge he reclined on atop the two-step dais.

His generous middle, rumpled robes, and slouched posture were anything but regal, much less inspiring of loyalty despite the opulent draping of immense quantities of expensive black and gold fabrics behind and to the sides of the dais. The decorations were meant to intimidate, and they would have, except for him.

I was little more than a peasant of peasant stock. I knew my place. But I'd applied myself and had, I'd thought, elevated my family's status a small bit by becoming a dream weaver. But I'd clearly deluded myself. I was no better than dung to him, at least based upon his treatment. I tamped down my emotions as I always did in the presence of my betters.

"So good of you to join me." A smile graced his lips but didn't reach his eyes. "I trust you are enjoying your accommodations."

I tucked my wings tighter, nearly making my muscles spasm with the strain of leashing my roiling emotions. My effort made his smile grow. No doubt he thought tucking my wings was my attempt to humble myself and pay him more honor. Let him delude himself.

"You are undoubtedly curious concerning the help I desire you lend our cause."

I breathed in and out, slowly. Better to focus on my breathing than his arrogance, which made my blood boil. He controlled my future and that of my family.

He chuckled at my continued silence but went on. "I have something very special planned for your charge, none other than the empress, herself."

The hair on the back of my neck lifted as my mind raced. I couldn't contain a gasp, but I schooled my expression a heartbeat later. Of course he would know Rasa was my charge.

"You will draw a mare to her."

My eyes went wide, and I bit down on my tongue to keep silent.

He smirked. "Much the same reaction as your fellows. You should see this as an opportunity to elevate yourself further. Why, with your assistance, there's no end to the positions you might hold in my service. Think of it: wealth, power, fame. It can all be yours."

I tamped down my disgust—sacrifice my charge for my own benefit? Never. No doubt he'd made the same offer to each of my fellow prisoners.

When I didn't respond, he nodded at the larger of my two captors, and I felt a hand grip that most sensitive spot at the top of my back between my wings. I had no choice but to comply as he forced me to the floor. His vice-like hold forbade so much as twitching as my cheek dug into the rough stone and pain blossomed as he continued scouring my skin against its course texture.

"I had considered giving you the option of doing things the easy way, but it's clear you prefer difficulty."

Sure he'd considered it. Any self-respecting dream weaver would object to what he sought. Wait, is this why my fellow prisoners all sported the marks they did? Were we all dream weavers who had refused him? The pieces fell into place. But why was he forcing us to misuse our charges? To what end?

The guard released me, then growled, "Stand."

My cheek stung and I felt warmth trickle down my face as I ruffled my wings and resumed my place. Once I met King Ambien's eyes, he commanded, "Acquire the empress's thought thread." His tone left no room for debate.

I would not. I would never compromise my charge, and certainly not to expose her to a mare. I didn't care what they did to me.

He wasn't stupid. He knew I wouldn't obey for he hesitated only a heartbeat before nodding to the guard.

A club struck the top of a wing and I forced myself to stand tall as pain raced through it and down my back. I clenched my jaw, barely holding in an explicative.

"Your king commanded you to acquire the empress's thought thread," the guard snarled.

Still I didn't move, nor would I.

Two zaps of intense pain shot through me a heartbeat later as both guards landed blows, one to the top of each wing, making my legs buckle. I closed my eyes, focusing my strength to remain standing.

An uppercut to my jaw snapped my head back, and I tasted blood. The hard floor punished my knees as I fell. "Respect your king. Never close your eyes to him."

It took considerable effort, but I pushed my legs up and returned to standing, then made my features neutral, refusing to allow them any satisfaction.

Clubs struck the backs of my knees, and I caught myself with my hands as I crumpled to the floor a second time, my knees again taking the brunt. I blew out a breath, recomposing myself. I would not let them get to me.

But in the blink of an eye, two boots struck, one to either side of my ribs, and knocked the wind out of me. I gasped, falling to my elbows, as I tried to suck in air, but it wouldn't come. It felt as if the room had emptied of it. Air, I needed air. I sprawled out, hoping to find the smallest trace. Panic threatened to overwhelm me. I managed to suck in just a whisper of air, but it wasn't enough. More, I needed more.

The guards' laughter barely registered against the buzz that filled my head.

Calm, I needed to calm. Despite the frenzy, I forced myself to attempt a deep breath, and the dam broke as air rushed in. I collapsed, panting. Sweet, sweet air.

"Rise."

I shifted my head to see the king scowl as my chest continued heaving. Let him scowl. I could no longer pretend they hadn't affected me, but I would not obey. They could hurt me, but they would never break me.

I pushed myself up, struggling to sit, then get my knees under me. Pain shot from my ribs as I straightened, and I couldn't help but grab my middle.

Putting my legs under me proved equally agonizing, but I managed it, then squelched a cry as I pushed up to standing, still holding my ribs. I hunched forward unable to stand fully erect, then lifted my eyes.

King Ambien drummed his fingers on the head of the dragon engraved in the arm of his lounge, his expression stony. No doubt my fellow prisoners had behaved similarly, and he grew bored. Tough. Call the minstrels. I wasn't his entertainment.

"You seem to have deluded yourself into believing compliance is optional," he said.

I set my jaw.

He looked me up and down, then exhaled heavily. "Very well, but remember this was your desire."

My desire? I held my tongue.

His feet found the floor as he sat up, frowning—oh, I would be even more irksome before we were done. The haunches of the gilded dragon as well as the tail that wrapped around the front of the chaise came into view as his robe fell away. I wished the beast would draw breath and devour him.

The guards propelled me forward, then pushed me down so my battered knees hit the top step of the dais, the edge of the stair biting my shin, but I held in the groan. A hand at the top of my head thrust it down and held it there so only the king's fat sandaled feet filled my vision.

Metal rings that adorned each of his fingers grated against my scalp as Ambien spread out his firm, cold hand. "Will you hand me the empress's thought thread?" His voice turned saccharine.

I tensed my arms, protecting my middle, and held my breath. What was he about to do to me? No, it didn't matter, I would never relinquish Rasa's thought thread. Certainly not to bring on a mare.

Stabbing pain lit my head. My hands reflexively sought the source, but one of the guards grabbed my arms, wrenched them behind my wings, and pushed them upward. It happened so fast that I couldn't stifle a cry.

"Perhaps you have changed your mind?" His tone was light, teasing.

I shook my head. Never.

What felt like sharp needles, extended, then scrapped ever so slowly across my mind triggering a wave of blistering agony that inundated my senses. My head was on fire, blinding white filled my vision, but my captor didn't ease his grip on my arms, and I barked as my weight stretched my muscles taught.

"You have the power to make your discomfort ease, but perhaps you are enjoying it. Yes?"

I tensed my stomach, my ribs biting. I could endure. I must.

When I didn't respond he said, "Very well, then let us continue."

Caustic burning overwhelmed my mind again as those needles, no talons, dug deeper, moving torturously, slowly. I screamed and collapsed forward, my weight yanking my arms in their sockets, where the guard still held them.

"Release him."

I could barely move my arms, certainly not in time to catch myself, and my nose smashed into the dais. My wings splayed. I barely squelched a groan.

"Sit up," King Ambien commanded.

I would endure, I reminded myself, but one of the guards slammed that damn club into my side again. I whimpered and drew a hand to cover.

"Did you not hear your sovereign?" the soldier growled, readying to strike again.

I labored to furl my wings, then worm my legs beneath me, pushing myself up to sitting. Every movement was misery. I tasted blood as I grit my teeth.

King Ambien again splayed a hand on my head. "I will continue as long as you wish."

I didn't reply, readying myself for the next onslaught.

"Very well." He shook his head.

I shrieked and writhed as those claws scrapped yet deeper. On and on and on the excruciating pain continued, eviscerating my mind and loosing my bowels.

"Hand me her thought thread. Now."

How I wished the pain would end, but I couldn't do that to Rasa.

The claws dug deeper still, moving faster, coming for yet another pass and another. Piercing. Harrowing. Rending. The world dissolved into white agony as every fiber of my being was consumed. I lost myself. I was on fire, alive only to pain.

A blow to my back jolted me but didn't stop the onslaught.

"Hand it here!" the king bellowed.

Fire, agony. I writhed and contorted longing to endure for Rasa, but when my eyes locked with his, despair overwhelmed me—he hadn't broken a sweat.

I couldn't think, I only reacted by spitting on those fat feet of his, then grit my teeth. "Never!"

He just smiled.

Chapter Twelve

Rasa

Pain shot from the soft flesh on the back of my arm, and I woke, then sucked in air. Where was I?

"I'm sorry, my empress. I did not want to hurt you, but you instructed us to… You were screaming but wouldn't awaken." Hutchin, my guard loosed his grip as if I'd burned him. "We must get you to safety."

I heard his words, but they didn't register as the daze of deep sleep continued to hold me.

Serlon, another of my guards, said, "Please, your highness, come quickly, we fear for your safety." He glanced back to the door of my bedroom. His leg bumped the book from my nightstand that I'd been reading last night, and he scrambled to restore it.

I still panted, startled awake as I'd been from a nightmare the likes of which I hadn't had since father's deeds. My heart raced and my thoughts were scrambled. I sensed danger. It radiated off my guards. They wanted me to go with them?

A cacophony of discordant sounds reached my ears from the other room. "What's going on?"

"Please, majesty," Hutchin repeated with more urgency, holding open my robe to me.

My stomach clenched as I slid out from under the thick, downy covers, knocking a pillow to the royal-blue rug in the process. Something was definitely wrong. I glanced through the sheer curtains to the right of the bed. It was still dark out, and the fire in the grate still burned, albeit only half as brightly as when I'd retired.

I drew my sash up and tied it, then nearly stumbled down the step atop which my bed sat. Hutchin and Serlon caught me, then directed me toward the door. Both men's jaws were tense as they flanked me.

Hutchin was a Fire sorcerer with a Terra secondary affinity. Serlon was a Metal and Ice mage. Both held out their hands after throwing the double doors open.

I froze, horror overwhelming me as I surveyed the chaos of my private dining room. Eight of my personal guards stood about the perimeter, two more at attention on either side of the door to the receiving room.

I ignored it all, sprinting across the room, my heart in my throat. Jathan, hair sticking up at odd angles, leaned over Kovis, trying to staunch blood that gushed from his shoulder, a pool of it coloring the marble floor. So intent was he on his task that he startled when I stopped beside him. An apprentice, judging by the length of the sleeves on her green robe, turned wide eyes on me and genuflected from her haunches beside the chief healer.

I waved her back to her duties. I was of no consequence. Kovis wasn't moving.

"Jathan, what can I do to help?"

He glanced up. "Nothing, we've got it."

Master Lorica cast furtive eyes toward me from the other side of the long table, then shook her head and refocused, pressing gauze to Kennan's neck.

Kennan moaned but remained motionless, and my anxiety built.

"Empress, please, we need to get you to safety," Hutchin implored from beside me, but I ignored him as the horrifying familiarity of the scene overcame me.

It couldn't be. It couldn't, yet I couldn't deny. Bile rose in my throat, and I barely swallowed it down.

Before me lay my nightmare… Mine. Every detail of it come to life and my knees threatened to buckle.

A guard rushed into the room and announced, "All's clear. There's no sign of them."

Them. "Two insorcelled dignitaries." The words tumbled from my mouth unbidden. It felt like a firedrake sat on my chest, and I struggled to breathe.

The guard's news had brought with it a collective sigh of relief, but my utterance made it shrivel and die. Those within hearing fixed their eyes on me. I drew a hand to my mouth. What would I tell them?

Master Gavin saved me from an immediate response when he bolted through the door. His eyes scanned the room, growing as they took in his fellow healers working on my siblings, then landed on me, and he hastened my way, stepping over the broken china and gold dinnerware that lay strewn across the floor.

"Empress," he implored. He held out a hand, directing me to a chair. "Please take a seat so I can assess your condition."

I didn't want to sit. I didn't have a mark on me. Somehow I'd caused lethal harm to my brothers, and I couldn't still, let alone sit. "Only after I know they will be okay. Don't worry about me. Please, help Master Lorica."

He opened his mouth, but my glare silenced him, and he joined her beside Kennan, who still had not moved.

You have to be okay, brothers. You have to.

I started pacing and reached the far wall, brushing against the tieback that hung limply from one of the floor-length, white silk curtains—the fabric as well as its royal-blue fringe bore a spray of Kennan's blood. I'd seen it happen with my own eyes, at least in my nightmare.

I looked across the room to find that the oil painting of my grandfather that hung in a gilded frame just outside my bedroom had been slashed. Kovis had barely deflected the blade with his winds, but the warrior had still plunged a dagger into his shoulder.

I felt bile rise again. My brothers hadn't stood a chance. They'd been sitting right next to the two insorcelled warriors. This was my fault. My worst nightmare.

How had it happened? I'd had small snippets of dreams play out in reality upon occasion, like déjà vu, but nothing remotely close to this scale, ever. My nightmare had somehow gathered my brothers from wherever they had been and dropped them into its machinations along with two insorcelled delegates.

Did it portend calamity that would occur in the next fortnight? I stifled the thought, refusing to grant it life, and continued pacing, around and between the ornately carved, upholstered, white chairs that had been righted but stood askew to the left of the table. My eyes bounced between Jathan, Kovis who still lay unmoving, Lorica, Gavin, and Kennan's still form.

Come on, brothers. I was the leader of this empire, but it didn't matter. I couldn't fix this.

I rubbed the soft flesh on the underside of my forearm. It still smarted from where Hutchin pinched me. It would no doubt bruise, but that was the least of my worries. The courage that man had shown to pinch me, his empress, awake… I shook my head. He alone had stopped anything worse from happening, and I had him to thank for my brothers' lives.

But by the gods, how... how had the horror of my nightmare been brought to life? Bits and pieces of the scene continued playing in my thoughts even now.

The dream had started out innocently enough.

"Welcome, welcome gentlemen," I said as the two insorcelled leaders strode through the doors and joined Kovis, Kennan, and me. Four of my personal guards flanked the room, eyes roaming, watching everything.

Unsurprisingly, as in dreams, I couldn't make out the faces of our two guests, although from the wrinkled skin on their weathered hands, they were older. I also noted that their delegations were not present but dismissed it as just that, a dream where things didn't have to make sense.

The pair wore the traditional dress of their peoples, fitted tunics with fine trims, coordinating breeches, and knee-high boots. A pair of swords hung, one from either side of their hips—my guards' eyes locked on me the heartbeat they spotted the weapons, but I waved off their concerns with the shake of my head. I would not insult our guests by asking them to remove what was a part of their formal dress.

Despite the detail of their clothing, without seeing their faces, I couldn't begin to guess which of the insorcelled leaders they were. It shouldn't have mattered, but it made my anxiety worse.

Restlessness, apprehension, and fear had beset me with the approach of the annum meeting of provincial leaders. I felt passionately about disbanding The Ninety-Eight, but the nonmagical half of the empire's provinces opposed my edict. I hadn't yet determined how best to defend my position in a way they would support, and my anxiety had spiked as a result.

It's why I'd invited these two tonight. I hoped to build bridges with as many of the nonmagical leaders as possible. The better we knew each other I'd reasoned, the better we could support each other's objectives.

A liveried steward stopped before our group with a tray of sparkling wine.

"Thank you," I said reaching for a glass, along with my brothers.

One of our guests waved a hand in dismissal, the other thrust his chest out, clearly offended.

Damn. I'd assumed the wait staff knew proper protocol. Never again.

"Is there something else I might offer you?" the steward asked, his gaze darting between the pair.

"Spiced mead," the taller of the two replied, crossing his muscled arms.

His fellow nodded, adding, "It is the drink of choice among we warriors." He tapped his foot in emphasis and ran a thumb across the hilt of his sword.

"Right away," the steward replied, swallowing hard.

I forced a smile, attempting to cover the diplomatic blunder as the steward disappeared.

"If you'll please be seated, dinner is ready." Another steward entered and said a heartbeat later, motioning to the table that commanded the center of the room.

Elaborate place settings graced the spaces before five of the ten intricately crafted, upholstered, white chairs.

I strode to the head of the table as Kovis invited one of our guests to take the chair on his right. The other warrior made his way to the remaining place setting, to Kennan's left.

As happened in dreams, no one uttered a word, but there was no mistaking tension rippling off the pair.

The first and second courses were served to mundane conversation. I knew the dance. It would take time before we got to anything substantive that might forge a connection between us, especially since we'd gotten off to a shaky start.

But as the entrée arrived, Kennan inclined his head and asked, "I'm curious, how did it come to be that the brutality of the battlefield, the blood and gore and carnage, decides virtually everything for warriors?"

Kovis and I shared a nervous look.

Leave it to Kennan to cut to the chase. I shouldn't have been surprised. He hadn't been nearly so proper since he'd returned to us. I'd only hoped to address the hippocampus in the room in a more diplomatic fashion.

Kennan held his expression neutral, but I could see the warrior beside him chafe, his hand clutching his fork more tightly. His compatriot put his utensils down and started drumming his fingers on the linen tablecloth.

The man beside Kennan sniffed loudly before beginning. "I'm glad a prince of the empire has deigned to ask such a question, for it appears an understanding of our proud traditions failed to pass from your father... to his children."

Kovis stiffened visibly at the slight. Only the fire crackling in the fireplace behind him made any sound. Grandfather, who stood proudly in the imposing portrait to the left of it, seemed to hold his breath.

After protracted silence, the man went on. "Since I was a boy, the warrior code of honor and dignity was drilled into me by my father. He never allowed me to back down from a challenge but taught me to fight hard and stand strong, no matter the cost."

He made it sound banal, but knowing warriors, those "challenges" had been brutal. My stomach clenched as I spied scars on the backs of both his hands. No doubt he bore more.

This was exactly the crux of the problem I had with The Ninety-Eight. It was a brutal competition with maiming and slaughter, for the sake of what? Proving who was physically strongest? What difference did it make? As empress, I could affect real and lasting change that would benefit every province regardless of who was physically or magically superior.

The warrior continued. "Unlike your upbringing... we were not coddled." Damn this dream for hiding his face. I'd no doubt a smug smirk lurked. "If not for virtue, for what would you fight?" The man put his fork down and settled back in his chair.

For the good of every citizen of the empire... I wanted to shout, but I bit my tongue and took a deep breath. Kovis cleared his throat. I prayed Kennan denied himself the satisfaction of a deft rejoinder.

Force is what these men understood, but force would accomplish nothing save getting us in a heated argument. These warriors viewed us as pampered and weak, and disrespected us as a result.

I debated only briefly but opted not to defend my dignity which he had impugned. "You know nothing of our past. It was not as cosseted as you might think, far from it."

The warrior beside Kovis drew his napkin from his lap and threw it on his plate, planting his elbows on the table and leaning forward. "Then why don't you explain it to us?"

"Not all battles for virtue are public," I replied. "Not all scars are physical."

"I will grant you that," he said. "But from what little I know of your upbringing, you cannot deny it was privileged."

Kovis didn't hesitate. "You speak of upholding honor and dignity, yet you have robbed your empress of such."

"You're hypocrites," Kennan added, nodding. "Unless dignity and honor belong solely to you."

The heartbeat the words left Kennan's mouth, both warriors sprang up from their places, and in the blink of an eye, Kennan shouted out a curse as blood sprayed from his neck. He grabbed for it as he fell from his chair. The warrior readied to strike again, but Kovis's winds tossed him to the marble and held him there.

Two of my guards closed in on Kennan's attacker, hands outstretched, but Kovis's winds failed as he loosed a bellow, clutching his shoulder and collapsing under the snarl of the insorcelled leader who'd sat beside him. The warrior towered over him, then bent down and ripped his dagger from Kovis's wound, making him cry out again.

My other two guards rushed Kovis's attacker but not before he'd drawn his sword and brandished it. Ice shot at the assailant, but as can only happen in dreams, it didn't wound.

Both insorcelled turned in my direction, and the one who'd wounded Kennan warned, "You have just proven what we knew, you are weak. You allowed us to assail your dignity without challenge—only the crown prince defended you. Dignity and honor are not polite. They are divisive. Let this be a lesson. Never—" He let the word dangle. "—call us hypocrites. We will defend our honor to the death if need be."

With that, the pair vanished, and pain bit into my upper arm.

I rubbed my arm again, rousing from the memory, but confusion plagued me. Had these events actually happened? Clearly part had, but were those two insorcelled warriors real? Why hadn't I been able to see their faces?

"Careful," Jathan warned, helping Kovis sit up.

I breathed out, relief flooding me, then glanced over to where Masters Lorica and Gavin attended Kennan. He moved a leg as the healers held their hands above his wound, knitting his flesh back together. My shoulders slumped.

It seemed my siblings would mend, but how had this happened to begin with? How had my brothers been brought to my chambers as part of my dream turned nightmare? What did it all mean?

My stomach twisted. I needed to talk to Ali. She alone might shed light on this, because it couldn't happen again, especially with the annum gathering upon us.

Chapter Thirteen

"Princess. Please wake." Urgency laced the words.

I pulled down the thick covers and opened my eyes a slit to see Allard standing beside me, kneading his hands. He'd lit our bedroom's candles and stoked the fire, no doubt with just a thought.

My mind slugged to awareness. Why was he here?

He glanced to Kovis, then back to me. "Please, princess, you must come, the prince has been stabbed. You must come quickly."

The words sloughed around in my mind until the bit about Kovis having been stabbed registered, and I bolted up to sitting, my heart accelerating.

My eyes ricocheted to Kovis, but he wasn't in bed. What? I'd been asleep in his arms, against his bare body.

I felt his side of the bed. The sheets were tepid.

"What do you mean he's been stabbed?" My voice rose.

"I am unsure of the details. Hutchin said the empress is calling for you. She's apparently in quite a state."

Hutchin was a stoic man, part of Rasa's personal guard. If he was relaying *that* message, things had to be bad.

Allard held open my robe, diverting his gaze.

I slid down from the tall bed, thrust my arms into the sleeves, and tied the sash.

My feet found my slippers, and I followed Allard out of our rooms, turned right, and ran down the hall, across the vestibule, and into Rasa's suites, skidding to a stop in the doorway of her private dining room. I sucked in a breath as I took in the chaos.

Masters Lorica and Gavin along with Jathan were supporting Kennan and Kovis as they struggled to their feet. Kovis's thrum seemed quieter than usual; I prayed it was only my imagination. All the same, it set me even more on edge.

"Ali," Rasa said, nearing from the far side of the overturned room. Her shoulders slumped, so unlike her.

"Rasa," I acknowledged, stopping before Kovis. "What happened?"

Kovis scrunched his face in pain. "I've no idea. I woke to find myself dining here."

"As did I," Kennan chimed in a heartbeat later from where Gavin steadied him with an arm around his shoulder.

Rasa rubbed her hands up and down her arms as she stopped beside me.

"You can chat later, my princes," Jathan interjected. "We need to get you both downstairs."

I locked eyes with my master.

As if reading my thoughts, he continued, "We've closed the wounds but need to check their channels and ensure they are unharmed magically. I expect them to both make full recoveries, but we must go."

"I'll be fine, Ali." Kovis forced a smile, trying to reassure me.

With his thrum diminished, he failed to achieve his desired objective. He'd been stabbed. Stabbed. What in Hades had happened?

I gave him a long look, silently voicing my concern.

He nodded. *My shoulder hurts, but Jathan will fix me up like he always does, really.*

I raised a brow and caught his eyes before leaning in and giving him a kiss. "I'll see you downstairs when I'm done here."

Kovis bobbed his head, then using Jathan for balance, hobbled out the door, Allard on his heels. Kennan and the masters, along with Amity, a fellow apprentice, followed.

"Leave us," Rasa commanded her guards.

In the tumult, I hadn't studied her, but as the guards left and secured the door, I took the opportunity. She looked pale and her jaw clenched. Dark circles shadowed her eyes. She drew a long, dark-ash lock behind her ear, then held herself again.

My relationship with Rasa had grown over the past moon as we'd spent more time together, and while I never would have hugged her early on, I felt compelled to. I stepped forward and enveloped her in my arms.

Rasa tensed, but as I held her firmly, unyieldingly, she loosed a ragged breath, and her arms rose to embrace me. Her next several breaths hitched as if she warred with herself to maintain composure, fighting not to cry.

As a royal, I understood fully. Crying was weakness, an inability to master yourself. Crying was a shortcoming that would lead subjects to believe the monarchy was unstable, unpredictable. Crying was improper decorum no matter the cause, both Mema and Father had drilled that into us.

But a heartbeat later, she loosed a whimper. A long outrush of air followed.

And something shifted between us, forever.

Her chin brushed the top of my head and her arms squeezed me harder. I hugged her more fiercely as her body trembled and agonized moans escaped her.

I choked back tears of my own. She was letting me see that part of her that she kept locked down and off limits. She was letting me in to see her as she truly was; she trusted me enough to be vulnerable.

It was a long while, but her quaking subsided and she inhaled deeply, stepping back and swiping her eyes and cheeks with the back of her hand. She forced a watery laugh, then excused herself to grab a handkerchief.

When she returned, she'd recomposed herself, the familiar emotional walls reconstructed. She and Kovis weren't all that different.

"I apologize. I do not make a habit of plaguing others with my burdens. I haven't shed tears before another in…" She furrowed her brow then shook her head. "I can't remember the last time."

"I hardly call this burdening me. If anything"—I drew a hand to my chest— "I'm honored."

Rasa sent me a puzzled look but didn't probe. I wondered if she felt embarrassed by the open display of emotion. Did she not realize it made her more relatable? She'd allowed me to see her as human with frailties just like me.

Before I had a chance to ask, she directed me with an outstretched hand into her bedroom, and as we drew our legs beneath us and faced each other on the ornately carved, upholstered, white sofa, she launched into an explanation of what had happened to bring her siblings to her chambers as well as how chaos had broken out.

I sat transfixed and drew a hand to my mouth as horror overwhelmed me. My mind whirred. I'd never heard of anything like this happening. Ever. Nightmares were abominable, but they didn't come to pass in real life. Did they? They didn't transport people physically either, no. Impossible.

Yet it had happened. My mind balked, unable to make sense of it. This had to be Father's doing. It was the only plausible explanation— he had to have gotten ahold of Auden, her sandman, and used him to accomplish this. I didn't know Auden well, but the little I did, he'd never struck me as the kind of male to allow something like this to happen to his charge. I shuddered to think what Father had done to coerce him.

Worse, if Father was the cause, Dyeus had not yet captured him. He was still out there wreaking havoc, pursuing his nefarious goals. Wake was not safe. My stomach threatened revolt.

At length Rasa paused, letting several heartbeats pass before she swallowed hard and confessed, "Ali, I'm afraid." She looked down at her hands that she fisted in her lap. "I fear this is a foreshadowing of what might come to pass while the leaders gather."

She was right to be afraid, but I couldn't tell her that. I needed to encourage her, calm her.

But before I could say anything, Rasa continued. "Ali, this nightmare was different than others I've had when I couldn't wake. I felt *utterly* out of control. I saw the insorcelled leader recoil at Kennan's sharp-tongued remark. I saw him reach beneath the table. Somehow I knew what he was about to do, and I couldn't do a thing to stop it. I felt frozen and forced to watch." She paused for several heartbeats before continuing. "It felt like when my father..."

My chest constricted as we locked gazes. She didn't need to finish the thought.

I knew what it felt like to be molested, but not repeatedly, over and over again, always the threat looming, unable to avoid the perpetrator, powerless to deny his advances, powerless to do anything to make him stop.

As the reality settled on me like a cold, wet blanket, it took everything in me to keep my stomach's contents down. My perspective had always been Kovis's. I'd fumed and raged as their father sucked the life from Kovis every time he indulged his carnal desires. I'd never wanted to think more deeply about the depravity of their situation. I'd never thought about how Rasa had coped. I'm sure Auden had, and tried to help.

This nightmare had triggered those memories. Memories of being utterly at the mercy of another's heinous whims and this time, she'd nearly gotten her siblings killed.

"A sennight ago, I had another nightmare my guards were also forced to use extraordinary means to waken me from. In that dream, a banshee hunted me outside the palace walls. I ran, but I couldn't run fast enough. It gained on me. My heart felt like it would explode from my chest, yet it drew closer, and just as it was near enough to leap upon me, it howled." Rasa shuddered. "They say a banshee is a harbinger of death, and I believe it. Its cry was mournful beyond any I've ever heard, and then it started shrieking and wailing."

My stomach flipped. A banshee.

Kovis and I had heard an eerie keening the night we'd had mind-blowing sex in the empress's garden. I thought back. It had been a sennight ago. No, it couldn't be.

Rasa added, "In the morning, I received word that a banshee had been spotted outside the walls."

I opened and closed my mouth like a fish out of water. I hadn't placed the nature of the creature at the time, but as she said it... yes, that had to have been it. It had been such an odd, mournful sound. But a banshee? A chill ran up my spine. Had Rasa's nightmare birthed and breathed life into such a beast? How was that even possible?

My mind reared like a horse refusing its master. It had to be Father. What was he doing? Had he somehow figured out how to make nightmares come to life? By the Ancient One. To what end? What would it allow him to do? My stomach twisted.

Rasa didn't notice my panic and continued. "Something else you should know."

No not more, I begged silently.

"It's felt like someone has been trying to warn me, in my sleep. I sense a threat, but it's always fuzzy. When I wake, I can never remember anything. What does it all mean?"

Auden had tried to warn her. It had to be.

She sat quietly, watching me as if waiting for a trusted counselor to make plain the situation and suggest possible actions she might consider. I wondered how many healers she had spoken with based on the trauma she'd endured.

"Have you ever talked to anyone about what your father did to you?"

She sighed. "Never. I haven't even told my brothers all of it. Kovis said you knew."

I nodded. "I know the parts he was involved in. He beat himself up every time he found out your father had his way and he wasn't there for you."

Her shoulders slumped.

I reached for her hand. "I'm here for you."

"Thank you. I appreciate that. More than you know. Right now, I need to understand what happened to cause the events of this night. We must take steps to avoid it happening again, and it seems you are the only one who can shed light on the situation." Rasa's eyes filled with hope.

My hands started twitching, and I fisted them. She'd been vulnerable, revealing to me her fears. I needed to trust that she could handle my speculations, no matter how frightening, so I laid out my thoughts.

By the time I finished, and she'd riddled me with questions, most of which I couldn't begin to answer, I was exhausted, and she looked haggard.

Questions aside, one fact was irrefutable, Kovis and I had tried our best to stop Father, but he was still on the loose, and Wake was about to come under siege.

Part II: Restless Sleep

Oh, Dear! What Can the Matter Be?

By Unknown
England Wake Realm

Oh, dear! What can the matter be?
Dear, dear! What can the matter be?
Oh, dear! What can the matter be?
Johnny's so long at the fair.
He promised to buy me a trinket to please me
And then for a smile, oh, he vowed he would tease me
He promised to buy me a bunch of blue ribbons
To tie up my bonnie brown hair.

Oh, dear! What can the matter be?
Dear, dear! What can the matter be?
Oh, dear! What can the matter be?
Johnny's so long at the fair.
He promised to bring me a basket of posies
A garland of lilies, a gift of red roses
A little straw hat to set off the blue ribbons
That tie up my bonnie brown hair.

Oh, dear! What can the matter be?
Oh, dear! What can the matter be?
Oh, dear! What can the matter be?
Johnny's so long at the fair.

Chapter Fourteen

My mouth went dry as the man repeated himself at my request.

"The delegation from Elsor has arrived, but the empress and princes are indisposed. They asked that you greet your guests and show them to their quarters," Gallien said again.

Gallien was a steward I'd recently become acquainted with. He'd been tasked with overseeing hospitality for the empire's leaders while they resided at the palace for the duration of the fortnight-long, annum meeting.

Kovis and Rasa had led as we'd greeted the magical delegations from Ice, Metal, Terra, and Fire as well as the insorcelled delegations from Yerevan, Praia, and Tirana over the last three suns.

"I see." I set the leather binder with Kovis's latest writing down on the sofa beside me and drew my legs from beneath me. The fire, dancing merrily in the fireplace before me did nothing to cheer.

I'd been intrigued by Nomarch Formig, the female leader of Eslor, during The Ninety-Eight. I'd wanted an opportunity to learn how a female had risen to lead the insorcelled province, but it had eluded me. Since then, I'd brushed up against insorcelled citizens during our wilderness wanderings and gained a deeper appreciation of nonmagical peoples. The experience had dampened my enthusiasm.

Now it seemed it had fallen to me to welcome them, by myself. Gallien shifted where he stood.

"Very well." As a princess, duty and I were old friends, or perhaps old enemies was a more apt description. "Let me go change."

Not long after, I descended the two floors. Echoing laughter greeted me even before I strode into the ballroom, chin held high.

Castle staff had abandoned the formal dining room in favor of the ballroom, due to the number of leaders and their delegations who would be attending.

The hulking crystal chandelier with altairn accents that hung from the rounded, recessed ceiling in the middle of the room, bisected the ordinarily empty, cavernous space. An army of round, white-linen-topped tables populated the far half. A single, oversize circular table occupied the near. Fruits and meats had been artfully arranged, and a dramatic ice sculpture of an altairn, wings splayed in landing, stood in the middle watching over the twenty or so guests from Eslor as they took their fill after a fortnight of travel.

Yes, a fortnight of travel. They smelled it, too. Pungent body odor filled my nostrils as I wended through the delegation.

To a one, they wore well-worn leathers much as we had when traveling rather than the immaculate dress uniforms I'd seen them sport in Eslor when they greeted us. Swords hung from either side of their hips. The scribes and chancellors among them had donned auburn capes that draped from their shoulders to the backs of their knees, setting them apart.

A boisterous laugh erupted from near the windows that ran the length of one side of the room and reverberated about the space, adding to the cacophony of discordant noise.

I spotted Eslor's two representatives to the Council who lived here in Veritas, no doubt exchanging news with several of their fellow Eslorians. I'd met the pair but hadn't gotten to know them yet. From what Kovis had shared, they were decent enough fellows but warriors through and through and not to be taken lightly.

I scanned others of those gathered, searching for Nomarch Formig, declining offers of champagne or spiced mead from liveried stewards. Yes, spiced mead—it seemed Rasa had ensured the preferred beverage of insorcelled peoples was in abundant supply. Perhaps some good had come from her nightmare.

I braced when I finally spotted the nomarch. No doubt she was as pissed as the rest of the insorcelled over Rasa's plans to cancel The Ninety-Eight, at least if the murmurings of those we'd greeted already were any indication. I hoped she didn't bring it up, but if she did I would do my best to smooth things over, or at a minimum, not make them worse.

I grabbed a flute of champagne to give my hands something to do, then stopped beside Formig. As when I'd seen her in Eslor, she wore leathers and a weathered, auburn cape that reached nearly to the floor. Unlike then, her long, raven hair looked like it could use a brush.

"Nomarch Formig, I'd like to welcome you and your delegation to Veritas," I said.

She shifted the plate that still held a variety of fruits to her other hand as she turned from the warrior she'd been conversing with. Her eyes moved up and down, scrutinizing my hair, then my face, my necklace, and my navy dress in its entirety.

Her expression was hard, the same as the one she'd worn when she'd greeted us in Eslor, that had left no doubt she'd earned every bit of her power and was not someone to trifle with.

I froze as I had then, but my hands didn't grow sweaty. I'd changed since then, become more confident, more assured, and I would not allow her to intimidate me.

At length, her eyes darted around the room but finally came to rest on me again.

She smiled, but it didn't reach her eyes. "Princess Alissandra, it's good to see you again. This is Dane."

"Good to meet you, Dane—"

"It seems you are alone in greeting us," Formig added.

Okay, how to navigate this without her feeling slighted, especially when Rasa and at least Kovis, if not Kennan, too, had greeted every other contingent.

I could do this.

"I've been fascinated by the fact that you... the fact that you're a..."

"That a female rose to lead our proud people," she finished for me. She drew her shoulders back and her chin up.

Her comrade furrowed his brow and frowned. With the swat of his hand, he dismissed a steward who offered to take his empty plate. I didn't know what to make of his displeasure. Had I unknowingly insulted her? It seemed he thought so.

"Yes, exactly," I replied. "I have nothing but respect for you, Nomarch. I can't imagine what it took." I ran a finger around the top of my drink.

Intensity filled her gaze as she passed off her plate to a steward and replaced it with spiced mead. Had my interest earned her favor?

As she took a sip, I added, "I'd hoped to get the opportunity to speak with you during The Ninety-Eight but never had the chance."

"Then we should rectify that within the next fortnight. I could never disappoint the crown's champion." She let my accomplishment linger before adding, "My people will try to keep me busy every heartbeat I'm here, but let's make time."

"I'd like that very much, Nomarch."

She valued my win, that much was clear, in what way, I couldn't begin to speculate, but the seed of an idea sprouted. Might I be the bridge between opposing sides in this divisive controversy? Might warriors rally behind the fact that I'd earned the ultimate honor on the battlefield where their rules dictated the outcome? They knew I'd represented the monarchy. Possibilities buzzed in my head.

"I understand congratulations are in order, Princess Alissandra," Formig said, halting my musings. "It hardly came as a surprise." She gave me a wry smirk.

I felt my cheeks warm and couldn't hold back a gleeful chuckle. "I suppose not. Prince Kovis wasn't exactly private with his feelings about me."

"First time I've ever seen the prince grin," she said.

Her expression turned wistful, and I wondered if she'd given up love to gain and maintain her position. At least I didn't think she'd married. I didn't actually know. Perhaps that would be some of what I'd learn about her when we chatted.

"I am happy for the both of you," she continued. "When is the joyous occasion to be celebrated?"

"Thank you, Nomarch. Prince Kovis and I have not yet set a date, but we'll be sure to include you on our guest list as soon as we do." I rubbed the back of my teardrop sapphire ring with my thumb. I wasn't about to tell her we'd chosen to wait to wed until Father had been dealt with.

Dane forced a polite smile and nodded, then scanned the room. "So where *are* the empress and princes?"

Formig's gaze bounced between her companion and me.

Crud. He wasn't letting it go.

"They were unexpectedly detained." Formig raised a brow and I hurried on. "They knew you would be weary after your long journey and did not want to inconvenience you. As a new representative of the crown, they asked me to do the honors." I forced a warm smile.

The nomarch's face took on a pinched look.

Okay, wrong thing to say.

"They felt horrible missing you." That didn't sound regal.

Dane's eyes turned cold, hard. "Why did you just not tell us that?"

I was making a mess of this. How could I salvage it?

"They will stop by your accommodations and personally greet you once they are available." I only hoped Rasa didn't object.

Formig tilted her head. "Will they now?"

Dane gave a cocky smile. "Have they personally greeted any other delegation?"

"No."

I sighed to myself when the pair nodded. I needed to get out of here. "I'd love to continue talking, but I'm sure you and your delegates would enjoy freshening up."

"We would," Formig said.

"Then allow me to show you to your rooms."

After leading the delegation up the one flight of stairs to the guest suites, I headed up one more flight and back to our rooms. I sank against the door when it closed, my nerves frayed.

What had I expected? I'd done my best under the circumstances. I'd had only one in-depth conversation with a warrior before this, Nomarch Kett. But one thing was clear, warriors were not people to toy with. They'd chew you up and spit you out.

My throat constricted.

Did Rasa truly understand who she was up against? How would she and Kovis ever get them to see things her way? What would this fortnight bring?

Chapter Fifteen

Two suns later, I wasn't sure how much Kennan had had to drink, but it was no small amount judging by his lack of coordination as the string of beads he'd attempted to toss to the cheering crowds on shore fell short and disappeared into the channel's water.

The sun was just peaking in the sky, and Kennan was unsteady on his feet. Things could only get worse.

Kovis frowned where he stood, he and Rasa flanking their sibling on our water taxi, turned royal float. It led a good four or five dozen parade floats decked out and drifting through the waterways of the artisan's district as part of the first half of the fortnight-long, empire-unifying festivities.

A hoot, then a holler erupted on shore, and a male bore his naked self, in all his glory, to us.

My eyes grew wide.

Rasa shook her head.

We had a festival of sandlings in Dream, but it was absolutely, positively nothing like this.

"Loosen up, sister," Kennan roared. "It might just get you a man." He grinned and rewarded the bare man by tossing a strand of shiny pink beads his way. But the momentum made him bobble, and he nearly fell over the knee-high side.

Kovis threw an arm across Kennan's chest just in time. Kovis's flaring nostrils told me he wanted to let his sibling swim for the comment about their sister.

"Thank. You." Kennan slurred the words.

"Hey, easy there," Kovis chided, clenching his jaw and forcing a smile, pretending nothing was amiss for the watching crowds as he steadied his brother.

In preparation for the sun's events, Kovis had warned me about the possibility of seeing things like this, but words of warning and actually seeing someone do it were completely different. He'd said both men and women bared themselves as a way to "earn" bead necklaces. When I'd asked why in the world they coveted the necklaces, he'd chuckled and said, "Status."

I'd burst out laughing. Call me naïve but who would want to be known for baring themselves?

Our royal float had been decorated as a one-man-tall bust of Rasa. Alfreda and I were perched up top in a tiny space beside Rasa's crown. I plastered on a smile and waved to the crowds on shore.

A group cheered raucously on shore as the float behind us passed—it was decked out in the finery of the insorcelled province of Juba. Three men and a well-endowed woman on shore earned themselves "status," and surprise lit my eyes as Nomarch Kett and Minister Wedgemore tossed them bead necklaces. I'd had a good conversation with Kett during The Ninety-Eight champion's dinner, and he'd seemed reasonable, so seeing his eyes light up and him grin was... unexpected.

Typical male.

I leaned over and asked my sister, "How long has Kennan been behaving like this?"

"Since that family dinner," Alfreda replied. She scrunched her face in disgust. "He's not violent. He usually just mopes."

I relaxed only a fraction. Nonviolence didn't make the situation with Kennan better, but at least, I didn't need to protect my sister. Had he been violent, I would have, in the blink of an eye, future royal brother or no.

"It's getting old," Alfreda said. "I've taken to finding things to do outside our rooms so I don't have to be near him."

"Good for you." She had enough to heal from without Kennan's issues.

Alfreda and I ducked as the craft approached another bridge that connected the two banks of the river. It was a good thing those who had constructed our float hadn't built it any taller, or we'd never have cleared the span. As it was, we had to crouch down as we approached each and every bridge or be impaled. Being on the small side had its benefits in this case, since they hadn't left us much room.

Kennan looked up as we cleared the bridge and began waving a handful of necklaces at those looking down on us. "Earn yourself some notor... notor... ety... fame."

A plump woman on the bridge, tore open her top and let her bare breasts bounce in the sunlight much to Kennan's delight. Several men around her looked drunk as they took their fill, too.

Kennan tossed the whole handful of shiny beads into her outstretched hands, and she shrieked, "I got 'em from the prince hisself!"

A grin, much like a cat who had devoured a tasty mouse, rose on Kennan's face as he ogled the woman's bosom. She continued shrieking her excitement as our craft moved away.

Kovis leaned over and said something to his sibling, but Kennan shouted back, "What? I'm fos..." He hiccupped. "...fostering the empire's culture."

Kennan twisted and plunged his hand into a barrel of bead necklaces that stood behind them. He came up with another handful of the treasures and waved them about, and at the top of his lungs shouted, "Who's next to get one from me?"

Rasa took a step away to avoid being struck by the baubles. Kennan didn't notice, only trained his eyes on the crowds on the bank and continued shouting his invitation. Kovis looked to be bracing to steady his twin again. I didn't doubt but what he'd need to.

"I'm sorry," I told Alfreda. Kennan's behavior was undoubtedly the result of my setting him straight, and while I would not shoulder the burden of how he'd taken it, I was sad that my sister had to bear the brunt.

She reached over and squeezed my hand. "I chose to come here. Neither of us could have foreseen this."

"If you ever need space from him, don't hesitate to come by."

Alfreda nodded. "I will."

"Woohoo!" Kennan bellowed, and quicker than I'd have believed, he dropped his pants, then grabbed two handfuls of necklaces and shook his bead-laden fists above his head.

Folks on shore hooted and hollered, and all manner of pandemonium broke out with men and woman alike shedding clothing.

"He's too modest, but being twins, we look identical!" Kennan exclaimed, then gyrated his hips.

The muscle in Kovis's jaw bulged as he stared daggers at his brother. The glint in Kennan's eyes told me he knew his brother wouldn't dare stop him—he'd risk alienating every insorcelled warrior if he did.

Movement drew my attention, and I watched folks on Juba's float following us, mimic the vulgar display that rippled through the crowds on shore. Sorcerers on Water province's barge behind them stared unmoving, but insorcelled on Tirana's water taxi that was next, joined in the revelry without reserve, including their leader, Nomarch Marson, if my eyes were true. I couldn't make out the floats beyond that, but judging by the increase in volume from shore, I could guess.

I squeezed Alfreda's hand as more and more watching eyes fell on her. Citizens knew I was engaged to Kovis so out of the five of us on this float, not counting our security detail or the Water sorcerer who provided the locomotion for our craft, it wasn't hard to guess whose "belle" she was. I barely leashed a growl. Jackass.

A quick look at Rasa had me marveling that she remained composed, directing the anger in her eyes at Kennan who ignored her with his continued exhibition. I couldn't believe she was able to maintain the appearance of calm. I don't know that I could have, but the vein bulging on the side of her neck betrayed her. Over the last moon, I'd gotten to know Rasa and had learned her tells. She could be scary when upset. And she was livid.

This incident was far from over.

Chapter Sixteen

Resplendent and pure notes from the harpsichord, rebec, and other stringed instruments at the front of the ballroom lilted above the ugly, poisonous words. Kovis and I ignored as we engaged Representatives Destrian and Alderman and their nomarch, Marson, of Tirana in conversation. I ran my finger around the top of my champagne flute feeling ever more on edge from Destrian's continual eyeing me up and down.

I tried to tamp down the chill that coursed through my body—his marauding gaze reminded me of the way *those* prison guards had lusted after me during my assault. It had been moons since I'd thought of it, and it made no rational sense that I'd remember now, but it didn't have to. Despite winning The Ninety-Eight, my body instinctively recoiled.

I glanced toward the doors. When would Rasa arrive so we could ditch this trio and take our places for this, the fifth dinner of the fortnight-long meeting of leaders?

I let my eyes wander to the nearby window, over Nomarch Marson's stiff shoulder, just as he pulled it back in response to Kovis's remark. I blocked him out and focused on the lights that danced above the Canyon as majestic as ever.

These three were from yet another insorcelled province incensed by Rasa's plan to end the biannual competition, and they were letting us know it, yet again, in no uncertain terms. It had become the theme of things before Rasa arrived each evening.

I'd asked Kovis why we couldn't just arrive later to avoid these confrontations, but he insisted everyone needed to feel as though they were being heard, whether or not it changed anything. Avoidance would accomplish nothing save frustrating them, and from experience, he knew when they felt frustrated, no good came of it.

"All bow for Empress Altairn," a liveried steward announced over the din as he stopped before the head table.

At last.

Silence blanketed the ballroom as the finely crafted, double doors to his left opened and Rasa strode through. She looked stunning as usual in a royal-blue, off-the-shoulder, A-line gown with a sweep train. The high front slit put her long, sexy legs on display and not a few men's eyes flitted to them before they bowed.

Males.

I rose again at Rasa's command, and Kovis excused us from that damnable conversation and drew his hand to the small of my back. I happily placed my hand on the royal-blue sleeve of his knee-length tunic and allowed him to direct us to our seats at the head table that stretched across the front of the room. Only five elaborate place settings occupied the spaces before the twelve chairs on our side of the table and Kovis located us right of center, where Rasa would sit.

Kennan, with Alfreda on the arm of his white tunic, found their places to the left of Rasa's, several heartbeats later. While Kovis's twin didn't pretend to be enjoying himself, he at least didn't appear inebriated. My sister made an attempt to appear engaged with the festivities, plastering on a fake smile that might fool everyone but me.

I caught her eye, and she jerked down the pretty burgundy-lace sleeve of her gown.

Yep, she was more than unhappy.

I nodded, hoping she'd interpret my show of support as just that.

Rasa's arrival beside Kovis stilled my musings, and the ballroom filled with the sounds of over three hundred chairs scraping across the marble floor as everyone took their seats.

Once stewards refilled everyone's libation, Rasa rose and held her champagne flute high. Attendees mimicked and a hush filled the room.

Rasa opened her mouth to begin the toast, but instead of words coming out, she swayed forward, blinking rapidly. She caught herself, barely, before listing right, her hand still holding her drink aloft.

Kovis grabbed for her but missed, and she crumpled to the floor behind his chair, her glass shattering against the marble.

Shouts filled the air, and stewards scurried.

Kovis eased his chair back. I bolted up and brushed the largest shards of glass away with my sandal, then fell to my knees and grabbed Rasa's limp hand. Healing still felt rusty after our long absence, but I grabbed Terra and Wood threads from a few attendees and focused my attention on her body trying to locate whatever beset her.

"Summon Jathan!" Kovis commanded, lifting his head from where he knelt beside me.

"Be seated," Kennan roared.

I blocked out the commotion. Trouble was, I wasn't finding anything wrong with her. She'd only had time for a few sips of her drink while stewards had refilled attendees' glasses. All the same, I suspected poison, but I wasn't finding any traces of the substances I knew in her system. It didn't rule poisoning out; there were a plethora of toxins I didn't know, but the most common were not the cause.

But a heartbeat later, I locked onto something foreign and dark, erupting from her head, and it sent a chill racing up my spine.

Rasa screamed and every muscle in my body froze as a black stick poked out of her ear.

I screeched along with Alfreda as a second curved, black stick protruded from her nose.

Kovis's grip tensed on my shoulder and he pulled me back as Rasa let loose another terrifying shriek. Long, narrow, plated pincers erupted from her eyes despite being closed. The protrusions looked eerily familiar.

No, no, no, please no, I prayed.

Alfreda recoiled and Kennan spun her around and enfolded her in his arms. She trembled as she clutched him fiercely, face buried in his chest.

Fear ravaged me. The head of a giant beetle had emerged and more of the oversize insect was bursting from Rasa's head by the time I looked back. It utterly and completely wrecked me as its antennae felt the air. A rock beetle. I'd have recognized the vile creature anywhere.

I shrieked, thrust my shoulder forward throwing Kovis's hand off, and scrambled up, tripping on the abundant fabric of my gown in my haste as the wings materialized. The thing was as big as the beetles I'd killed in the cave, maybe bigger. Only the press of people stopped me from running.

"Stay back!" Kennan's command fell on deaf ears as the roar of the crowd encircling us reached fever pitch.

"The Empress needs air! Move back!" Kovis shouted.

Kennan shook his head, fear and disgust filling his eyes, then eased Alfreda aside and let loose his flames at the crowd.

The press roared louder, but edged back.

Kovis pushed them farther as he added his winds.

I looked on from where I clung to the edge of the crowd, terror biting into me. This could only be Father's work. First the nightmare come to life that got Kovis and Kennan stabbed and now this? He was still loose. My stomach twisted. What was Auden suffering to accomplish this?

Rasa thrashed as the remainder of the creature freed itself from her head and set the last of its six hairy feet on the floor, it's torso hovering above her still face, brushing her with the disgusting hairs that protruded from its underbelly.

I was only barely keeping it together as wave upon wave of terror washed over me.

I need to help Kennan hold people back. You can do it, Ali.

Rasa and others would die in the thing's deadly pincers if I didn't master my raging emotions. I took a deep breath, swallowing my fear. I'd killed two rock beetles. I had. I could kill this one too.

One step forward. It's all I took before the beetle eyed me.

The creature mimicked, but took three steps toward me, opening and closing its pincers. Like the beetles in the cave that had come to my thigh, this creature was a plate-covered fighting machine, but bigger—it came to my waist.

It raised its iridescent wings—their color shifted from emerald to cobalt. The thing might have been beautiful if not so terrifying. It was readying to fly at me.

My blood raced, and it grew increasingly hard to breathe. I couldn't stand these abominations. Evil and death coursed through their veins.

I took a fighting stance and stretched out my hands, forcing long, slow breaths.

"Get back unless you want to be struck!" Kovis yelled, strengthening his winds.

I waited only a heartbeat for the circle of onlookers to step back before letting loose a stream of ice needles that shredded the creature's wings. It's stumps only quivered by the time I was done.

"Back!" Kennan bellowed.

The beetle was big, but it wasn't quick, and I darted behind it, formed an ice dagger, and released it. But in that same heartbeat, the disagreeable Nomarch Marson rolled on his side, into the circle. Idiot. He'd found a way below Kennan's flames and Kovis's winds.

He leapt up, ran three quick steps, drew his sword high, and plunged it down, into the creature's back, just behind its shredded wings.

I diverted the ice blade I'd just released, with my winds, only barely missing the warrior. My weapon shot up to the coved ceiling that an artist had taken great pains with, and impaled itself, lodging in the painted arm of a winged god as he reached down to a man's extended hand. I hoped whichever of my Dream relations it was supposed to depict never found out.

Plaster sprinkled to the floor below.

The rock beetle took one step before its spinally legs buckled and it slumped to the floor, black blood oozing from where the tip of the blade protruded from its abdomen. I nearly retched.

Kovis and Kennan killed their magic as silence fell. No one so much as shifted, every eye transfixed by the site until thundering shouts of celebration by Representatives Destrian and Alderman shattered the quiet.

As one, every insorcelled warrior roared in praise of the heroic act of their fellow leader. Magical representatives cheered, but not as heartily. Their eyes bounced between Tirana's leaders and me, their looks telling me they believed Marson had robbed me of the kill that was rightfully mine.

Let them have their victory lap, I cared more about Rasa. I nodded and hopefully communicated my willingness to forego glory, happy that the abomination had been killed.

Jathan emerged from the tightly paced throng, raced past me, and fell to his knees beside Rasa.

Kovis reached me at the same time and drew me close with an arm around my shoulders.

Well done, my love.

I squeezed his hand and glanced among those still watching and my stomach clenched. Rasa was coming around, but a twinkle danced in Representative Destrian's eyes. Heartless bastard!

I spotted no fewer than nine more insorcelled leaders who shared his excitement, and I grew incensed. How could they rejoice at a time like this?

They intend to exploit what happened, Kovis said. *I can hear their spin already—the empress was possessed and loosed a deadly killing beetle on her own leaders.*

Are you kidding me?

I wish I was, Kovis said, as he rubbed my shoulder.

Father. He had to be the cause... and poor Auden. I shuddered, not wanting to even consider what might happen next.

Chapter Seventeen

I'd been naïve, and my stomach had tied itself in knots over the last seven suns since I'd welcomed Eslor's delegation. I'd told Nomarch Formig I wanted to get to know her more. I had, too, before she'd bared her teeth.

But the appointed time had arrived.

Clad in my leathers, I walked into the busy Pits as the sun sank to half its height above the horizon—I'd questioned Formig's request that we meet here, where sorcerers trained, despite her not being one. Why would she ask to meet here? And how did she anticipate having a conversation with all the noise?

Crowds packed the observation decks above the three large pits, and I heard sounds of battle emanating from the fourth, the smallest. A roar went up from spectators watching the match in the second pit, underscoring my concerns.

Several sorcerers, dressed in training garb in a host of colors depending upon their affinity, acknowledged me with a bow despite the fact that I wasn't yet, officially, royalty. I reciprocated with a nod, and they went back to what they'd been doing.

"Favian, Koal," I said, smiling at two sorcerers whose muscled, tattooed chests still heaved from exertion. Kovis had introduced me to these best-of-the-best sorcerers ages ago. They'd been among the ones who, along with Kennan, had helped me discover my affinities.

I still remembered Koal nearly besting me, chasing me around the pit, pelting me with a funnel of water until the floor swam. But I'd turned the tables, transforming the soggy mess into quicksand, and stuck knee-deep in the bog, he'd had to concede.

Since our return, Kovis or one of them trained with me.

"Like to join us?" Favian said, wiping his brow. The tattoo on his bare chest turned blue—trust and loyalty. "Prince Kovis isn't here at present."

"Actually I'm meeting—"

"I thought we might speak woman to woman," Nomarch Formig said, her boots hitting the stone as she strode to a stop beside me. She brushed her auburn cape over one, then the other shoulder as Dane and five others of her delegation stepped beside her, also clad in worn leathers.

The nomarch ran her eyes over my sparring companions' chests, then lower, much lower, lingering there, before returning to their faces. A corner of her mouth rose.

They grinned.

I felt my cheeks warm. Sure I enjoyed sneaking glimpses of Kovis in the same way, appreciating his toned muscles, his lithe body, as well as... other parts. I had, even before we were engaged, but I'd never... She was so brazen. Did she regularly satisfy her desires with beautiful men such as these? Is that what her delegation was, at least in part? The rogue thoughts refused to be harnessed and heated my cheeks all the more.

And here I'd had visions of being some kind of pure and honorable bridge between the monarchy and warriors as the crown's champion. I'd significantly underestimated the situation, that much was clear. Sunshine and rainbows, that's what my siblings had called me. It seemed they were right. I was much too innocent and naïve to compete on this playing field.

"I would count it an honor to spar with the crown's champion. I thought we might, oh, I don't know, have you show us, firsthand, your skill against... us." She surveyed her companions.

So *that's* what this was about.

Favian's and Koal's eyes grew large.

My eyes shot to the six warriors—four men and two women—who stood with hands clasped behind their backs. Even the smallest female towered above me. While I couldn't see weapons on them, I had no doubt they'd come armed.

Seven against one. I'd faced worse odds in my rounds at The Ninety-Eight. Of course, I'd saved myself fighting in the final when I put several of them to sleep.

As if reading my thoughts, Dane said, "We'd ask that you not put us to sleep."

Formig nodded.

Fine. "I had wanted to converse," I said as I inventoried the affinities of the sorcerers around me, assessing the powers I'd have to draw upon.

"Oh, we will," Formig replied. "You indicated you wanted to get to know me better. I just thought this might be more fun than just sitting and chatting."

More fun. For who?

I scanned her group again. To a one, they held serious expressions. They'd be tough, but they lacked magic. And I could still throw a dagger with deadly accuracy, not that I'd try to kill them. "Very well."

"Wonderful." Then turning to Favian, Formig said, "Would you be so kind to clear one of those arenas? We'll need room." She waved a hand at the three large ovals.

Favian looked to me with a raised brow, but I nodded him into action. No doubt word of our match would spread like wildfire.

In no time, I braced in my fighting stance, arms extended, boots dug into the sand. My opponents had spread out around the oval, occupying the apexes—they'd ensured I'd have a blind spot.

Eager crowds clogged the platform above as I'd expected. Several shouted encouragement to me, others to my opponents.

Favian, standing with Koal on the upper edge of the oval, dropped the starting stone. The heartbeat it hit the sand, I drew up my winds, building a wide, protective hedge about me.

My Air magic repelled seven daggers that greeted me in the blink of an eye, tossing them to the sand.

Cheers echoed above.

The four males at one end, raced for me.

I added sand to my winds. I didn't care that it clouded my view. Good luck broaching this barrier.

"Princess!" Formig shouted from behind me. "Let's talk."

"Great!"

The males dropped to the sand, crossed their arms over their chests, and rolled on their sides, trying to breech my cocoon like Marson had with Kovis's winds while battling that rock beetle. The image sent a shiver down my spine even now, no doubt intentional. I brought my winds down, even with the sand, but the men didn't stop.

"Warriors aren't upset about The Ninety-Eight," the nomarch said.

Surprise bit, and I lost concentration on my winds for a heartbeat as I pivoted to face her. "You could have fooled me."

I felt movement behind me and whirled back around. One of the males towered over me, inside my cocoon, knife poised. Damn!

He'd slid under my barrier when Formig broke my concentration. Her comment had been calculated. The trickle of blood oozing down the warrior's cheek where sand in my winds had kissed him, didn't slow him.

"The Ninety-Eight represents our culture, what we value."

I kept my sand cocoon up and locked eyes with my opponent, then drew a thread of Water from Koal and let loose, much as he had me, ages before. The knife flew from my opponent's grip, and he threw his hands up to shield his face.

I lowered the wall of my cocoon to waist height, readying to toss him across the pit, but Formig and the two female warriors had anticipated my move.

"Warrior provinces protect Elementis, the magical provinces. Would you not agree?" Formig asked, as she and her companions leapt my lowered sand wall in a heartbeat.

Surprise killed my concentration. It killed the Water magic, too, and the crowds gasped as the trio of women and the hulking male converged and brought their blades down in unison before I could react.

The force of their punches jolted me—one to my chest, one to a shoulder, one to the middle of my back—but the blades bounced off my leathers. I drew my winds up and pushed them back, but not before Formig's blade found the back of my exposed hand and dug in, piercing muscle. "Would you not agree?" It came out a growl as we locked eyes.

She'd impaled me! Formig had impaled me!

Anger replaced shock as pain shot up my arm. Any notion that she'd been playing evaporated like mist, and my heart began to race.

The other three warriors had joined them by the time I wrested Fire magic from Favian. I felled one male and one of the women until they no longer moved, then I willed my flames to separate the five remaining foe—yes foe—my ire grew with the heat of the magic.

Pain wracked my hand from the still-impaled blade as I lost more and more blood. I seethed as I backed them up, step after unrelenting step. All five fought me even after I pinned them against the oval's walls where I held them with Fire.

Cheers erupted from above.

"Would you not agree that Warrior provinces protect the magical ones?" Formig shouted her question.

With the pain, coherent thoughts proved a challenge, but I spit out, "Yes, you protect Elementis."

"Yet the monarchy does not value us," Formig's voice again emanated from across the oval.

I grit my teeth and yanked the blade from my hand. Agony shot up my arm and more red flowed down my fingers.

Several onlookers yipped.

"Just because the empress wants to eliminate that deadly competition doesn't mean warriors aren't valued," I ground out, nursing my wound.

"Look out!" Shouts drew my attention. Three, four, five, six daggers flew at me with deadly aim forcing me to leap, bob, duck, and sidestep to avoid being impaled.

Flames weren't enough to neuter them it seemed.

"What does one do to show they value another?" the nomarch asked. Her question taunted.

How in Hades would I know? I'd never stopped to ponder it.

Roars erupted as two of the males, the largest of the seven, breached my fire walls and the repugnant stench of singed hair erupted. Not even burns marring their faces slowed them.

"Behind you!" a spectator cried.

Another warrior was nearly upon me.

Enough! It was time to end this. Formig hadn't been playing, I wouldn't either. I extinguished my flames and again drew Water magic from Koal. I enhanced it with more magic from another five Water sorcerers in the crowd, then sprayed my attackers, drenching the pit in the process. I added my winds for good measure, holding nothing back. But release did little to ease my fury, and while my opponents struggled in the deluge, they didn't stop.

Formig wanted an answer, I'd give her one. "You invest in and spend time with those you value," I snipped. "Elementis invested much in Eslor, all the insorcelled provinces, and what thanks do we get?" I eyed Formig as she battled the pummeling water. Good. Struggle a bit. "And I honestly wanted to get to know you better. I didn't do it to prove anything. You all seem to always have mixed motives." I didn't add a gripe that my overture at friendship seemed to have fallen on deaf ears.

Despite being pelted, the five warriors roared with laughter as they took labored step after labored step, drawing closer.

They'd rejected my reply.

And stoked my fury further.

I located three Ice mages in the crowd and pulled a thread of magic from each. Kovis had stopped me by freezing the wet sand, I would stop them.

A thought was all it took to kill the pounding water and fierce winds. Another thought froze the soggy, sandy mess the floor had become.

Silence blanketed the Pits as everything settled, but shouts soon banished quiet as onlookers took in the scene.

Ice coated the five warriors from their necks down, making them look like frosty statues standing in a circle, mid stride, three men's height from me. Only their heads jerked, nostrils flaring as they fought their frigid bonds.

It wasn't in my nature to gloat, but I would make an exception. I was fed up with being attacked. All I'd wanted was to sit down and have a nice chat with the leader.

Instead, my hand dripped blood from Formig trying to *kill* me. I'd certainly gotten to know her better. Boy, had I. Any questions I'd had about how she'd achieved her position had been more than answered.

I clenched my jaw.

Acting blatantly seemed a key component of the bluntness warriors understood, and I had a message to send. I clutched my bloody hand to my chest and swaggered over to Nomarch Formig.

Unlike her fellows, the leader didn't struggle. Rather she locked eyes with me, and in an even tone said, "If you believe investing in and spending time with people are the only ways you show you value warriors, it is no wonder the situation is what it is. The monarchy has indeed invested, but it has certainly never spent time trying to understand warriors."

I furrowed my brow, as the leader went on. "Valuing another requires far more. It requires listening to them, being interested in what interests them, acknowledging them publicly, saying thank you every now and again, treating them equally, giving them opportunities to use their talents to further the empire's goals, and gods forbid, praising them for a job well done. *That* is what it means to truly value another."

My anger shriveled a bit as I opened and closed my mouth like a fish out of water. She made a strong case.

The crowd grew uneasy.

A corner of Formig's mouth rose. "Make no mistake, Champion." She paused and let my title linger. "There are malcontents in every province who would shake off what they view as the bonds of captivity to this empire, but those are the few. Eslor and the other warrior provinces have increased in prosperity as a result of becoming part of the Altairn empire, but we will not stand for being viewed, much less treated, as second-class citizens."

Hoots and shouts erupted from the observation deck as warriors agreed. Sorcerers shifted, drew back, and lifted chins in an attempt to appear above Formig's correction.

Was she right? Did most warriors only seek to be valued as she'd said? She wasn't wrong that the monarchy didn't go out of its way to express appreciation. Rasa viewed them as barbarians. I speculated she didn't believe they cared about recognition. More and more questions rose, and my anger fizzled.

Eslor's nomarch cleared her throat, drawing my attention back. "We yield." She looked down at her frozen form.

I drew in a breath. They'd yielded. I dissolved the ice in a heartbeat.

"Think about what I said, Champion," she said, flicking ice shards from her leathers as her compatriots approached.

I braced, holding my aching, dripping hand closer. They'd tried to kill me; I wouldn't forget it.

The biggest male stopped before me and pulled my uninjured arm away, in his meaty hand. I fought his grip until he said, "Thank you for the honor of this competition, Crown's Champion."

Wait. What? My brain tangled itself up.

"I shall treasure this contest all my suns," another added.

"We knew we wouldn't beat you, but thank you for doing your best against us," one of the women said.

"It's clear you gained your title honestly and with honor," the smallest male added.

The rest included other slants to their praise, but I couldn't deny it was genuine, and they rendered me speechless.

The nomarch grasped my forearm and bobbed her head. "Thank you for the honor, Champion. I shall cherish our friendship."

Friendship. Friendship? This is how warriors treated friends?

I begrudgingly replied, "Thank you for helping me understand."

She nodded, then motioned her warriors to help the two fallen. I watched as they did, then mounted the steps of the pit to roaring cheers as they carried the fallen. I still couldn't process it all.

Nomarch Formig had used my desire to know her better to further her own objectives. What did that say about her? I didn't know her motives. Had she done it to bring peace between warriors and sorcerers? Or to further her position among the nomarchs by battling the crown's champion? I couldn't begin to reconcile it.

But another thought froze me: Rasa, Kovis, the other nomarchs, Council representatives, no doubt every citizen of Veritas and beyond would hear tales of what had happened.

What had I done? What might I have started?

Chapter Eighteen
Rasa

One last dinner, just one more before this fortnight-long meeting was over. But how would the final banquet go on the morrow? My throat constricted.

The Canyon's lights rippled above me in all their glory against the starry night sky. They'd been doing it for eons—my life was as a gnat's compared to them. I breathed in the fresh, cool air trying to calm my fraying nerves. I'd come to Mother's garden to get some perspective.

I brushed a pale primrose petal from the edge of the fur blanket stretched out beneath me.

Delegates would leave, and we'd have our home back. I wouldn't miss seeing some of these unsavory characters in the halls at all times of the sun.

The breeze made ripples in the pond's waters. Nothing like the rhythmic sounds of lapping water to calm. It was a potion for my weary soul.

Speaking of... I exhaled. Jathan hadn't found anything wrong with me despite observing me for nearly a sun. He'd concluded I'd been deep in sleep, much as Kovis and Kennan when Ali tested Somnus on them, and suffered a day terror, he'd said. The facts hadn't expunged the resulting nightmare brewing with Council members. Nor had they eased my worry that it could happen again, at any time.

Cold fingers traced my spine, and I drew my cloak tighter. I wouldn't pretend it was to ward off the chill. Hearing that an enormous rock beetle had erupted from my head, nearly sent me over the emotional edge I thought I'd distanced myself from.

Breathe in. Breathe out. Slow.

But Kennan... I'd wanted to knock sense into him for his behavior during that parade. It had been inexcusable, but after lengthy contemplation, I'd chosen to bite my tongue.

My heart ached for him. He hadn't been himself since he returned. I couldn't fathom the trauma he'd endured—unimaginable danger from all manner of beast, starvation, and nigh freezing to death in that godsforsaken wilderness. Sanity had been the price of his return. Would we ever get him back?

I blew out a breath. I'd asked myself the same question about Kovis many a time, too. Until Ali had rescued him from himself. Would Alfreda rescue Kennan? I'd seen no evidence of it thus far.

Scuffing footsteps on the pebble path drew my attention.

"Good, it's just you, sister." Kennan shook his head, approaching.

"Evening to you, too, brother." I chuckled. "Who else would it be?"

My sibling frowned as he stopped at the edge of my blanket. "I stumbled upon Kovis and Ali..."—he cleared his throat—"making love."

My cheeks warmed. "Here?"

He nodded. "As naked as the sun they were born."

"I see."

Anger flashed in his eyes, but quickly gave way to pain that lingered. I wouldn't probe. I'd once been able to read him like one of his beloved novels, but not anymore. Since he'd returned, he'd explode as easily as have a civil conversation. Would he talk to me tonight?

I patted the fur beside me.

He hesitated for a heartbeat but finally nodded and took a seat, pulling up his knees and hunching forward.

We sat soaking in the silence for a long while until Kennan said, "I owe you an apology."

I furrowed my brow.

"While on that parade float."

Ah yes, that.

"In my drunken state, I told you to loosen up. That it might just get you a man." He hung his head. "The heartbeat it left my lips I wished I could pull it back." He shook his head.

I picked at a thread caught in the hairs of the fur.

"It was cruel, and it's tormented me. I'm not that kind of a man, at least I didn't used to be. I'm not sure who I am anymore." He lifted his head and turned toward me. "I'm so sorry, sister. Can you ever forgive me?"

I met his eyes and let several heartbeats pass before I said, "Perhaps you were right. Perhaps I should loosen up a bit."

He tilted his head.

"Make no mistake, I don't condone your wild behavior. It was unbecoming of your station and your role, but perhaps it took you being uninhibited to say what you really feel. As you've been doing of late about so many things."

A grin slowly rose on his lips.

"I would like to wed one sun, but you're right, I'm a bit prickly. Ali's the first person I've had the courage to let in."

A scowl obliterated Kennan's grin.

I pursed my lips in response. I didn't know what I'd said to change his mood so radically, but unless I wanted him to explode, I needed to change the subject. "How are you doing, Kennan?"

He gave me a long look, then turned back and started bouncing his feet.

I didn't think he'd answer, but at length, he slumped and said, "Honestly... I feel like I'm in a castle with thousands of doors. I keep opening new doors hoping to find my way out of this nightmare, but every door I open leads me right back to where I started. I sense Kovis and Ali are in grave danger, and I'm searching and searching for them—*nothing* but finding them matters. I try and I try, but I can't search fast enough. I wake panting, sometimes screaming because I know something horrible has happened to them, and it's all my fault because I was too slow."

"Oh, Kennan..." I drew a hand to my chest. I'd no idea things were this bad. I longed to comfort him, but how? I resisted an idea that sprung to mind. I couldn't share... no not that...

My stomach clenched.

Yet I'd found the courage to open up to Ali. Her receptivity had only encouraged more.

Kennan stared at the water unaware of my inner turmoil.

I took a deep breath and let it out slowly. It would be worth it, if it helped restore him.

Resistance be damned! I opened my mouth and forced the words out. "I felt lost after Father killed himself..."

Kennan turned toward me with an incredulous stare.

A sudden coldness hit my core, but I pressed on. "I'd been thrust into my role as empress. While Father had prepared me for it, I didn't feel at all ready. I felt hollow, a shell, with no idea who I was... not after..."

I tossed my head from side to side, reliving the despair. I sucked in a deep breath.

"I wanted to rule well, wanted to lead this empire to be stronger than it had ever been. To be more peaceful than I could ever remember."

Kennan opened his mouth, then closed it again.

"Mercifully, I had only our mourning moon to come to grips before my coronation. It sped my recovery. Because I knew, down deep, I couldn't rule well—not the way our people deserve—the way I was." I forced a smile. "So what changed?"

Kennan nodded.

"I realized that I could let my lostness control me, or I could control it. The realization came when I was looking out the conservatory windows at the mountain behind the castle. Snows had left, and all I saw were the imperfections of the trees against the ground—broken branches, bare limbs, exposed rock. I couldn't change it. I couldn't make it beautiful like happens in spring.

"But then I saw my reflection in the window as I looked out. Shadows lingered beneath my eyes. My cheeks were sunken. I lacked joy. In that heartbeat, I realized I was seeing two ways at the same time, getting two perspectives if you will."

Kennan didn't flinch, only continued staring.

"And for the first time, I understood I had power to focus on my reflection over the ugliness of the mountain."

I let my words linger.

"Changing my perspective wouldn't alter that mountain, but it would allow me to focus on something that *could* be beautiful."

Silence reigned until Kennan leaned over and swallowed me in his arms. Into my shoulder, he said, "I'd no idea. I knew you lacked confidence, but... thank you. Just... thank you."

We held each other. His strong arms that had been absent for so long eased some of my angst, and I lingered. We both did.

I finally pulled back and swiped the back of my hand across my eyes. Kennan mimicked and let out a choked laugh.

"How are *you* doing, sister?"

We'd been transparent with each other, he deserved to know I struggled so I ran down my litany of concerns.

"Have you heard any chatter on the grapevine concerning Formig's match with Ali?" I asked at last.

"Warriors think it was a stroke of genius. Sorcerers seem split. Why?"

"I accept Formig's premise. We haven't praised them for the value they provide the empire, but I'm concerned that giving them too much recognition will make their heads swell and render them impossible to deal with. If you thought eliminating The Ninety-Eight was a challenge, just wait."

Kennan nodded.

"We need to find a path to recognize their contributions while keeping them reasonable. I won't recognize warriors to the exclusion of others. Peace and strength come when everyone works together for the good of all, and while we'll never please everyone, pleasing more is imperative."

"But how?"

Yes, how. That *was* the question.

We sat in companionable silence as my mind mulled. The rainbow of colors continued dancing across the pond. Water lapped the shore. Scurrying sounds across the pebbled path—no doubt a furry coypu—rose not far off.

At length, an idea rose. And Kennan might just be the man for the task. I hesitated. His behavior had been erratic of late, but giving him something productive that would benefit the empire might give him a goal and restore meaning to his life. Yes, I'd give him the opportunity.

"Kennan..."

He turned from the knee-high baby dragon, complete with fire blazing from its mouth, he'd been constructing in the sand. No doubt there would be an entire family, treasure horde and all, before long.

My smile drew a corner of his mouth upward, and he shrugged. "It's nothing."

"What would you say to helping me develop greater cultural intelligence concerning warriors?"

"I'm listening."

"I'll be the first to say I don't have any depth of knowledge to draw from to make them feel more valued, and until I do, we will be at a disadvantage."

Kennan shifted. "What are you suggesting?"

"I want to show the people of every insorcelled province that we care about them, that we seek to understand them and appreciate the diversity of their cultures as part of this empire."

"Okay. It's what Formig not so subtly hinted at."

"Exactly. I'm needed here in the capital, as is Kovis. But you have more freedom." Kennan's jaw tensed. "You could go to the warrior provinces on a goodwill mission. Spend time with them, experience their culture, get to know them. When you return, I'd hope to implement some warrior-inspired traditions that will better unify this empire."

Kennan ground his teeth, starring at the fur blanket. "A job for the spare."

"What? No." My voice rose at his accusation. "You could provide valuable insights that would strengthen this empire for eons. I'd go if I could, but I can't. You know that."

"Right."

"Kennan—"

He stood, wiped his hands together, and brushed sand from his pants.

"Kennan—"

His boot connected with the baby dragon's round belly, and left nothing but a V in the sand as he strode off.

"Kennan...." I sighed.

Chapter Nineteen

Kennan

"She made it official! Gods damn her! She knew I didn't want to go on some 'cultural intelligence' tour."

Alfreda's eyes roamed our rooms seemingly worried someone would overhear my ranting and report my treasonous explosion to Rasa. I hoped they did.

A button flew off my royal-blue tunic as I ripped at the neck that felt as though it grew more and more constricting, tighter and tighter, like a snake squeezing the life out of me.

"Another job for the spare," I said, fuming.

Frustration welled up in me—at this, at Alfreda's constantly "organizing" my rooms so I couldn't find anything, and over not feeling like myself anymore. Enough was enough, I was fed up with all of it.

"I'm sure she didn't mean it that way," Alfreda countered. She hadn't moved from where she gripped the carved top of a chair at the dining table.

I turned my anger on her. "What would you know? Of course she did! She *knew* I didn't want to go back out there."

Alfreda's knuckles turned white as I strode toward her, fury fueling my steps. She backed into another chair making the skirts of her long gown flare out against its legs.

I didn't know what I'd to do to her, but rage egged me on. "She hasn't known *what* to do with me since I returned. She thinks I'm out of control! Ha! She should look in the mirror! Sending me away seems a *very* convenient way to deal with yet another situation she has no clue how to address."

Alfreda cowered.

I ignored, nearing to within two steps of her. But movement out of the corner of my eye drew me up short. By the time I turned, one of my largest paintings had risen up of its own accord, then walloped me hard enough so my head broke through the canvas. It pressed down until my arms were bound firmly at my sides.

Alfreda's eyes grew wide.

"What?" My fury raged ever hotter as I jerked about, fighting my bonds.

"I'm... I'm sorry." A look of horror crossed Alfreda's face.

I threw a shoulder forward. "Why are you apologizing?"

"I... I was desperate. I wished something would stop you... and it did."

I stopped struggling and wrinkled my forehead. "What are you talking about?"

"I think I caused that." It came out a whimper.

"You?"

She bobbed her head. "You scared me."

I drew in a breath, then sighed as reason reasserted itself and I calmed. "I'm sorry."

I shifted my shoulders, trying to extricate myself, but the damn painting held firm, even constricted a bit if I wasn't imagining things. It behaved as if magic controlled it, but Alfreda didn't...

I turned piercing eyes on her. She bit her lip, studying me.

"Your sister recently manifested her magical powers."

She nodded, then cocked her head.

"I may have scared you to the point yours just did, too. I'm sorry."

"My powers?" Her eyes grew as large as saucers and she drew a hand to her mouth.

"Magical powers don't acquiesce to easily revealing themselves. They hide until something dramatic outs them." I exhaled heavily. "I may have scared you to the point your affinity manifested. If that's the case, like your sisters, it seems whatever power this is, is not of the Canyon."

"It's not?"

I shook my head, then huffed, irritated with myself. I'd scared her, badly. This was not the man I was, not the one I wished to be at least. "I'm sorry I frightened you. I was just so angry."

"I'm sorry your sister upset you."

"I haven't been feeling like myself of late. Please forgive me."

Alfreda slowly bobbed her head, eyes still locked with mine. No doubt she didn't trust me enough to take her eyes off me.

I could have burned the canvas off with my Fire magic, but after scaring her, I didn't want to make things worse. "I promise I won't hurt you. Do you think you could help free me?"

She studied my face no doubt looking for tells that I lied, but at length, she stepped forward and helped me wrestle the canvas up and over my shoulders. Yes, wrestle, it took considerable effort to pry the painting up and over my head.

Gripping it by the edges, I looked at the rough hole through the middle. The idyllic gazebo surrounded by flowers now flapped limply. "Guess I won't be hanging this up after all."

She tried to hide a smirk, but failed.

Served me right. I deserved to be laughed at. I tossed the ruined painting onto the table.

Alfreda gave me a frown. I'd messed up her clean tabletop, so wound me.

Questioning welled up in me. "You wished for that painting to stop me. Let's see you do it again."

"I don't understand." She worried her lip.

"Moving things usually requires Air magic, but I didn't feel any breeze, so I'm guessing it's something else."

Her mind raced, I could see it in her eyes, no doubt considering what she'd done.

"I've got Fire and Metal magic," I said. "I know how to coax those to life, but I've never seen this kind of power, so I'm not sure how to help you repeat it, but if its magic, you'll be able to."

"How do I try? How should I start?"

I moved beside her and assumed a ready position, shoulders relaxed, feet apart, hands outstretched. "Stand like this."

I couldn't tell if her feet were in the correct position what with her long skirt, but the rest of her posture looked right.

"Magic is directed with thought. When I want to ignite a flame, I think about starting a small fire in my hand."

"Show me?"

I turned my hand palm up and did what I'd just explained. Alfreda gasped as a tiny flame erupted.

"Doesn't it hurt?" Her voice rose.

I chuckled. "No, fire can never hurt me because I bear its magical essence."

Alfreda brought her hand close to the flame. "It feels hot."

I drew my other hand above the flame, then lowered it for several heartbeats before pulling back again.

Alfreda grabbed my hand and ran a finger over where my palm should have been burned. "That doesn't hurt?"

I shook my head. "Not at all."

"And you think I can move things?"

"It looks that way."

She gave me a long look. "How do I position my hands?"

"Hold them palms up, at least until we know if there's a better position."

She nodded, then mimicked me. "Okay, what's next?"

"Perhaps focus on an object and think about moving it. Command it to obey you."

"Okay... I'll try to move that book." She fixed her gaze on *Love Sonnets* resting on the end table beside the couch. I was rather attached to the tome; it had been my great-grandfathers. Its binding was fragile from both our use.

If she could move objects, what else might she do with her talents? My mind mulled as I waited for the book to move even a finger breadth.

At length she exhaled heavily. "Nothing's happening."

"How did you command it?"

"I just told it to move."

"Did you tell it where to move? Perhaps you need to give it more direction."

"I'll try that." Alfreda drew her arms back up and tried again.

But at length, she pressed her lips tight. "It's still not working. I told the book to move to the sofa."

I took a deep breath. "Okay, maybe try this. Maybe you need to feel more urgency. Envision me attacking you."

She nodded.

"You're terrified, yet I'm still coming at you. Stop me in my tracks by throwing something at me."

A single bob of her head, and she went back to work.

I hadn't coached many newly manifesting sorcerers; instructors did most of that, and I was rusty. It'd been ages since my powers had manifested. I took them for granted; they'd never failed me.

When I'd worked with Ali, the question had been which powers did she possess, not how to conjure and control them. Alfreda already demonstrated a power; the question was how to wield it. How did I give my flames life? I thought about it for several heartbeats, concluding that I told them where to burn as well as how big the flame should grow and how hot it should get. The key was being as specific as possible.

Alfreda rubbed the back of her neck. "Still nothing."

I drew a finger to my lips. "Maybe… maybe you also need to tell it how fast to move."

She lifted her chin and pondered, "So I should tell it *everything* about what I want when it moves."

"Perhaps so."

"So I pick an object, tell it where to move, and how fast. Anything else?"

I shook my head, unsure. "Give it a try."

She scrunched her face. She was rather cute when she concentrated like this.

Movement out of the corner of my eye drew my attention as the lute that rested on the sofa took flight… and careened directly at my head. What was it with these sisters hurling objects at my head? Ali had beaned me with a flowerpot.

I dodged right and snatched the instrument from the air before it could strike the mirror or impale itself in the wall behind me. I started when it lurched in my hands, and I tightened my grip.

Alfreda's jaw dropped as it jerked again. "Maybe if I take it?" Her voice rose and she reached for it.

Just as I let go, the thing quivered in her hands and Alfreda gasped. "What do I do?"

"Maybe tell it to stop?"

She glared at the lute, and in a stern voice commanded, "Stop."

The lute stilled and Alfreda exhaled.

"Nicely done."

She quickly laid the lute on the table as if it might bite, then rubbed an eyebrow.

"New powers call for a new name. I think we should call it Motus powers."

"Motus?"

"As in 'to move.' I just wonder if you have other powers, too."

"Others?" A look of disbelief raced across her face.

"Let's get Motus under control first shall we?"

A corner of her mouth rose.

"It might just come in handy when we're traipsing about in the wilderness, since it seems my sister is intent on banishing me." I bit back a growl. "That is what will happen you know. If I have to go... you have to go, too."

Alfreda frowned, looking none too happy about the prospects.

Chapter Twenty

Noctus… It sounded ominous, shadowy.

"Noctus!" I said, adding a hint of doom to my utterance.

Kovis lifted his head and ran an ink-smudged hand through his unruly chestnut locks where he sat at his parchment-covered desk. A smile played on his lips as he lowered the quill. "Imitating a hippocampus sneezing?"

I snorted and shifted my legs beneath me on our sofa. A fire danced merrily in the fireplace before me. "No, silly, Alfreda named her new affinity Motus. I think Velma should call hers Noctus. Doesn't it sound dark and mysterious?"

He chuckled. "I think you should let her name her own affinity, after all, it is hers."

I rolled my eyes. "You spoil my fun. Very well, we'll let Velma name her affinity. Please… continue writing."

"Thank you for your permission, kind lady." Kovis winked then picked up his quill.

I turned my attention back to the round, decoratively carved, gold case that fit in my palm that my aunts had given me. I opened the front and watched the two toothed wheels circle as if of their own accord, as they had since the first time I'd set eyes on it.

"A little something for when you most need it," Aunt Nona had said. The scene came to mind as if it were just the sun before. They'd given me this trinket because they believed I'd done something commendable in coming to Wake; they said I'd put aside self-interest, for Kovis's sake. I had, but I still didn't see it as anything extraordinary. There'd been no choice.

Nona hadn't said more, and I'd been too awed to ask what it did, so to this sun I still had no idea. It didn't matter, I treasured the piece all the same. It gave me hope, reminding me that Velma and Alfreda lived despite Father's cruelty.

I'd taken to finding comfort from it since Alfreda had left with Kennan a sennight before. How I missed my big sister. I hoped they were safe and that with more concentrated time together, she'd be able to help him heal, and he, her.

Speaking of healing, I'd been working with Velma to better control her powers, and it seemed to ease my lingering angst over what I'd done to her. I didn't know if I'd ever get completely over it, but it was a start.

A knock at the door interrupted my reflections.

"Enter," Kovis said.

Rasa strode in.

Kovis and I stole a quick glance as I bounced up from the sofa. Rasa never knocked, she always barged in. It amazed us that she'd never interrupted us... enjoying each other.

I enveloped her in a sisterly hug, which she reciprocated, then stepped back. "The sun is shining, the birds are singing, and with all of those delegates gone, I feel free, but I'm cooped up." Rasa frowned. "Ali, I was wondering if you might join me for a ride." She pushed a stray lock behind her ear, then bit the inside of a cheek.

With a lack of friends growing up, Rasa had never had to develop the subtle social skills that friendship demanded. Ordering people around didn't require finesse. I'd noticed her working on it since our friendship began, but it was clear she still felt awkward when she didn't dominate a situation.

She's almost cute when she's unsure of herself, Kovis said.

Cut her some slack. I love that she wants to spend time with me rather than by herself.

"That sounds good. I'd love to," I replied.

Rasa exhaled, and her eyes brightened.

Kovis cleared his throat. "Is it ladies only or can a rogue tag along?"

She turned to me. "What do you think? Should we let him?"

Mischief danced in my eyes. "Oh, maybe."

"What? Maybe?" Kovis feigned affront, drawing an ink-stained hand to his chest. He strode over to me, bent me backward, and started tickling me.

"Ah!" I shrieked.

Rasa laughed.

"Okay. Okay. If... If—" I shrieked again. "—If she... she doesn't mind, you... you can come, too." I forced out the last words, trying desperately to capture his fingers, but failing.

Kovis stilled his hand and planted a claiming kiss on my lips before standing me back up. "I thought you might see things my way." He waggled his eyebrows.

I cuffed his shoulder.

Rasa grinned. "Then let's change."

Not long after, clad in leathers, we rode out of the stables followed by our usual contingent of guards. Rasa rode her stallion, Arion. Kovis sat tall atop his charcoal destrier, Alshain. Kovis had helped me mount a young palomino mare named Snowmane since Fiona had gotten a stone stuck in her shoe and had a tender hoof. She'd be fine, but the groom cautioned against riding her for the time being.

The air was crisp as the sun rose. My breath fogged as I exhaled as we followed the path to the left at a slow walk. Our conversation and laughter mingled with the horses' hooves hitting stones on the bare path. Spring wouldn't be long now, or so Kovis promised. I smiled feeling at ease. It was so different from my tenseness during my first ride with Rasa a couple moons before.

At the fork, Rasa took the lead and charged Arion up the steep hill. Snowmane followed on his heels, seemingly filled with boundless energy. Alshain brought up the rear.

In not long, Arion picked up the pace, trotting up and around a handful of switchbacks until Rasa gave him free rein to race hard up the balance of the steep incline. Snowmane and Alshain seemed equally thrilled to be running, exerting themselves outside again judging by their quick pace.

The horses' sides heaved like bellows stoking a fire once we crested the rise. We stopped to admire the view of Veritas, and Snowmane pricked her ears forward. I'd come to know Fiona's tells enough to know my mount sensed something, but after scanning the area I saw no threats and dismissed it, then lost myself, enjoying the breathtaking view.

Sometime later, Rasa said, "Shall we?"

She directed Arion toward the trail again, but the heartbeat I turned Snowmane to follow, a fat pheasant flew up from the tall, dead grass. I ducked, but its wingtips brushed my mare's ears as it sounded a very loud, very excited two-note cry.

Snowmane squealed, then reared.

I flew backward.

Only reflexes I hadn't used since our wilderness wanderings saved me as I instinctively formed a cushion of air and caught myself on it. My heart pounded, and I stayed put for several heartbeats as my breathing slowed. At length, I stood and, with a thought, disbursed the pillow of air.

Rasa approached, clapping. "Nicely done. Very impressive."

I giggled as I curtsied. "Thank you so much."

"Good job," Kovis said.

Rasa stooped and picked up my trinket that must have flown out of the pocket I'd stowed it in. She looked it over, then handed it to me. "Yours, I presume? It's beautiful."

"Thank you. My aunts gave it to me."

Kovis grinned, no doubt remembering his experience with them.

Rasa's gaze bounced between the two of us and she chuckled, then asked, "Are these the same aunts that have a few... *proclivities*?"

"You told her?" My voice rose.

"I cannot tell a lie." Kovis drew a hand to his chest.

"He did indeed. He told me about your search through a number of booksellers—" She cleared her throat. "—for certain *interesting* reading material."

I rubbed the trinket, laughing, as I felt my cheeks warm. "Oh, stop."

Rasa's laugh cut off suddenly, and I furrowed my brow, looking up.

Kovis's eyes rose to his sister, then bounced to me when she remained unmoving, her face frozen in a broad smile and her hands stilled, not quite finishing a clap.

"What...?" I said, stammering.

Rasa continued smiling, staring blankly.

Kovis waved a hand before her eyes, but she remained frozen.

"Rasa," I called, to no effect.

The horses bobbed their heads as if questioning equally, but remained several paces away where Kovis had left them.

"*What's* going on?" Kovis asked. His voice held an edge.

I scanned the area. Our guards remained a ways back, ever vigilant. The fact that they had not approached, told me they detected no danger. And nothing else seemed amiss.

I made to slip the trinket back into my leathers.

"Wait." Kovis raised a hand. "Can I see that?"

I shrugged and handed it to him.

He opened the cover, and we both gasped. The two toothed wheels no longer rotated.

I looked to Rasa and back again, fear twisting my gut. "You don't think…"

"Rasa had just handed this back to you. What did you say to her?" His voice rose.

"She was kidding me about my aunts' eccentricities."

"Yes, and then you said something. What was it?"

I thought back. "I said, 'oh stop.'" My mouth dropped open, and incredulity spilled out. "Did I freeze her?"

Kovis looked back at the trinket. "Have these wheels ever stilled?"

"No." Horror filled me as I looked back at Rasa who still beamed and nearly clapped.

Kovis's eyes ping ponged between the trinket and his sister.

"I froze Rasa…" I swallowed hard as reality walloped me on the head. Hard.

I'd frozen her like Aunt Ta froze Mare-Rankin, all the mares, at the Palace of Time when he'd been disrespectful.

"How is that possible?"

We needed Rasa. Needed? I couldn't picture the world without her anymore. She'd become another sister. My love for her had no measure. And now I'd somehow frozen her?

"Do you suppose you can unfreeze her the same way?"

Kovis's words barely registered as my mind whirred with anguish, despair, and self-loathing.

"Ali." His firm tone recaptured my attention, and once I'd focused on him, he asked, "Can you unfreeze her the same way?"

Unfreeze her. Unfreeze her. Reason pierced the malaise. "But how?"

"Maybe tell her to unfreeze?"

How I hoped this worked. I studied the trinket in my palm, then looked up at Rasa. I'd told her to stop. "Continue."

I held my breath.

Rasa's smile shattered as her hands met, but a furrow rent her brow. "What…?"

"Yes!" Kovis and I shouted together, making Rasa's head jerk back.

I jumped up and down, then threw my arms around Kovis. He grinned and hugged me back.

Still holding me, Kovis said, "Sister, you're never going to believe this, but Ali's trinket can freeze time. It froze you." I noticed he didn't say I'd frozen her.

"What…?" She sputtered.

Kovis recounted everything that had happened, and Rasa drew a hand to her brow, shaking her head.

"May I see it again?" Rasa asked.

I looked down at the face before handing it to her. The two wheels were again moving. Incredible.

Rasa's eyes grew large as she examined it. "You said your aunts gave this to you."

I nodded.

"Who… who exactly are your aunts?" She caught Kovis's eye.

He launched into an explanation, I added details.

"You seemed to have overlooked a few particulars, brother," she said after we explained.

Kovis shrugged and laughed.

She shut the cover and handed the trinket back to me, shaking her head.

My aunts had gifted me with an instrument that controlled time. They'd entrusted me with a chronometer of immense power. Clearly they believed I wouldn't misuse it. The thoughts awed and overwhelmed me.

But why?

Nona had said the trinket was "for when you most need it."

My stomach grew hard as I considered such a dire situation.

Chapter Twenty-One

Ambien

I roared in laughter. "That's right, princeling, follow your gut."

"Are you sure?" Alfreda asked, fingering the reins of her buckskin mare.

She worried her lip despite Mother's best efforts to instill proper etiquette in my daughters.

It was too perfect. Manipulating the logic this human employed was proving great fun now that I'd activated the seed I'd implanted many moons before.

About time, too. I'd patiently waited, but no longer. It was time.

"Look, all these gifts are bulky and just slow us down. It's taken a fortnight and more to reach Flumen because of them," the human replied. His raven-color horse bobbed its head, not happy at stopping after spotting a walled city rising from the plain.

Smart beast. It knew abundant food and shelter awaited, perhaps a treat or two as well.

"But your sister was insistent that warriors would prefer these over money." She met my eye, well not mine, but the human's.

I'd patted myself on the back when I discovered the human's eyes weren't even cloudy like they were when I used other methods—I'd discovered it when Princeling had combed his hair before a mirror, and I'd guffawed. At times I amazed even myself.

Alfreda hadn't a clue. I grinned.

My daughter frowned at the man.

Princeling waved his hands, silencing her. "We'll find buyers for these wagonloads of goods at the market. Currency will be much easier to carry. Trust me."

"But..."

"Think of all the uses they'll find for money versus,"—he motioned behind them, to the umpteen covered wagons brimming with treasure—*"a gold vase, decorative swords, statues, jewelry. Oh, and don't forget that royal-blue frosted-glass bowl on a gold and silver stand surrounded by five antelope. Yeah, that's a winner for sure."*

Alfreda scowled. "But she picked each of those items specifically for each province."

"She was the first to admit she didn't have a clue concerning warrior preferences or culture. I hardly think they'll turn down currency. We'll tell them to buy something nice." Princeling chuckled. "At a minimum, we won't offend them with something inappropriate."

Alfreda shook her head.

I stirred a bit of the fury that still blazed just below the surface of this human. So weak and emotional, he'd not gotten past his anger at being banished to the wilderness, and it was proving a delightful way to influence him.

"You must trust me." The human locked Alfreda with a piercing gaze, and she slumped her shoulders.

"That's a good girl," I whispered, rubbing my stubbled chin. "Don't thwart my useful little soldier. The empress was so kind to fund my campaign. How could I possibly refuse such a gift?"

Princeling reached over and patted Alfreda's leathered thigh. "Look, for better or worse, we're in this together. Can't you just support me?"

My daughter returned a heavy sigh. "Very well."

"Thank you." He gave her his winningest smile. "Then come on. We have much to do before our dinner with Nomarch Formig at sunset."

Alfreda cocked her head. "You think we'll sell all of this before sunset?"

"We'll at least begin." Princeling smiled then looked to the lead guard, nodded him into action, and the caravan soon advanced.

"But we've only been in Flumen a sennight," Alfreda protested. "Do you really feel as if we've gotten a good grasp of Eslor's culture? Enough to make recommendations to Rasa for how to honor Eslorians, specifically?"

Princeling smiled. "I want to get to know its citizens. Formig can tell us anything she likes, but I want to see for myself if what she claims is true."

"Why would she misrepresent her people?"

The human held up his hands. "I'm not saying she's doing it intentionally."

Nice argument. I couldn't help but laugh. Such an obedient human and so easy to direct. A little prompting was all it took before he embraced my ideas as his own.

"You really think so?" Alfreda asked.

"Only one way to find out."

A cacophony of roars and bellows drew my attention from the fun I'd been having with the human as the heavy wooden door swung shut.

"My liege?" Orven, my commander, bowed low before me.

"Rise." I lifted my hand from the gold-inlaid arm of my throne and motioned him up. My throne here, in Rolse's creature compound, might not be as big as elsewhere, but what it lacked in size, it more than made up for in ostentation.

"My liege, you asked me to inform you when the remorrigan census reached three hundred ninety-five in our reciprocal compound. It just did, sir."

A grin spread across my face. Just five remorrigan to go in Eslor, and sooner than I'd expected. Dream weavers had done an admirable job of getting us to this point. I'd have to congratulate my sand people in Rolse personally. Perhaps while there, I'd also gather their humans' thought threads and form another mega remorrigan. I had three already, a fourth would make a nice addition. The only question, should I direct it to Eslor's Wake or Rolse's Dream compound? Decisions, decisions.

I roared with mirth.

But enough fantasizing. Having anticipated this development, Princeling was already headed for the wilds of Eslor. It would take only a nudge to direct him to their creature compound to assume command.

Lightness filled my limbs. A prince of the realm itself leading my pretties on this quest. I almost couldn't believe my luck. No, it wasn't luck; I'd worked hard to achieve this, and things were shaping up nicely.

"Dismissed."

As soon as Orven left, I returned to Princeling's head. "Ditch your guards and head into the mountains, just you and your lady. It'll be a great adventure where you're sure to meet lots of Eslor's finest. Wouldn't it be nice to become intimately acquainted with their warriors, an expert even?"

Chapter Twenty-Two

Alfreda

I fumed. It had been a simple question… "How much farther?" If Kennan told me to "trust him" one more time, I might strangle him.

I barely restrained my foot from stomping; it would only exacerbate the blisters that had blisters, some of which were bleeding, and he'd no doubt call me a child. I'd ceased caring; I was at the end of my patience with him.

He grinned at my fury. "You're very cute when you're mad."

My vision turned red and my palms, sweaty.

A beast howled off in the distance. I ignored it.

"Ready to continue?" Kennan asked, extending his arm to indicate the unending path before us.

I huffed, ignoring his proffered hand, and stood, then picked up my walking stick, grumbling to myself.

The rocky ravine that we'd entered as the sun rose was bare save for a few hardy plants that persisted despite the harsh conditions. Several dead trees clung by their roots to the wall, above us.

I rubbed my stomach as we traversed a rocky ledge. Snow melt had made the river below swell, at least that's what Kennan had said, and the sound of water rushing over rocks in its path drifted upward.

The river had been our lifeline with its abundant minnows that swam in the smoother shallows. If not for them, we would have starved by now, but it took considerable patience to catch enough to fill my belly. Larger fish followed the current downstream it seemed, because we'd found only a handful.

Another howl sounded, a bit closer, sending a shiver through me. "You don't think...," I asked, my breath catching.

Kennan scanned the terrain.

We'd nearly succumbed to five, count them, five vile monsters since Kennan, in his infinite wisdom, decided to lose our guards back in Flumen. The first had nearly loosed my bowels; the others were just as bad with their dripping saliva, hideous bulging eyes, and ferocious fangs... and their stench that nearly emptied my stomach.

"Doesn't seem so, but I can't really tell," he said at length. "Good thing you're becoming skillful with Motus. With you here, I'm not too worried."

I frowned and under my breath mumbled, "He's not worried. That makes one of us." Desperation had fueled my magic, and I'd gotten lucky. Who knew if I could actually do it again. I'd nearly killed us with the last landing. Thinking of our narrow escape from that ugly, plated, forked-tongued monster again sent a shiver up my back. Too bad I couldn't just whisk us away from this godsforsaken place.

Puffy, white clouds floated against the blue sky. A scavenging bird hovered on the currents, searching for a newly dead morsel. The stone walls amplified its echoed caw.

"Go away. We're not your next meal," I mumbled.

Kennan turned toward me, and the corner of his mouth edged up. "We really are almost there, I can feel it."

My eyes narrowed as he turned back, and I glared. Never had a dream charge vexed me so. I barely stifled a sharp retort.

"Almost there." "Almost there." We weren't "almost" anywhere. We were completely lost, and he refused to admit it. Men. We'd been following that godsforsaken river, wandering farther and farther into these damn mountains.

The scavenging fowl continued hovering, searching, adding to my angst at our lostness.

I nursed my grievances as we stumbled across unending loose rock, my feet paining me with every step. I'd been perturbed like this only once before in my entire, previously immortal existence—with Father in that cave. It, like my footsteps, still pained me.

Step, ouch, step, ouch, step, ouch. Only leaning on my walking stick kept me moving.

"Thank the gods." I sighed with relief as we *finally* emerged from the canyon as the sun crested the sky. The ground took on a rough but flatter typography. We hadn't cleared the mountain range, but we'd at least been granted a respite.

"How you holding up?" At least he had the decency to look contrite. I'd grown quiet as I hobbled. It was the only way I could cope. Apparently he'd noticed, but it wouldn't change a thing.

I held my tongue.

Caw, caw, caw.

The calls which had grown closer, drew our attention upward.

Four birds had joined their fellow, hovering. At length, they all dove.

"They must have finally found food," I said. "About time."

But rather than landing as I'd expected, they swooped and flew directly at us.

"Kennan?" Wariness filled my voice.

"I see them." He assumed a ready position, palms outstretched.

I stopped beside him, mimicking his stance.

The five fowl landed several men's height away.

I barely stifled a shriek when four of the five transformed into huge, smelly, purple-haired beasts, filling me with horror.

Kennan tensed and alarm filled his voice. "Where'd they go?"

"They're right there. Can't you see them?" My voice rose.

Kennan worried his brow and wrinkled his nose. "No. And what's that... stench?"

The remaining bird took on the form of a too-familiar man in uniform. A *very* familiar male—the guard who'd watched me in Father's cave. He strode forward with a grin, clearly recognizing me, too.

"They're my father's mares." My voice quaked. It felt as if insects crawled across my skin.

It had been *them* guarding, *touching* Velma and me back in that cave. I'd known Father had taken to domesticating mares, but...

Mares. He'd used mares. Mares had coerced me to comply. Mares had forcefully restrained me when I'd refused. Mares had held me back from stopping...

I sucked in a breath.

Mares had cleaved Velma's wings.

My heart raced.

"We've been expecting you. Follow me." The uniformed male turned and strode away.

I scanned the area. "We have to get away," I whispered.

Kennan nodded.

He didn't hear the mares behind us growl as they prowled closer when we didn't budge.

My stomach clenched. I wasn't yet so proficient with Motus that I could whisk us away, and even if I had been, I had no doubt these beasts would transform back and pursue us.

Still, I had to try. Desperation and frustration collided, and I grabbed Kennan's hand. A heartbeat later we stumbled forward ten men's height away. At least we'd cleared the mares.

Snarls rose.

"Get them!"

I closed my eyes and focused, blocking out the sound of paws spraying the loose gravel as they raced after us.

We stumbled again, landing roughly. I'd moved us another ten men's height. I had to propel us faster. But before I could try again, a vice gripped my calf from behind. I screamed as I fell forward, and the gravel dug into my hands.

"Warn, don't wound!" The mare leader admonished the brute, stopping short, a pace away.

I kicked, trying to shake the beast loose, but it held fast. It shook its head as I attempted rolling over, keeping me on my belly. Thank the gods for leathers or the thing would have amputated my leg.

Another mare growled at Kennan who lay sprawled beside me.

"Get up!" the soldier commanded, fists on hips, feet planted firmly.

The mare opened its mouth, releasing me. I thrust my boot at its snout with every ounce of energy I had left.

A whimper escaped, then it snarled and was on me in the blink of an eye.

"Drogo, stop!"

The mare gnashed its teeth but eased back, growling, canines barred.

I scrambled to sitting as Kennan stood, dusted himself off, and extended a hand to me, still not seeing the enemy.

"Move!"

I frowned as I rubbed stones from my palms before complying.

Father was behind this. He'd manipulated Kennan into coming here. But how? Kennan kept telling me he sensed we were near, but when I asked "near where?", he hadn't been able to say, he'd just insisted we continue our course.

How had Father manipulated Kennan? He hadn't used me, not like he'd tried with Ali, influencing Kovis's thoughts via his thought thread. Kennan's eyes weren't cloudy, either. How had he done it?

Absorbed in my musings, I nearly stumbled on the uneven ground, and Kennan reached for and steadied me. His look told me he berated himself for our predicament.

"Separate!"

Two mares were on us in a heartbeat.

I shot a scowl at the leader, but Kennan loosed my hand.

"Move!"

A small round hole in the enormous rock wall we approached soon appeared. Roars and bellows emanated from it, ricocheting across the stone as we neared.

My heart picked up pace and my steps slowed. A cave. Not another cave. Not with mares.

Worry filled Kennan's eyes as he glanced at me.

"My father..." I shook my head. I couldn't do it. I couldn't go in another cave, especially with mares.

Growls erupted behind us, but I ignored them.

Sensing that we didn't follow, our guide turned around and glared.

I didn't care. I couldn't do it.

"King Ambien..." He let the vile name linger as if it would convince me to comply. "...requires your obedience."

I shook my head. "No. I won't."

Kennan stiffened and closed the two steps between us. His jaw clenched, and he raised his hands, then pushed me. Hard.

It happened so fast that I hit the ground.

Kennan towered over me. "You will obey." It came out a growl. "You're nothing more than a spoiled *former* royal. Now get up!"

I pushed myself up to sitting, and with eyes wide, looked Kennan up and down.

"Get up!" he shouted, locking fury-filled eyes with me.

What was happening? Kennan might not be the sanest man I'd ever known, but he'd not been physically violent, well other than when he'd coaxed my powers to manifest, but that wasn't the norm.

Reality hit me. Father. He was controlling Kennan like he had before.

Kennan grabbed my arm, yanked me up, then shoved me forward. "Move!"

I barely caught myself.

The four mares closed in, teeth bared, saliva dripping. I thought I'd retch from their stench.

"Kennan?" My pitch rose. He was my dream charge. Father couldn't have him again. I had to reach him.

"Silence!" the leader ordered.

Kennan strode ahead and joined him.

Terror welled up inside me as I sloughed toward that dark, circular void in the rock. I gasped for breath, but air refused to fill me.

My knees buckled.

Breathe, I needed to breathe, but breath eluded me.

"Walk!" Two mares shifting into soldier form surrounded me in the blink of an eye.

I felt myself fall but couldn't catch myself.

Air. I needed, air.

My head struck the rocky ground.

White streaked my vision.

"Carry her!"

Darkness overwhelmed me.

Chapter Twenty-Three

Kovis

Was this really a good idea? My insides constricted as I stepped inside to the bell's jangling. The situation demanded trying something unconventional... this was certainly that. The empire needed to be unified as we faced Ambien to have any hope of defeating him. If we didn't stabilize the crown, I didn't know how we'd cope with the threat.

"Welcome. Welcome. Come in, my prince! What a lovely surprise." Madame Catherine shut the door behind me and bowed. I waved her up and she pecked both of my cheeks, then motioned me forward.

"Is the princess enjoying the garments I sent recently?" She grinned as we entered the area where ladies tried on gowns and other garments. Two of the three circular platforms before which several floor-length mirrors captured every angle, stood empty. "More importantly, are you?" She wagged her eyebrows.

I chuckled. "Yes, very much. Thank you."

A wide-eyed councilman's wife watched us from atop the third platform. I recognized her with a nod—her husband was one of our few loyal supporters. One of Catherine's girls was pinning the hem of a gown she modeled.

Catherine stepped behind the counter and straightened several parchments. "How may I assist you? A few pieces for nighttime, perhaps?"

"Might we speak somewhere more private?" I asked, my voice low.

Always unflappable, Catherine tilted her head, but replied, "Of course, my prince."

I followed her through the fitting rooms, which seemed to be empty, and into a room abounding in all manner of fabrics. Row upon row of textiles stood tall on rolls, organized in a manner unknown to me. Trims overflowed cubbies that lined the walls floor to ceiling save for the space necessitated by the four windows on one side.

"Please." She pulled out a chair at a round table in the corner and motioned for me to sit, then swooped in and picked up two stacks of fabric from the tabletop, placing them in a cubby. She closed the door, then took a seat opposite me.

"I didn't mean to impose."

She swatted the air. "No imposition at all. So tell me, how might I help you, my prince? You've piqued my curiosity."

"I'm wondering if I might beg a boon."

Madame Catherine drew a hand to her chest. "From me? Now you've really got me going."

"No doubt you've heard stories of what happened to the empress during the recent gathering of leaders, how a rock beetle climbed out of her head."

"Ah. That. Yes. The shop was buzzing about it for a full sennight. Several of the ladies still bring it up amongst themselves. I make it a habit to keep my nose out of such idle chit chat."

I gave her a long look. "Unfortunately, it wasn't idle."

"As I'd gathered. I'm so sorry."

"So you have heard what happened then."

Catherine gave a slow nod.

"A few leaders and their representatives seemed eager to exploit the calamity," I said.

"What they're saying is treasonous, if you ask me." Catherine slid a swatch over and began fingering the frayed edge.

"I'm sure." I raised a hand. "Have no fear, I will not ask who said what."

She met my eyes.

I shifted. "Who are your customers?"

"Mostly council members and their spouses, the occasional dignitary, and of course the healers who saved my son's life several annums ago."

"Would you say *every* council member patronizes you?"

She thought, then said, "I would."

I nodded. As I'd expected. "You have no small amount of influence over them, then."

"True, they trust me to ensure their fashion meets prevailing sensibilities. It seems I have become responsible for every season's designs." She sat up straighter, pulling her shoulders back. "Imagine, me, an insorcelled seamstress."

I smiled. "And you should be proud. You've worked hard and earned their respect."

"Sometimes I still can't believe my change of luck. If we hadn't had the opportunity to make a new life here in the capital..." She shook her head. "My family struggled to make ends meet in Vaduz, had for generations. And my son..." She closed her eyes.

I stilled her hands that continued shredding the edge of the sample. "You have greater influence than that."

She furrowed her brow.

"Councilmen don't want to tick you off."

She grinned. "You're right about that. They know better. They'll find themselves facing *unpleasant* consequences of, shall we say, a very personal nature if they do. Happy wife, happy life and all that."

I chuckled. I'd never want to go up against Madame Catherine. She understood what men *truly* cared about.

I withdrew my hand and said, "Which brings me to that boon."

She sighed and said, "You want me to talk to their wives about the empress."

"Not quite, but you're close. The council smells weakness unlike ever before. That episode fueled their lust for power. I see it in their eyes. If we can't speak reason to them, there's no telling what they'll do and where it will leave the monarchy, let alone the empire. I'd like you to address the Council."

She looked to me, then stood and wandered over to a stack of fabric, then started running a hand back and forth over the topmost piece as she starred out one of the windows.

I'd never taken time to study this woman who I'd come to appreciate; but in this heartbeat, I looked past her impeccably coiffed hair and fashionable attire and noticed the wrinkles on her face and the hunch of her back.

"Have I ever told you about when we left Vaduz?" Her feet stayed planted as she turned toward me.

"No." We'd never spoken much beyond business.

"When we told our family and friends of our plans, they branded us traitors and accused us of capitulating to the enemy. After that, they shunned us, seeing us as traitors siding with our oppressor, so when we left, we left everything, including family…" She let her words linger. "…to make a new start."

"And allying with the crown could jeopardize your shop."

I hadn't intended to put her in a difficult position, but it seemed I had. I wanted to tell her I'd be more than happy to make up for whatever business she lost if she worked with me, but it would insult her. She'd worked hard and earned her reputation honestly, as was the warrior way.

"I always thought I'd be able to stay nonpartisan. Fashion is a language all its own that bridges differences between people. It's why I love it so much." A wistful look filled her eyes as one of her hands squeezed the top swatch. "But it seems I was naïve."

"This is not a royal edict."

"Oh, I know. I trust you. You'd never do that to me."

All I could do was nod.

She brought her other hand down sharply on the top of the stack as if making up her mind. "Let me discuss it with my husband, if I may."

"Certainly."

"I'll send word with my next delivery." A smile lit up her face. "I've been working on something very special for that lady of yours."

"I look forward to it." I strode over to her, placed a hand on her shoulder, and locked eyes. "Thank you."

She reached up and placed a hand on my cheek. "Thank you."

I'd never fully appreciated this woman, certainly not what she'd just revealed of herself. She was a gem. And I'd asked her to offer up her livelihood for the sake of the throne as well as the empire.

Her and her husband's response would reveal whether they believed we were worthy of such a risk. I hoped we measured up, because if not, I didn't know what the future of the empire held with Ambien on the prowl.

Chapter Twenty-Four

Kovis

Smiles on council members' faces set me on edge the heartbeat I arrived. They never smiled. What trouble would these vipers manage to stir up this sun?

I took my seat beside Rasa—Kennan's to her left, sat empty— directly below the imposing wall sculpture of an altairn that marked the head of the chamber. Light illuminated the beechwood against which the embellishment hung. The effect created a glow behind us that was supposed to make us appear godlike—a visible reminder of the power my siblings and I wielded.

They ignored the reminder.

I stole a glance at Rasa. She put on a good show of being relaxed, but a muscle in her neck bulged. We both braced for the worst.

Lord Beecham, head representative from Ice, approached the podium below us and called the chamber to order. His jowls jiggled as he announced, "Due to unforeseen events, I am choosing to break with protocol and advance a more pressing matter for discussion."

The gallery at the back of the chamber began murmuring.

I scanned the twenty-eight representatives—two from each province—who sat stoically around the large, circular table that owned the center of the room. None looked surprised by the news.

My stomach tensed, but like Rasa, I didn't react.

The round man with no neck, turned and snuck a triumphant glance at us before turning back. "While my insorcelled colleagues appreciate the renewed attention the monarchy is showing them with Prince Kennan's cultural intelligence tour"—several nonmagical representatives bobbed their heads—"events before, during, and since the annum meeting compel me to submit a motion"—he pivoted his head around the circle of delegates—"to depose the empress."

The gallery erupted.

Two representatives stood.

"I warned you, Beecham," one of our supporters said.

"You can't do this!" another shouted, raising a fist.

Others of our advocates frowned, shaking their heads. Most of the other representatives remained passive, unmoving. They'd known.

Rasa remained still. I wondered if her heart raced like mine.

Beecham's tunic was the latest fashion with stiff ruffles that rose up to his jiggling chin and would have strangled him if we'd been fortunate. As it was, we weren't. I'd have to talk to Madame Catherine about changing designs just for him.

He raised his hands calling for silence. "When a leader puts his or her people in danger, it is the duty of responsible representatives to remove said leader from power. Empress Rasa has put us all in grave danger." He let his words linger. "Many of you saw it yourselves, an oversize rock beetle emerged from her head."

Gasps rose from the gallery. "Rock beetle?" "From her head?" These and more exclamations wafted up.

"If not for the courageous actions of Nomarch Marson, who knows what might have happened to the empire's leaders?"

Lord Josef, of Terra, one of our two vocal supporters, argued, "How can you hold her responsible for that? You think she wanted it to happen?"

Beecham glared at Josef. "Intention matters not. It's actions that speak loudest. She's possessed by some strange beast. Who knows when it might happen again?"

"She was unconscious!" Lady Krea of Wood province shook her finger at Beecham.

"Matters not. I repeat, who knows when it might happen again?"

Beecham locked eyes with the lady, then looked down his bulbous nose. "A banshee was spotted outside the castle walls several fortnights ago. The empress herself believes she had something to do with its creation."

I sucked in a breath. Rasa's knuckles turned white as she gripped the arm of her chair. How had he learned of Rasa's conversation with Ali? Ali said they were alone.

"Now see here, Beecham! That's quite enough," Josef objected. "You're sounding like a crazed lunatic going on about mythical harbingers of death."

Krea leveled piercing eyes on the council leader.

He ignored both and persisted. "If you think I'm crazy, explain to me why both princes were treated for stab wounds received in the empress's chambers. Prince Kovis was treated for a wound to the shoulder, Prince Kennan for a wound to the neck… in the middle of the night."

More gasps rose from the gallery.

"You're grasping at straws, Beecham," Josef shook his head. "Has your desperation to usurp more power rent the few remaining threads of your sanity?"

"My sources are irrefutable," the leader defended. "Shall we have the crown prince show you what's left of his wound?"

Protests rang from the back of the room.

Flippant, blasphemous, and profane. Like usual, Beecham stirred them up, but I'd had enough. I rose and took the podium that stood to my right.

Rasa's eyes swept the room as it quieted.

Beecham turned to face me, forced to look up to meet my eyes. Good.

"Lord Beecham, we've given you your due despite your treasonous slander." I let my words linger until murmurs rose from the gallery. "But enough is enough. We both know you have no irrefutable source to back up your claims, certainly not one you haven't paid to be your mouthpiece."

The lord's ears turned red, and he clenched his fists, then opened his mouth, but I cut him off. "You've had your opportunity, sir. Now I will say my peace."

Not so much as a peep emanated from the back of the room.

"Lord Josef, Lady Krea, members who support the empress, I thank you."

Friendly council members nodded, unfriendlies scowled.

"I could stand here and defend Empress Rasa's reputation from the slander that vipers like the lord here espouse." Beecham shifted where he stood. "But I think you already know how I feel." I smiled, and chuckles sounded from gallery members. "So I'm going to let a woman who we *all* greatly respect and *eagerly* follow, say a few words on the empress's behalf." I drew out the words.

Necks craned. Several representatives leaned over and whispered to a neighbor behind cupped hands.

I looked to the door through which Rasa and I entered the council chambers and extended my arm. "Madam Catherine, please come and address the Council."

Surprise echoed throughout the chamber as Catherine, shoulders back, chin up, strode toward me.

Beecham slunk to his seat, shaking his head.

It had been as much of a surprise to Rasa as everyone else, but she quickly schooled her features, rose, and embraced the dear woman.

Catherine joined me, and I let a corner of my mouth rise as I asked, "You have a few things you'd like to say?"

"I most certainly do, my prince."

"Then by all means...." I smiled, then retook my seat.

Madame Catherine gripped the sides of the lectern and slowly swept the room with her gaze, nodding at some and smiling at others. Despite her short stature, she commanded respect as I knew she would, for none so much as whispered.

"Greetings, friends."

Her cheerful demeanor disarmed those with raised brows, and they settled back in their seats.

"I don't pretend to understand all your politics, and I haven't come this sun to offer design expertise, but I was hoping you'd indulge an old woman in listening to my story.

"Most of you have been coming to me for annums, practically since my family arrived in Veritas. Some of you are newer, but I count your patronage no less dear. I consider each and every one of you a good friend, and as a good friend, I want to share the story of what brought my family here. None of you know for I've never shared it."

No one fidgeted. None whispered. Everyone sat spellbound.

"I come from a proud line of insorcelled of Vaduz." A gleam lit her eyes. "My family have been tailors for generations. It is a humble trade, but they did it with pride for it kept us all fed.

"But one sun, the plague visited our people. I was but a child, but I remember how it ravaged our kingdom. It quickly claimed Grandmama and Grandpapa, and I vividly remember Mama and Papa mourning so many others who perished. I lost four of my playmates, and it claimed nearly three-quarters of our people before it ended."

Catherine shook her head. "Some things you never forget."

"With so many having perished, you can imagine how my family was affected. People focused on rebuilding. They made do with the clothes they had, made their own, or mended them, and saved their meager resources for sustenance.

"Hunger became our constant companion. Time went on, but nothing changed. Papa took ill at some point, I think the constant strain and worry wore him down. He passed on not long after. I was only coming into my maidenhood, but with no means of supporting us, Mama married me off so she had only herself to feed.

"The gods blessed me though, for my husband's family welcomed me in as a daughter. He, along with his family, were smithies and earned a decent living, and invited Mama to live with us. Life took on a regular routine until Emperor Altairn began a campaign to enfold Vaduz into the empire.

"Our brave warriors fought back, but to no avail. Empire troops were better equipped and had far greater resources, and they quickly overwhelmed us. I well remember the despair that fell upon us all.

"But money and more resources than any of us had ever in our lives seen soon began pouring into Vaduz. The empire repaired some structures and built new ones. They constructed aqueducts to provide running water and sanitation for the first time. They built roads to facilitate trade with the rest of the empire's provinces, and so much more."

Madame Catherine paused.

"Some contended the emperor 'bought us off,' placating us at best, enslaving us at worst."

Agreeing grumbles erupted from several listeners.

"Friends and neighbors echoed that mantra, disgust and distain lacing their words—we were proud warriors and would continue our proud traditions, subject to the will of none."

"As if there's something wrong with that." A snipe erupted.

I gazed across council members but couldn't identify the source.

"There is nothing wrong with that. Absolutely nothing," Catherine cautioned. "But my husband and I *chose* to see things differently."

She scanned the audience.

"Call us young and naïve, but… we dared to dream." She drew out the last four words, making eye contact with each and every representative.

"We wanted more from life. We sought to improve our lot, sought to rise above the ordinary, sought to wring every measure of good out of life, to suck the very marrow from it." Madame Catherine's voice rang out. "We dared to thrive."

She brought a hand down on the podium.

"We decided anyone who had the resources the emperor did and who *valued* Vaduz as his gifts showed would surely have a place where we could realize our dreams."

Murmurs rose from representatives, and the gallery hummed. Emotion added fuel, and the volume increased.

I suppressed a smile. Like Beecham, she knew how to stir them up, but I welcomed her poking.

Catherine raised a finger. "Mind you… " She spoke softly and the room soon quieted. "Our family and friends didn't see eye to eye. They shunned us. Called us traitors."

She choked back hurt and raw emotion, and my heart constricted. All that they'd been willing to leave behind.

Her eyes shown with tears as she caught mine. We both understood this was the crux of what our challengers fought against—leaving behind what they rightly treasured, not to forget, but so they could embrace… more, embrace the peaceful empire Rasa sought, where all might prosper.

Catherine took several measured breaths and composed herself. "We were committed to realizing our dreams. So we came. It took lots of honest, hard work, but little by little, we began to realize what we had sought after. And I honestly have to say, it was worth it." A corner of her mouth turned up.

"You know what happened." She drew a hand to her chest. "I am more fulfilled than I ever thought possible, and I count myself *richly* blessed having each of you a part of realizing the dream that guided us."

I tried to swallow, but it proved difficult. All that dreams could achieve. I'd never dreamed like she and Montagu, her husband. My position forbade it. I'd known my future since my earliest annums.

But she and Montagu had dreamed. She'd become the foremost fashion diva, and he'd earned my respect many times over as my most trusted smithy crafting all of my family's weapons. He was that good.

To think what all of us would have missed if they had succumbed to expectations.

Listeners hadn't missed her meaning—this monarchy, led by our family, had created the opportunities she and her husband had seized and benefitted from—and the gallery erupted in applause, drawing me from my musings. Magical representatives and a handful of insorcelled rose and joined in. Those who didn't sat quietly.

I'd never know, but I chose to believe the quiet ones were showing respect for the accomplishments of a fellow warrior and her husband, accomplishments achieved only because they'd dared to dream and embrace opportunity, against the odds.

I hugged Madame Catherine after Rasa. Words to express my appreciation failed me, but her eyes twinkled as she said, "If this doesn't do the trick, I know what men care about." She winked.

Laughter erupted from my belly. Rasa tittered.

The question now was, what impact had Catherine's moving account effected and would it be enough to quiet murmurings among the power hungry?

Chapter Twenty-Five
Kennan

Detestable, weak.

It's all I could think and feel as I jerked my hand away from Alfreda, who still slept, and threw my legs over the side of the bed. My bare feet hit the freezing stone floor, and I slumped forward, rubbing my face.

I felt eyes bore into me, as they had since guards showed us to our "accommodations befitting a prince," as they'd called them, four suns before. One of the pair of guards shifted where he stood at attention before he bolted the metal door.

They might just as well have cast us in a cell.

That could be arranged, Princeling. A chuckle.

I ran my hands through my hair. *That door.* I had no memory of anything on the other side. I barely remembered anything on this side. Life had become a haze.

A drop of water hit my head, and I scowled at the chiseled rock ceiling. Clumps of stalactites populated the damp plane like stars in the sky.

A reverberating roar, off the stone corridor outside, snuck through the crack beneath the door.

Dress. You have work to do. The words filled my mind.

I tensed my legs, resisting, struggling to keep my feet planted, to stop myself from rising, and failed as my feet betrayed me again, walking me to the chamber pot where my bowels forsook me.

Another bellowed roar filtered into the room.

Despite the futility, I fought my body that strode to the wardrobe where we'd stashed our leathers before bed. They soon covered my braies.

My breathing hitched as I approached the guards who shifted aside, opening the door.

Frustration had me draw on my Fire magic as I neared. What I longed to do to these beasts for their part in this charade.

But as I walked into the chiseled, stone-lined corridor, my fury quieted and I wondered what had angered me.

Yes, prince, why would you seek harm to your own troops?

I drew a hand to my head. "I don't know."

The scuffing of boots on rock drew me from my quandary.

"Another remorrigan just arrived," Galleron, Eslor compound's commander, said, stopping beside me. The burly officer gave me a hard look. "Eslor's rebels will begin arriving in three suns, and you have yet to master control of even one of these creatures. How do you think you'll earn the rebels' respect if you can't even harness one of these beauties?" He shook his head.

I'd been a spare my whole life, but no longer. I'd lead a rebel force along with a herd of remorrigans against the crown and claim it as my own if it was the last thing I did. I fisted my hands. "I will master it."

"See that you do. This sun." It came out a growl, and without another word, he strode off.

I eagerly followed past torch, after torch, after torch.

I would do this, I told myself.

Shouts, followed by shrieks and yelps reverberated as one, two, three corridor fireplaces came and went, the stench of straw and feces strengthening, then waning.

Angry bellows emanated from a hallway we approached. We were nearly there. I could do this. I would claim that crown. My siblings would never know what happened.

As it had every time before, my breathing labored as self-doubts, fear of death, memories of Father standing over Rasa, touching her, bloody beatings, terror as Kovis and Ali succumbed to billowy shadows—the images coalesced, hitting me like a wall, and I stopped.

I hadn't even seen the remorrigan, yet I felt its unmistakable terror.

It's nothing but the embodiment of human fear and frailty. You will control it, Princeling. You're a wobbly human. You've shattered with each and every attempt thus far. You're pathetic. Utterly pathetic. Perhaps the shock of having a prince of the realm itself usurp the crown isn't worth all this hassle.

No. It was worth it. I was worth it, and I would do this. I beat back my loathsome fears. I *had* to go further this time. I stumbled forward.

Galleron slowed, then met my eyes. "Content to be a spare the rest of your life?"

"No!" I forced my feet to pick up pace.

High-pitched screams and shrieks echoed from around the corner.

I shook my head. Something felt different. The notion registered, then flitted away.

Oh yes, different all right, fragile princeling. The stakes just got higher. You can't help but rise to them now.

I sucked in a breath.

We turned right, and my heart raced as I took in a hideous, hairy, eyeless creature that rose to waist height. Fear rolled off the thing in waves. The passage was wide, but its whiskers, no fleshy tentacles, flailed from where a nose should have been, blocking the corridor. Massive, black claws that matched the color of its wiry fur, grabbed at the air. It loosed an angry bellow as one of the seven guard's long prods struck home, keeping it in place.

"Kennan!"

My eyes landed on Alfreda, arms shackled above her head, just beyond the horrid abomination.

Weak. Pathetic, the reflexive thoughts again filled my mind.

No, treasured. You must save her.

I must save her. I must. I would. No matter what.

Blonde hair askew, she fought against the bonds that tethered her wrists to the wall in nothing but braises. Tears streamed down her cheeks.

Her shriek drew the creature's attention, and it whirled around, fleshy tentacles whipping erratically. The guards scrambled out of the way. One screeched in pain, then dropped to the floor holding its arm when one of the whips found him.

Treasured. That was Alfreda. I swallowed hard at my rising panic. I scanned the space, frantically searching for any way to stop that monster even as crippling fear and images of Father touching Rasa reasserted themselves.

"Prove you're worthy to lead." Galleron's voice thundered.

Step by despicable step, the creature crept toward Alfreda, tentacles flailing.

A guard strode toward her, stopped beside her, then reached up, as the fear-inducing abomination drew closer.

Alfreda jerked at her bonds. "Kennan! Help me!" Terror laced her words.

The guard turned and grinned at me, then grabbed her breast.

"Stop!" I yelled.

Alfreda unleashed another blood-curdling screech, kicking at the guard. "It's a mare! This guard is a mare. Kennan!"

Still that tentacled monster slunk closer to her.

Flame erupted from both my palms, hugging the ceiling as it hurtled for Alfreda's attacker. I made my fire dip so it also singed the furry-terror-incarnate along the way.

The guard at Alfreda's feet bellowed as my flames devoured it, replaced in the blink of an eye by a slumped, long-haired beast whose coat was wholly singed.

I barely had time for horror to register—I'd never seen anything so grotesque—as the black-haired monster pivoted toward me, tentacles flying. It plodded toward me, claws clicking against the stone floor.

Terror mounted as images of Kovis and Ali screaming, swirling shadows swallowing them whole, overwhelmed me. Fear rippled off the monster as it drew ever closer, step by agonizing step, its tentacles undulating everywhere.

My heart felt as if it might explode from my chest.

Click. Click. Click. Click. Still that abomination came for me.

I conjured dagger after dagger, thrusting them rapid fire at the beast, but it continued its unrelenting trudge forward.

"Kennan!" Alfreda screamed again.

I glanced up. She jerked at her bonds as two new guards flanking her, tore at her top.

She was a treasure. I had to save her.

Tentacles waved in my vision.

How could I free her?

"Alfreda! Motus!"

I prayed she understood as flames fiercer than anything I'd ever unleashed erupted from my hands. They filled the corridor, incinerating everything in their path.

A heartbeat later, I cut my fury off and held my breath as I surveyed the devastation I'd wrought.

Seven blackened corpses lay strewn, smoking. A mound of blistered and burned flesh blocked half the corridor.

Alfreda hovered prone, at the ceiling, wrists still bound to the blackened wall. She turned toward me, and a small smile mounted her lips as she lowered herself and stood.

Yes, she was a treasure.

Footsteps behind me made me jump. I inhaled sharply and starting coughing as I whirled around.

Galleron stopped, then shook his head. "The idea is to control the remorrigan, not kill it." He scowled. "You're supposed to lead them, remember?"

You will learn. The voice chortled.

I would learn. I gave a curt nod.

Turning to a guard beside him, Galleron barked, "Again."

Chapter Twenty-Six

My hands strained, clutching the sofa pillow, arms above my head.

"Oh, Kovis. Dreambeam." It came out a moan.

I felt his lips turn up against my bare stomach.

"Say it again, love." He kissed his way upward, then latched onto a straining, pebbled tip.

"Oh! Kovis!"

Rapid knocking at the door sounded.

Kovis sucked harder.

"The door." It came out breathy.

"They'll go away." His fingers found my core, and I moaned.

More knocking.

So close. A whimper escaped me.

The door flew open.

My arms flew downward, covering my nakedness, despite the back of the divan that protected me from sight. Kovis straightened, but remained kneeling. The red of his tattoo shifted brighter still.

"Oh! Oh! Sorry," Rasa said. "I'll... I'll come back."

I giggled. *So much for her not catching us in the act.*

Kovis grinned.

"No, sister, stay." He shook his head. "Whatever it is has to be important. Just give us a heartbeat."

I tilted my head.

He smiled. *She's not looking, love.*

I grabbed the back of the sofa and sat up to find Rasa staring out at the Canyon's lights, back turned.

Kovis kissed my nose, and we exchanged grins before heading for our bathroom.

Rasa was pacing, skirts swishing, gripping a parchment in one hand, when we emerged.

I gave my white robe's sash a final tug, then ran a hand through my gnarled hair.

Her cheeks turned rosy when I reached to give her a welcoming hug. "I apologize. I..." she stammered.

"No harm done." I smiled and pushed a golden lock behind my ear.

She blushed more, then closed her eyes and drew a hand over her face.

Kovis grinned and drew the soft white fabric of his robe tighter, then cinched the sash about his waist. "So what's got you all wound up, sister? Care to sit?" He extended his arm toward the sofa we'd warmed.

"No. No, I'd rather stand. Thank you. This letter arrived not long ago, from Nomarch Formig."

Kovis wrinkled his brow, then accepted the parchment. His slippered feet stopped before the sofa, and he sat. I followed, sitting beside him and drew my legs up under me. Rasa continued pacing.

I looked over Kovis's shoulder as he opened it and read:

Empress,

The prince and his lady proved quite the
entertaining company over a sennight, so I was
saddened when they chose to continue on so soon.
I had many more provincial visits lined up for
them to discover Elsor's proud and ancient culture.

Kovis ran a hand through his hair. I bit my lip. They were to have been in Eslor a full moon.

Imagine my surprise when my warriors informed
me that the two apparently slipped their guard
and disappeared, leaving only a note claiming they
were headed north to Praia.

They'd done what? Rasa's skirts continued swishing.

Their guard was up in arms as you might well
expect. With all due respect to the prince, it did
seem rather odd behavior.
So, on a hunch, I dispatched my warriors who
know the terrain well, to track them, with orders
not to interfere.
The prince and his lady headed due east, into
the heart of the mountains.

I twisted my hair. Kovis frowned. Why had they lied about their destination?

> After wandering for suns, they met up with
> soldiers bearing bright-red accents on black
> leathers...

I sucked in a breath. Kovis paused and caught my eyes. Bright red on black leathers. It was the uniform of Father's troops.

> ... and disappeared into a cave from which strange
> roars and howls continually erupt.

Howls and roars? "Continually erupted?" That didn't sound like mares. But if not, then what? My gut clenched.

> If that's not bad enough, rebels have begun
> arriving, adding to their numbers.

My breathing labored. Rebels. *What* was Father up to?

> Our troops continue to observe, and I will update
> you as soon as I know more.

My heart raced. Kennan and Alfreda had joined Father. Formig's troops had heard growls and roars. Continuously. From some cave. Out in the middle of nowhere. And rebels were joining them. I couldn't wrap my mind around it. Father had possessed Kennan before... I shook my head, not wanting to consider.

In closing, many thanks for your generous
monetary gift. I will put it to use in a manner
befitting your intention, and that of their visit.

With all diligence,
Nomarch Formig

Rasa stopped behind us. "I picked out an elegant, silver-handled sword as a gift for the nomarch, but it seems it never reached her. That hardly seems important, at this point, though. What does he think he's doing?"

I turned around and met her eyes. "Rasa, those troops they met, they're my father's."

"How do you know? What are you saying?"

"Please, sister. Sit," Kovis said.

"Fine." The empress sat down, back rod straight, on the edge of the upholstered chair to our right.

"I've seen those uniforms plenty. Trust me."

"But how?" Kovis asked. "Your father is in Dream realm. How could he have troops here?"

"He sent mares after me, remember? Why could he not have troops here? Remember the uniforms of the guards in the cave? They were dressed like that."

"Yes, but that was in Dream, and they had wings." Kovis studied the letter again. "Formig would have mentioned wings if they had them."

"Look, I don't know how they're here or why they look a little different, but I know they're my father's. I just do."

Rasa's eyes grew large, and she stood. "Why would Kennan and your sister join up with him? After your father possessed him... no, you don't suppose…" She threw a hand over her mouth and shook her head, slumping back into the seat.

Horror filled me. Had Father possessed Kennan again?

"I don't know," I replied. "With Alfreda here, my father shouldn't have been able to possess him again." I rubbed my brow, at a loss for words. Father couldn't have possessed him again. He couldn't have. Yet the facts would allow no other conclusion.

I had no doubt Father had been behind the abomination that had erupted from Rasa's head. If he could do that, he was more than capable of possessing Kennan again, whether I understood how or not. My stomach twisted as I spit out the foul words. "I can't imagine Kennan would seek him out, otherwise."

My breath hitched. If Father had again possessed Kennan, what did that mean for any of us, Kovis and me included?

"If word of this gets out, you know what they'll say?" Kovis ran a hand through his brown locks and clenched his teeth.

Treason. The word ripped through my mind, and I touched my throat. Rasa hugged herself.

"You thought the Council was bad with that rock beetle and your dreams, sister? Just wait to see the gleam in their eyes when they charge Kennan with treason. He puts the monarchy in jeopardy."

Kovis crumpled up the letter and slammed it on the low table that spanned the length of the sofa. It bounced off and into the fireplace. Thankfully, a fire hadn't been lit.

"Dyeus hasn't captured Father. He couldn't have," I said, thinking aloud.

"What are you saying?" Rasa asked.

"Dyeus is hunting him. If he had captured him, I doubt my father would be able to possess Kennan. As I've told you, he wants to conquer Wake. It seems he's on the move, and who knows what he's cooked up."

Knocking at the door interrupted the tension.

"Enter!"

"Beg pardon, Empress, this just arrived for you." The steward bowed, panting, as he held out an envelope. "The courier said it was of the utmost urgency that you read it."

Rasa stood, strode to the door, and took the letter. "Thank you."

Allard closed the door, and Rasa tore open the missive, reading it as she meandered back to us:

> Empress,
>
> Word just reached me. My troops have spotted the source of at least some of the strange roars and howls they've been hearing.
>
> Three abominations equal in horror to the beast that emerged from your head, briefly came forth from that cave.
>
> Prince Kennan directed them.
>
> Preparing for conflict,
> Nomarch Formig

Rasa dropped her arms, stopping beside our sofa.

Bile hit the back of my throat. I only just swallowed it back. "We've got to return to Dream and stop my father."

Rasa shook her head. "No, Ali. *You* need to return to Dream and stop your father. Kovis needs to lead Wake's armies against whatever he's sending against us."

"Against your brother?" My voice rose.

"Kennan isn't himself right now." Rasa exhaled heavily, then set her jaw. "It seems your father controls him, so yes."

Kovis opened his mouth as if to object, but closed it again. He didn't have to tell me. Rasa was right.

But Kennan… and Alfreda. I raced for the bathroom and only just made it as my stomach dispatched its contents. So intent was I with retching that I didn't hear Kovis come in, but he fell to the floor and held my hair back.

I wiped bile from my mouth and panted, before the basin. "They've been through so much." I shook my head as Kovis rubbed my back.

It couldn't end this way.

Rasa couldn't… Kennan was her own flesh. They'd been through so much together. So much. Alfreda… I couldn't think it. Wouldn't.

"Hey…" Kovis stroked my hair. "Trust me when I say that decision will forever haunt Rasa. Honestly, I don't know if I could have made it."

Rasa. She was in an impossible position with the empire pitted against family. Yet as empress, she had a duty to protect citizens, no matter the personal cost.

But my sister… I'd lost my family once, lost Velma twice. My stomach made to purge itself again, and I clutched the side of the vessel.

When the urge at last passed, I collapsed on the floor. Kovis wiped the tears from my eyes with his thumb.

"We've no choice," Kovis whispered.

I bobbed my head. "I know." My voice cracked.

Kovis wrapped his arms about me and held me, kissing the top of my head.

War was again afoot. At least in Wake, but this time it wasn't Emperor Altairn calling for the conflict. It was Father, because Dyeus hadn't stopped him.

But I had to, before… I shook my head.

It had taken multiple Dream regents to stop Father both times before.

How did I expect to?

Chapter Twenty-Seven

Kovis and I had so much to do, but that meant saying goodbye with no guarantee either of us would make it back.

I swallowed, hard, as I looked up into Kovis's blue eyes. Their hazel centers still set them apart and made them beautiful to me.

His heart sped as he grabbed me, swallowing me in his strong arms one last time, then planted a claiming kiss on my lips. He finally eased back and brushed a few of my stray locks behind an ear. "Be safe, my love."

I raised my hand between us and the diamonds surrounding the teardrop sapphire of Kovis's mother's ring sparkled. "I intend to hold you to this promise."

"There's nothing I would love more." He drew me close and held me tight again, running a hand up and down my back as we lingered. I'd thought I loved Kovis before I'd come to Wake. I had, in a way, but my love for him, right here, right now, was so much greater than I could ever have imagined.

In Dream, my feelings for him had been one sided. It hadn't seemed so—not with all my fantasizing about him and his bulging muscles and the thrum of his power. But beyond that, I'd felt deeply connected with him because of the similarities in our situations, our longings to feel loved by our parents, and that connection had made it feel like we faced our common problem together, as a team.

But sharing vulnerability, being open to being wounded, hurt, even emotionally destroyed—that connection that only two damaged people could share with each other—had added a dimension to our love I could never have imagined had I not come. And despite the trials we'd faced, I wouldn't trade the heartache I'd experienced for the very world itself.

Kovis eased back and studied my face as if searing it into his memory. At length, he brought a hand up and cradled my cheek, then planted one final, tender kiss on my lips.

"All my love," he whispered.

"All mine."

With drooping shoulders, he turned and left to go help Rasa plan.

The door snit shut, and I wiped away a tear. My eyes scanned the space that had once just been "his" rooms, but had become "ours." How well I remembered my trepidation the first time I'd stepped through that door. Longing to see him, his eyes, his muscles, in person, experiencing him for the very first time. Hearing his thrum before he came into sight, the way he'd stalked toward me, making every nerve in my new body tingle. Even now my heart picked up its pace, and I smiled.

The dining table to the right, where we'd enjoyed our first dinner together, uncomfortable and unplanned as it had been. His desk, where my nosiness had discovered that Kovis wrote novels of his adventures, of narratives I'd given him while helping him cope.

The ornate glass doors to the balcony where we'd watched the Canyon's lights, listened to their energy crackle, and I'd let him decide if we'd kiss to aide his sleep.

And this couch, yes, this couch. I stopped and ran a hand over the back. It had experienced so much of us—lovemaking to be sure, but also Kovis's sulking over that torturous time when he'd wrestled with letting me fully in to his frozen heart.

It was all here, the memories captured in my heart.

I rounded the sofa and picked up the cloth sack with the six naughty books I'd purchased for my aunts that lay on the short table. A smile tugged at a corner of my mouth.

I ran a hand over the lump in the pocket of my blue and white print dress—their trinket that stopped time. "A little something for when you most need it." That's all Aunt Nona had said as she'd closed my hand over the metal case.

If not now...

I stepped back around the couch and grabbed the navy cloak I'd draped over the back, tossing it over an arm.

I exhaled sharply as I glanced quickly about the space one final time. I was as ready as I'd ever be, no point in dithering further.

"Good morning, princess," Allard greeted with a cheery smile, when I opened the door.

"Good morning, Allard. Lovely sun."

"That it is."

How appropriate that he would be on duty. He'd been there the night I'd first met Kovis and so many others since, including during The Ninety-Eight in Flumen. Somehow I felt like I knew him best of all our guards.

Allard closed the door behind me, and I meandered down all five flights of circular stairs, appreciating the artwork, the familiar sounds, the comforting smells. I'd lived here not quite an annum, but it had become home, especially with my sisters joining me.

I dallied as I passed through the treatment rooms, greeting Haylan, Hulda, Swete, Arabella, Myla, and others of my apprentice friends; they were unaware that I was really saying goodbye. I prayed I'd see them again.

I climbed the two flights of stairs to the third floor of the healers' suites and turned right. It was quiet as I strode down the hall. Everyone was working downstairs or sleeping after a night shift. My old room, across from Haylan's, still bore my name plaque on the door. I stopped before Jathan and Velma's rooms, at the very end, and knocked.

Velma enveloped me in a hug the heartbeat I stepped in. I hugged her back, fiercely. I'd lost her twice; I prayed the same would never be said of me by her. I pushed the thought aside and stepped back.

Jathan, donned in his green chief healer robes, forced a smile, as he closed the door.

Sun through the four large windows illuminated shelf upon overflowing shelf, crammed with books that adorned two walls, floor to ceiling, the centerpiece of their rooms. I inhaled deeply. I'd loved spending time with Velma here.

Jathan drew Velma close with an arm around her shoulders.

"So it all comes down to this." Velma met my eyes.

I nodded. I couldn't speak or I'd break down. Whatever happened, Velma had Jathan's love to support her. She wouldn't be alone. Somehow that helped ease the pain in my throat.

Velma had breathed over me to send me here the first time. She'd do it again, but to Dream. I still didn't fully understand how it worked, something about language holding the power to change things and envisioning, like the Ancient One had at the beginning of time to create our world. Kovis and I had returned to Dream, trekking through Porta, the last time. I just hoped envisioning and language worked in reverse, too.

"Let's do this." I forced back the quiver in my voice as I tied the string of my cloak around my neck.

Velma gave me a long look, but finally bobbed her head, then stepped forward and clutched my shoulders and looked into my eyes.

"Land me in the palace of sand maidens," I said. I clutched the bag that held the six naughty books. I only hoped my aunts would be willing to help. They had before.

"Say hi to Mema and our siblings for me. Tell them… tell them how much I love them." Some invisible damn broke and tears started streaming down Velma's cheeks.

"I will," I said, tears threatening to overwhelm me as well.

Velma inhaled and let her breath out slowly. "Are you ready?"

Hurry back. I want to marry you with all haste, Kovis said through our bond. His voice cracked.

Ravish me, too? I forced a chuckle.

Most definitely, wildly and passionately, every sun of our lives.

I fingered the books and nodded at Velma. Jathan drew his lips in a line.

She gripped my shoulders tighter, closed her eyes, then breathed over me.

My navy cape vanished in a heartbeat, replaced by blinding pain that lanced my back and I shrieked. Mind-numbing. Agony. Not a dagger. Far worse.

I'd forgotten.

Golden locks whipped my face.

My skirts flew up. Flapped. Smothered me.

I flailed. Free arm. Skirts. Down.

Breathe.

Blackness swallowed me. Disorientation slammed into me.

I clutched the books. My back. Stabbing, stinging. Searing. Couldn't hold them.

A wail. Near me. My throat. It burned with fury.

Pain shot up through my shoulders and traced my arms, igniting my fingertips.

My legs. Set afire. Pain. Agony.

I screeched. Squealed.

Weight. My back. Familiar.

I panted as the pain ebbed as quickly as it started, easing to a dull throb.

I yipped as I sprawled on the marble of the entry in the palace of sand maidens, my full, onyx wings splayed. My bag of books clipped my wing as it thudded on the floor then belched its contents.

Kovis! I made it! I'm safe.

A long exhale filled our bond, and Kovis replied, *See that you stay that way, my love. I'll let Velma and Jathan know.*

I love you, Dreambeam. My shoulders slumped. Our bond worked even when we were in different realms. We'd worried it wouldn't.

And I love you.

I got my wings back. I ruffled them, despite igniting a twinge.

Are they as big as mine were? A chuckle rumbled down our bond.

I snorted. *You're such a male. No, they're not, if you must know. I'd never be able to drag them around.*

Kovis loosed a full-bellied laugh.

Two guards rushed into the foyer, eyes fierce, swords drawn.

I recognized Baldik, the largest of my family's guards, but not the other one.

Baldik, along with Rowntree, had accompanied Kovis and me in retrieving Velma and Alfreda from Father's clutches. A wave of sadness hit me as I again remembered Rowntree's ultimate sacrifice.

Baldik pulled back and squinted. "Princess?" He drew an arm across his fellow guard.

I scrambled up, but a spasm from the weight of my newly formed wings, pulled me up short. I frowned as I clutched my chest to keep the bodice of my dress in place. Another dress ruined thanks to my new wings sprouting; but I didn't care, I had my wings back. I beamed as I ruffled them again, sending another twinge through me.

The guards sheathed their weapons, and Baldrik said, "Fortnight family dinner is underway." He nodded at the closed dining room doors just down the hall. "Perhaps you would like to freshen up before joining them?"

I bobbed my head.

The other guard advanced and gathered the spilled books. A corner of his mouth turned up as he caught the titles.

My cheeks pinked as I made to snatch them away.

He handed me the bag and I stuffed the incriminating evidence away. "I'll… I'll go change."

"Shall I announce your arrival?" Baldik asked.

"Please tell them I'll join them in the sitting room." We always reclined there, chatting, after family dinners.

"Very well."

I turned and headed toward the foliage-and-fountain-filled atrium. I'd arrived safely; I only hoped the rest of this quest proved equally uneventful.

But a heaviness beset my stomach. So much rested on my shoulders, and I could not fail.

Chapter Twenty-Eight

Kovis

Ali was safe. I exhaled as I leaned over the table, a map of the Altairn Empire before me in the War room. Black as well as red markers cluttered the features of Eslor, Juba, and Vaduz. Red alone flagged the other four insorcelled provinces that bordered Elementis.

Father had conquered the nonmagical peoples to provide a ring of protection for the seven magical provinces of the empire. Currently, abominations like Nomarch Formig described had been spotted in three. Rebels massed in all.

Red markers still cluttered the features of all seven of our magical provinces—Ice, Air, Water, Terra, Wood, Metal, and Fire, the ones the Canyon, the source of every sorcerers strength, ran through.

I growled as I crumpled the parchment that had just arrived and added black tokens to Astana.

"I'll bet we'll add black markers to each and every one of our nonmagical provinces before this is over," Colonel Merek said, adjusting his spectacles. The man trained the Inquisitors, which until recently, Kennan had led.

Who knew if they'd ever be under my brother's command again. I struggled to push the thought aside as I stared out the window, overlooking the mountainside that rose behind the palace. Like the storm clouds, his prediction was ominous and exactly what I'd hoped to avoid. I blew out a breath.

"Colonel Merek, when will we have your scouts' reports on the other provinces?" Rasa asked.

The officer studied the map, his eyes darting about as he did silent computations. "Within a sennight, Empress." He adjusted his spectacles.

Rasa huffed.

Blue markers, those indicating the positions of our forces, were clumped throughout Elementis where they'd been keeping rebel insurgents at bay, away from critical infrastructure in our magical provinces. There was only a smattering of blue in insorcelled areas.

"So which troops do you plan to redeploy to address the new threat?" Merek asked.

"First things first. Do we anticipate discovering these abominations in Elementis?" Rasa asked, crossing her arms.

That was *the* question.

I frowned. "If we send aide to our insorcelled provinces, just to find the menaces in Elementis, we won't have enough strength anywhere to best them—not to mention, we leave ourselves open to more rebel attacks in the magical provinces."

Merek pushed his spectacles up his nose. "On the other hand, insorcelled will be up in arms if we hold our troops in Elementis and leave them to fend for themselves."

"When must we decide our course of action?" Rasa asked, pacing.

A knock came at the door. "Enter," Rasa and I barked together as I strode for the door.

Two servants panted as they genuflected, then rose, holding out envelopes.

"Thank you," I said, taking the missives. The pair bowed again, then turned and left.

I flipped the first envelope over to find the seal of Metal province. "From Minister Letam." Examining the second, I added, "And Formig."

Rasa's knuckles turned white where she gripped the edge of the table.

"We may discover our situation sooner than expected," Merek said, scratching his chiseled chin.

I broke the seal on Letam's dispatch first, and pulled out a single parchment. Clearing my throat, I read:

Empress,

It is with grave concern that I report the sighting of two dozen, perhaps more, vulgar creatures of unimaginable darkness emerging from caves in the mountains of our fair province.

Troops attempted to approach to discern more, but were stopped by crippling fear.

I furrowed my brow and glanced about. Rasa's and Merek's brows mimicked mine. I clenched my jaw. I'd see these soldiers severely disciplined.

I know this sounds like dereliction of duty. I thought the same, but officers implored me to experience the horrors. With significant doubts, I ventured forth to see with my own eyes.

What they reported was not half the horror I experienced—terrors that excited my very soul—when still afar off. My worst nightmares pale in comparison to the awe, dread, panic, and shock these creatures elicited.

Anathema. Worse by thrice, maybe more, than the abomination that emerged from you, Empress.

I await your instructions for I know not how you wish us to proceed. I fear they will spread within our province and beyond.

In your humble service,
Minister Letam

Jaws dropped. Every eye bulged. My breathing sped. Two dozen of these things? Perhaps more.

"Shit." The collective expletive exploded.

Colonel Merek swallowed hard, pushing his spectacles up his nose with a shaky hand.

"*What* has Ambien unleashed?" Rasa murmured, fisting her hands.

Merek cleared his throat. "Well, that clears that up. Seems they're in Elementis as well as our insorcelled provinces."

Rasa sucked in a breath. "What's Formig say?"

How much worse could this sun get?

I forced my hands to still as I opened the nomarch's missive and read:

Empress,

Prince Kennan has left the mountain hideaway and is leading nearly four hundred abominations along with rebel forces toward Flumen. At their current pace, we anticipate their arrival within a fortnight.

Nomarch Formig

My stomach went rock hard. This sun couldn't get any worse. Two dozen abominations had had that effect on Letam, and there were four hundred, *four hundred,* of them loose. Correction, Kennan led them. Somehow he was immune to their powers. It could only be Ambien's doing.

"There's no time to dispatch troops to aid them." Merek yanked at his chocolate brown locks.

"How many creatures have been spotted in Juba, Vaduz, and Astana?" I asked.

Colonel Merek straightened, then pulled off his spectacles and rubbed the bridge of his nose. "My intelligence reports fifty, at a minimum, probably more."

"Are they on the move?" I asked.

Rasa froze from her pacing and in a monotone said, "You said Ambien had designs on taking over Wake realm. If Kennan's leading his forces—" We locked eyes. "—they're headed here, to Veritas."

My heart raced as she walked to the map and pointed. "They'll be here within a moon."

Chapter Twenty-Nine

Thunderheads billowed up in the night sky, lightning bolts alone illuminating our way as rain pelted us. I prayed the foreboding scene was not a foretelling of what awaited at my aunts. They'd helped before... Wake was completely screwed if they didn't this time. My stomach cramped.

A clap of thunder, off to the left, too close by, made my wings shudder where I flew in my leathers between my brothers, Harding to my right and Rankin to my left. Baldik, the largest, and three other heavily armed family guards surrounded us.

My brothers had volunteered to join me the heartbeat I told my family what had transpired in Wake. So dire was my recounting that even Mema had supported my plan to visit our aunts. With any luck, Father had no idea I'd returned to Dream, so while we didn't anticipate interference going or returning, we'd armed ourselves well. We weren't about to take any chances. Not after the last time.

"Palace of Sand," Rankin yelled, and our group shifted to an easterly path. Light flickered from the spires of the sprawling palace complex as we neared.

I wondered how Selova, our region's dream stitcher, fared. I'd never heard the result of her dispatching messengers to her counterparts in the other provinces of Dream, alerting them to Father's activities and instructing them how to break the permanent bond Father had formed between dream weavers and their human charges. I stifled a growl even now.

I'd definitely stop by and find out. Perhaps I'd even sneak a heartbeat or two for a sandling fix. It would surely relieve some of my angst and no doubt improve my mood.

Tremors shook my body, and I wiped away the wet cascading down my face. Had timing not been critical, I would have waited for better weather, but we didn't have that luxury.

I glanced at the hilly terrain flowing past beneath us. Vegetation, spots of black and gray in the dim, varied in density, growing thick in parts and thin in others. Unsurprisingly, no one was about in this foul weather. Only the flickering lights of scattered residences waved as we passed.

I was soaked to the skin and chilled to the bone when the towering edifice of my aunts' home finally came into view against the backdrop of dark clouds and lightning. All height and virtually no width, their castle rose no less than thirty floors. A multitude of ornate spires jutted from irregular, wart-like protrusions bulging from its sides. Spiky... all the way up to its pointy top. They still reminded me of boney fingers. Last time, I'd learned that the castle added to its height of its own accord as the number of humans and their time pieces necessitated.

The wind picked up as we set down in the shadowy courtyard, but only the sounds of thunder and rain greeted us. Limbs on the massive tree in the middle, swayed violently. Combined with the lightning, the shadows looked scarier than I remembered, and my heart sped.

The hulking wooden door to the castle was unguarded as it had been every time before. No surprise, you'd have to be a few notes short of a full measure to be out in this weather, let alone consider threatening my aunts.

I scurried toward it, anxious to get out of the elements. Baldik reached it first and put his broad shoulder to it. A heartbeat later, the door's hinges creaked in protest, but granted us admittance.

I'd never been here at night, let alone during a bad storm. If not for the four lit torches clustered on the walls just inside the door, the pitch blackness would have left us blind. A strong gust tried snuffing them out and one of our guards slammed the ancient door shut again.

A collective exhale sounded.

I wiped my face with a hand, then took several steps forward, unfurling my wings along with the others, and shook the wet off. Our movements stirred up the layer of thick dust blanketing the floor and several of us started sneezing.

"Aunts really could use a housekeeper or two," Harding said, covering his nose.

"Why don't you suggest that when we see them?" Rankin grinned.

I chuckled.

A corner of Baldik's mouth rose. He'd escorted me along with Kovis the last time and knew some of this palace. The rest of our guards exchanged wide eyes, fingering the hilts of their swords.

"Shall we?" I asked, nodding toward the pair of winding, dust-covered stairs across the high-ceilinged foyer. All those footprints... this place had seen more traffic of late than in eons. Our guards grabbed the four torches, and we mounted the left set of stairs, like every time before.

I hugged the bag of books under my arm as we crested the first flight. The corner of my mouth rose, remembering the playful trouble my brothers had given me the sun before when I wouldn't let them see the titles. Nope. No way.

We reached the next landing and continued up the stairs that clutched the rounded walls. Up and up we climbed. Around and around. I stopped counting as a stitch bit into my side.

Harding looked back, panting, and smiled. "This is a good place to train. Perhaps we should come more often."

Rankin huffed out a snort behind me, along with our guards.

We hadn't yet reached Aunts' floor—I couldn't tell how many more steps we had to climb—but movement drew my attention as we trudged to halfway up the next flight.

"Stop. Look." My chest heaved, and I waved to Rankin behind me, then pointed. Baldik and another guard, along with Harding, paused and looked back at me, then turned back around, following my finger.

A pair of black-robed stewards crossed their arms before a hulking set of closed doors on the next landing. Their eyes roamed up and down our party, but otherwise they didn't move.

I forced my breathing to even as we reached their level. Odd. Every time before, we'd seen no one around except on the floor where my aunts directed activities from their ancient rocking chairs, and this wasn't that. Had they moved down to this floor for some reason?

I wove my way through our party and stopped before the pair. "Hi, I'm Princess Alissandra."

"We know who you are," the wiry steward on the left said, frowning.

"Are my aunts here? Have they moved?"

The pair just stared at me.

"Excuse me." The voice from behind was soft and feminine.

I glanced back. A slight, long-black-haired, tan-robed attendant squeezed through our group. I stepped out of the way, but her big brown eyes caught mine as she passed, seemingly pleading with me to take her place. Her hands trembled as she grabbed a long-handled mace that leaned against the wall.

I cocked my head. She was so small. How would she wield such a weapon if she had to?

The attendant clenched her jaw and raised the mace before nodding to the black-robed attendants.

The males bobbed their heads, then the one on the right grabbed a massive door handle and heaved it open.

Whistles and fizzing and sizzling sounds poured from the room into the hall.

"Back! Back!" the female shouted in a high pitch.

My eyes went wide as I peeked in and gasped. My heart raced as I drew a hand over my mouth and clutched the bag of books more tightly to my chest.

Damn, she was fast with that mace, but that poor attendant. She'd gone in willingly.

My eyes bounced between the two males. Would she be okay?

My heart crawled into my throat.

The door's thud echoed against the hard stone of the multi-storied atrium and set my nerves further on edge. They wouldn't have let her go in there if she would be harmed. Surely not.

I exhaled heavily. My aunts were *definitely* not in there.

"Are my aunts okay?" Panic laced my words, and I waved my hands.

The wiry steward frowned as his eyes again traced our group. "Your aunts are unharmed."

I exhaled.

The steward crossed his arms again and said nothing more.

"That's it? What'd you see?" Rankin asked, alarm making his voice rise.

I shook my head. I would not speak *that* into being. I motioned to keep climbing.

"Ali, what did you see?" Harding asked two flights up, from behind, beside Rankin. His voice held an edge.

I wagged my head as a shiver raced up my back. I continued climbing, not looking back.

Harding grabbed my shoulder at the next landing and spun me around. "*What* did you see?"

His scowl, coupled with his raised brows, told me he would no longer tolerate my silence, and I exhaled heavily. "Fine."

Rankin set his jaw, beside him.

My gaze bounced between my brothers, and I rubbed my arms. "You've… You've seen the timepieces in the hall of time." They'd been here, along with the rest of my family, rescuing me when Father's mares dragged me here the first time.

They nodded.

"They measure the suns Aunt Ches sets for each being," Rankin added.

"Yes. Hourglasses, metal balls rolling down zigzagging tracks, contraptions with dripping water, candles, whatever the device, Aunt Nona crafts the clocks. They're mechanical, some simpler than others, but handcrafted." My stomach tensed as I met their eyes. I opened and closed my mouth and fisted my hands.

"Glowing black orbs float in that room. More than I could count. Slits, like with feline eyes but reversed, in red, aqua, orange, and other colors, stare as if they're giant eyeballs." My body twitched as I saw it again in my mind. "Black mist, like smoke, pours out of the top of each."

"Why'd that female arm herself?" Rankin asked.

"Yes, and yell at something to 'get back'?" Harding raised a brow.

"Those glowing orbs… swarmed her. She whacked them back with the mace. I shudder to think what happens if one reaches her."

Their jaws dropped.

My breathing labored. Speaking had made the horror all the worse, as I'd feared.

"I can't imagine Aunt Nona crafting them." Another shiver raced down my back.

"If not her…" Harding's voice wavered.

"Then who… or what did?" Rankin's face turned ashen.

"And how'd they get here?" I swallowed hard.

Chapter Thirty

I panted. My heart would explode from my chest. Thirteen...
Fourteen... Fifteen... more blasted flights of stairs. I was not prepared
for this. In more ways than one. My mouth went dry. What if my
aunts refused to help? What if they couldn't shed light on the
situation. What if Father... I shook my head. What if... what if...
what if.

I bent over, hand to knee, clutching the bag of books with the
other. I sucked in air after finally reaching the floor my aunts
inhabited, the only one with a hallway with a row of windows to the
left that permitted scant light, especially with the dark weather
outside.

Lightning brightened the hall like the sun for a heartbeat, and
movement at the other end drew my attention. I yipped as thunder
crashed—it was so loud this high up, close to it. The hard-stone walls
amplified its echo.

Another flash, and I made out Jansha or Rinion, one or the other of the two black-robed stewards who stood outside the Hall of Time, pacing. Yes, he was pacing. Thunder's boom amplified my fear.

I'd never seen either of them do anything other than stand there, on either side of the set of open doors from which artificial light and all manner of low mechanical noises emanated. They'd looked me and my party up and down and scowled a good deal—although Jansha had been more pleasant the last time—but they'd never paced.

First those floating spheres, now this? My muscles started twitching—it had to be from the climb. Yes, the climb.

"Shall we?" Rankin asked, raising an eyebrow, no doubt at my hesitancy.

I bobbed my head and followed my brothers. Our guards, muscles tense, alert to everything, started after us.

We'd made it only halfway down the hall when one of the stewards spotted us, paused a heartbeat from his pacing, no doubt identifying us, then scurried forward.

Jansha's black robe swished as he stopped suddenly before my brothers and drew a hand to his chest. "Thank the gods you're here."

"Jansha, it's good to see you," I said, stepping forward, between my brothers.

The steward extended a hand, gripping my forearm. "Moirai will be happy to see you. Come."

Jansha held firm to my arm, turned, and headed toward the Hall of Time. I clutched the bag of books as my feet struggled to keep pace with him. Rinion bobbed his head as we passed—a first. He'd given me an evil eye every time before. It just underscored how not normal things were. I bit my lip.

"You four will remain here," Rinion said to our guards. I glanced back over my shoulder. "And you two will surrender your weapons. Brothers or not, there will be no armaments in the hall."

Jansha didn't pause, and I missed the exchange as we strode ahead, between the ancient rows. They didn't care that I had weapons on me? I wouldn't ask.

Tan-robed attendants still flitted about, ensuring my aunts edicts were adhered to. I caught their furtive, worried glances.

Light from the lightning burst through the large windows in the far wall, but with the ancient shelves that stretched floor to ceiling, much of it was thwarted. Torch light augmented the dim.

The smell of incense again greeted me along with the low sounds of the various timepieces that ensured every mortal got each and every heartbeat of life Aunt Ches allotted them.

We traversed the width of the room, and my aunts Nona, Ches, and Ta came into view on the dais, erect and rocking vigorously in rocking chairs, conversing. Their stringy, white hair still fell over their plain gray robes with overlong sleeves. My limbs turned shaky. I'd never seen them so active, not out here for all to see.

"Moirai." The steward stopped, then dragged me down as we bowed low.

The repetitive creaking of the three chairs ceased in a heartbeat.

"Alissandra, rise child." Aunt Ta, I recognized her voice.

I obeyed, along with Jansha who finally let my arm go. The steward turned on his heels and headed back out.

All three of my aunts were standing, eyes locked on me.

My breath hitched.

"Come," Ches said, rubbing her brow.

What? Why the rush? I needed time for my siblings to join me. I opened my mouth to object.

Nona frowned as she followed her sisters to the right of the dais, toward that circular door that swirled in a host of colors.

I sucked in a breath and let my protest die on my lips as I followed. One did not debate, not with my aunts. Not if they wanted their help. I'd had wonderful times getting to know my aunts, but I could never allow myself to become casual with them. They embodied power and deserved the respect they'd earned. I could never forget that.

All the same, I glanced about the hall when I reached the opening to their hideaway. Where were my brothers? My stomach clenched, and I gripped the books tighter, swallowing hard. I'd faced my aunts alone before, I could do it again if I had to.

No more stalling. I turned and stepped through the swirling colors. And stopped short. Not at the expansive floor to ceiling window that filled virtually the entire far wall with the clear, blue sea despite the storm and elements I'd experienced. Not at the huge crackling fireplace to the left before which had been arranged three sofas with a short, wood table in the middle. Not at the colorful rugs scattered about. Not at Nona's cluttered workbench to the right. I'd seen all this before.

No, what brought me up short was the shiny ball that stood on an intricately carved wooden stand between me and that huge, bright window. It was much bigger than the swirling spheres several floors below and lacked that eye slit, but smoke still swirled, albeit within rather than wafting up, but these pieces were too similar not to be connected... somehow.

I clutched the books to my chest and ruffled my wings as I stepped down the three steps, never taking my eyes off the swirling cloud within. The sphere would have risen to my waist without the stand. With it, it towered over me.

Aunt Ta huffed as Ancel helped her remove her gray robe from around her black wings and replace it with a navy one. "Lovely isn't it?" Sarcasm filled her voice.

I glanced between her and the sphere. "I... I..."

"It appeared not long after your last visit," Aunt Ches said, giving the sash of her turquoise robe a rough tug. Bright purple flowers had been woven into the fabric. She chucked her sandals before descending the steps and strode to the swirling ball, hands on her hips.

Aunt Nona glanced at the ball and shook her head, joining us. She pulled one of *those mechanisms* from a pocket of her lime green robe, and gave it a spin.

Ta glanced at the contraption and frowned but didn't correct her sister as she'd done every time before.

"I brought you these," I said, holding the bag of books out to Aunt Ta.

"Thank you, dear. That was very thoughtful of you." Ta accepted the bag and handed it off to Nona who strode over to her workbench and dropped it, then rejoined us.

My shoulders tensed. They'd made such a big deal about ensuring I brought them *specific* reading material to fuel their passions. My hands turned sweaty. Did they know about Father? Had what he was doing made them forget even their odd proclivities? I'd known it was bad, but... My breathing hitched.

"What... what does it do?" I asked, nodding at the swirling ball.

Aunt Nona wrinkled her nose and placed an open hand on the sphere. The gray smoke stopped swirling and began to coalesce into a shape. No, not a shape, a life-like image.

A squeak escaped me, and I'm sure my eyes grew large. I hugged myself as a monstrous griffin—huge wings, long beak, feathered head, and twitching lion-like tail—stared at me, exercising its very long talons. In, out, in, out the curved daggers moved from its altairn-like feet.

"That's a new one," Aunt Ches said.

"New one?"

"All manner of vile and vicious creatures have appeared. No doubt another sphere just materialized." Nona curled her lip.

"Another sphere? You don't mean... downstairs?"

"She does," Ta said. "So you've seen them."

"Just a peek, but it was enough... How...?"

"Our tower shook something fierce as another floor was added. We thought nothing of it to start, but we felt our powers being taxed.

A little at first, but more and more. Imagine our shock when our stewards reported… glowing spheres in the new area."

"Unnatural they are. Creatures for which we have been forced to measure life." Ches brought her head down sharply.

"Forced?" My voice rose.

"Indeed." Ta huffed.

"Unending." Ches glanced at Ta.

Unending life? That thing was immortal, like I'd been?

"*And* I have no power to cut it off." Ta started pacing.

She'd tried? When I'd hinted at modifying the length of Father's life, she'd told me she didn't prefer to alter any life because one never knew what unintended consequences might result.

She lifted her hand, and the image dissolved back into swirling smoke.

There had been hundreds of spheres floating around in that room. Hundreds. My stomach went rock hard. These had to be the abominations roaming about Wake. Abominations from which fear rippled. Creatures like the one that had emerged from Rasa. I'd only known about a handful before now. But hundreds? *Kovis!*

"Do… do you know where these creatures are?" I asked.

"Throughout Dream and Wake," Nona said, putting a jerky hand to her mechanism and giving it a spin.

"What? Both?" Panic laced my words.

Ali, are you okay? Kovis asked a heartbeat later.

I'm with my aunts. There are hundreds of those abominations, Kovis. Hundreds.

Yes, we just received a report from Metal that told us the same.

No, Kovis. They say they're throughout both Dream and Wake. Throughout.

Shit! Okay, I'll… I'll talk to you later. I love you. Stay safe, love.

I love you, too, Dreambeam. And you stay safe, too.

I shook my head, refocusing. "Do Dream's regents know?"

Ta shook her head. "Had Selova's messengers reached their destinations, the regents probably would have discovered Ambien's plans by now, but they didn't."

"What? None of them?" My heart raced.

Ches shook her head. "The regents know all about their citizens going missing, but none as yet have a clue about what lurks in each of their territories."

"In *each* Dream territory? No, you can't mean that." Father couldn't have. He couldn't.

"Yes, in each and every territory of both Dream as well as Wake," Ta said, continuing her pacing, hands behind her back.

"Couldn't you just…" I paused when all three locked wide eyes with me. "Couldn't you just stop… my father's timepiece?"

Nona's shoulders fell. Ta went back to pacing.

"That's the first thing we thought of, too," Ches said, picking up my hand and rubbing the back. Her skin was wrinkled and soft, that of an old person, like Mema, and soothed my fraying nerves. "Unfortunately, there is some sort of invisible shield surrounding his basin, and we are unable to even touch it."

My mouth dropped open as my mind whirled. "Then how do we stop him?"

"That, Alissandra, is why we are so glad you came." Ches continued petting my hand. Nona forced a wrinkled smile beside her.

I felt dizzy and my knees turned weak. They didn't know how to stop Father.

Ta stopped next to me and picked up my other hand. "We're counting on you, Alissandra."

I made to pull my hands away, but both held tight with surprising strength.

"No, you can't mean… I can't… I don't know how…"

Chapter Thirty-One

Alfreda

I'd never been so scared in my entire life. Time was running out.

Out of the corner of an eye, I caught one of our cursed captors glance our way, and I slammed my eyes shut.

My arm trembled as I shifted my grip, holding Kennan's sweaty hand. He hadn't moved in ages and his breathing was slow and even. *Glad he could sleep.* Sarcasm edged my thoughts as another one of those abominations bellowed, adding to the cacophony of discordant sounds that never stopped, even in the dark of night. Covering my ears didn't begin to silence it, I'd tried.

The fire raged in the pit not far off. I hadn't heard so much as a bird chirp much less a frog croak since we'd emerged from that cave suns before. I shuddered. Animals weren't stupid. They'd no doubt fled the fear that rippled off these things before we were anywhere near. How I wished I could, too. The torments that had beset my thoughts every heartbeat of every sun, these beasts were definitely to blame.

That cave. Just the thought of it made my stomach twist all the more. Bile threatened to show itself again. I clutched my leathered abdomen. How many more times could I retch?

I should have been glad to be out in the open air. I should have, but we'd reached someplace near Flumen, which meant we had little more than a fortnight until we reached the capital—Kennan had shouted our destination, fists raised high, as he rallied those cloudy-eyed rebels just before we set out. My breathing again hitched at the fire in his words. Threats, plans to unseat his siblings and claim the throne for himself. This was definitely Father's doing. My sisters would come to grave harm, I knew it.

I jumped as a snort erupted too close behind me. The male mumbled something, then fell back to snoring. I couldn't get used to these... warriors. Bawdy and course. I couldn't get far enough away from them.

I drew my blanket closer, under my chin, with a shaky hand.

I didn't know how Father controlled Kennan, but instinct—no experience—told me Kennan's very life, my sisters' lives—depended upon me freeing him. My breathing labored. Father didn't care one whit about my charge. Kennan was nothing more than a tool to him. He didn't care if Kennan lived or died.

But *I* cared.

I studied Kennan's features in the firelight. He seemed so peaceful. Nearly like he'd been those nights I wove his dreams after he'd discovered his love of painting or mastered the lyre or citole or rebec to his own satisfaction.

A corner of my mouth rose.

The lines of fierceness and aggression he'd worn since this nightmare began had smoothed and vanished from his face as he slept. His eyelids with their long, full lashes were closed against the starry night, and his breathing was deep and regular, all the muscles in his lithe body calm. His chest barely rose and fell with each breath, such was the depth of his slumber. Kennan was completely at peace, at rest, restoring his mind and body... before the start of yet another sun of chaos.

I barely stifled a growl.

I returned my attention to Kennan's face. I'd waxed poetic just now. Perhaps I cared more for him than I'd admitted even to myself, despite his behavior toward me of late. I frowned.

No. That wasn't Kennan, not the charge I knew intimately. Not the one I'd endured so, so much with. *That* was Father, controlling and oppressing him, again. He didn't deserve this.

Kennan had been pleasant enough, chatting with and encouraging me, escorting me to functions before Father reasserted governance over his mind and dragged us into this godsforsaken wilderness.

Another shiver raced down my back.

Kennan couldn't come to harm. He couldn't. But it's what would happen if we made it to Veritas. He was as vulnerable as a Pegasus before a dragon, as were my sisters.

I *had* to free him.

I fisted my hand. I'd tried, the gods knew I'd tried. I'd attempted to understand how Father controlled him, but every theory, every effort so far had failed.

What had I missed?

Ali and Kovis talked to each other through the bond they shared, or so she'd said. She'd grinned, telling me about her love for Kovis. I was happy for my little sister. That sounded nice, to be that connected to another. I smiled. Kennan and I shared a bond, too, but we'd never used it.

I pressed my lips together as Ali's tale of tunneling through their connection and seeing through Kovis's eyes, rose to the forefront of my mind. I shook my head. Imagine.

I mused on the idea. Yes, imagine. I exhaled lightly.

Wait. Imagine indeed. The tale continued swirling, filling my thoughts.

Father controlled Kennan, yet his eyes hadn't turned cloudy like the rebels. He *had* to have done something to Kennan's mind, directly. It was the only way without me to allow him access to Kennan's thought thread. I sucked in air. If he could do that to Kennan, we were all at risk. I clutched my leathers.

I *had* to free him. Now. I had to figure this out once and for all.

Could I access Kennan's mind through our bond? And if I did, could I save him from Father?

I set my jaw. I had to try.

How to find our bond? I didn't have a clue.

I'd accessed Kennan's mind through his thought thread after reaching out to the dream canopy.

Is that how it worked? It seemed my only option.

I closed my eyes and pictured reaching out to the dream canopy, then gliding down to the palace in Veritas… but he wasn't there. No, of course he wasn't. He was here.

I tried again. I imagined the dream canopy, then pictured flying over those mountain peaks we'd trekked across, riding the winds above the thick pine trees, then hearing our party, then coming upon us, seeing the host of rebels stretched out on blankets around the roaring campfire. There we were, Kennan beside me.

I imagined setting down, furling my wings, and kneeling down behind Kennan's slowly rising back. I reached out and pressed a hand to the side of his head, looking for his thought thread.

Kennan groaned.

"It's fine. All is well," I whispered. "Show me your thought thread."

Kennan tossed in his sleep.

"Show me."

He mumbled.

Nothing.

I huffed.

I was getting nowhere. Again.

I opened my eyes.

How had Ali entered their bond? When I'd probed her further, she'd divulged that she'd been worried to death about Kovis. She hadn't heard the thrum of his power and had been terrified that she'd hurt him irreparably. She'd *longed* to see how he faired.

Was that it? The longing? I certainly understood longing. I had to get into Kennan's mind, before... I bit my lip and closed my eyes again, picturing Kennan's thought thread: it was a dark tunnel that led to his thoughts and memories that flowed freely there.

"Kennan, I *must* search your mind. Let me. I beg of you." I said it in little more than a whisper, soaking, saturating, pouring every measure of longing I possessed into my words. So much rested on this.

I envisioned that dark tunnel between us, between our minds. Step after careful step, I envisioned making my way across it. When I reached his side, I shouted desire—*Kennan, let me see your beautiful mind. Let me experience the fullness of who you are, the warm and loving, the giving and sacrificing man you have become. Let me experience the man I know.*

I sucked in air when a rainbow of colors burst before my mind's eye. Woah, how was this possible? I opened my eyes. I still lay beside Kennan. He still slumbered. But... I closed them again and the kaleidoscope of colors again filled my vision.

Our bond. It had to be. I'd done it. I'd somehow tunneled through it, and I was seeing with physical eyes in my own body as well as with my mind into his, at the same time. And in brilliant colors. His, all my charges, thoughts had only been grays. Is this what Ali experienced? My heart beat faster. It was beautiful, magnificent, but also disorienting.

Kennan shifted. I froze. *Stay asleep, Kennan.*

He settled, and I exhaled, enjoying the multicolored display that bested the Canyon's lights. I recognized the strands where his thoughts and memories flowed. I'd tapped into them with regularity, but I resisted the urge to do so now. I had more important work to do.

I'd somehow made it into Kennan's mind. Now to find... what? I didn't know what I searched for. Something that looked out of place.

Kennan shifted and moaned, shifted and moaned, shifted and moaned, time and again as I searched and searched for... something. I'd looked everywhere I knew, multiple times. I'd left no area around or near his memories unturned, yet I'd found nothing out of the ordinary.

Yet Father controlled him, I couldn't give up. But if I didn't hurry, Kennan would wake, and I'd have to wait until sleep again claimed him. Another shiver raced down my back. We didn't have that luxury.

Where? Where? I shook my head.

Where had I not looked? My pitch rose as frustration reduced me to whining.

Nowhere. I'd covered it all.

Where had I never looked? My breathing labored as the rogue thought rushed to the forefront of my mind. I'd only ever been in a relatively small area of any of my charges' minds, but Father could have done his dirty work... anywhere. It would take suns... suns... to search every nook and cranny of Kennan's mind.

I longed to curl up in a corner and wait for this horrible mess to blow over. But I couldn't. I *had* to do this.

Despite the need, defeatist thoughts ran wild, pillaging and plundering. I wasn't up to this. I couldn't do it.

And my sisters would die because of it.

I sucked in air and forced myself to let it out slowly.

No, I couldn't let that happen. I had to be strong. My muscles tightened.

I'd overcome the overwhelming malaise that had ravaged me after Velma... after *that* cave.

I could do this. I had to do this.

Without giving myself time to reconsider, I plunged into the unknown.

Like the area with Kennan's memories, the path I chose was bright and well lit. Muted colors swirled around me as my mind ventured down one tunnel, then another, looking, gazing, taking it all in. Searching, scanning for what didn't belong.

I paused as Kennan again shifted in his sleep. If I was Father, where would I hide something I didn't want found? I chuckled. Probably the very center of his mind.

I gasped. The center of his mind. No one would expect it. And it'd be the most secure there.

The sound of Kennan's heavy breathing reasserted itself, and I glanced about. Where was I? I'd headed toward the back of his mind. I turned around and corrected course, toward the center.

So many beautiful shapes, abstract designs, freeform patterns in colors I'd never seen nor imagined. The relatively small area Kennan's memories were confined to didn't hint at this vast array of creativity. Sparkles, stars bursting, the images took my breath away as our bond allowed me to forge a mental path to the core of Kennan's amazing mind.

Kennan groaned, then tossed, then moaned again, the frequency increasing as I continued on. Was I closing in on whatever it was? Is that why he grew ever more restless? My heart lightened, and I hastened my steps, no longer stopping with each sound or shift he made.

There. Just ahead. His core. At least it would be if my sense of direction was correct.

I emerged into a smallish cavity. Its rounded walls glowed in the purest white I'd ever beheld. While the beauty of the whole of Kennan's mind truly defied words, I nearly gagged despite not being able to smell. My eyes landed on a black, roundish seed of sorts. Grotesque... evil... yes, loathing overwhelmed me... visceral... pure evil emanated from it. My throat burned and a shudder rocked my body. So, so, so vile. That *had* to be it. It was so different from every other aspect of Kennan's mind.

Kennan tossed and turned. I had to work fast.

I'd learned how to move things with my thoughts, but could I do it with this? And could I do it fast enough, before Father knew and woke Kennan? I'd yank it and retrace my steps. Wait, did I remember how I'd come?

I replayed the path I'd taken. Yes, I remembered.

Kennan groaned and my mouth went dry. This had to work.

My skin crawled as my mind reached for that odious seed.

I locked on. Burning and pure agony shot through my mind, through our bond, in the blink of an eye as I yanked it.

Run!

Chapter Thirty-Two

We were royally screwed. My aunts didn't know how to stop Father, and they expected me to save Dream. I'd never forget the feeling of horror as realization dawned. I still hadn't shaken, I couldn't shake, the coldness that had hit my core.

No pressure.

I couldn't settle despite the comfort of my family surrounding me after I'd told them all that our aunts had said, over fortnight family dinner at the palace of sand maidens. So I paced as all twenty-two of us, my siblings and I plus Mema and Grandfather, conversed in the sitting room after dinner.

"Maybe we ask Dyeus for his help again?" Clovis, my baby brother, asked, picking at a stray white thread that had come loose from the sofa that stretched below the row of windows. Like every dinner, he'd styled his black hair. He'd formed it into the shape of a globe this time, saying it represented the world that Dyeus had forced Atlas to carry for eternity as a punishment for wrongs committed.

Did he hope that's what the chief of gods would do to Father when he caught him?

I raised my brows as I gazed his way. Several others did too.

"Aunt Dite told me just the other sun that her father has been unable to find Ambien despite his stewards ongoing search," Mema said.

"They're still looking?" I asked, pausing my pacing. "I figured they'd given up."

Mema frowned. "No, not after what he did to Velma." She shifted, crossing her legs. "Despite our families' differences, it's become something of a beetle biting under his robes from what she said. He won't let it go; or put another way, it won't let him go. Either way, he's still searching."

"But the chief of all gods hasn't found Father." I hugged myself.

"No." Mema fingered the collar of her navy dress.

Grandfather drew her closer, wrapping an arm around her shoulders on one of the smaller divans. He clenched his jaw and said, "Perhaps it's time we reach out to some of the other gods." His grip on the arm of the sofa tightened.

My knees went weak, and I hastily took a seat on the upholstered footstool. I gave Grandfather a long look. For him to even suggest it... "Are... are you sure?"

The favors that would be expected, required, for such help... by him and the rest of my family. Nothing came free with the rest of the gods.

Mema stared at her skirt, then drew a hand to his thigh and patted it.

Grandfather covered Mema's hand and gently squeezed. "He is our son as much as he is your father, and I will not have my granddaughter responsible for ending what he started." He drew his lips in a line. "These... abominations he's created must be stopped. Morpheus's delusions of power can no longer go unchecked."

Mema glanced up at his face with sadness in her eyes.

I inhaled sharply, several of us did. Grandfather had used Father's given name—the name he and Mema had given him—not Ambien, or any other of the names he'd adopted, then shed over time as it suited him. And in that heartbeat, I realized Father had disrespected Grandfather and Mema, not just his offspring. He'd changed his name umpteen times to pander to one set of humans or another—Greeks, Romans, the list went on. I'd never heard either of them say a word about it, but their expressions revealed their hurt, especially Mema.

Rankin, my second oldest brother and a born leader, had sat silently beside Clovis, but in this heartbeat, he drew his wings that rested over the back of the sofa, tighter and cleared his throat. "Before you ask for help from the other gods…"

Every eye locked onto him.

I sat up straight.

"Father has been stopped in his campaigns twice before. How?"

Ug. Those awful, bloody wars. I grimaced.

"Several regents banded together," Wynnfrith replied from the opposite end of Mema and Grandfather's couch.

"Yes, but he didn't have those… those… things before," I argued. "Rankin, you've never seen them. They're pure evil. Fear ripples off them." Shivers raced up my back, and I rubbed my arms. "Aunts said there's hundreds of them. Hundreds."

"Be that as it may, the regents still stopped him." Rankin leaned forward.

"What are you suggesting?" Grandfather asked.

"I believe the threat is grave, but before we ask the other gods for help, we ought to exhaust *all* of our options. They're, pardon me,"— he drew a hand to the back of his neck—"arrogant bastards at times and will want to do things their way. They don't know the situation like you do, Ali, and we can't afford to have them screw it up."

I couldn't help but chuckle. He was right.

"They have been known to let their pompous asses bumble more than a few things upon occasion," Grandfather agreed.

Several snickers erupted. Mema elbowed him although a corner of her mouth hitched.

"So what do you suggest?" I asked.

"You said Selova's messengers never delivered their missives." Rankin rubbed his hands.

"Yes, that's what Aunts said. The regents know some of their citizens have gone missing but have no idea about Father's monsters."

"I think it's time they discover all that has been happening under their noses. If memory serves Arret, Doow, Latem, and Erif of Dream's reciprocal magical provinces stopped Father the first time and Naverey, Anarit, and Abuj from Dream's reciprocal nonmagical provinces, the second."

My mind whirled, unable to remember who'd done what. I'd tried to forget the bloody mess.

"Do we know how they stopped Father?" Harding asked, wings tight, ankles crossed where he stood, leaning against the end of the sofa, near Clovis.

"We do not, but I believe it's time we find out," Rankin grinned. "My guess is they'd be very open to a request for help if it means keeping Father from meddling in their stew pot."

"But what'll we do about those creatures?" I fingered the lace of my dress. "We don't have much time."

"First things first," Rankin said. "The regents need to know the threat they're up against. Then we can discuss strategy."

My stomach clenched, and I bobbed my head slowly. There was no good plan it seemed, but Rankin's was better than none, which is where I'd been.

"There are fourteen provinces and nine of us," my brother said. "I suggest we divvy them up— "

"I'm going too," I interrupted. "There's no way I'm sitting on my hands waiting for you males to be manly while I stay here in safety and ease."

Ailith, Beval, Deor, Farfelee, and Wasila also insisted they go, pushing back shoulders and giving Rankin curt nods.

Mema held herself, her stare distant.

Our brother hunched like a turtle peeking from its shell, then held up his hands in surrender. "Very well. Then there's *sixteen* of us and fourteen provinces." He went on and divided us up into groups of twos or threes along with guards, assigning territories to visit. We would leave as soon as we gathered supplies.

I just hoped it wasn't too late.

Father had Kennan marching toward Veritas in Wake. My gut told me he'd be mobilizing his minions in Dream too...

If he hadn't already.

Chapter Thirty-Three

Kennan

My eyes shot open beside Alfreda's writhing form. Confusion ravaged me. My head pounded as if someone beat on it like a drum.

Alfreda shrieked.

I threw my arms around my head and slammed my eyes shut. What was happening to me? I groaned with the continued pummeling... But the daze, the brain fog that had blocked out awareness, perception, the haze that had plagued me for suns... it lightened, faded... I could feel it. How? I forced my eyes back open.

Alfreda stilled, panting. Her golden hair was wet with sweat, an arm's length from where I lay.

Guards bolted for us, swords drawn, converging with roaming eyes and flaring nostrils.

My chest heaved as I struggled for words. Another stab of pain shot through my head, and I clutched it tighter. *My* words. I'd heard a cacophony of them, sometimes a hum, other times a buzz, as words spilled from my mouth. Yes, I'd spoken. I knew it like I knew my name. What had I said? Why could I not remember? What had happened to me? The pounding in my head eased a tad.

"Bad dream," Alfreda said, drinking in air.

The guards grumbled, then ambled away.

Brushing locks of damp, messy hair behind an ear, Alfreda pushed herself up to sitting and looked me over. She clutched at her chest, eyes wide.

Alfreda. I didn't remember much of the last... I didn't know how long, but disgust didn't swell in me like it had of late when I looked on her. Wait. How did I remember that? What had happened to me? I sat up and gazed at her—her dirty fingernails, the dirt smudged on her cheek, her bare feet. She still held my hand as she did every night, all night, but no revulsion rose.

Roars, howls, and growls rumbled through the night air, and a feeling of fear, no terror, unspeakable horror, assaulted my senses, and my eyes went wide. "What?"

"You don't remember them?"

I couldn't envision whatever it was, but my body definitely did, and a shiver raced through me. I didn't want to remember at this rate.

"What happened?" I struggled to keep my tone even.

She leaned in. "That's a long story. How do you feel?"

"I... I feel..." I cocked my head and looked around. "I'm clear headed." I gave her a *very* long look.

Alfreda bit her lip.

"You?"

She nodded.

"How... how did you do it?"

"I accessed your mind through our bond."

My jaw dropped.

"I found a seed of sorts. It felt like pure evil, and I knew it couldn't be yours. It had to be something my father somehow put there."

Her father? Ambien? He'd possessed me a second time? I bared my teeth.

One of the guards who paced nearby gave me a long look.

Alfreda waved her hands at me. "It doesn't matter." There she was wrong. It mattered. It definitely did. "What does matter, is that I used my magic to yank it out."

I drew a hand to my temple. Ambien had somehow planted something in my head without me knowing... or at least remembering? He'd controlled me, *twice* now. How? Could it happen again? My stomach twisted. Was I to be his game piece forever, whenever the whim struck?

Alfreda shook her head. "I have no idea how he did it, especially since I've been here, and he couldn't get to you the way he did the first time—"

"You're not making me feel any better."

She forced a smile. "However, if he ever does it again, I'll know how to... rescue you."

"Assuming he doesn't change tactics since you found this... seed thing."

Alfreda sighed.

But she'd freed me. I looked up into her big brown eyes. "You'd free me again, even after—" I looked down, at my hands. "—how I treated you?" How could I remember that? I'd been horrible to her, but little else?

"Absolutely!" Her face had taken on a ferocity I'd never seen before.

The guard approached, a scowl making his ugly face even more so. "Enough talking."

We both lay back down, and he turned away.

But Alfreda wasn't done with our conversation, and in an ardent whisper, arm folded beneath her head, she said, "You were my dream charge. I'd never let anything, especially Father, happen to you."

I raised my eyebrows at her vehemence. Her chin dipped down, and she drew her blanket closer, under her chin.

"Hey, look at me," I said, returning her whisper.

Ever so slowly, she raised her head, and even in the glow of the hot coals, it was clear her cheeks had taken on a pinkish hue.

"No need to be embarrassed."

She bit her lip and pulled at the blanket. "I'm... I'm not."

"Thank you for caring enough to save me."

She closed her eyes and nodded.

I glanced about, confused as to how we'd come to be... wherever we were. "I presume it was I who got us in this trouble. I can't imagine you'd lead us out in the middle of nowhere. Here."

She shook her head. "Not you, Father."

"You honestly believe that?"

She nodded. "I do. He controlled you. That wasn't you."

"So where are we?"

"Around Flumen." She went on to give me the lowlights of the last fortnight and more.

I shook my head, my eyes grew wide, and I flared my nostrils as my anger grew throughout her telling. Ambien had possessed me. Again. And he'd forced me to lead his minions against those I most loved. I was the spare, but there was no way I'd seek the crown for my own. My stomach clenched. I'd committed treason.

Coughing, just behind us, made us both jump.

"It won't be long until your father realizes he doesn't control me any longer. We need to get out of here," I whispered.

Alfreda bit her lip and nodded.

I scanned the campsite. The fire in the center near where we lay had dwindled, and only red coals flickered. A sea of slumbering men curled up in thin blankets, surrounded us. Clumps of guards, in twos and threes, watched every goings-on from around the perimeter as well as throughout the campsite.

More roars, howls, and growls rumbled through the night air, again sending chills up my spine. Alfreda had described the creatures, but I was content never to see one.

"How are we…?" Alfreda whispered.

"Where are the horses?"

"Far edge of camp, away from those… things. They spook the horses and keep them on edge."

I glanced about, still not seeing any equines.

"That way." Alfreda bobbed her head. "But how—"

"Pretend you need to pee. Then skirt around to where they are."

Her eyes went wide.

"Select two that look like they can run like the wind. Do you think you can move them with your magic?"

Alfreda tilted her head and grimaced.

"That's okay. Then I'll meet you there, and we'll figure it out. Now go."

"How are you—"

"Don't worry about me."

She gave a curt nod, put on her scuffed boots, then got up and meandered through the maze of slumbering men. I opened my eyes a slit to see a guard stop her not long after, but a quick glance at me and my still form had him nodding her on.

I waited until she'd reached the edge of prone men and turned right, toward our objective, then I stretched and yawned, pretending to have just awoken. I stood and wandered toward the opposite side of camp running a hand through my messy hair.

"Stop." The growled command came from behind. "Turn and face me."

I did and the soldier looked me up and down, then glanced over to where we'd slept. "Where's your lady?"

"I presume tending to the same thing I wish to."

"Then I'll walk with you." The soldier grinned.

"That's not necessary."

"Oh, but it is. We wouldn't want our commander to get lost would we?"

Commander? I forced a chuckle. I could play along. "No, we wouldn't. Then shall we?" I waved an open hand.

"Oh no, after you. I insist."

I led the way between sleeping lumps, unsure where I was going. I looked ahead for a smallish pit dug in the ground and a trowel standing in an upturned pile of dirt beside it that would mark my destination. My heart picked up pace the longer I looked.

"Hey, Commander. Where do you think you're going?" my companion barked.

I shrugged. "I can't remember where—"

The guard huffed, then grabbed my arm and shoved me forward. "There. Behind the bushes."

The shrubs offered a modicum of privacy. "Do you mind?"

The guard scowled, but turned.

I hated to do this—who was I kidding, no I didn't. Not after what Ambien had done to me, twice. Anger ignited in a flash, and I conjured a dagger, then threw it with fury-laced might. This guard wasn't Ambien, but he carried out the god's orders. It felt good. It felt right. A small vindication. The soldier didn't have time to make so much as a sound before my knife embedded itself in the back of his neck and he slumped to the ground.

I'd drag him behind... I barely stifled a yip as he transformed into a large, purple-furred, wolf-like beast.

What in Hades? Between the sight and the stench, I nearly retched.

Movement to my right refocused me in the blink of an eye, and I turned on quiet feet and dashed left, widening my berth around the camp's perimeter as I did. The horses had to be here somewhere.

Shouts erupted behind me, and I prayed Alfreda had our mounts selected. The string of horses came into focus, and I exhaled as I spotted her crouched not far from the tree line. I followed her gaze to

● ● ●
240

five guards who huddled not far away from her. *Crap!* I dove behind a tree, panting. No good. Five against one. And I'd need to protect Alfreda.

Correction, eight against one. The five guards roused at an approaching commotion. Three more were headed directly for her from the opposite direction.

I sucked in a breath. *Alfreda, move!* She needed to before they spotted her.

Alfreda startled, glancing about. What'd she see?

My toes curled. *Behind you!*

Her head pivoted, scanning the area, but she must have heard approaching footsteps because she scurried behind another clump of bushes, with no time to spare.

I exhaled.

Kennan? Is that you?

I looked about. *Alfreda?* How was I hearing her? She was over there.

Yes. It's our bond. Ali told me she can talk to Kovis through it when she really, really longs to.

My eyes went wide. *Our bond? She'd rummaged through my mind with it to extract her father's "gift" and now she used it to talk to me?*

Guards raced past my hiding spot, bringing my attention back. They'd circle around in no time.

We needed those horses. We couldn't rely solely on Alfreda's magic to get us back to the capital. It'd exhaust her.

"Halt!" a low voice growled behind me.

Chapter Thirty-Four

Kennan

I felt myself launch, then fly through the air. Trees and shrubs raced by below. I braced as the rocky ground reached for me.

Thank the gods for Motus powers, wholly unique to Alfreda. Thank the gods for her.

I stumbled but managed to stay upright as my boots hit the flat of the small clearing amongst a host of tall trees. Shouts erupted a ways off.

Alfreda!

She landed on top of me, in the blink of an eye, bowling me over. I grunted as we fell into a heap.

"Sorry. Are you okay?" she asked, scrambling up and off me. She stood, then looked my crumpled form up and down.

I smiled. "Never better, thank you."

Shouts drew closer. No doubt Ambien's minions would blanket the surrounding area and scour every handbreadth.

I rose. "How much power do you have?"

"What about horses?" Alfreda's feet bounced.

"We'll find some to 'borrow,' on our way home."

She rolled her eyes, but grinned, then scanned the area. "I'm not sure how long my power will last, hopefully I can get us far enough away…"

I bobbed my head and held out a hand.

I wasn't sure why, but Alfreda gazed between it and my eyes, and a small smile rose on her lips, but she didn't say anything as she took it, closed her eyes, and I again felt weightless as my feet skimmed the treetops.

The further we flew, the lighter my heart felt. Visceral fear had gripped me back there. I'd realized it, but as it faded as Alfreda put more and more distance between us and Ambien's forces, I felt as if I could breathe once more. He no longer governed me, and I felt more alive than in forever.

Alfreda set us down near a stream and bent over, panting. I practically leapt for joy. I was free. Free. Truly free.

Because of her. My eyes roamed over her hunched form as the thought rose. Yes, this was only possible because of her.

Alfreda's power lasted *nearly* two more jumps—we crash landed in a thicket the second time, her power completely spent. Eyes closed, Alfreda's chest heaved and sweat rolled from her brow where she lay after the shrub she'd landed on collapsed beneath her.

The bush I'd landed in, clawed my face as I rolled over and out, but nothing seemed broken.

I crawled over to her and pushed her golden locks away from her face. "Alfreda, are you okay?"

She didn't move other than to raise a finger as if asking me to give her a few heartbeats to recover before speaking. I beamed. She could have as long as she wanted. She'd given us her all. I'd ask for nothing more.

I lay down beside her and listened. Her breathing slowed. Birds sang. A pair of small somethings argued in high pitched squeaks not far off in the sun's growing light. Leaves swayed on trees in the slight breeze. No shouts. No growls or roars. Blessed serenity. I drank it in like a parched man getting his first taste of water.

Alfreda's breathing grew long and slow, not surprising with all the energy she'd expended, so I rose and scouted the area while she slept.

The sound of tinkling water drew my attention, and I hastened my steps to find the suggestion of a stream. While its waters were not abundant, they tasted sweet on my tongue. I drank my fill, then surveyed the thinning trees at the edge of the wood. No berries or mushrooms or any edible plant showed itself.

A crowing sound in the brushy meadow just beyond drew my attention. A drumming sound—wings beating together—followed a heartbeat later, and a pheasant flew up from the wispy grass.

I conjured a dagger and crept to the woods' edge, ducking behind a tree, then sat down and waited. Where there was one pheasant, there had to be more.

My mind returned to the turmoil my thoughts had become since Alfreda had woken me early this morning, extracting that seed.

She'd saved me even though I'd been such a bastard to her. With everything that had happened, how was it I remembered that not so small detail, but not much else?

I picked a blade of long grass and sucked on it.

Ambien. I loosed another growl. The first time he'd controlled me as I'd wandered about in the chill wilderness, I'd been obsessed with Ali. She was all I'd thought about—how she could complete me. I stared down at my hands, the ache from her admission that I owned no part of her heart, still there. I'd been nursing feelings of betrayal and loss this whole time, and I'd been miserable, despondent, irritable.

A crow and rustle drew my attention back to the meadow, but too late. The bird had flown.

The malaise of my wilderness wanderings had vanished back at the palace, and I'd thought he'd left, but... My stomach twisted.

I remembered Alfreda had tried telling me stories about him as I'd endured forced bed rest, but I'd cut her off... I'd nearly cursed her because... it felt as if she'd been defaming... *me!*

Damn prick, Ambien was demented. He'd never left. He'd let me believe he had, but he hadn't. I'd been his playing piece the whole time. I'd probably been quite the entertainment for him. And no doubt he'd even "encouraged" my... delusions about Ali.

I ground my teeth.

He probably enjoyed my fury, my angst, my despair, and even the hurt I still felt.

I scanned the meadow, taking in the pair of black birds that flew above, smelling the pine scent, hearing the caws and chirps. I picked up a handful of fallen pine needles and let them sift through my fingers. My mind felt clear. The world was crisp and sharp again. Yes, I was myself once more. Alfreda had well and truly removed him from my mind.

I blew out a long breath.

Alfreda. My throat felt thick. Since she'd come, she'd been nothing but encouraging. I'm sure I didn't remember everything, but what I did was plenty. I shook my head, guilt making my chest tighten. I'd treated her poorly. I didn't treat others that way, not without cause. But how was I remembering that?

If Ambien had been controlling me, as it seemed... Was the guilt I felt, the real me railing against my behavior? Was my mind shouting that my actions didn't match my beliefs? Is that why I remembered? I put my head in my hands.

The grass rustled not far off, bringing me back. I drew my dagger back, then let it fly as the pheasant took flight.

It dropped like a rock as my blade struck true.

With a heavy heart, I deplumed, then gutted the bird. I cleaned its gizzard in the stream, cauterized one end with my flames, then filled the sack with water. I guzzled and refilled its contents several times as I gathered wood and built a fire, all before she woke.

"Kennan?" Alfreda sat up and stretched as the sun kissed the horizon.

I sat down beside her. "How do you feel?"

She rubbed her eyes. "Good. Rested. Hey, something smells good. You've been busy."

"We have pheasant for dinner."

She raised her brow. "Do tell."

"Are you hungry?"

"Umm, yes."

I kept sneaking glances at her in the firelight as we ate.

She took her time licking the fat from her fingers, then finally dropped her hands and locked eyes with me, frowning. "Why do you keep glancing at me?"

Where to start? Emotions had swirled in my heart while I'd worked. "I want to apologize." She held up a hand, but I waved it away. "No, let me speak. I've been thinking a lot while you slept." I told her everything I'd deduced about Ambien still controlling me until this morning. "I'm sorry for how I treated you. I know you know it was your father, but I can't live with myself until I've apologized properly."

Alfreda drew her lips into a line. "Then I accept."

"Thank you." I pressed my palms to my eyes and exhaled. Based on her earlier reaction, I'd known she'd accept; but all the same, relief washed over me, and I took a deep breath.

Alfreda smiled.

"Which brings me to another realization."

"Goodness, so much reflection." Her eyes danced.

I nodded. "You were my sand maiden, and I've taken you for granted. Never once have I appreciated all you've done for me." I swallowed. She tilted her head. "I imagined how you helped me cope all those times by shifting my narratives about one thing or another as I slept, giving me hope, how you focused me on creative pursuits through which I could ease my pain. That was you, wasn't it?"

"I can't take full credit, but a part was, yes."

"You saved me time and time again. Saying 'thank you' falls far short, as does 'I owe you my life' but it's true."

Alfreda wrinkled her nose and chuckled. "That sounds so staid. You were my responsibility, and I did my job happily."

"I suppose so, but you did it for *me*." I thumped my chest. "You made a difference in my life."

The corners of her eyes turned silver, and she bobbed her head. Her voice trembled as she said, "I've never sought thanks from a charge." She sniffed. "But you're welcome."

My eyes ran up and down her. Alfreda was pretty—even now with all the grime and dirt—but true *beauty* had little to do with outward appearances. No, beauty was inside, at the heart of a person, and Alfreda exuded it. She was a flower of rare beauty, splendid and exquisite.

I flicked my wrist, conjuring a metal replica of the bloom I envisioned her to be.

She sucked in a breath, and I grinned as I held it out to her.

She cupped it in her hands and studied it as she drew it back toward her. "It's beautiful." A smile mounted her lips, as she examined it further. "Thank you."

We woke with the sun and trekked up hills, across rocky terrain, through pine forests, around deep ravines and more, following the path of the sun. Veritas was due west of Flumen, and as long as we kept to this course, we'd reach the capital in the least time possible.

"Ha, look at that." Alfreda laughed as we came upon a tree with mushrooms growing up the side. "I loved going to the mushroom caves." She proceeded to regale me with stories of her and her siblings going and getting tipsy after ingesting them.

I couldn't help but laugh at the thought. But by the time she'd recounted several trips, adding a stagger to her steps as she did, my stomach hurt.

She told me about flying. Even told me about Kovis sprouting wings and how he'd crash landed a few times on his last visit. My mouth dropped open. He hadn't told me. No surprise, I'd been a regular bugbear.

Alfreda was the thirteenth of twenty-two children. Deor, one of her older sisters, was her roommate. She loved the smell of coffee and freshly baked bread. Her favorite celebration was the solstice with aerial dancing and all the colorful dresses she and her sisters got to wear.

She screeched when we ventured upon a snake in the path, which my fire quickly dispatched.

More than once I caught her admiring that metal flower when she thought I wasn't looking.

And there were always more and more and more stories of her and her family. Of being immortal and the daughter of a god. Hearing her tell of the bonds they shared, of the comfort and strength she drew from their mutual support and encouragement. She had a lot more family members than me, but it was clear we both shared a closeness, an intimacy, with them.

So passed the next seven suns as we walked and leapt, with Alfreda's help, from sunup to sundown. We hadn't come across any towns from which to "borrow" horses, and our feet had started to complain.

But of greater concern, that army of nefarious creatures grew closer to Veritas with each passing sun, and the longer it took us to reach home, the less time we would have to prepare… if there was anything that could even be done to stop it. Judging from all that Alfreda had said, I wasn't so sure.

Chapter Thirty-Five

Kennan

The ground rumbled and a horse whinnied, waking me where I lay beside Alfreda—still holding hands, so I could sleep—near the ash heap that had been our fire the night before.

Another horse and another whickered, growing nearer. I sprang up. *Please don't be. Please don't be.*

"What?" Alfreda sat up, rubbing her eyes, hair flying at odd angles.

I raced through the wood and caught sight of dust billowing up from between thinning trees. The herd ran toward us, toward the meadow just beyond.

I prayed it wasn't our enemy finding us as I dashed to meet them, summoning fire. If it wasn't the enemy, if I could separate two from the herd, we'd reach Veritas a whole lot sooner.

I skidded to a stop and ducked behind a tree at the edge of the meadow. The ground's shaking intensified. They'd be on me in no time. Was I crazy? Probably. I swallowed hard, bracing.

In the blink of an eye, the first horse galloped into view, then the next and next, and I exhaled. Only horses, no riders. It wasn't our enemy finding us.

I ran out into the meadow and into their path, then took a ready position, hands out.

The lead stallion veered right when it spotted me. Several followed his lead, but others didn't and continued careening toward me. Snorts and squeals sounded as my flames erupted in a wall before them. The three in front threw up dust as they stopped abruptly, the horses following merged into and between them in a messy clump.

I expanded my flames into a wide arch to corral them, eliciting more squeals. Their eyes went wide, and their ears flattened. They trotted left, then turned, tails swishing, and pranced right, within my flames. Ten of them.

The lead stallion circled around behind me in the open meadow and vocalized support.

"It's okay. You're okay." I took slow steps forward but succeeded only in scaring the ten more. The horse closest to the wood snorted, then wheeled around, bolting through where my flames couldn't reach lest I ignite trees, back from whence it came.

Four others followed.

Five left. One, a golden mare with matted blonde mane and burr-ridden tail, wore a rope halter. Had she escaped from a farmer?

I dimmed my flames, but the horses continued cantering back and forth like an undulating wave, eyes wide, within my flame corral.

The lead stallion reared up, then roared behind me, charging. I killed my flames and dove left just before it reached me.

My captives trotted back toward their waiting companions, whinnying and brushing necks when they reached them.

But I wasn't done fighting. Even one horse would do.

The lead stallion followed me, not far behind, head down, no doubt readying to bite. So I ran, circling around, then charged for the herd. Those nearest shied away, but in the chaos, not all spotted me and as I reached the edge of the group, I leapt, praying I'd find a horse beneath me when I landed.

Legs spread, I straddled two when I came down—a painted, white and brown and that golden one with the rope halter. I scrambled onto the golden as the tightly packed group shifted. My hand just barely grabbed hold of its matted mane and I conjured a flame with my other.

I waved my hand behind me and the horses following, moved away.

"Whoa, girl. You're okay." I patted her withers.

Once the herd distanced itself, I turned the mare toward the woods and stopped her, then let my flames fly. Shrieks and whinnies and the rumble of feet echoed as the stallion led his band away.

Clapping rose from the tree line where Alfreda stood grinning. "My conquering hero."

I bowed, atop Hermes. Yes, I'd name her that, after the winged god of wealth and luck. We'd need luck, and then some.

As it turned out, Hermes had been domesticated and had a pleasant disposition. It beat having to break in a mount as I would have had to if I'd picked the painted horse I'd landed on. I judged she was nigh three annums, and with her sleek but sturdy bearing, she'd get us to the capital within two suns.

"How well do you know your gods?" Alfreda asked, my arms around her waist where she sat in front of me as we cantered toward home not long after.

"Certainly not as well as you, but a fair bit. Why?" I shifted the makeshift reins we'd crafted from pliable grass in the meadow, then attached to Hermes's halter.

She chuckled. "Hermes is also known for being one of the cleverest and most mischievous of the gods."

"Is he now?"

She nodded. "But—" She raised a finger. "—he's also known for…" She snickered.

I nudged her waist with my elbow. "For what?"

"Fertility." She burst out laughing.

I felt my cheeks warm. "He is?"

She bobbed her head.

"I thought that was only Aphrodite." My voice wavered.

She slapped her leg.

"So you're saying we're riding fertility." I couldn't help but chuckle.

She giggled.

She was having entirely too much fun at my expense. I reached up and tickled her chin.

"Hey!" She grabbed my hand and stilled it.

Hermes snorted, as if laughing at our antics as we reached the bottom of another rolling hill.

Time to turn the tables. "You said you saved me from your father because I was your dream charge."

She nodded, releasing my hand.

"I've been wondering…" My eyes twinkled, remembering how her cheeks had pinked as she vehemently declared she would save me from her father if, gods forbid, he possessed me again. "Is that the only reason?"

"Isn't… Isn't that enough?"

"Of course. I just wondered if there were, oh, I don't know, any *other* reasons?"

Birds chirping filled the void as she grew silent. She pulled at the collar of her leathers.

My stomach took to quivering. I shouldn't have asked. "I'm sorry, I—"

"I thought it was." Her words spilled out. "We've been through so much together. You tramping about the wilderness, half frozen to death. Father in that cave—" She shook her head. "—and what he got me to do to you, I still hate myself for it. What he did to Velma"—she looked down— "that sparked my coming."

I drew my arm tighter around her middle, and she leaned back into me. Into her ear I said softly, "We've both been through a lot. I shouldn't have joked about it."

"It's fine. You're fine asking." She drew her arms around mine.

Our conversation steered clear of this and similar topics the rest of this sun and the next, but Alfreda continued leaning against my chest. For my part, I didn't loose my hold of her. It felt good to have her there, swaying to the regular rhythm of Hermes's cantor, and clutching me as I made our steed gallop—I might have made Hermes run a few more times and a bit longer than I ordinarily would. I might have.

I'd known we were close, so when the white spires of the palace came into view between the treetops, over the crest of the steep hill we climbed, warmth radiated through my chest and I hugged Alfreda. "We're here."

She sat up straight and scanned the horizon. "Oh! I see it."

The sun had begun its descent by the time we stopped at the overlook, but we'd made it. All in Veritas, in the valley below, seemed quiet, at least for now, but my stomach clenched. Time was running out.

A quick check at the palace told us Kovis and Rasa were down at the council building, so we surrendered Hermes to a groom and soon sat astride Onyx—I declined the man's offer to saddle another horse for Alfreda. She'd just smiled.

I tied Onyx to a post, then helped Alfreda off my stallion when we reached the spherical-shaped building. Water bubbled from the top, cascading down to a trench around the base. The few citizens milling about on the plaza gave us curious looks, no doubt at our unkempt appearances. It didn't matter, we'd clean up after we delivered our news.

A steward dropped his jaw, but opened the doors, then quickly bowed. "My… my prince."

The council was in session judging by the few who mingled in the wide hallway that wrapped around outside the main chamber. They, too, shot us strange looks, but I grabbed Alfreda's hand as we strode past.

I opened the door to the private, royal entrance and waved Alfreda forward, then followed her in, again taking her hand. Lord Beecham, representative of Ice province and head of the council—the blowhard—bloviated. His voice echoed down the curving corridor.

Kovis came into view through the doorway, seated to Rasa's right, on the raised platform directly below the imposing wall sculpture of an altairn that marked the head of the chamber.

I squeezed Alfreda's hand, then strode into the chamber and to the podium beside Kovis, and his eyes went wide.

The gallery lining the back of the chamber erupted. Lord Beecham followed their pointing and turned around. A scowl erupted on his face.

I scanned the twenty-eight representatives—two from each province seated around the large, circular table in the center of the room. Jaws dropped, gasps rose, heads shook, representatives leaned over and whispered to their neighbor.

I smiled, waved, then shouted above the noise. "Empress, Prince, representatives, and guests, thank you for your warm welcome." The chamber quieted.

Kovis sat stiff, clutching the arm of his chair. Rasa's eyes were wide, knuckles white on the edge of the curved table.

Alfreda shifted beside me.

"We have just returned from our cultural intelligence tour and come bearing grave news." I went on and delivered the highlights of all we had endured, my stomach rolling as I relived each piece.

Rumblings and whisperings from citizens in the gallery along with representatives, put my stomach on edge by the end. Neither Rasa nor Kovis had yet said a word.

I cleared my throat, then raised a fist as I concluded. "We must move quickly if we are to defend ourselves from the onslaught that is about to reach us."

Lord Beecham, who had stood at the lower podium throughout, said, "Prince Kennan, thank you for that moving account. Thankfully, Nomarch Formig and others have already informed us of events and preparations are underway."

I exhaled. Thank goodness. We might actually have a chance depending on what measures they employed.

"But," the round man with no neck said, "You have also confirmed for us what the nomarch accused."

Rasa closed her eyes. Kovis leaned back, shoulders slumping.

My eyes darted about the chamber.

"You are a traitor."

I sucked in a breath as the gallery erupted. What was happening? There was no time for this. Alfreda grabbed my hand and squeezed.

Beecham nodded at two guards.

My eyes went wide as the pair was joined by four others, striding my way.

"You are hereby under arrest," one of them announced, stopping near. Although they wore no weapons, they could easily take one dual affinited sorcerer down.

Alfreda squeaked and clutched my hand tighter, and I drew her close.

"You will stand trial for your crimes at a time of our choosing," Beecham added. "Now take him away."

Rasa and Kovis rose but didn't approach. I knew. I saw it in their eyes. They couldn't override the will of the Council, not on their own. They had to let them take me and rise to fight another sun.

"Step aside," one guard commanded Alfreda.

She thrust her chin up. "He will not suffer alone after what he's been through and for the good he is doing."

"As you wish." The man shook his head, then pushed me forward. "Move."

Part III: Night Terror

Little Disaster

By Unknown
England Wake Realm

Once there lived a little man,
Where a little river ran,
And he had a little farm and little dairy O!
And he had a little plough,
And a little dappled cow,
Which he often called his pretty little Fairy O!

Once his little maiden, Ann,
With her pretty little can,
Went a-milking when the morning sun was beaming O!
When she fell, I don't know how,
But she stumbled o'er the plough,
And the cow was quite astonished at her screaming O!

Little maid cried out in vain,
While the milk ran o'er the plain,
Little pig ran grunting after it so gaily O!
While the little dog behind,
For a share was much inclined,
So he pulled back squeaking piggy by the taily O!

Then to make the story short,
Little pony with a snort
Lifted up his little heels so very clever O!
And the man he tumbled down,
And he nearly cracked his crown,
And this only made the matter worse than ever O!

Chapter Thirty-Six

Kovis

Shouts woke me.

"What now?" I mumbled, then yawned, rubbing my sore, sleepless eyes. It'd been the way of things since Ali's departure and our insufficient preparations despite her nightly ministrations to me through our bond. And with Kennan imprisoned… I shook my head. He'd sounded like his old self the times I'd visited him over the last sennight—Alfreda had nearly convinced me she'd freed him from Ambien's control. But how to free him from a farcical trial and penalty?

Rapid knocking.

"Enter!" I hoped my shout reached the petitioner. The sun hadn't yet risen, and I didn't want to either.

The double doors to my bedroom swung open, and Bryce stopped and bowed, beside Cedric. Two of them. This couldn't be good.

"Rise." I took in their wrinkled brows and Cedric's gaze that flitted about the room but never settled, as I struggled to sit up.

"My prince, they've been spotted. To the west of the city."

He didn't have to specify who he spoke of. My heart sped, recoiling at the news.

"They're about to sound the alarm," Bryce informed. "The colonels are readying the troops and our citizens are moving to safety like we drilled."

"Thank you."

The pair saluted and turned.

"Has the empress been told?"

"Yes, my prince."

I nodded and they strode out, men driven with purpose.

I'd known Ambien's minions would show up to the west. No one would be crazy enough to attack from the mountain side. It would be too much effort for his troops to scale that steep slope among all those trees, not when our western side was so exposed.

I drew my robe about me and tied the sash as I headed for my desk. I grabbed my long-range glasses as I passed, threw open the ornate glass doors, and walked out onto the balcony.

Clouds, gray in the dark, blocked much of the moon's light, but in the Canyon's undulating colors, I could make out a boundless, black mass off in the distance. I scoured the horizon, hoping, praying my eyes betrayed me in the dark, but the harder I looked, the clearer the scene became. While definition eluded me, I sucked in a breath and my stomach turned hard as a rock. There seemed no end to them.

My hands turned clammy and I clutched the rail. I'd experienced, firsthand, the nature of the creatures out there, as one emerged from Rasa. We'd been told of their numbers. I'd prayed that reports had been exaggerated of the fear those abominations wielded, but seeing made dread, unlike any I'd known, coil about me, constricting, squeezing like a thick, hungry viper.

Ali? I called down our bond, struggling to keep my voice even. I needed to hear her. I needed to feel her close, even if I couldn't hold her.

Kovis, what's wrong? You should be sleeping. She chuckled. *Or would you like me to add a bit more 'suggestion' to my last lullaby?*

A corner of my mouth turned up. *No, my love.* I hesitated, bracing. Speaking of it would give life to the bone-chilling fright out there. I sighed. *They're here, a ways off, but within sight. Innumerable.*

Ali sucked in a breath. *Kovis...* A wave of raw emotion roared down our bond.

We knew they'd eventually get here, love. My throat constricted.

Yes, but there's a difference between worrying, knowing they're coming, and the terror of them arriving on your doorstep. Innumerable? Her voice quaked.

I love you, Ali. I coughed, choking on emotion. *I'd still be lost without you, my heart frozen. But you—*

Stop. Just stop. Her tone turned pleading. *Don't say any more. We'll see each other again.* Silent tears clouded her speech. *Promise me.*

Ali, I...

Just promise me. Demand filled her words as her voice turned brittle, like the last ice of winter.

I gripped the balcony railing. *I promise, my love. I promise.* I gritted my teeth, loathing lying to her.

She choked on tears.

The sound of Alshain's shoes on cobblestones sounded above the shouts and calls of grooms as my guards and I raced from the stables not long after. The swords sheathed on either hip brushed my legs as I bore left at the fork. I'd donned my leathers quickly, but not before stowing a host of daggers and other weapons.

We headed down the sloping switchbacks that painted the mountainside leading up to the palace. I directed Alshain around and between scrums of citizens making their way up, where they would take refuge behind the palace's stone walls.

There wasn't space for all our citizens to shelter in advance; so we'd devised and practiced an evacuation plan. I prayed all went according to plan now that the enemy was at our doorstep.

The sphere of the council building shifted from glowing water to fire, lighting up the night as I neared. A woman shrieked. A soldier called, trying to calm her as he, along with fellow soldiers, hurried her and others toward a refuge.

Representative Destrian, of Tirana's insorcelled province, came into view. A pair of swords hung, one from either side of the warrior's leathers. We'd never seen eye to eye, but as I galloped past, he dipped his head, his rugged features and mean brow softening. Perhaps in this, we'd at last found common ground.

Other representatives, magical and insorcelled alike, had donned leathers and weapons and descended from their homes on the hill above the council building, directing more frightened citizens toward safety. That facility would double as an infirmary during this conflict, and it's where Rasa would lead a portion of the healing efforts, well away from the front lines.

We turned left and followed the path toward the river and the merchant, artist, and food districts beyond. Water taxis bearing Water, Fire, Air, Ice, and other affinitied sorcerers were moving into positions along the river.

Soldiers hurried wide-eyed citizens toward stone bathhouses and designated sturdier structures.

We rode on toward the sprawling residential district. Streets were waterways in most of this area, the quaint river having been diverted for aesthetic purposes. In any other time, I loved the smells and tranquil sounds it created, but not now. Now, the watery streets slowed citizens' exodus.

But I took heart when I spotted troops in crowded crafts, on more than one occasion, shuttling trembling citizens to safety. With any luck, every citizen had found capable hands to aid their escape according to plan.

We stopped briefly as a uniformed officer flagged me down. "My prince, we've got this area nearly evacuated. We'll have everyone to safety before dawn."

Good news. I saluted and we moved on.

The scene repeated itself time and again as we neared my destination—the outskirts of Veritas and our chief defensive positions where the bulk and worst of the fighting would take place. It was also from where I, the most powerful sorcerer in the Altairn Empire, would direct the front lines.

"Where's Colonel Ranulf?" I yelled to a uniformed soldier as we slowed to a trot. The battle-hardened man supervised the training of my troops, and I'd tasked him with leading our center forces.

The young soldier saluted then pointed. "Midbulwarks, my prince."

My troops had erected a series of bulwarks in concentric arcs starting at the steep mountains to the right, fanning out and sweeping across the exposed plain where our farmers raised crops and livestock. They included steep earthen walls followed by pits filled with metal spikes that pointed toward the sky on the opposite side; metal pikes perched at angles that would hopefully gore the monsters as they charged; buried rock beetle bombs that would explode when trod upon, and more.

But my stomach soured. I'd never conceived of the numbers these fortifications would need to fend off. There weren't enough. Not nearly enough.

I waved my thanks and motioned my guards forward.

We passed a host of insorcelled soldiers digging into positions, readying, before a swarm of sorcerers came into view coming and going, executing orders around the very fit, dark skinned, battle-hardened officer I sought. Ranulf viewed the white scar that ran from his eye to his chin as just another of his medals. I'd always joked that I wouldn't want to meet him in a dark alley. I only prayed he had the same effect on our enemy this sun.

"Report," I commanded after dismounting.

He scanned the pinking skies. "My prince, our right and left flanks report their insorcelled archers and footmen are in position, their riders are ready. He ran down the list of magical and nonmagical roles we'd assigned based upon the topographical advantages as well as deficiencies we faced.

I looked to the skies. "What of…"

"Colonel Bliant reports that our aerial ranks will be in position very shortly."

Ali and I had learned the fine art of using our Air magic to propel us forward some distance off the ground as we'd traveled to Porta. Once we'd returned, I'd taken that knowledge and begun training mages with dual affinities of Air and another magic, forming an elite aerial squad. This would be their first true test.

"There are vast numbers arrayed to meet us, far more than we ever dreamed," I said in a hush, when he finished.

He grinned, a crazed look flitting across his face. "All the more fun to be had."

I patted his shoulder and smiled. "I'll be by your side every step of the way."

Lord Beecham, the head of the Council, stopped atop his mount not far away. He fisted and unfisted his hands, watching the horizon.

Ranulf cocked his head, catching my gaze. I rolled my eyes.

"Best get yourself out of harm's way, my lord," the colonel suggested.

Beecham frowned. "I'm more than capable of taking care of myself thank you, or have you forgotten my prowess with Ice?"

I shook my head and exchanged a glance with Ranulf.

"Fine, get yourself killed," my companion mumbled, so only I could hear.

A corner of my mouth rose.

"My prince." A scout stopped abruptly, beside me.

I nodded for him to go on.

"My prince, the empress asked me to tell you that she's"—he clenched his fist— "she's in position, as requested."

"She let you know of her displeasure, did she?" A corner of my mouth turned up.

"Ye... yes, Commander." The man shifted.

I shook my head. She'd wanted to fight, demanding that I understand that she'd never get her agenda implemented if insorcelled council members didn't respect her on the battlefield. She'd begrudgingly agreed not to fight only after I'd laid out the good she could do leading behind-the-scenes efforts with healers just as she had at the front during Father's war.

"Thank you, soldier. Dismissed."

Rasa had no idea the carnage and bloodshed that was about to unfold. She may be unhappy, but better that than dead.

Yes, than dead. I surveyed the hurrying soldiers, those positioning catapults, others stacking projectiles. How many would stand when this was over?

My stomach twisted.

Chapter Thirty-Seven

"Ambien was spotted heading toward Satirev," the liveried steward reported, arms clasp behind his back in the doorway to the dining room. He looked to Mema. "With your permission, madame..."

She frowned, but nodded for him to go on.

"The males of your family request that if any of you ladies wish to accompany them to meet him, that you ready yourselves. They will be arriving shortly." His news hit us no different than if he'd poured freezing water over our dinner conversation, and we all sat in stunned silence.

They'd found Father. Dyeus hadn't had any success in accomplishing the feat in moons, but my brothers' scouts had. If you wanted something done, you asked the little guys.

But Satirev. My breathing labored and my heart sped. It had to be more than coincidence that Kovis was just below in reciprocal Veritas. My gut twisted. Father had been jealous of Kovis—I doubted he'd ever gotten over me fleeing Dream to protect him—and now he flew not far above him. This could not be good. At all.

Kovis! Father's been spotted, heading to Veritas.

Damn!

"Thank you, Emory," Mema said, wiping her mouth with a linen napkin, then setting it down. She scanned the table, no doubt catching our set jaws and tight muscles, then exhaled heavily. "Those of you who wish to join them may be dismissed."

I'm going with my brothers to fight him, as soon as they get here.

Fight smart, and stay safe.

You, too...

Only the sound of chair feet on marble rose as eight of us pushed back, wings twitching. I surveyed the long table, Mema at the head. Two of my four remaining sisters bowed their heads as if in supplication, the others watched with wide eyes, their lips trembling.

Much would undoubtedly change before we sat around this table again, and I longed to sear the peaceful image into my memory, but resolve forbid me lingering.

I threw my shoulders back, raised my chin high, turned and strode out, my sisters on my heels. Father was close to Kovis. Too close.

True to their word, my brothers arrived not long after. We bid farewell to Mema and our lingering sisters, then along with our guards, headed out the front door of the palace of sand maidens, no one saying a word.

I patted the trinket that stopped time that I'd tucked in my leathers. I'd put it on a gold chain and hung it around my neck; I wasn't about to risk it falling out of a pocket. In a way, I was taking my aunts with me, hiding them above my heart. Kovis couldn't be here, but I had my aunts close. They were old and feisty, unafraid, and their examples gave me courage.

Speaking of courage, as I'd dressed, an idea had sprouted. It was something we hadn't considered before, and I knew if I didn't at least check it out before I joined the battle, I'd always wonder "what if."

"Everyone ready?" Rankin asked as the door shut behind us.

I raised my hand. "I had an idea that I need to investigate. You go on ahead. I'll meet you in Satirev."

Rankin forced a smile over my siblings' furrowed brows. "What is it?"

I shook my head. It was the last place I wanted to go, but I would if it might mean the difference between winning and losing, between saving Kovis or... My mind refused to finish the thought. "I'd rather not say until I know if it really is an opportunity to help."

Rankin frowned, but said, "Very well, little sister. Baldik, Wallis, escort Ali to this mystery place of hers. The rest of us, let's go." And with that, they rose into the lightening sky, my sisters giving me long looks.

"Ready?" I asked my guards.

"At your bidding, princess," Baldik said.

Anxiety bit into me as we climbed into the sky. This was a very bad idea. My body agreed, for it felt as if beetles crawled over my skin beneath my leathers.

I tried to distract myself from this fool's errand as we flew. We'd returned from our travels of nearly a moon, two suns before. In the provinces that Rankin, Harding, and I had visited, we'd tracked down and rescued their missing citizens; so they'd been more than happy to pledge their support to helping defend Dream from Father.

News from my siblings had been similarly positive. The regents they'd visited had pledged their support as well, after their citizens had been returned to them. Well, that and they feared the numbers of loathsome creatures that they'd discovered inhabiting their lands in the process.

An approaching bird brought my attention back, but it posed no threat, passing with only a look. I glanced about. The sun from behind made the shadows of my guards and me appear mammoth over the buildings of Sand City as we approached. I made the shadow of my arms look like one of those monster's jaws and chomped down on building after building, pretending I killed Father's abominations.

On we flew. How I hoped and prayed that the gods found favor with our cause. Surely Dream realm was worthy of being saved.

It wasn't long after that my destination came into view along the rugged coastline we approached. There was no mistaking the creepy palace with its cracked masonry gargoyles leering down from the roofline and overgrown vines that grabbed for you. I was just glad we visited in sunlight rather than in the dark, like the last time. All the same, a chill ran down my back.

Yes, this was probably a very bad idea, a fool's errand, but I'd come this far.

I gazed over my guards after mounting the steps. Their thumbs twitched above their sword hilts, and a vein bulged from the side of both of their necks.

I took a deep breath, then reached for the ghoulish doorknocker—a skeleton hand with moving eyes for "fingernails"— mounted to the burnt orange front door. I tensed when a loud moan erupted as it struck the wood. I wasn't alone in my fear, judging by my guards' inhales.

A heartbeat later, the hinges of the door creaked and a gaunt steward peered out the cracked door.

I cleared my throat. "I'd like to speak with my Uncle Thao. Please." I tried to still my fidgeting feet, to no avail.

The man's beady eyes looked me and my guards up and down before closing the door without a word.

I bit my lip. Was he retrieving Uncle or not?

My legs started bouncing as I turned around and took in the thickly treed wood just beyond. Did Uncle do morbid things in there? My hands trembled at the thought, and I turned back around. Yes, this was definitely a fool's errand, but we were here.

The door shrieked as the steward eventually thrust it open, making me jump.

"Uncle Thao, it's so good to see you," I said, forcing a lightness I didn't feel. Uncle Thanatos, Grandfather's twin and Death incarnate, stood before me.

Uncle's gray eyebrows furrowed. I forced my smile to remain.

He narrowed his eyes, studying me, then frowned. He didn't recognize me.

"It's me, Uncle. Ali. Ambien's daughter."

He rubbed his chin, still remaining silent.

"I… fled… to Wake. I became mortal in the process. It also changed my height and hair color." I pulled my hair back so he could see just my face. It had worked with others. Hopefully, he'd recognize me, too.

His blank look morphed to recognition in a heartbeat, and he pointed with a bony finger. "You… you took over my music on Autumn Equinox."

I held up my hands. "I know I did, and I'm sorry to have offended you."

He huffed, making some of the stringy hairs in his gray beard fly up. "And then you hired Easton away. He was my favorite musician."

This was not going how I'd hoped. I couldn't win this argument. "Uncle… Uncle, I have an opportunity I think might interest you."

He pulled back. "An opportunity." Sarcasm filled his voice.

"You love battlefields filled with fear and terror." I knew it to be true, I only prayed mentioning it, diverted his interest.

He cocked his head. "True enough, blood spiced with fear is rather tasty. Far better than without, tangy, you know."

"Are you hungry?" I held my breath.

He gave a hesitant nod and uncrossed his arms, stepping aside. "Come in, child."

"Thank you, although I can't stay long."

"Of course not. No one in this family enjoys my company."

I stepped across the threshold, into the high-ceilinged entry hall. Six flaming torches illuminated the windowless space. It grew even darker when the steward closed the door behind me and my guards, and I swallowed hard.

Uncle led us down the torch-lit hall and turned right into a sitting room. A musty smell assaulted me, but I willed my hands to stay at my sides—I'd breathe through my mouth. Weapons with dried blood still on the blade, adorned two of the walls. I sucked in a breath when my eyes landed on an arrangement of bones stacked on the mantle—two gargoyles stared at me, one on either end—above the heap of charred bones and ashes in the grate.

Another shiver raced up my spine, and I quickly found an upholstered chair, then sat on my hands to keep them still. I'd make this quick.

"Tell me more," Uncle Thao said, stretching his scrawny arms across the back of the sofa to my right.

"I'm wondering if you might enjoy the taste of fear without blood."

"Speak plainly."

"I've no idea how, but Ambien has created abominations from which fear ripples. They're terrifying to even be near."

Thao leaned forward. "Did he now? Clever boy."

I swallowed revulsion. Even breathing through my mouth couldn't blunt the stench of his foul breath.

I coughed. "Problem is, he plans to take over both Wake and Dream realms with them."

His eyes started to sparkle. "Sounds as if it will be quite the feast as his beasts do battle."

I waved my hands. "Uncle, no, you don't understand. If he takes over, he'll rule everything. Everyone will do only his will."

"Not me." He sat up straight.

"Not directly, but he can make life difficult for you if he chooses." I wasn't sure if Uncle had been the one to alter my aunts' timelines on more than one occasion, those random "accidents" as they'd called them, but I took a chance. "Do you really think he'll let you take humans at your convenience, anymore?"

Uncle pressed his lips together. "Upstart boy."

"Exactly." Perhaps it wouldn't be as hard to convince him to help as I'd feared.

He sat back and crossed his arms. "Why should I believe you? No one in this family ever asks for my opinion, much less my help."

Then again, maybe not...

"I'm telling the truth." The words spilled out before I could rein them in.

He raised a brow. "Seems he's not the only upstart in the family."

I closed my eyes and slumped my shoulders. "I'm sorry, Uncle. Please forgive my outburst, but I'm telling the truth."

He started tapping his foot.

Time to change tack before I lost him completely. "How would you like to taste *real* fear—" I drew my arms wide. "—to *experience* the full flavor palate of it?"

He tugged at a worn sleeve, not meeting my eyes.

I hurried on, outlining my plan for him to feast on Father's monsters.

He opened his mouth, no doubt to criticize, then closed it again.

"Have you partaken of just fear, without the blood? Ever? Some of his monsters are mammoth, others small. How might a leviathan's fear taste, different than a rodent's?" I was making this all up, but if it worked to sway him he might help our cause. "Perhaps big fear is gamier tasting, while small fear is more concentrated, sharper. Think of it, Uncle. You could gorge on all of them and see which you like best."

His eyes softened. Was my plea working?

At length, he said, "You are right, niece. I've never tasted fear by itself. It might just prove to hold unique flavors." He bobbed his head, considering.

"So are you interested?" *Please say yes.*

Thao cleared his throat. "I wasn't so sure about your proposal to start. You shouldn't be surprised to learn that there are several in this family who haven't shown me much respect." He rubbed the sleeve of his robe. "You'd think they'd respect Death, but no." He huffed. "But I can see earnestness in your eyes. You took time to think about what I might enjoy, even helped me see it, rather than getting huffy." He brought a hand to his chest and gazed into my eyes. "This is the first time anyone has thought to reach out and include me in family drama. Thank you, child. It means so much." Uncle bent forward. I stifled a shiver as his shriveled lips brushed my cheek, and he squeezed my shoulder. "I shall repay your kindness."

"Oh, no need, really. It's... it's my pleasure."

"I insist." He licked his lips and rubbed his wrinkled hands together. "So, when do we start?"

Yes!

"His abominations are gathering over Satirev as we speak. It's where we're headed, if you'd care to join us."

He bounded up from sitting and barked, "Wymond, bring me my weapons!" Then turning back to me, he said, "I shall save you tastes of the rarest and best fears, then lavish you with them as a token of my appreciation." He brought his head down sharply, seemingly believing he'd settled the matter for both of us.

My stomach clenched.

Chapter Thirty-Eight

Kovis

Ambien would soon be in the skies overhead, in Dream, if he wasn't already.

My fingers twitched, the Canyon's powers begging to be unleashed. I struggled to calm under the onslaught of panic and unrelenting terror that rippled off the perverted abominations among Ambien's vast army marching toward us.

"Easy boy." I patted Alshain's neck trying to still his dancing feet and bobbing head beneath me.

Nearly here. They were nearly here.

I gripped the reins tighter, drawing a protest from my mount. "Sorry, boy."

A rumble ran through the ranks and soldiers pointed. I followed their gazes, and my heart lightened despite the oppressive fear. Our aerial squad rose from the heart of the city behind, glorious as they flew in formation. They made a pass over the city, then headed toward us where they'd wait for the battle to begin in earnest—they'd monitor fighting and lend aid where needed as the battle raged.

Roars and guttural bellows from the sea of grotesque monsters reverberated across the plain; the waves of fear were palpable, building the closer they drew.

A crazed look—blood lust, terror, a tinge of insanity perhaps— filled Colonel Ranulf's eyes as he massaged the scar that ran from his eye to his chin. Lord Beecham, atop his towering mount, clenched his jaw along with his hands, his eyes darting beyond Ranulf.

Nonmagical foot soldiers gripped sword hilts behind round shields. Sorcerers flexed fingers, in, out, in, out, shifting from foot to foot, trying to cope with the growing terror as they waited to engage.

Troops wiped clammy hands on their leathers as the unrelenting drum of hoofbeats pounding dry ground grew, dust kicking up as cloudy-eyed rebels raced for us atop steeds at the front of the enemy's ranks.

Just a little closer, and I'd commanded our troops to engage.

Still the dread grew; that wave of fear nearly climaxing, nearly bursting. So close.

Mage foot soldiers just ahead of my line licked their lips as the dread mounted, ready to engage as soon as I gave the order.

Waiting. We were waiting for the enemy to reach us. It was always one of the worst parts of a battle.

But without warning, a wave of terror surged over us, sparing none. Soldiers loosed soul-rending howls, crumpling to the ground, writhing, then whimpering as their worst fears overwhelmed them.

Alshain reared up. I pulled back on the reins, my knuckles turning white as images of Father's hands on Rasa ripped through my consciousness. Father's hands moved up and under her green robes. She fought, but he held her down. I had to save her, but when I tried to move, an invisible hand held me in place, forcing me to watch in horror. I fought, thrashing, swinging.

Maniacal cackling to my right broke through the nightmare's stranglehold, and I regained my faculties despite the unrelenting horror that continued pummeling. Arms raised, Colonel Ranulf's head was back, pealing chortles toward the sky.

My guards, before us, grasp hair, clutching themselves, or bent forward over their mounts.

The wave stretched skyward, hitting our aerial ranks; they bobbed like a rope bridge above a ravine.

Ali! The attack's begun!

Shit!

The single word filled our bond, but I couldn't focus on it.

"Attack!" Lord Beecham yelled, his round body scrambling up from where his mount must have dumped him—the creature was nowhere in sight. Two riderless horses cantered by, behind me, eyes wide with terror.

"Attack!" Beecham ran in front of us, waving his arms.

I'd known these monsters embodied terror, but I hadn't anticipated this wave of fear. Our forces were in disarray as the assault went on, unrelenting.

"Attack!" the lord's voice shrieked with panic.

Several soldiers stumbled up and retook ready positions on unsteady feet. Their heaving chests betrayed their continued distress. They took in the lord running about, then looked to me.

I met my soldiers' eyes and attempted a slow nod, hoping they understood my command to calm, to breathe. Who was I kidding? I could barely control my own terror.

I scanned the plain. The enemy was nearly upon us. Jitters bested my limbs, my angst growing.

"What's wrong with you, soldiers! Attack!" Beecham's arms flailed.

I barely stifled a cry as a vision of Ali, pinned to the ground beneath the paw of a writhing monster again stole rational thoughts from my mind. Saliva dripped from its open maw as she struggled under its weight, but couldn't escape. The beast lowered its head, then bit down, severing her head from her shoulders.

My heart raced as a shout brought me back.

I needed Kennan. Right here. Right now. I couldn't command the army in this state. I barely leashed my own fear. How long could I last? I didn't know if Kennan would fare any better, but Ranulf was in no shape to command.

"Soldier." I pointed at a lanky young sorcerer. He stumbled, unsteady with fear so palpable.

"Get Prince Kennan from prison." I forced the words from my mouth. "If anyone tries to stop you, tell them they can take it up with me." My words had venom I didn't intend, and the troop stepped back. I had to calm down, hold it together.

Beecham continued his antics, swaying as if he'd been in his cups as he came my way. He'd failed to rally any followers. He halted before me, breathing hard, face red with anger. "I forbid it!"

"Go, soldier!" I barked.

"Don't you dare!" Beecham snarled.

The sorcerer's eyes bounced to Beecham, then up to me, mouth agape.

I dared a peek at the enemy. Closer still. Their fear was crippling despite not yet reaching us. But they'd be in range of our weapons in nigh more than a heartbeat.

"Go! Now!" I bellowed, sweeping my arm.

"Yes, Commander!" The man's hand shook as he saluted, then bounded off.

"Stop!" Beecham called, clenching a fist. Turning, he pointed a shaking finger at me. "You'll regret that, Prince."

"And you'll regret your attempt to commandeer our army." It was hard to hold a look of contempt with the fear inundating as it was, but I did my best, and he withered under my glare. "We'll take it up if we both survive," I added, then turned my attention away, dismissing him without a word. The lord huffed, then stormed off.

"Troops!" My legs took to trembling as that wave of fear continued pummeling.

My ranks, most of whom stood on legs as shaky as mine, gave me their attention as I rose in the saddle, locking my knees. I willed my voice to remain steady as I said, "It's time we answer their attack. Are you with me?"

A roar rippled up and down the lines, spreading across our center ranks, out over both flanks, and up into the air. A rumble in the affirmative returned.

"Let's do this!" I raised a fist, then threw my arm forward, igniting our rallying cry.

Warriors manning catapults stumbled into action as the front line of enemy rebels plowed into the beginning of our bulwarks.

Terra sorcerers dropped the ground out from beneath more. They weren't as quick as in practice, but they were doing their best under the circumstances.

Archers on our left and right flanks rained arrows on enemies who strayed too close. Though more arrows than usual flew astray, many hit their target. It would have to do.

Fire sorcerers lofted shaky arcs of flame into the midst of the oncoming horde. Single affinitied Air sorcerers enhanced their flames, making them burn hotter and spread wider.

Water wizards blasted other enemies, pummeling them with unrelenting streams, knocking rebels off their horses. The hordes of enemy following trampled them.

Aerial mages sped forward but stayed clear of the rest of the army's attacks.

More and more terror washed over us the closer our enemy came. It leveled our soldiers, bludgeoning, nearly crippling all of us with unrelenting fear.

Like air to a flame, terror stoked my imagination and the image of Kennan crazed and out of his mind, attacking Rasa, pounced, then overwhelmed me. I imagined turning my Ice on him, but he melted it with his Fire.

Pain shot through my foot and up my leg, breaking the evil spell. Ranulf's horse had slammed into Alshain. My stallion whinnied and bobbed his head as I came to my senses and reached to steady the colonel. He grabbed for the pommel of his saddle, then screamed with rage. He battled his own inner demons; that much was clear. He steadied himself and managed to loose a stream of Ice over our front lines.

His troops, along with Lord Beecham who had calmed, followed suit launching a magical assault of their own—Water, Air, Fire, Terra, Ice. They split the oncoming swarm and left a swath of dead and dying humans and beasts.

Our left and right flanks mimicked.

But the enemy crush didn't stop. They trod the dead under foot to mend the tears in their lines as they continued surging toward us.

Explosion upon explosion upon explosion ripped across the bulwarks as our enemy found buried rock beetle bombs, but still they came.

They were so close, and the terror they unleashed knew no bounds.

A horn sounded, piercing the din. This was it. That heartbeat our armies met.

I sucked in a breath, bracing as shouts and cries echoed on the battlefield. Our nonmagical troops raised their shields, weapons, and voices, then charged to meet the approaching horde.

I longed to cover my ears. There was nothing like the awful crash when our soldiers and the enemy met, plowing into one another. Metal against metal. Violent. Brutal. Savage. Raw power unleashed. A clap like none other. I'd experienced it time and again in Father's battles.

I'd never get used to it.

Chapter Thirty-Nine

Ambien

Squawks and bellows followed close on my wings, but waves of self-doubts, fears of death, overestimations of catastrophes, certainty of dire calamities, rippled toward me, threatening to overwhelm.

I pivoted, nostrils flaring, looking over my shoulder at the host of winged creatures following. I locked my gaze with the fear-inducing culprit, an overlarge beauty—another remorrigan I'd birthed from gathering the terrors of more than a dozen weak, human minds.

She *dared* challenge me, again, even now. I bared my teeth. Her vast, membranous, gray wings and the pallor scales that covered her breast made her look like death incarnate. A wraith of a most magnificent sort. But she'd picked the wrong fight. I would never allow her even a hint of triumph. I'd prepared, subduing beauties like her and others, time and again.

The corners of her lidless, black eyes crinkled in her leathery-skin-covered, avian skull, believing she affected me. Believing I was her toy.

Unlike others I'd mastered, I would not command she sleep; I couldn't have her falling from the skies. No, that would never do. Some might chide that I overcompensated with the number of beasts I controlled, but that very fact meant I could afford to teach her a lesson leaving her *nearly* at her best for the errand we'd embarked upon, but she'd be obedient.

I slowed without warning, and before she could react with her lumbering size, she drew up beneath me. I reached down and grabbed the hollow bone at the top of a wing.

One might wonder if a being made of fear could know fear. She beat her wings faster, attempting to dislodge me. I loosed a bellowed laugh. Answer enough. How quickly things changed.

I eased my dagger from its sheath at my side, then plunged it through the leathery flesh below.

Her shrill squeak nearly pierced my ear, but I held on. She would know, once and for all, I was her master. Enough challenges.

I drew my knife down, in a line, two, three, four handbreadths, tearing the membrane, before extracting it again. Only a trickle of blood oozed from the cut that was long enough to impede easy flight, but short enough to heal—a memorial scar. If she was as smart as I expected, she'd challenge me no longer.

I resheathed my blade and brought my fist down hard on the top of her bony skull, locking eyes. She held our gaze for a heartbeat and more, refusing to submit even after that. Damn, arrogant female.

I curled my lips and again reached for my dagger. I couldn't do this all sun, but she didn't know that.

She averted her gaze, whining in surrender.

I thumped her skull once more, but she refused to meet my eyes. About time. "Never again, darling. Never again."

I looked ahead as I rose to retake my position leading this flock of sorts. In a way, she was a picture of the challenge ahead. It would take humans as well as my subjects time to learn obedience, but they would, I had no doubt. They would submit to my bidding, just as my lovelies had; pain was a marvelous teacher. I just needed to guide them at a pace that would satisfy me.

With the rising sun, sea gave way to land below—Ria province—and I glanced back, marveling once more at these amazing, fear-inducing creatures my ambition had conceived of and brought to life. I beamed. At times, I amazed even myself.

We'd be at Satirev shortly, over the human capital, Veritas. Ah, Veritas. The name meant 'truth.' How appropriate, for the truth would soon be revealed that I would be sovereign over all.

I breathed deeply, savoring these heartbeats. I'd toiled for annums and all my hard work would shortly come to fruition. I'd learned from my mistakes. The past had been a cruel taskmaster, but this time… yes, this time, I'd anticipated every eventuality, every possible misstep, and the overwhelming force of my terrible pretties would more than compensate for any minor weaknesses that dared hide from my consideration. Never again, never, ever again would I taste defeat.

I chuckled. I'd even abide by the dictate I'd spelled out eons before. Dream territory could only be taken after the reciprocal Wake region had changed hands. I'd never said it had to be *a human* conquering the Wake territory before Dream's reciprocal could be taken. While efficient, gods forbid I be accused of illegitimate conquests by taking Wake and Dream territories at the same time. No, we'd take Veritas, then Satirev and spread out from there in both realms, taking great care to ensure we controlled the Wake area before that corresponding in Dream. A laugh rumbled out of me, but I cut it short before I felt its full pleasure.

I had a score to settle with several Dream provinces. I gnashed my teeth. They'd stopped my earliest campaign, during the conquests of King Altairn as he consolidated the seven magical nations into Elementis. I'd make sure they knew I hadn't forgotten. And as for the regents of those nonmagical territories who had stopped me more recently during Emperor Altairn's quest, oh, they'd be experiencing my displeasure, too. Yes, each and every one of those despicable regents' time had finally come. I guffawed as the image of them groveling at my feet, played in my mind.

Several of my lovelies screeched, bringing me back. Ahead, a kettle of vultures swooped and dove, scavenging. They must have found something particularly satisfying judging by their numbers. No, wait, those weren't vultures. I glanced down. We'd reached Satirev. I growled. My mares were to have transformed into large altairns—I'd thought it a nice touch considering our objective—and be waiting for me to give the order to pierce the dream canopy and join their ground-bound fellows. I snarled. How hard was it to form ranks? I'd need to instill harsher discipline in my soldiers at this rate.

I fumed as we flew closer, but my frown quickly turned as a host of black winged beings launched and engaged my mares. It seemed Dream realm citizens were trying to stop us. I grinned. Good luck with that. I'd forgive my troops not following orders, this time.

No doubt these citizens had been compelled by my children, but it mattered not. It seemed their work to thwart me had produced at least a weak result for they'd found a small following. I had to give my offspring credit; they had heart.

A corner of my mouth turned up. They were so like me, going after something with every bit of energy they had once they set their minds to it. Yes, my blood definitely flowed through their veins. Too bad, for it would only cause greater bloodshed. If my soldiers didn't do these acolytes in, my pretties would in short order. I just hoped my offspring weren't among them. Their betrayal would need to be dealt with expeditiously, but I had more pressing matters to focus on.

One, then two beings spiraled down, wings splayed to the winds. A pity to lose them… or perhaps not. No doubt citizens like them would only test my patience, stirring up dissent. No, I'd had my fill of that. It was time to restore order and obedience, no different than with my mares.

I spotted Urian, my commander who'd I'd tasked with marshalling our troops through the dream canopy, not far ahead and motioned for him to meet me on the ground.

I tapped into the collective thread joining my flying monsters and communicated a silent command—circle but do not engage—then I dove to meet him.

"Report," I said, landing.

He morphed back into his guard form and saluted. "My liege, all is in readiness."

"What of…" I waved toward the fighting.

Long canine teeth appeared over his lips as he smiled. "Nothing to worry about. We stand ready, on your command."

"Very good." I drew in a long breath, surveying the skies, taking in my troops in action, my pretties soaring above; searing the images into my mind. I would relish this, time and again.

"Then begin."

Chapter Forty

Kovis

"Brother!"

I jerked my head to find Kennan atop Onyx, galloping toward me. His eyes were open so wide I could see white all the way around the center, even at this distance. Crazed. Definitely crazed.

Maybe this was a bad idea.

Alfreda wore a fierce expression keeping pace on her mount beside him. Maybe she would ensure he kept it together. I could hope.

My heart leapt into my throat when I spotted Jathan. Velma followed close after, wearing equally stormy looks. What were they doing here? Jathan was a healer. He knew nothing about fighting!

"I hope you don't mind me bringing reinforcements to the party." Kennan beamed, that deranged look set in his eyes.

He couldn't be in his right mind, but it was too late to change course.

Perhaps a bit of insanity was what we needed, Ranulf case in point. Live or die, we'd all go down together.

"Kennan! Your timing is impeccable." Despite the screams around us and the pummeling terror, I forced my voice to stay even.

The four spread out, joining our line of mages. Kennan unleashed Fire toward the enemy, over the front line. Alfreda raised her arms, and for a heartbeat, I wondered what power she wielded. My jaw dropped when Kennan's magic shot farther than I'd ever seen, then hopped. His flame actually hopped. *What?*

I watched as one, two, three crawling monsters stopped in their tracks, then slumped under his fire. Black charred bodies were all that remained when he eased back.

My eyes grew wide as I realized, these fear-inducing abominations could be stopped. They could be killed, no different than all living things.

"Motus!" Kennan yelled, eyeing me, then cackled. Beecham and several nearby shot wary looks, his laugh no doubt enhancing the overwhelming fear we all battled.

Kennan and Alfreda repeated the feat.

"Die filth, die!" He waved animatedly sending more flame at the enemy. Alfreda directed, then redirected his power, felling more abominations.

Maybe there was something to be said for insanity. Perhaps it alone could overcome fear. He seemed more limber than any of the rest of us. As if to underscore the point, my body lurched, every muscle spasming for a heartbeat as the image of Rasa, bloodied and slumped over, raced through my mind. My mouth grew dry, the fear continuing its unrelenting assault. I shook my head, forcing away the thoughts. It was a lie. Rasa was safe. She'd be tending to the wounded.

I diverted my attention to our aerial mages raining down magic on the massive enemy ranks, not far from where Kennan and Alfreda's magic worked. Go! Go! Go! I cheered silently, distracting myself. Between them, Kennan, and Alfreda, they'd slaughter many, creating chaos and hopefully confusing the enemy. It would give our front foot soldiers a boost.

I did a double take as a cloud... no, a void of light, a swirling blackness, began growing to the left, over a bit, but still behind enemy lines. It swallowed up the enemy. What in the gods' names? Magical blackness? Who? Wait.

A quick glance to Velma revealed her atop her mare, hands outstretched, eyes fixed ahead. Jathan sat in the saddle behind, arms wrapped tightly about her waist, eyes closed. He'd climbed onto her horse. But why?

I well remembered teaching Velma to control her manifesting powers. They were as wild and powerful as an untamed stallion. Was it her doing that? If so, what was Jathan doing?

As a healer he possessed Terra and Wood magic. Wood... it made living things grow. Was he somehow making Velma's shadows grow?

The writhing blackness grew, stretching farther and farther.

I watched, mesmerized, waiting for the enemy to emerge from the black cloud. Five, six, seven heartbeats. Eight, nine, ten. The first horse backed out, its soldier turned around in the utter darkness. Our waiting warriors cut him down.

I raised a fist in celebration.

But movement in the skies directly above wrested my attention. I drew my hand up to block the sun. Ranulf and Beecham followed suit.

I sucked in air, my heart pounding from more than the fear that raged. A great, gray-winged bat swooped, then dove. Where had it come from? The thing had to be huge judging by its size even at this distance.

Closer and closer. It wasn't alone. No, other, smaller winged creatures appeared seemingly out of nowhere. More and more and more of them. Their numbers grew with each passing heartbeat, like ash falling from the sky.

Sweat beaded my brow. My muscles were tense already from the terror, but this wound them even tighter.

Ali? I drew out her name.

More and more airborne creatures dove. My eyes strained to take them in. And then I did. And my bowels nearly loosed. That huge bat... wasn't a bat... it had no fur. It was a monster unlike any I'd seen before. Its bony skull, membranous wings, and the pallor scales covering its chest made it look like the embodiment of death, come to claim us. They were abominations, taken flight.

Kovis, what's wrong?

Monsters are falling from the skies!

Are you serious? Shit! I'm on my way to Satirev with Uncle Thao as we speak!

What? Your Uncle Thao? My voice rose.

Long story, but if they're the same as the ground beasts, Uncle can probably stop some.

The guy was a morbid lunatic.

Ali, be careful.

I'm trying.

Closer and closer the monsters flew.

My fingers itched to unleash my power, but not yet. I needed to save myself for when our troops flagged.

Aerial troops had spotted the winged creatures, too, and raced to meet them. Terra sorcerers among them raised fist-size crystals above their heads, and a rainbow of color shot up into the sky. Healers knew the powers of crystals to restore, but they could also destroy, liquefying a person's insides. I prayed they would succeed with these abominations.

Dozens of the flying beasts ceased beating their wings, as if stunned, then dropped, and I exhaled. The winged beasts could also be stopped it seemed. But with so many of them and so few aerial troops... I didn't finish the thought.

Water, Ice, and Fire magic stretched for the creatures, felling more.

But that mammoth beast flew right through our airborne magical defenses. Closer and closer.

Alshain whinnied as he danced beneath me.

The creature's shadow grew longer as it opened its beak and gobbled two of our troops whole as it shot through our aerial squad. Its wings slammed into several more making them free fell.

Catch yourself. Catch yourself. I fisted a hand, rooting for the three soldiers it had hit. Two stopped their fall. My gut twisted as the third…

The monstrosity swooped, then rose up, plunging through our crumbling air formations again, gobbling another troop as it did. They couldn't fire on the thing when it was below them, or risk hitting ground troops.

My limbs begged me to unleash the Canyon's power surging in my veins. Still I ignored.

A squawk sounded behind me, and I whirled around. One, two, three, four, and more monsters swooped over the city. They weren't as large as the behemoth besieging our aerial guard, but they still hunted. Mages aboard barges greeted them with force—Fire, Water, Ice, and Crystal magic. Several dropped but were quickly replaced.

Off in the distance, one abomination flew up and up with a wriggling soldier in its talons. It soared above the top of the theater and higher. A heartbeat later, the troop plummeted toward the ground.

I squeezed my eyes shut, fear growing in my chest, knowing what his end would be.

My attention darted back to the monstrous winged creature as it plunged back down through our aerial squad, eating another troop and scattering still more as it headed our way.

I ducked. The whole of our lines did too as the thing's giant wings beat the air directly above our heads, readying to blast upward through our troops again. Alshain and other horses squealed. The rancid taste of palpable fear soured my tongue, and the image of Ali's crazy uncle plunging a bloodied sword through her back, hammered my thoughts.

I beat back the paralyzing horror, and my magic surged. Enough.

I clenched my jaw, pushing off the ground with my Air magic; Alshain whinnied as he ceased bearing my weight.

Despite the terror leaching off the pallor-breasted beast, I dogged it in a heartbeat, unleashing Ice and Water at its tail feathers. No more. It would be stopped, and I would be the one to do it.

I dipped when I diverted some of my Air to pelt its now-frozen feathers. I shouted when several snapped off. Oh yes, it would succumb to me.

It turned back toward me as I rose back up, but I was close enough that its beak couldn't reach me. I shot more and more Ice at its tail feathers, then another burst of Air, and more feathers cracked, then fell. Again and again, I pelted it with magic. It flapped more dramatically, trying to rise, but without its tail feathers, it couldn't.

"Yes!" I loosed another shout.

Around and around we flew. Never did I let up on my Ice and Water magic. I sheared off nearly all of its tail until one more blast of Air would prune the rest.

Then I waited, for it to turn toward the mountain, just below the palace. When it did, I blasted the last few feathers off. It could no longer turn much less slow. It shrieked and flapped wildly as it saw its own death nearing.

I raised fists above my head as it plunged, beak first, into that mountain. But my celebration was cut short when two more flying creatures headed straight for me. I cut the Air beneath me and plummeted. A Fire and a Terra sorcerer aboard barges cut my pursuers down as I caught myself again handbreadths above the ground.

Chest heaving, I rose on Air once more and surveyed the city. The sky was still dark with winged creatures, the sun struggling to peak through. Bodies lay at odd angles on the ground as well as on rooftops or wherever they'd landed after being mauled. A good many wings, still and unmoving, jutted up from abominations as they burned, alongside homes that their corpses had ignited. A haze of fire and smoke along with the stench of burning flesh had settled over Veritas.

I scanned our front lines. More bodies littered the ground, but abominations as well as cloudy-eyed rebels fought on. My stomach hardened when I refocused and realized that the enemy had reached the line I'd held with Colonel Ranulf. He along with Kennan and the rest fought, magic flaring nonstop.

But the enemy kept coming.

That blanket of fear still strangled, and though our troops waged on, it was not enough. The sheer size of Ambien's army...

Would anyone be left? Heaviness, like a weight, pressed down on me.

Kovis, don't think that way—Ali's voice.

Love. I choked up, other words escaping me. Even with the battle raging around me, flying monsters swooping and diving not far off, Hades unleashing everywhere... For a heartbeat, it was just the two of us.

I just got here. It's chaos. I can't talk. Just don't give up. Please. For us.

The knot in my stomach eased just a bit. *Only for you, my love. Only for you.*

I'd been fighting to squeeze all the joy I could out of life of late. How badly did I want to experience it with her? The thought pulled me up short. I wanted to. No. No, no, no, I craved to. I yearned, ached, lusted after it. After her. With every fiber of my being.

If I gave up now, all the suffering... all the anguish... all the misery I'd endured... all of it... would be in vain.

I fisted my hand. No matter how grim the battle looked, I would keep fighting. I'd endured too much not to. I would fight... I would collect on Dite's promise of blessing... for Ali and me.

Another oversize abomination caught my attention, slithering through our left flank.

Troops scurried to fill the gap, but their pace had slowed as they tired.

That flying creature had looked like death with wings. This one was equally hideous, snakelike with green scales and a forked tongue that flicked in and out. It rose up, opened its large maw and struck, grabbing a soldier, tossing her up and catching her again, then swallowing.

In a heartbeat, I was on my way. But another winged creature had other ideas, locking onto me in the blink of an eye.

I dove.

It followed.

Chapter Forty-One

I'd heard the squawks and caws, shouts and cries, and felt a heaviness and palpable fear that sunk deep in my bones long before my guards and I, along with Uncle Thao, spied the battlefield.

But dread and alarm bit into me as we landed and my eyes took in the scene.

A vast, grassy plain stretched from Satirev. The usually bustling city that had grown with its reciprocal, Veritas, the capital of the Altairn empire, was eerily quiet.

Kovis had mentioned flying monsters. He hadn't exaggerated. They swooped and rose, filling the sky as high as I could see above the city, nearly blotting out the sun.

I breathed in, but with terror blanketing the air, I felt as if I suffocated, and I drew a hand to my throat.

I didn't know if Kovis knew about the giant altairns that also filled the skies—Father's morbid sense of humor, no doubt, having his mares bedeck themselves in the Empire's symbol—I prayed not. These abominations were bad enough.

But where were the crawling beasts? I knew they were here in Dream, I'd seen them as Harding, Rankin, and I visited the provinces. Nothing hideous crept or stalked the ground, not that I was complaining, but it added to my angst. When would they show themselves? And how?

Our leathered, black-winged warriors clashed with Father's minions, but there were so few of us. Why weren't there more? All fourteen Dream regents had pledged their support to stop him. My brothers would have notified them as soon as they got word of Father's whereabouts. I prayed they were on their way.

Uncle Thao ruffled his wings beside me, running his fingers up and down the smooth wood of his scythe handle as if fondling a lover. "Odds seem a bit lopsided if you ask me."

I scowled, trying to push aside the stifling fear. "I didn't."

He gave me a long look.

"But it's why I invited you. Kovis said those monsters were raining from the sky down into Wake."

"He's probably sending them through the dream canopy."

I turned furrowed brows on Uncle. "He can do that?"

"Of course."

"How do you know?"

"I go through it, too. All the time."

"*Through* the canopy?"

He chuckled. "I get a little dizzy, but it works."

My jaw dropped. That nauseous, dizzy feeling I'd experienced when I danced with Father during the Solstice ball, raced to the forefront of my mind. We'd flown higher than I'd ever been, into the dream canopy itself, for my dance with him as solstice queen.

"How do you think your grandfather and father managed human sleep and dreams eons ago?"

"I… I never thought about it. I thought you became mortal if you went through it. I did."

He smiled a yellow-toothed grin. "Not necessarily. It's a bit complicated." He reached over and patted my arm. "Your intentions, the role you play, and the like, it all comes into play when you pass through the dream canopy."

I furrowed my brow. "What do you mean?"

He chuckled, seemingly delighted that he'd drawn me up short. "Do you remember the creation story?"

I bobbed my head.

"At the same time, the Ancient One created the world, he created the gods to help steward his creation, I, being one of them, and gave us access to humans to carry out our assigned duties."

"Okay, but…"

He held up a bony finger. "I'm getting there. Honestly, I'd never even thought I could be made mortal by going through the canopy until your father and grandfather retired. The first time one of you dream weavers breeched the canopy to weave the dreams of a charge, thunder, from Dyeus, roared through the heavens."

I stared at Thao, mouth gaping. I remembered that sun. It had been terrifying as the palace shook, the sea turned red, and Dyeus' lightning bolt kept racing across the sky. Father had dismissed it saying Dyeus was a bit upset over something, but he'd never elaborated.

"Dyeus was raving mad because in teaching others the craft that your father and grandfather had been entrusted with by the Ancient One, they'd desecrated sacred knowledge set apart for only them. Dyeus understood why they did it, but that didn't fix the situation. As a consequence, he declared that henceforth anyone who attempted to go between Dream and Wake would be judged for their intentions against the role they held. There's a few other criteria he stipulated, but that's the gist of it."

I closed my mouth. Our, my, weaving dreams was wrong? Unsanctioned? Unholy even? How was that even possible? Yet it seemed to be—I'd been made mortal when I'd gone to Wake. I shook my head. I wasn't sure how I felt about that but knowing didn't change a thing.

"What would happen if my father passed through the dream canopy, now?" The words spilled out.

Thao moved his head side to side, contemplating for several heartbeats. "I'm not sure. Could go either way."

Either way. Either way.

Thao scanned the battlefield again, lust filling his eyes. "May I?" He motioned toward the chaos.

"Oh, of course."

He grinned.

But I held up a finger and locked eyes with him. "None of ours. Not. One. And abominations first. Understand?"

Thao rolled his eyes. "So many rules. You take all the fun out of it."

"You'll have plenty of fun. Now promise me."

Uncle huffed. "Fine."

"Then go." I laughed as he whooped, then launched.

Fear-inducing bodies fell before him. I didn't think Father's monsters could become more hideous, but I was wrong as Thao left a trail of mutilated gore in his wake.

The farther he flew, the more chaos he carved into their ranks. Abominations paused midflight, eyeing him, then shrank back, as if sensing Death come for them.

My skin tingled. These creatures embodied fear itself, yet they were no different than any other living thing. They wanted to live. Even Fear sought to live. Several shrieked, then headed the other direction.

I tore my eyes from the scene above. I hoped Thao enjoyed gorging himself, but Father was here, somewhere, and I had to find him.

I ran my hand over the trinket tucked safely under my leathers. I wished I could just command every abomination to "stop." They'd plummet to their deaths, but I doubted Aunt's magic would discriminate between good and bad beings.

"Let's go find Ambien," I said to my guards, then with a mighty downbeat of my wings, I lifted off.

Kovis, I'm hunting for my father.

Silence greeted me for a heartbeat before he replied, *Be careful, love. Use my powers if you need to.*

Your powers? You think they'll work here in Dream?

I pushed my magic to you through our bond when you were ill.

He'd thought about this, about me, here. As I flew on, I opened and closed my mouth, marveling at the possibility of having magic at my command while here in Dream. *Let me try.*

We were within reach of a black-scaled, vulture-like beast that had its sharp talons locked onto a warrior's leather-clad shoulders. I reached for a thread of Ice through our bond. My heart sped when I felt it come at my command. Not too much, Kovis needed his power to fight.

I directed a stream of magic at the creature's head, coating it fully. It kept flapping its wings, but its movements became irregular. The dangling female sensed the change and looked up, catching my eyes. I held up a finger, hoping she understood my intended message, to hang on.

I drew a thread of Air from Kovis and blasted the beast's frozen head. Blood sprayed as the decapitated appendage fell free. It, along with its flailing body, plummeted. The female's mouth dropped open as she darted out of the way, then hovered as we watched the carnage smash into the plain below. Her wide eyes found me, and I grinned. She'd never seen magic.

She gave me a shaky salute before she turned and rejoined the battle.

You're brilliant, Kovis.

He chuckled. *Glad to be of help, love. Now stay safe.*

I spotted my sisters below, not far from where the abomination had fallen, tending to wounded. I was glad they'd come.

But I had to find Father. My guards and I lifted up once more. Up and up and up we flew, despite the terror that raged around us.

We passed my brothers and other warriors locked in conflict with grotesque winged creatures. Several warriors looked bruised and beaten, cuts marring their faces. A few wore dirty bandages. I furrowed my brow, the scene not making sense with fighting having just broken out. How could they have soiled bandages?

And where were our reinforcements? There weren't nearly enough troops compared to Father's beasts. My angst grew at their absence. We had to find Father.

We rose farther, and those on the ground started to look like ants.

I spotted Auden, Rasa's sandman, swinging his blade at an altairn who tried grabbing him with its talons. It clubbed him with a wing making the sandman's wings splay, but he fought to right himself before it grabbed him. I raced for him, my guards on my wings, and unleashed Ice at the altairn's head and followed with a puff of Air. Blood sprayed, and we watched it drop, taking out another abomination on its way down.

Auden's chest heaved as my guards surrounded us. "Thanks," he said. "Nice trick. You need to teach me that sometime."

"My pleasure."

I looked him up and down. He sported a gash across a cheek along with a nasty bruise, and he looked thinner than the last time I'd seen him.

Sensing my examination, he sighed. "Ambien tortured me, several of us dream weavers."

I grit my teeth and shook my head.

"He wanted us to hand over our charge's thought thread."

I closed my eyes, anticipating his story.

"I... I tried so hard to fend him off..." His shoulders slumped.

I held up a hand. "I've experienced his wrath, too. I understand."

He jerked his head back. "You? But you're…"

"It doesn't matter who you are, not to my father. Not if you stand in his way." I drew a hand to my chest. "Trust me, I know. But how'd you get away?"

"I'm not sure what precipitated it, but soldiers from Arret stormed the prison he held us in and freed us earlier this sun. They told us Ambien was on the move over Satirev so I came directly. All of us did." He waved a hand at warriors contending with the enemy… bearing bandages.

Perhaps that's why there were so few warriors fighting on our side. Were they continuing to rectify Father's abuses? It seemed so.

"I'm hunting him. Want to help?"

A feral grin blossomed across his face.

Chapter Forty-Two

Kovis

A horn blast, sharp and blaring, pierced the noise of battle.

I went still, like the green-scaled slithering abomination I'd just felled, beneath my feet. I panted, feeling the thinness of my remaining power and prayed I had enough to last, for Ali.

Another blast and another from the city... from the palace.

I whipped my head around.

There... from the ridge behind it... across the summit...

I scanned the soldiers, hundreds and hundreds of them, spread out. I knew who they were the heartbeat their capes came into view—auburn, honey, teal, lapis, and more. Seven colors, some more in number than others, but all seven—warriors from every insorcelled province. Despite the abominations that crept in their own territories, they'd come without being asked, and they'd scaled that forested mountain—the last place I'd expected any force to rise from.

I blew out a breath. They gave us a slim chance, dare I think it, a small shot at turning the tide of this battle, of curbing the slaughter.

I wouldn't question why or how they'd known to come. Stories would be exchanged if we survived. No, *when* we survived and lived to tell tales.

With raised fists and a mighty roar, the warriors raced forward, capes flying, creating a rainbow of colors, down that mountain, around the mammoth flying abomination I'd forced to meet its end there, they looked like ants overtaking a find.

Their dash broke the spell over the flying monsters many of which had paused to take in the spectacle. Several shrieked, then dove, straight for the new arrivals.

I grimaced as those minions grabbed the first warriors they reached in their talons, lifted them skyward, then let them fall.

But as the next round of flying monsters appeared, warriors met them head on. Shrieks and squawks erupted, and wings beat wildly as talons succumbed to weapons. The first abomination dropped and was swaddled in a blanket of blades in the blink of an eye, until it stilled.

My attention tore away as Ali drew on my power and I fisted my hands. Gods above, my power had to last.

I scanned the bloody battlefield and sucked in a breath, then launched.

Alfreda cowered where she'd fallen, beneath the stare of a fanged, brown-plated abomination. It raised up on hind legs and Kennan charged, sword raised.

If he'd resorted to forged weapons, he'd exhausted his powers. Alfreda, too.

Kennan's blade bounced off the terrible beast's chest. The thing swatted him with a massive paw, and he yelped, then flew back, crumpling to the ground as I landed hard.

My twin grimaced, then jerked his head back as he caught sight of me. His shoulders slumped, and he exhaled.

"I've still got magic," I said. "Not much, but some." It would last, it had to. I nodded, directing him to see to Alfreda.

Fear filled his eyes, but when I bobbed my head toward his dream weaver again, he grimaced but started dragging himself along with his sword toward her.

I raised my hands and loosed terror of my own in a blast of Ice. "You cannot have them," I growled.

My ice flew wide as the fanged abomination morphed, becoming a gray, cat-like creature with a mouth full of long, dagger-sharp teeth.

Alfreda shrieked at the spectacle, then sat up and threw her arms around Kennan's neck, clinging to him.

"Are you okay?" Worry filled his voice as he dropped his blade, drew her into his lap, and started stroking her back.

The beast lunged at me, mouth gaping wide. It tumbled back as I met it with a burst of Air three men's height away.

"You're okay. You're okay." It sounded like Kennan said it as much to reassure himself as her.

The beast growled as it righted itself, scowling with narrowed, silver, otherworldly eyes.

"You said before that you saved me from Ambien because I was your dream charge." Urgency filled Kennan's voice.

I glanced quickly at the pair to find Kennan staring with longing into Alfreda's eyes.

"I don't know if we'll make it off this field…" Kennan continued.

"No, don't say that," Alfreda whimpered.

"You need to know…" His voice turned insistent.

The abomination hissed, then leapt at me, claws extended from massive paws. I met it with Water, sidestepping, then pivoting as it flew past. It recoiled as it landed, caterwauling and hissing. Like most cats, it seemed this overgrown kitty didn't like water.

"Alfreda, you came. You chose to give up immortality"— Kennan's voice cracked—"for me. For me."

I missed the next few words he spoke, as I doused the creature with more and more Water. Its ears flattened and it hissed until it morphed again.

"I'd no idea what a treasure had dropped into my lap that sun. But I know now," Kennan continued, back turned to me at this angle.

I panted. How much more power did I risk using? I drew my sword.

A bare-breasted female warrior materialized, her auburn-hair dripping. Naked clear down to her waist, she held a scythe in one hand. She grabbed her wet locks and tossed them over a creamy shoulder, then rested her fist on a black-leathered hip. A grin, exposing a mouth full of pointed teeth, banished any seductive pretense.

I stole a quick peek at my sibling. I couldn't see Alfreda's face, blocked as it was behind Kennan's body. "Alfreda, you... make me whole." He struggled for words, emotion filling his voice.

The creature raised her weapon and sauntered forward, full, milky-white breasts jiggling as she closed to two man's height away.

I raised my blade, taking a ready position as she drew to within a man's height. But in the blink of an eye, she brought her scythe up, and I felt the air part, then felt the sting of her blade across my thigh.

"I love you, Alfreda."

The words barely registered as I stumbled back, pain shooting from my leg as I nearly tripped over Ranulf's still form, his eyes staring blankly to the skies, but I managed to catch myself.

I'd been stupid letting that woman get that close. No, not a woman. "Kennan!" I shouted, eyes fixed on the half-naked female.

She chuckled, then stalked forward. A blade that size should have been cumbersome, but she handled it with ease. I hadn't even started to block her strike when she cut me.

Agony and burning exploded as I put weight on my leg, but I had no choice. I loosed the full force of my powers on her, and she bobbed and ducked, but I followed her every movement, unleashing my fury. Until, in a heartbeat, she drew up short, eyes growing wide, a choking noise coming out of her, as a silver blade broke through her throat, spraying blood.

She crumpled into a heap at Alfreda's feet, clawing at the protruding knife.

Alfreda turned fierce eyes on her, bent down, and thrust the blade to its hilt, through the back of the abomination's neck and growled, "Don't you dare touch him."

Kennan grunted as he crawled toward her, but before he reached her, Alfreda fell to the ground and retched over our unmoving enemy.

Kennan rubbed her back until she stopped heaving, then enfolded her in his arms and kissed the top of her blonde head. "I love you." He sucked in a breath. "I love you." It sounded nearly like a prayer.

I didn't know what had transpired between them, but clearly something had. This wasn't our half-crazed brother who Rasa sent on that pseudo mission because she didn't know what else to do with him. It had been a long time since I'd seen him behave with such tenderness toward another. For that matter, I'd never seen him show affection like this to Alfreda.

I felt for any lingering embers of power and found only the thinnest of threads. That last burst had nearly exhausted what little I'd had left. I ran a hand through my hair. I'd put Ali in jeopardy, all to kill one more creeping abomination. Other than Kennan, Alfreda, and I, no one cared, not when so many more still slithered, roamed, and swooped along with cloudy-eyed rebels.

I surveyed the killing field. Our right flank had collapsed after its twin, our front lines swallowed whole in the still coming horde. Only a fraction of our aerial guard fought on.

Kennan looked me up and down as he roused Alfreda to sitting. His eyes locked on the blood coursing down my leg. "You need the healers."

"I could say the same of you, brother."

Alfreda shrieked, as she took in something behind me.

A shadow darted, then wings brushed my head and I felt talons pierce my leathers, sharp claws squeezing, then digging into my shoulders, and I rose.

"No!" Kennan and Alfreda screamed, in unison.

Chapter Forty-Three

Auden, my guards, and I soared up and up, into a cloudy layer, the dream canopy itself, and dizziness assaulted my head just as it had during that Solstice ball. I couldn't tell which way was up or down and bile rose in my throat.

I wasn't alone judging by my companions' expressions.

Flying abominations were thick as seaweed soup up here, and we had no time to indulge our weaknesses. I inhaled deeply despite the choking fear and let it out slowly, settling my head a tinge.

Auden along with my guards took to hacking heads and talons off as enemies threatened the higher we soared. I didn't want to use too much of Kovis's power, so I searched the skies for Father instead.

Ahead, a dozen or so altairns herded squawking abominations into a group, then pressed them forward, and the winged terrors disappeared in the thick cloud.

My jaw dropped. Was this how...?

I was about to intervene when I spotted Father and froze.

Auden followed my gaze, and his nostrils flared the heartbeat he spotted him.

Black hair and wings, black leathers, black boots. On the surface Father looked like a nightmare, enhanced by that full, black cape fluttering behind him. He beat his wings, hovering, malevolence in his dancing eyes, a feral grin spread across his face as his winged terrors headed down to Wake.

He used to be such a beautiful male. Big and strong, svelte, every feather of his stunning, black wings ordered and in its proper place even after flying, but ambition had changed all that. The girth of his belly had increased, lust had risen in his eyes, blackness had taken root in his heart and grown over time. He'd transformed into someone I barely recognized.

And to think I'd idolized him. I shook my head. I'd deceived myself. I'd wanted to know his unconditional love and acceptance so badly that I'd shut down any contrary opinion. But what I hadn't considered, never, ever contemplated, was whether he was capable of what I so longed for.

Velma had been right, everything was about him. I swallowed hard. And it always would be. And what that would mean for Wake and Dream... was unconscionable.

I had to stop him.

I nodded to Auden as I pulled the thinnest of threads of Ice, Air, and Water from Kovis that I could.

Surprise lit Father's eyes as we neared, but he quickly schooled his features, putting his grin back on. He eyed me, then Auden, then looked my guards up and down.

"Couldn't get enough?" he said, eyes fixed on Auden.

The sandman drew in a long breath.

"I think we've all had enough, Father," I said, before he could goad Auden into action he'd regret.

"Oh, I think not. The party is just beginning."

I felt wings close in behind, surrounding us, but Father raised his chin, holding his altairn-looking mares off.

He chuckled. "A nice touch, don't you think, daughter? Altairns?"

"I'm afraid I see no humor in it, Father."

He sighed, feigning disappointment. "You never were one to appreciate my levity."

"You can't do this." I motioned to the flying beasts.

"Ah, there you are wrong, daughter." He nodded, almost imperceptibly and his mares began herding us, slow step after slow step, toward him.

"Aren't my creatures amazing?" He watched the abominations swoop and dive. "Made from the nightmares of frail humans, their own terror radiates from these beauties." He sighed. "A stroke of my genius."

I felt a push as his soldiers crowded us.

Auden and my guards raised their weapons. I wheeled around and sprayed Ice and Water at the five enemies' heads, following up with a puff of Air.

Father's jaw dropped in mock affront, but in a heartbeat, he reached for me, grabbing my arm, then pulled me flat against his chest, smashing my face into his leathers. I beat my wings as memories of him doing the same in our dining room just before I'd fled Dream, raced to the forefront of my mind. I'd learned nothing.

As a mortal, I was smaller than I'd been, and no matter how hard I pushed against his chest, his arm was stronger.

And then I heard the distinctive sigh of metal on leather as he drew his dagger. My heart picked up pace. Would he shred my wings as he'd threatened before?

"I wouldn't if I were you," he said to Auden, and my guards as I felt the cold blade kiss my neck.

I flailed. If he shredded my wings at this height…

The trinket. The thought catapulted forward. I needed that trinket. My aunts had promised me it would help "when I most needed it." It would work. It would. They'd somehow known. If only I could reach it.

"Ali, I'm so glad you've come to aid me in this cause. I'm sure you can convince that prince of yours... to cooperate. Surely he understands he's come between a father and his favorite daughter. And I just won't tolerate that."

The seams of his leathers bit my brow and my cheek, and his forearm clamped down on the back of my neck, making it ache.

His favorite daughter, this again? He'd sworn me off. He was delusional, utterly and completely.

I strained, pushing against his chest, beating my wings.

"Yes, he robbed me of your optimism, your devotion, your affection." He sneered. "A mere mortal."

"That was your doing, Father."

"I think not. He corrupted your mind to the point that you lowered yourself and took on temporal flesh."

I pressed my hand between our chests, straining for my collar. I just needed to touch the trinket.

"And so, I shall be forced to forever mourn your loss."

"I'm not dead yet!" Just a little higher.

"Compared with eternity, you shall wither and die as the grass."

There, the chain. I strained, pulling and felt the metal case rise against my chest.

"You're so dramatic, Father. If you'll forever mourn my loss, that must mean you loved me. So how come you didn't care to spend time with me or my siblings when I was immortal?" Still, I beat my wings.

He sighed heavily. "Alas, some lessons one can only learn from their mistakes."

It was nearly free. "You're saying ignoring us was 'a mistake'?" My voice rose. "What about Mother. Failing to marry her was also 'a mistake'?" I took on a sarcastic tone. "I'm sure she had hopes of you committing yourself to only her." *Though I fail to fathom why.*

"Your mother is a matter altogether different," he snapped.

I steeled myself, even now, as I said, "Is she? When I was young, all I ever wanted was for us to be a family, for all of us to live together." Smashed as my neck was against his chest, my throat smarted as I yanked the trinket past.

He chuckled. "Sunshine and rainbows, just like your mother."

I beat my wings and the token dropped into my waiting hand. This would work. My aunts would not fail me.

"Father…" My voice was light, like when I was little, as I stilled, then shifted, looking up at his double chin, as if making to peer into his eyes with adoration.

He loosened his arm just a little, then looked down.

"There's one thing you don't understand."

He frowned.

"I'm not sunshine *and* rainbows. I've never been. I was always only sunshine, undimmed as it is by clouds. Yes, me in my naivety, and you took advantage of it."

He scowled.

"A rainbow only shows itself after the adversity of a rainstorm."

He furrowed his brow.

"I have experienced that storm." I clutched the trinket tight. "I have become a rainbow." I growled. "And you will never use me, or harm those I love, again."

Father had no time to react before I said, "Stop."

Chapter Forty-Four

Kovis! I shouted down our bond, panic building, as soon as the searing pain of losing my wings eased. I couldn't find his magic, not Air, not Ice, not Water, nothing. I'd found only a parched desert when I'd tried to pull a thread just now.

Oh. Wait.

I called to my Air magic, and it surged to my fingertips, just waiting to do my bidding, and I sighed with relief. My powers had returned as I transitioned.

I looked over. Father's eyes stared blankly, frozen in time like the rest of him, thanks to my aunts.

His wings had stilled in the blink of an eye, and he'd dropped—we both had when I stopped beating my wings—straight down, like rocks, plummeting through the dream canopy.

Uncle Thao hadn't known how the transition would treat Father since he no longer wove dreams. I'd discovered, firsthand.

Justice had been meted out.

I looked away, repulsed by Father's stiff, naked, wingless, blonde-haired body as we tumbled. He'd shrunk a bit in stature, just as I had, and was as mortal as me. I'd kept my clothes. The transition had claimed his, like it did with everyone the first time—like being born anew.

Ali! What's wrong? I'm a bit indisposed.

I've fallen through the dream canopy, and I'm mortal again.

Silence.

Kovis?

He grunted. I was distracting him. *Kovis, I'll find you on the ground once I land.*

The artist's district has the least fighting, he said.

Perfect. Stay safe, Kovis.

Down and down and down we fell. It reminded me of the last terrifying heartbeats of my solstice dance with Father. We'd been falling, and the ground had raced for us. I'd motioned for him to untie the band around my ankles that joined us for the dance, but he'd shaken his head and beamed, saying, "My favorite part."

My heart raced, remembering.

I'd kicked my feet, trying to free them as the ground approached.

Father again had shaken his head. "You need to trust me."

I'd swallowed hard as we drew still nearer, but Father had remained calm, only asking, "Do you trust me?"

I'd tried bending to reach my ankles, but our increased momentum forbade it.

"I'll take care of us as soon as you trust me. Show me. Relax," he'd said.

My breathing had sped, and I'd fought harder against that tether.

He'd locked eyes with me and said, "Trust me, Alissandra."

A command. I'd heard it, squeezed my eyes shut, and, against my best judgment, gone slack.

My legs had freed a heartbeat later, and I'd screamed as I free-fell.

I sucked in a breath, trying to calm my breathing, even now, trying to forget that horror as we'd dropped.

Things had been so different then. I'd been naïve and overly trusting, especially of Father, but I'd learned. It had been jarring and painful, but I had... and I was different now. I'd been put through the refiner's fire and my impurities—my naivety—had been burned away. I'd come out changed and perhaps not hardened but stronger, more resistant.

Father had done so much to hurt me—he'd terrorized and abused me, verbally and mentally. It hadn't been in me to seek revenge back then, but in this heartbeat, all I wanted was for him to feel just a taste of what he'd done to me.

"Let him move just his eyes," I yelled, above the noise of the wind. I didn't know if it would work or not, whether this trinket was an all or nothing proposition, but it was worth a try.

Father's eyes grew huge, darting about, taking everything in. Every other part of his body remained still and unmoving, save where the wind buffeted it.

I didn't smirk or grin as I meted out my justice. This wasn't a time to celebrate. But as panic consumed him, wholly and completely, my anger, my frustration, my feeling like a victim, eased just a little.

Down, down, down we careened.

I looked up. Small mercy, abominations seemed to have stopped spilling through the canopy. A few flew even with us, heading downward, but it was a trickle compared to before. Perhaps Father becoming human had fractured his hold on the creatures.

We raced past clouds and as the ground grew closer, Veritas came into view and my heart sank as I took in the devastation—the burning buildings, the bodies, the smoke. A mass of crawling monsters still surged through gaping holes in what had probably been the front lines; no one on our side was left to defend them.

We approached several more flying monsters, swooping and soaring, and fear rose in me. But bless the Ancient One, the things seemed more interested in the goings on below than in us and steered clear.

I spotted the artist's district and eased us in that direction with my winds. The smell of burning buildings and flaming flesh hit me as we neared, and I about retched.

I looked over at Father. White surrounded the center of his eyes making him look crazed. Good. He needed to experience the terror I had. I'd let him sweat a bit, like he had me.

"Trust me, Father." A corner of my mouth edged up, and his eyes locked on me. I couldn't resist.

I scanned the ground. We were nearly there. But movement, then a shout not far below drew my attention, and I took in a group of warriors… flying… fighting three flying abominations, a good distance above the ground. My jaw dropped. Had Kovis… I couldn't help but grin. Brilliant. Truly brilliant.

But a bellow sounded far off, and my heart climbed into my throat as I took in a flying monster… with Kovis in its clutches.

I shrieked when it dropped him, and he plummeted but didn't slow himself—his powers had to be exhausted… and I was too far away to reach him in time.

See him. See him. See him. I silently begged those aerial troops as they fought against the three monsters.

The trinket swung and smacked my neck. Wait. Could it… ? I grabbed hold but hadn't so much as put into words my desire when one of the three abominations dropped. One of the aerial soldiers pointed, and two of them raced after Kovis.

I blew out a breath when they caught him.

But there was no time to relax, I needed to slow us and fast.

I drew on more of my Air magic, directing us over residential waterways, past burning abominations, through smoke that made my eyes water, toward the theater.

Father's eyes could grow no wider.

"Do you trust me?" I asked. It was mean, but I couldn't help myself. I would no longer be a victim. He squeezed his eyes shut.

Only then did I conjure a pillow of Air.

I set down on the theater's deserted square, then stood. I *might* have let him feel the bite of impact.

Only devastation and ruin greeted us, not a living soul was in sight. The fighting had ended, at least here, at least for now.

Father opened his eyes and looked about, clearly stunned that he still lived.

"You didn't trust me, Father." I shook my head, frowning. "If I'd treated you like you did me, we'd both be dead."

I wrinkled my nose, not at the stench, but at his nudity. Time had not been friendly to him and despite my feelings toward him, I'd at least grant him a modicum of modesty—it would spare my eyes.

Several troops as well as abominations lay strewn at unnatural angles. I tucked the trinket back inside my leathers as I strode for the nearest soldier, then knelt. This man had paid the ultimate price for Father's nefarious ambitions, and I had only respect for him. I reached over and closed his sightless eyes. "May your soul rest in peace and may you find your way to the gates of Light realm." I truly hoped he did.

I opened his cold hand and gently lifted the hilt of his sword. Then I loosed the two fasteners, one on each shoulder, that secured his royal-blue, butt-length cape and slid it from beneath him.

Gripping the fabric, I told him, "I'm sorry. He doesn't deserve this, but thank you." I gave the fallen soldier one more long, appreciative look, then turned and strode back to Father.

Father's eyes followed me. I was tempted to throw the cape over his head and let him think I'd leave him to die this way. Yes, to die, frozen, naked, and utterly disgraced, but I didn't. I threw the cape over his midsection, then stepped back.

He was mortal. My father, the god of dreams, this being who had imposed his will on myriads of innocents, was mortal.

I let that sink in as he stared unblinkingly at me.

He couldn't take over Wake, much less Dream anymore. Laid out as he was, he wouldn't be hurting anyone, anytime soon.

But I couldn't leave him like this. He might deserve it, but I wouldn't. It'd be something he'd do, but I'd never become like him; I'd never stoop so low.

I pulled the trinket back out, then took a deep breath, and said, "Resume."

Fire lit Father's eyes, and he bolted up to sitting, gripping the cape, then moved to rise.

I drew the point of the sword to his neck and held it there.

"Alissandra." Fury laced his words.

In the past, I would have cowered, but no longer.

"You made me mortal!" He spat the words.

I didn't respond. He would have loved to draw me into a verbal altercation, but I wasn't biting. Let him fume, it served him right.

He shook his head. "You've ruined everything. You've no idea what you've done."

"Oh, I know what I've done. I've protected humans everywhere. I've saved Wake from your schemes. You can't hurt anyone, ever again."

He shook his head. "You're naive. Can you not see that this conquest was for the benefit of the citizens of Dream?"

I furrowed my brow. He'd lost it.

"I am... I was... king." He fumed. "It was my duty to shepherd and protect my citizens. Many of them are still suffering under the dictates of those conniving regents that I—" He gritted his teeth. "—failed to oust during two separate opportunities."

"Suffering? I've visited three Dream provinces within the last couple moons. Those citizens were far from suffering. No, they were prospering."

He curled his lips. "You're ignorant. You saw what they wanted you to see, but I know them." He loosed a growl. "They didn't show you how they produce the prosperity you saw, did they?"

I cocked my head.

"No doubt they pledged their support to help you in your campaign against me, but when you needed them, they weren't there for you. Were they? Were they?" He locked piercing eyes with me.

I drew in a breath.

His tone turned testy. "Your interference means my citizens will continue to be subject to those calculating bastards. Why do you think I tried so hard to oust them? Why do you think they fought so hard to stop me?"

My mouth opened and closed. Had I... had I been wrong this whole time? No. It wasn't possible. It couldn't be. "You hurt your subjects," I countered. "You imprisoned them and made them do all manner of evil to their charges."

His eyebrows pinched together. "They were my subjects, willingly serving their sovereign, helping me succeed. They didn't fight me... unlike some."

I hadn't talked with any of the beings we'd freed in the provinces my brothers and I had visited. I'd no idea if he was blowing smoke or telling the truth. But... had I been wrong? Was it even possible? I shook my head, he spoke lies. "You hurt Auden." The words tumbled out. "He's your subject, and you hurt him."

"Those that fought me, I corrected." His voice was as hard as stone. "I could not let him or any other citizen best me, their sovereign. I had to maintain respect. Surely this is not hard for you to understand." He thumped the side of his head with the heel of his hand. "What do you think would happen if others saw me as a pushover? Alissandra, I can't be seen as weak or chaos would reign."

I bit my lip. Had Father really been trying to care for his subjects all along? No... it couldn't be. Could it?

"You wounded Velma." I would never forgive him for that.

He exhaled. "I was attempting to steer my wayward children down a better path. Doesn't every elder want that?"

"Steer your wayward children?" My voice rose. "You hacked off her wings!" Delusional, he was delusional.

He drew a hand to his chest, anger lighting up his eyes. "I did not wish to. Her continued rebellion forced me to use extreme measures. I could not suffer to let her ruin her life, much less drag the rest of you with her."

My muscles quivered and my heart raced with the fury that filled me.

"Never once, before this, did I direct my actions toward Wake. I don't suppose you ever noticed that." His voice turned quiet, menacing as death.

"Not true. You tried to get Aunts to change Kovis's timeline." I drew a fist to my hip.

He held up a hand. "A notable exception. The *only* exception." He growled. "He'd come between us, a mere mortal, and I wasn't about to sit back and take it."

My mind whirred. Were the regents really as bad as he claimed? I hadn't had time to get to know them, our visits had been quick. Had he really been trying to… "What about the rebels? You controlled those humans."

"They certainly didn't fight me," he spat back. "I am not responsible for human desires. They hated the empire. I facilitated them achieving their objectives."

I closed my eyes and shook my head.

"Calm yourself, daughter." He huffed then motioned for me to sit.

I'd do no such thing. I drew the tip of my blade closer, letting him feel the sharp point.

"You think you know everything." Sarcasm filled his voice. "You've no idea what I hoped to do once I conquered Dream and Wake."

"I don't care. No good could ever have come of it."

"Don't be so sure." He raised an eyebrow. "Because I planned to retire. I've grown tired of ruling, but you've ruined all that."

I burst out laughing. "Right. Sure. Your actions are a loud announcement that you plan to do anything but."

He shook his head. "There you are wrong, daughter. I didn't feel right about retiring until those regents were ousted. Wake was at peace and there was no sign of things changing, so to remain in adherence with my own declaration that Dream territory can only change hands when Wake territory changes, I started this war. War isn't a crime. It's not right or wrong. It's a means to an end."

A means to an end. I snorted. "And lots of beings die!"

I couldn't have been wrong. I couldn't have. No matter how bad those regents might be, he was worse. "I won't listen to this nonsense. You planned to turn everyone in Wake into catatonic beings to do only your will."

"No, Alissandra. Never once did I say that, but you certainly have, on more than one occasion. That was never my intention."

I shook my head.

"That was the story you told yourself to justify hating me for the corrections I have enacted on you and your siblings. Being an elder is not an easy task."

I glared at him. No, he was lying. He had to be... but what if he wasn't?

"I'll admit, at times, I haven't been the easiest being to be around, but your rejection hurt all the same. Every father longs to be loved by his children."

"So if not you, who would rule?" I hissed.

"Newly appointed regents who respect and honor me. I'd put in place a system whereby provincial rule would change every so often so things couldn't devolve back to how they've become."

"So you'd just ride off into the sunset like Grandfather." Cynicism filled my voice.

"Well, I don't enjoy sleep so much. My first love has always been weaving dreams." He smiled. "I remember when I used to sprinkle opium from that old orange bag on a charge. I'd send them to sleep, then weave their dreams, but I never had the chance to linger and really get to know those humans. I had way too much work to do.

"Once your Grandfather and I designed the new system, there was no need for us to participate, and I've never had the opportunity of fostering a single human charge of my own, really getting to know who they are. I think I'd like that. I don't want the workload I had, but I'd like some responsibility with a human or two." He snorted. "But again, you in your supposed brilliance have made that impossible."

I clenched my teeth. He was either talking crazy… or he was telling the truth. How was I to know?

"So you expect me to believe that all this"—I swept my arm—"is you conquering Wake—so you stay in compliance with your damn edict—so you can retake the reciprocal Dream territory and depose the sitting regent, all so your citizens are freed from some perceived tyranny, before you retire." I scoffed.

"That about sums it up, yes," he snipped.

"And what of Wake? What happens to all the humans?"

He waved a dismissive hand. "Let them do what they wish. Let them live whatever life they choose for themselves."

I stomped a foot. "I don't buy it. I think those two defeats at the hands of your Dream regents still eat at you. I think you're desperate enough to do anything to defeat them, to put them in their place. I don't know if you really planned to retire or not. It doesn't matter. This was nothing but some perverted attempt for you to feel better about yourself."

He snarled. "I can understand how you might think that with that small mind of yours, but I've told you the truth, not that any of this matters anymore."

I ignored his insult, let it roll right off me. He couldn't hurt me anymore, not unless I let him.

He was wrong that none of it mattered. Whether he told the truth or not, he'd cost countless humans their lives, and justice needed to be served.

But my stomach kept twisting with uncertainty.

Chapter Forty-Five

What was I to do with Father? I scanned the square. A penalty had to be paid when a wrong was committed, and he'd certainly wronged a whole lot of people.

Uncle Thao had underscored the point when he'd told me that despite Dyeus understanding why Father and Grandfather had passed the sacred knowledge of how to weave sleep and dreams on to us, he'd still enacted judgment because a penalty had to be paid.

I shook my head. Father was mortal and the blood of innocents and brave warriors cried out for justice here in Wake. How did one consider his actions in light of the totality of the world, both Wake and Dream… *if* he was telling the truth?

I huffed. There'd be time for discussion and debate. This wasn't it.

"Let's go." I motioned with my blade for him to stand. With so many abominations filling the skies, I deemed it inadvisable to use Air magic to fly us.

He starred at me for several heartbeats but finally rose, clutching the cape about his midriff. "Where are you taking me?"

"To the prison."

"So, it's come to this." He curled his lips as he gave me a long look.

When I didn't answer, he drew his chin up and turned.

I took it slow as we navigated around and between corpses, my blade near his back. His tender, bare feet kept hitting sharp objects, and his body lurched, but he held his face neutral, pretending nothing phased him.

Flying abominations still swarmed the skies a ways off. I prayed they ignored us as we meandered through the destroyed artisan and food districts because my search for threads of magic, of any affinity, was proving futile. Most sorcerers were nearly, if not completely, spent. Warriors and sorcerers alike that we passed battled abominations with forged weapons.

The top of the council building was just coming into view through smoke that rose from several of the trees lining the riverbank. Nothing had been spared it seemed.

Roars and bellows rose as fire erupted from the spherical-shaped building. Citizens had to have taken shelter there. I strained to see. The outside of the building normally shifted between displays of the seven affinities, Fire being one. Was that what I saw or was this real? Was the building on fire? *Please oh please oh please, just be the usual show.* But it looked so real.

Several long heartbeats passed before I exhaled when Fire died and Ice replaced it. Safe. The council building was still safe.

But four, no five flying monsters thought differently, and my heart picked up pace as they dove. Roars rumbled through the trees. Barks, bawling, and howls from creeping abominations rose up to meet them. Crawling beasts had made it all this way it seemed.

Father turned around, eyebrows raised, questioning our course that drew us ever closer to the chaos.

I directed him right, up the steep mountain the palace sat atop, hurrying our steps. No way would we go closer.

I wrinkled my nose as we came upon and skirted around some mammoth avian abomination that had planted its beak into the hillside.

Up and up we climbed. Heart in my throat, I gazed back at the attack unfolding on the council building. More and more abominations circled, then dove as crystals—depicting Terra affinity—replaced the foliage of Wood magic.

One, then two, then three winged beasts flew low above us, and we dove, hitting the ground, covering our heads. They passed in a heartbeat, intent on the council building, but my hands trembled all the same.

"We need to hurry." My voice quaked. Those monsters were busy for now, but what would they turn to next? I just prayed the building held.

We passed soldiers carrying wounded on stretchers, all of us headed for the palace, they to seek healers, I to... imprison my father. At least for now.

I emerged again from the palace after turning Father over to the single guard. The man had given me a very long and very strange look when I'd pulled him aside and warned him that I didn't know what powers Father might wield and told him to be extra vigilant. I could only hope he took me seriously.

I scanned the skies. Abominations kept flying. They looked like pepper against the sun that had crested and made it halfway back to the horizon. I still had nearly all my strength. Where to reengage to biggest effect? But first things first, I had to know Kovis was safe.

Kovis?

Yes, love.

You busy? Am I interrupting anything?

He chuckled. I'm not busy, no. Just getting put back together.

I sucked in a breath.

Just a scratch.

Panic rose as I tunneled down our bond and looked through his eyes. I recognized the treatment room in which he lay atop a table—he was in the healers suites here, at the palace.

Kovis... My pitch rose as I gasped. *I'm coming.*

I hadn't withdrawn from our bond and disoriented as I was from being in two bodies at the same time, I still tried to hurry to him, alternating between watching where I was walking and keeping an eye on him through our bond.

Two healers were bent over him, one working on his leg, the other, on his arm. Hulda wiped one of their brows. Judging by the bloody cloths strewn about the floor, he'd bled considerably.

That's no scratch, I protested.

Ali, please don't worry. Jathan says I'll be fine. Speaking of which...

The chief healer, my master and Velma's beau, strode in with a worried expression. The fact that Jathan wore bloodied leathers piqued my curiosity. He looked like he'd been involved in the fighting, which made no sense. I furrowed my brow as the two healers pulled back, and Jathan inspected Kovis's wounds. At length, he nodded, and the pair went back to work.

Jathan said, "You're fortunate, my prince. Any deeper, and you'd be mending naturally instead of magically." He patted Kovis on the shoulder. "Let them finish, then give it a bit before you try rejoining the battle."

Kovis smiled. "I will. Thank you."

Kovis? You're hurt. You can't go back into battle.

Ali, I'll be fine. Really. By the way, Kennan's here, too.

He... he is? How bad?

He got off easy. What have you been up to?

Long story. I'll tell you about it when I reach you.

Pain shot from my stomach and I drew my hand up, ending the trip into Kovis's mind.

"Sorry. Sorry." Distracted as I was, I'd slammed into a stretcher—one of many lined up against the walls—bearing injured awaiting treatment. The place was in chaos.

A moan was all the wounded woman offered as Haylan came to an abrupt stop beside me. My best friend in Wake, and fellow apprentice, she looked a fright, her straight, dark-brown hair flying in her round face, the front of her green healer's robe, brown with drying blood.

"Ali." A smile lit her face, and she offered a one-armed hug. "The prince is in treatment room one," she said quickly.

"Want me to help—" I nodded toward the soldier.

"I've got her. You're the crown's champion and have more pressing matters to attend to, like stopping those things." She looked me up and down, no doubt checking for wounds. "The sooner those creatures are dead, the sooner the injured will stop coming." She sighed, then hugged me fully. "Ali, stay safe."

I squeezed her shoulder, then wound my way through the shrieks, groans, and chaos headed for Kovis. I needed to hurry. Too many had been injured, and I could prevent more, but I had to see Kovis.

Velma grabbed me from behind and swallowed me in a hug when I neared the room Haylan mentioned. "You're safe," she murmured in my ear, strengthening her hold.

At length, she released me and pulled back. "No one knew where you were. Prince Kovis said you'd returned, but no one had seen you." I'd barely noticed she wore leathers when Alfreda bounded to a stop beside us and squeezed my arm. She, too, was clad in leathers. Blood-spattered ones. They both looked exhausted.

"I was dealing with Father. Have you been fighting?"

Velma's eyes grew wide, and she nodded. Alfreda covered her mouth with a hand.

"We have, but what happened with Father?" Velma asked.

I looked them over for wounds. Bless the Ancient One, they looked uninjured, and I exhaled. "Father's mortal."

Alfreda gasped. Velma's head jerked back.

"It happened when he fell through the dream canopy." I quickly recounted a summarized version of the tale. They marveled throughout my telling.

But before they could fully grasp the news, a soldier halted abruptly and yelled above the din, "Those creatures have breached the council building! The infirmary there is under siege!"

Velma grabbed my arm as if steadying herself. "The empress is down there."

My stomach clenched, and I pivoted. I'd see Kovis later. He'd be fine. He'd be fine. I'd convince myself of it because Rasa and so many others might not.

Chapter Forty-Six

Kovis and Kennan caught up with me a heartbeat later, limping and sheathing their weapons, faces grim.

"Kovis, you're injured. You can't go down there." I grabbed his arm.

"Like Hades I can't." His voice quaked.

He stopped only long enough to embrace me in his strong arms and kiss the top of my head, then continued on. Kennan didn't stop despite Alfreda's pleading.

I hurried after. My sisters followed.

The sky was thick with abominations swooping and diving above the council building when we emerged from the palace. I heard Kovis's heart pounding through our bond—mine was no calmer—as we descended the path.

A third of the dome was gone, yet the building kept changing scenes between the various powers. Every time the color scheme changed, flying monsters roared and more dove.

The changing color is attracting them!

Damn! Kovis's only reply.

The entire structure would collapse before long at this rate with the constant pummeling of those beasts.

An abomination dove at us. Kovis and the others ducked while I blasted it with my Air, sending it somersaulting back. Threat gone, we continued on, Kovis and Kennan stumbling with the exertion.

"Steady them," I told my sisters as I lashed out, repelling another threat.

Alfreda grabbed Kennan around the waist, and Velma did the same for Kovis as we pressed on, the path never feeling so long. Snarls and roars increased in volume as we neared.

How I wished I had other powers at my disposal because all I accomplished was diverting a particular abomination for a time, but I wasn't killing anything. How would we ever defeat so many?

Another portion of the dome disappeared as a monster swooped down, severing more of the failing roof with a wing as it disappeared inside. A heartbeat later, the creature reappeared with a struggling, bandaged soldier in its talons, flying off, only to be replaced by another and another, claiming more of the roof and wounded in their wake.

I raced ahead of the others. I could staunch the flow.

I stopped not far from the chaos and raised my hands, then loosed my winds toward the gaping roof, blasting any beasts threatening from the sky. Soldiers who had been battling aerial enemies spotted me, then threw thankful looks before turning and engaging the creeping ones.

But these abominations kept coming and my magic would expire at some point. And then what? I'd no idea if they'd become mortal when they passed through the dream canopy, but we needed a way to kill the lot of them, immortal or not

I kept buffeting the monsters as Kovis and Kennan fought their way down the rest of the hillside, then disappeared into the council building. How to kill these things?

"Look out!" Alfreda yelled behind me.

She and Velma ducked, and I blasted the enemy, then pivoted back.

An abomination had taken advantage of my lapse and swooped down. It squawked and cawed when my winds found it before it could dive into the nearly roofless building. I hurled it into two of its brethren.

But how to kill them? It seemed impossible.

My mind whirled as I continued pelting the enemy.

Velma had accomplished the seemingly impossible when she first sent me here to Wake, leveraging her understanding of the creation story. Perhaps Uncle Thao's mention of the Ancient One and the beginning of time had sparked it, but the thought brought me up short. "Velma!"

She and Alfreda stepped beside me.

"Remember when you were first thinking about how to send me here? How you worked through the creation story and deduced that by envisioning what you wanted to happen—"

Velma nodded. "Yes, thinking the words in my mind, then willing it to be, I envisioned transforming you into a human and sending you to your charge—"

"And it worked. Can you do something like that, for this?" I waved my finger about.

Velma furrowed her brow. "You want me to envision getting rid of these things?" She glanced around.

"Yes."

Alfreda bit her lip.

My eldest sister scanned the skies, then bobbed her head. "I don't know, but let me try."

My winds thwarted another three flying abominations from breeching the council building as the decorative display of powers disappeared.

Got it! Kovis exclaimed.

Did you do that, kill the changing colors?

He exhaled heavily. *Yes, hopefully those monsters won't get so excited by it anymore and will go away. We're going to go find Rasa.* His voice caught.

Kovis, how bad is it?

It's not good...

My stomach twisted. *Try to stay safe.*

He chuckled. *Always.*

"Perhaps..." Velma said, pondering aloud. "It might be possible if..." She shuffled her feet. "It'll have to be done differently though. We want to destroy, not send them somewhere."

Alfreda glanced between Velma and me.

I blasted another three abominations that neared the council building, but their numbers were thinning. Killing the changing colors seemed to be working.

Velma mumbled, "If we..."

Alfreda locked her gaze on our eldest sibling.

"No... Wait... maybe if..." Velma worked through some sort of logic known only to her. I just wished she could hurry it up a bit. My Air magic had started to thin.

Velma tapped her mouth, until her eyes went wide. "No... couldn't be..."

My heart picked up pace listening to her. I redirected two more aerial monsters.

Velma tilted her head as she continued to think.

"Look out!" Alfreda squealed as a creeping abomination crawled up the hillside.

I blasted the giant shelled creature until it drew its extremities back into its shell, and I sent it rolling down the hill. I wiped my brow. She needed to hurry. My magic was nearly spent.

"Yes... yes, that just might work." Velma refocused, looking between Alfreda and me. "I'm... I'm not sure what to make of it, but I think we might indeed be able to kill all these creatures. *If* my thinking is correct." She shook her head. "Only the Ancient One could have accomplished this. I still can't believe it. I'm in awe."

Alfreda furrowed her brow. I blasted another monster away from the gaping building, then, panting, locked my gaze on Velma.

"Ali, have you ever thought about your powers?"

"How do you mean?"

"Simulus, Somnus, and Air. Simulus is the amalgam of the Canyon's powers. You embody every magical affinity of Wake."

"Okay." I drew it out.

"You could say Somnus embodies Dream with the power to put people to sleep. Ali, you're the perfect blend of both worlds. Put another way, Ali, your powers represent the two realms these abominations pillage."

I didn't say anything, neither did Alfreda, we just let her speak.

Velma drew a hand to her chest. "I have Noctus powers. What do blackness and shadow represent throughout ancient stories?"

"Evil or fear," Alfreda said.

"In this case, fear. Yes. Exactly. These creatures are fear, embodied. It ripples off them."

I nodded.

"Alfreda, you have Motus. You can move things. I hadn't considered it until now, but when you move something, what do you do?"

"I imagine whatever it is, sliding or hopping to another spot."

"Could you picture these abominations sliding or hopping into utter blackness, or oblivion?"

Alfreda cocked her head. "I... yes, yes, I think so..."

I shot a blast of magic at another beast, then inhaled deeply from the exertion.

Velma's face lit up. "So you see?"

My gaze bounced between my sisters, no different than Alfreda, not comprehending.

Velma waved her hands. "Ali, with your powers, you embody the essence of the world. My power is the essence of fear that fills the world. Alfreda, you can move these abominations out of this world."

"Into utter darkness," Alfreda said.

Velma bobbed her head. "If we combine our powers, I believe we can vanquish them. Only the Ancient One could have known we would face this situation, and if I'm right, it's no accident we ended up with the powers we did."

"There's one problem." I said. "I've got no Simulus power, every sorcerer nearby is drained dry."

"I don't think it matters. It's what your powers, together, represent that matters. Use what's left of your Air."

I mulled, trying to grasp the enormity of it. Was it really possible to obliterate all of these countless monsters this way? Had this really been divinely ordained?

My skin began to tingle at the immensity of the thought. "That's too perfect..." It was. I'd given exactly zero thought to why we'd ended up with the powers we had. They'd seemed random. Never once had I considered there might be a reason. They weren't of Wake realm, any of them, they were "other." If she was right... they had been divinely ordained. I drew a hand to my cheek.

Alfreda covered her mouth.

Our unique powers. Not from the Canyon. For a battle unlike any other before or to come.

"Let's try. But we need to make it quick." I motioned toward a horned, armor-plated abomination that was a good twenty men's height behind Velma, but crept closer on cloven hooves. "I can't blast it and have enough energy left to try this."

Alfreda's face turned ashen.

We quickly joined hands and Velma said, "Ali, you and I need to focus our powers into our joined hands, envisioning them mixing as they flow through the circle we form. Alfreda, you need to do the same while imagining moving these monsters into utter darkness, both flying and creeping. Will it with every fiber of your being."

"That won't be hard," she said quickly, eyes locked on the fanged monster that drew ever closer.

Velma swallowed. "I've no idea how this might affect us..."

"There's no other choice," I said, and shut my eyes.

"Begin," Velma said, voice tense.

I reached out and pushed the last shreds of my power into Alfreda's hand, then pushed it into Velma's, back to myself, into Alfreda, then Velma, then myself.

I sucked in air as my power sputtered, but I willed the thinning thread on, on, into Alfreda. Into Velma. Through me. I started panting. Into Alfreda. Nearly gone. Into Velma. Through... My heart raced. Through me. Into Alfreda. I pushed. Into Velma. I ground my teeth. Back through me. Harder, every hint of it. Into Alfreda. I gasped for air. Into... Velma. Blackness nibbled at my mind. Into me... More. More. All... Into Alfreda...

I collapsed. Cheek. Rough ground.

Blackness.

A wail.

I eased my eyes open.

Another torment-laced cry. Someone wept.

I lifted my head. Alfreda lay still, not far off.

Velma pushed herself up and found me.

Soul rending weeping.

I scanned the hillside and awe replaced my haze.

I turned my head this way and that, hardly comprehending the scene before me. Silence, deafening silence except for that weeping, blanketed the area, replacing the unending drone, the cacophony of bestial roars. They were gone.

Lightness filled my limbs. The choking fear, too.

I scanned the skies, hardly daring to believe.

Not one flying, not one creeping abomination remained. None. Not even their corpses. Gone.

Sobbing. Gut wrenching pain.

It returned my focus, and I sucked in a breath as realization pounced, then dug in its claws.

Another anguished cry followed in a heartbeat, through my bond with Kovis.

"Shit!" He'd gone to find Rasa.

Chapter Forty-Seven

I bounded up in the blink of an eye, and had to catch myself, a bit unsteady. "Rasa..." My voice choked.

Velma closed her eyes and bowed her head, understanding in a heartbeat. "Go..."

Kovis, I'm coming! My heart sped as I hurried down the path, past bloody corpses, past panting and dirt-stained soldiers whose limp hands barely held blades.

Several men and women alike stumbled about, as if in a daze. Some wore leathers, others soiled and tattered clothes. Their stench hit me even at this distance, as if they hadn't seen a bath in ages.

Rebels. The thought darted through my mind as if on a wind.

But another agonized cry focused me before I contemplated further.

I raced up what remained of the council building steps, around the fallen and debris, my heart in my throat. I strode through what had been the hallway circling the council chambers, sunlight illuminating my steps with the roof gone. Portions of the chamber walls still stood, but much had succumbed to calamity. I climbed over a huge chunk of what looked to be roof that blocked my path. How could anyone have survived?

Sobs.

I stepped on one of a pair of ornate doors that had served as the main entry and stopped dead in my tracks. A thick layer of white dust blanketed nearly everything, the living, the dead, animate, and inanimate alike. Several white-dust-covered healers quietly picked their way through the rubble, bending down and feeling for any signs of life with each bandaged person they found. A few soldiers helped, following murmured requests, pushing or lifting large chunks of debris so healers could reach victims.

The hum of quiet tears being shed rose from searchers who had found the one or ones they sought. Dust motes wafted about, adding to the surreal surroundings. With the sun lending its orange rays, it felt like a giant, gods' blessed tomb.

A shrill cry drew my attention to the right. A woman, who had been searching, dove to the floor, wailing.

Where was Kovis? He'd quieted in our bond. I looked close, eyes scouring everything, but didn't spot him.

Kovis? Where are you?

Behind the center roof section. His voice waivered.

The roof's crown, where the buttresses supporting the walls joined, had fallen down, into the middle of the space, rising a man's height.

I sucked in a breath, then wended my way, avoiding still hands, bandaged, unmoving arms, splinted legs in the path, trepidation building with each step.

I rounded the hunk of debris... and a whimper escaped me. Tears sprang up, and I drew a hand over my mouth. I shook my head not wanting to believe.

The building's crown pinned Rasa, just below the waist, arms spread wide, partly atop a female warrior whose shoulder had been bandaged—it seemed she had tried to shield the woman, but neither had lived to tell the tale.

No… no… it couldn't be. It couldn't. My breathing labored, as much from the suffocating dust as the sight before me.

Rasa's dark ash hair was sprayed asunder, streaked white with dust. She looked nearly like one of those haloed beings from Light realm portrayed in children's storybooks.

"No…," I squeaked, then dissolved into sobs, my tears smudging and muting the harshness of the scene. If only they really could.

Kovis eased back to his haunches and found me behind him. Tears stained his cheeks. Kennan's body shook where he hugged his sister's still form, mewling softly.

My hand fell, brushing my chest, and I felt the bump of the trinket. I inhaled. Could I… Was it possible? It controlled time.

Kovis furrowed his brow as he rose and joined me.

I grabbed the chain around my neck and drew the watch-like trinket up.

His eyes went wide. "Is it possible?" His voice rose, and he swiped the back of his hand over his face.

Soldiers and others were making their way in, helping with rescue or recovery efforts.

I closed my fingers around the piece. Kovis enfolded my fist between his cold hands, then looked to Rasa where Kennan still shuddered, clinging to her.

My eyes fluttered shut, and I clenched my jaw. I dared to rip her from Uncle Thao's clutches. He couldn't have her. I didn't care if he got pissed, didn't care if it divided the family because of this. I'd let him gorge himself on fear-laced blood. He owed me this.

"Continue." My voice was cold, hard, leaving no room for argument. I wasn't asking. I demanded.

Kovis squeezed my hand, willing, pleading for this to work.

I opened my eyes. She had to move. She had to.

We waited. Hoping.

"Resume." It's what I'd told Father to get him moving again. *Please aunts, please.*

This couldn't be her appointed end. She'd endured too much for it to be. She needed to live, to suck all the marrow from life.

I stared, frozen, begging life back into her with every fiber of my being. *Move. Please move. Breathe.*

I hadn't stopped time for her, maybe I needed to say something different. Think. Think. What had Aunt Ches said when she unfroze Mare-Rankin back in the Hall of Time when Father had had his mares abduct me? "You may rise."' Yes. That's what she'd said.

"You may rise." My voice waivered.

This couldn't be one of those random accidents that ended Rasa's suns before the fullness of those allotted by Ches that my aunts had mentioned. I shook my head. It couldn't.

"Rise, please." My volume increased.

Yet she ignored, still and unmoving.

"Damn you, Rasa. Move!" My voice squeaked. "Move!" I waved my hands.

Kovis drew his arms around me and pulled me tight against his chest, his chin pressing down on my head as if I might vanish if not fully anchored.

"No. No," I sobbed.

"Dyeus, no! No!" shouted Alfreda. Absorbed in my own grief and loss, her words barely registered as she arrived.

Still Kovis held me, his body quivering along with mine. I waved my arms, but they finally found their home around his waist, and I hugged him tight, clinging to him as much as he clung to me.

How could this be? Rasa needed to live. But she was bowing out. How could she do that? To me? To Kovis? To Kennan? To the empire? She couldn't. But I couldn't stop her.

My gut spasmed as a new wave of tears overwhelmed me. I'd just started to know the real Rasa, beneath all those protective layers. She'd scared me silly at the beginning with her gruff demeanor, but she'd started to warm, to thaw in a way, no different than Kovis. Far more than a friend, she was… my newest sister.

How long Kovis and I lingered, holding each other, I didn't know, but when I finally pulled back, Alfreda hugged Kennan near Rasa, and Velma stood holding herself an arm-length away. Fist to her mouth, she looked to be struggling to maintain composure.

Movement drew my attention. A soldier—a tattered, lapis-color caped warrior—knelt down, then bowed his head, joining a host of others doing the same amongst the bodies and debris, in a circle around us. Insorcelled warriors beside magical sorcerers, they all knelt in silence.

"Emperor Altairn."

I turned to see Nomarch Formig step forward, face grim, and I sucked in a breath.

She swept her soiled auburn cape back over a shoulder, then took a knee.

Chapter Forty-Eight

Excruciating emptiness.

The feeling of loss threatened to overwhelm me as Kovis and I sat, staring blankly into the cold fireplace, holding each other. We'd returned to the sanctuary of our rooms and cleaned up, going through the motions in a fog of despondency. Water could only wash away physical dirt; it couldn't begin to cleanse the dry ash my heart had become. It felt as if a breeze was slowly scattering the shards on the wind.

I'd experienced my share of grief with each of my dream charges as they passed on. While it was never, ever easy to lose one, I'd known from the start that each of their lives would be relatively short, even if they lived to the fullness of age. But Rasa… grief at losing her was altogether different. She was my sister. Yes, my sister… and this was an emptiness neither tears nor words could ease.

Through my malaise, worry about Kovis had begun to nibble at me. He'd endured so, so much pain throughout his life. He'd made progress after Aunt Dite had intervened, devouring each and every opportunity to experience joy in life. But this... would he ever find a light out of this darkness? Or would it prove to be the blow that made him give up on life, finally surrendering to despair?

Rasa had told me her story of overcoming her father's abuse, in the suns since we'd started growing closer. She'd never told a sole, not even her brothers. I'd considered it an incredible honor and a sacred trust that she'd opened up to me, alone.

The painful process had been what changed her perspective from that of a victim to one of overcoming—refusing to view life through that lens any longer—and embracing happiness. She'd had no choice. She'd known deep down she couldn't rule well if she saw herself as a victim. To Rasa, victimization was self-focused, ruling was anything but.

The circumstances were different, but just like Rasa, Kovis needed to rule, and he couldn't do it if despair won. I knew Rasa would approve of me sharing it, so I didn't ask if he wanted to hear her story, I just began.

"After your father killed himself"—Kovis stiffened—"Rasa didn't know how to process the fact that he was no longer a threat to her, along with the fact that the responsibility for an entire empire and its people would be thrust upon her within a moon. The thought staggered her. She felt ill prepared to handle such responsibility after all she'd endured."

Kovis squeezed my hand.

I squeezed his right back, remembering her telling. My voice cracked as I said, "She cried as she confided in me how utterly worthless she felt, her self-esteem at rock bottom." I cleared my throat, choking down tears that longed to flow. Her confession had hit me hard.

Kovis's breathing labored.

"She cringed, even as she told me, waving her hands as she spit out, 'Who was I? What was the meaning of my life? I needed answers.

I knew the gods had slated me to rule, but why? Why me? My shit was a mess. And I... I was supposed to rule an empire? Ha!'"

Kovis met my gaze. "Why are you bringing all this up?"

"Bear with me, and I think you'll see."

He nodded, his expression strained.

"Rasa sought answers, desperately. She told me your father had raved like a lunatic in his suicide note. It was so at odds with how she remembered him when she was little, and she couldn't stop wondering what had turned him into the evil monster he'd become. She needed closure; she needed to understand what could have possessed him to do the despicable things he had to her. She found his journals, all the way back to when he was a young man, and started reading them."

Kovis's face was pinched.

I coughed, recomposing myself. "Apparently he was *quite* passionate as he courted your mother. He wrote sonnets about her, obsessing about her beauty and marveling at her goodness and capacity to love even the least lovely." I rubbed his hand. "Kovis, he was head over heels in love with your mother. Rasa showed me that journal. He practically worshipped the ground she walked on. It's why he commissioned... this ring. 'A rare and precious ring of the utmost beauty, like her,' or so he wrote."

Kovis's eyes fell to the blue, teardrop sapphire that graced my finger.

"When your mother told him they were expecting their first child, he was over the moon. He saw Rasa as an heir to secure his line but much more, the physical embodiment of their love. He'd been an only child, and he spoke over and over and over again about his optimism for the future."

I took a deep breath, but my voice took on a squeak anyway. "I cried when Rasa told me, because I believe the same... with all my heart." I drew a hand to my heart. "Children are promises for the future." A tear trickled down my cheek. "No matter how awful he became, he wasn't always that way."

Kovis cleared his throat, and his voice cracked when he asked, "So what happened to him?"

"An annum after Rasa entered the world he was thrilled that they were again with child. He went on and on about it in his journal—'Babes from my beloved! *Two* of them, and boys! I love that woman with all my heart. She is my very soul. The gods have blessed us. I can feel it.'" I paused and let the words wash over Kovis, perhaps it could be part of his healing, too. "Kovis, I've read it myself."

He set his jaw and shook his head. "Until Kennan and I… killed her, birthing us."

I didn't respond. I prayed he knew he and his twin couldn't be blamed for the circumstance of their births, yet the lie was what he'd lived with since his earliest age. "Rasa said she didn't see him for some time after your births, but when she finally did, he wasn't the same. His cheerful, sunny disposition had fractured, replaced by anger, hatred even. She thought she was the cause because no one would let her see her mother. The nannies finally told her that her mother had passed on. They tried reassuring her that she was in no way to blame, but without your father's reassurances, she found it hard to.

"Your father was furious with the gods for taking your mother, and he despaired of life. He felt he had nothing to live for—he was existing, merely filling time. Bitterness and anger obsessed and fueled him.

"He threw himself into the war that he had started, to build a protective barrier of provinces around the magical Elementis, hoping he would die in the conflict. At least that's what he wrote. Yet the gods refused to take him. He railed at them for that, too."

"Selfish, self-centered bastard," Kovis murmured. "As if his children weren't something to live for. Ali, must you continue with this story?"

"Please, I'm nearly to my point."

He waved his hand for me to continue.

"When the war raged on and he still didn't die despite several close calls, he became brash and decided to test the gods... by abusing his children, or put another way, by abusing the gifts they'd given him. They'd taken the love of his life, and in his way, he told them to 'fuck off.' It was the only power he felt he had against them for what they'd done to him."

Kovis caught my gaze once more. "He said that?" His voice rose.

I nodded. "It's all in his journals."

"Bastard! All that with Rasa... *that's* why he did it?"

"And you and Kennan. I wouldn't have believed it if I hadn't seen it myself."

"That's just twisted!" He fisted his hand.

"It is."

"How did Rasa take that, when she figured it out?"

"She was shocked. She'd never viewed him as a victim since he was the aggressor. But *that's* what helped her put everything in perspective."

Kovis furrowed his brow.

"She realized he saw himself as a victim... just like her."

Kovis opened his mouth to object, but I waved him silent. "They weren't the same. At. All. But he saw himself as one nonetheless, a victim of the gods."

He shook his head.

"That discovery made her loathe feeling like a victim anymore. She feared she would become like your father, bitter, angry, and vengeful... self-centered. She realized victims are just victims. They couldn't change anything because they had nothing to do with what was done to them."

Kovis nodded.

"She understood that she couldn't rule, at least not well, if she continued to view everything from the perspective of a victim. She knew she needed to go beyond herself and take charge of her life if she was ever to be happy. And that's what she wanted, desperately, to be happy… after all that time. It wouldn't change what happened, but by overcoming, it would be her way of telling your father to 'fuck off' for all he'd done to her."

"Good for her!" Kovis exclaimed, swiping the wet that trickled down his cheeks.

I nodded, then sat in silence, letting Kovis ponder.

"You told me this… because you don't want me to become a victim… of the darkness," he finally said.

I met his beautiful blue eyes, their hazel centers as alluring as ever. "Yes, she told me she never forgave him, but she did her best to move on."

"She never said a word." Kovis exhaled.

"You've been doing so well at seizing life after what Dite told you." I picked up his hand. "Rasa's passing…" I sucked in a breath. My voice cracked as I said, "Call me selfish, but I can't stand to lose both of you."

Kovis let out a shaky breath, and I snuggled close.

We both needed to grieve, then heal. Would Kovis embrace Rasa's legacy? Would he see it as an opportunity for her to live on, in him? I honestly didn't know.

Chapter Forty-Nine

Tears streamed down Kovis's and my checks as the sound of stone sliding across stone rose in the warming, nearly spring air. I swiped at mine, Kovis let his fall.

He bent over Rasa's grave, to the right of where her elders lay, and placed a simple bouquet of white primrose below the altairn emblem that had been engraved in the smooth gray stone. Kennan stepped forward and did the same, then returned to Alfreda's side, and she clutched his hand once more.

Kovis cleared his throat. "I hereby declare that a moon of mourning shall begin."

Onlookers standing four and five deep outside the stone walls of the ancient cemetery murmured blessings to their fallen empress, wishing her speed and safety on her journey to Light realm.

Seven long and draining suns had passed and much of the carnage of battle had been cleaned up, the rank stench of burning flesh only now fading. Families of the fallen who could be identified had received back their dead, but so many soldiers had been mangled beyond recognition by those abominations, and only flames could pay tribute to their sacrifices.

The buildings and surroundings would take longer to restore and would serve as a reminder of the chaos that had been unleashed, for time to come. The Council building had been declared a total loss and would take the longest to restore between clearing the debris and completely rebuilding it.

I stepped forward and joined Kovis, processing back toward the cemetery's gate, Kennan and Alfreda following. Despite official protocol that frowned on displays of emotion, Kovis took my hand in his as we strode past nomarchs and ministers who had lingered after the battle, as well as surviving Council members, arrayed in a semicircle around the grave. Lord Beecham eyed Kennan up and down as we approached.

I barely stifled a growl.

Pay the villain no mind, Kovis said, squeezing my hand.

Beecham frowned and shook his head as I stared him down, catching my very clear message—if he did *anything* to prosecute Kennan after all he'd done to aid the battle, he would suffer my wrath. No matter the solemnity of the occasion, people like him only sought to care for their own political agendas. It was sad, really. He was a sad human being.

I refocused as we headed back down the steeply sloped path in silence, leaders and citizens following us.

Despite his grief, Kovis had been pressed into service almost immediately after Rasa's passing, along with Kennan, and I'd seen little of him, so I wasn't surprised when he informed me that he was needed elsewhere when we reached the palace. I hated "duty" for what it was doing to him, giving him no time to sort through his grief. I only prayed he'd heal in time.

Velma embraced me along with Alfreda when we reached the dining hall where a memorial reception for all citizens was being held. Jathan squeezed my shoulder, showing his support, and shook

Kennan's hand as the musicians began playing music befitting the solemn occasion.

After exchanging pleasantries, Kennan and Jathan went to retrieve sustenance for "the ladies." When they returned, Kennan handed me a plate brimming with what he said were traditional foods of remembrance and blessing. I took to picking at it, not at all hungry, as I watched Kennan interact with the others. He seemed calm and rational as he chatted, even smiling as he fondly recounted a story about he, Rasa, and Kovis. Hope grew in me that he might actually be healing from the trauma he'd endured at Father's hands.

My feet ached by the time everyone attending had shared their condolences with me and Kennan, who stood beside me. Velma, Jathan, and Alfreda had left us ages before so as not to intrude on well-wishers. I was just glad no one could see me trying to wiggle life back into my sore feet beneath my long skirts.

"Can we talk?" Kennan leaned over when only a few lingered in the hall. "In private?"

I raised an eyebrow.

While his disposition had been pleasant toward me throughout the proceedings, we hadn't talked since he and Alfreda had returned. It seemed things between them had changed, for the better by all indications, but Kennan's explosion at that family dinner eons before still lingered between us.

"Do I dare suggest my rooms?" I asked.

Kennan chuckled, clearly remembering that stolen kiss when we'd been alone in his. I'd never repeat that mistake.

He offered me his elbow, and we strode out of the nearly empty dining hall, heading for the stairs.

I threw off my shoes the heartbeat Allard opened the door for us, then motioned toward the sofa. Kennan took a seat and smiled as I threw my bare feet up on the short table before the cold fireplace, beside him.

Kennan sat up straight and cleared his throat. "Thank you for heading off Beecham."

I bobbed my head. "The bastard. He's a thorn in all of our sides." I lowered my voice. "Too bad one of those abominations didn't find him."

Kennan shook his head. "Even they weren't crazy enough to savor his bitter flesh."

I laughed, and pregnant silence fell between us once my smile faded. He'd initiated this conversation, so I clamped down on my fidgeting as I waited for him to say what was on his mind.

At length, he took a deep breath. "You need to know what happened while Alfreda and I were away." He recounted how my father had possessed him a second time and how Alfreda had finally figured out how to remove the seed he'd implanted in Kennan's mind.

My head was a whirl by the time he finished. It explained so much of his erratic behavior of late.

"I want to apologize for how I behaved during family dinner a while ago. I was... crazy." He shook his head.

I put a hand on his arm. "You were, but I doubt whether I would have behaved well either." He forced a smile. "I'm just glad Alfreda figured out how to stop my father's hold on you."

He blew out a long breath. "I wouldn't wish that on my worst enemy." His shoulders drooped, clearly still upset with himself.

When he hadn't said anything more in several heartbeats, I said, "So... it seems things have changed between you and my sister." It was my attempt to lighten the mood. I wanted to understand where they stood, from his perspective. Alfreda had already given me her version.

But instead of lifting the seriousness, Kennan grabbed my arm, then met my eyes. "Ali, I..." He exhaled loudly and paused for several heartbeats before continuing. "When that beast attacked Alfreda on the battlefield..." He closed his eyes, reliving the horror.

I waited patiently for his words to catch up with his mind.

"After she freed me, I still had many of my memories and I looked back, viewing events sanely instead of as a lunatic, and I saw what had really happened." He swallowed hard. "When she first came, I was cold to her. She'd given up immortality... immortality... to come to me." Silver welled up in the corners of his eyes and he looked down at his hands. "I'm not worthy."

"That's not for you to decide."

"I'm not. No matter what she says." He clenched his jaw. "After all she gave up, I treated her with coolness. Yet she stuck with me and supported me." He shook his head.

"Are you saying you love her?"

He sucked in a breath, but after a few heartbeats, a corner of his mouth edged up. "I am. I love that woman with all my heart. She's loyal and determined, funny and smart. It would be impossible not to be drawn to such a strong person. It's more than that though, so much more. I've never felt about another the way I do about Alfreda...." He snuck a glance my way.

Not even you. He didn't say the words, he didn't need to. Frankly, I was glad he hadn't. But he'd acknowledged our strained and at times painful history.

"I feel connected to her... in my very soul." He patted his chest.

The fact that he didn't refer to our past, told me he'd finally accepted that no apology, no matter how sincere, would ever atone for his actions. He wasn't a bad person, his judgment had just been flawed. And he'd compounded it by lying about that intake manual.

He sat back. "I wasn't planning to ask right now..." He sighed. "But Rasa's passing has made me more aware than ever that we don't know how long we have. I want to love, honor, and cherish Alfreda for however many suns we have." He gave me a long look. "As my friend and future sister, would you give us your blessing?"

I forced a chuckle. "Kovis bypassed my father's blessing, too."

Kennan snickered.

I smiled, but my thoughts continued to whirl. Could I look beyond our past and give him the blessing he sought? He'd acknowledged his mistakes at the risk of losing any remaining relationship with me; that was something.

I didn't fault him for making mistakes. I'd made some pretty big ones with Kovis and paid the price, but more importantly, I'd learned from them. Had Kennan? His silent acknowledgement of our strained and at times painful history told me he had, or he was at least on the journey of learning and I sensed he'd never repeat the mistakes he'd made with me.

So the big question was really, would he treat my sister well? They'd both been through Hades and back and deserved a happily ever after. Kennan was a good man at heart, fallible, but good. I knew down deep.

I placed my hand on his arm. "Kennan, you have my blessing."

His eyes grew soft. "Thank you. You don't know what that means to me… coming from you."

I bobbed my head. "Just make her happy. She deserves it."

"Definitely."

I hesitated to change the subject, but based upon our conversation, it seemed a good time to bring up something that I'd been pondering. "I won The Ninety-Eight if you recall."

Kennan furrowed his brow. "Actually, I don't, but—"

I laughed. "But you do know that I won."

He gave me a lazy smile. "I'd heard something to that effect, yes."

"Well, I hadn't figured out what I wanted to do with my winnings, until now."

He cocked his head.

"I want to start a network of shelters for women suffering abuse, throughout the empire."

Kennan locked eyes with me.

"I plan to name it in Rasa's honor. People will think I'm naming it because she recently passed. They won't know the depth of her story, but—"

"No one need know but us." He shook his head. "I can think of no more fitting a tribute."

"We all need new starts, Kennan, and this will be mine, pouring my energy into something significant and meaningful to me." Something that would continue to foster my own healing while helping women like me, or those worse off.

The look Kennan gave me told me my comment had hit its mark—I'd found a constructive way to work through our past, but he needed a new start, too. Alfreda would be a part, but not the whole.

Chapter Fifty

"He deserves to hang," Nomarch Formig said of Father, frowning.

Kovis and I, along with Nomarchs Formig and Kett stood on the balcony of our rooms taking in the repairs underway on so many of the homes and buildings of Veritas. We sipped our preferred beverages as the sun set, and I tugged on my cape, warding off the chill. The night would be cool, but the air had finally started to smell clean again, and I drank it in.

Nomarch Kett nodded, beside Formig. "We lost a good six-hundred warriors to those abominations."

I'd never forgotten my conversation with Kett over The Ninety-Eight champion's dinner. He'd passionately defended the competition that Rasa had wanted to end, believing it necessary to help sorcerers understand and even appreciate warrior culture. Kovis and I hadn't yet discussed the competition nor how he felt about it. It was just one more mantle he'd have to take up.

"He deserves a fair trial, like everyone," I replied, staring them down.

I hadn't yet heard back from the inquiry I'd sent my brothers to see if Father's claims were founded—that he'd behaved as he had to rein in the supposedly corrupt regents in the other provinces—and public dissent grew. I wasn't yet sure how to weigh his crimes in two different realms against the calamity he'd brought to Wake, nor was I sure whether it would matter to anyone but me, but no matter what Father had done, I needed to know his treatment would be just, not the result of public outrage.

"Your wounded are healed enough to travel?" Kovis asked, changing the subject.

"Many. They'll go in two groups. The first will leave on the morrow, the others will travel when all are able," Formig said. "I'll remain until after your coronation."

"As will I," Kett added.

"Thank you. And thank you again for coming," Kovis said. "When that horn sounded and I saw you all arrayed across the mountaintop…" He shook his head. "I'd questioned whether—"

Nomarch Formig straightened, standing taller.

Kett dipped his head. "This is our empire, and as warriors, we will defend it."

"How did you know to come?" I asked. "The empress…," I sighed, "she'd told everyone what to expect and encouraged you to defend yourselves as best you could at home."

Kett drew his chest up, seemingly proud. "Madame Catherine."

Kovis furrowed his brow. I drew a hand to my heart.

"Her origins may have begun in Vaduz," Formig said, "but she's a warrior as well as a citizen, and when she overheard talk of preparations to combat those abominations that were headed your way—no thanks to the nervous chatter of councilmember's wives in her shop"—she frowned, no doubt at the Council's loose lips—"she sent word to every warrior province asking us to send help."

Kett chimed in. "We'd heard about her address to the Council. I must say, it was a noble gesture to elevate her identity, as a warrior."

Kovis bobbed his head. "So when we received her missive we took the threat seriously and contacted our fellow nomarchs. We dispatched our fastest troops as a matter of course after that, hoping we'd make it in time."

"Well, your timing was impeccable," Kovis smiled. "And your influence seems to have brought those warrior provinces who don't yet see eye-to-eye with the monarchy into line. They've at least been cooperative since the battle."

"We're hoping to see the monarchy embrace warriors and our culture, more," Kett said.

Formig nodded.

Nothing subtle there. The nomarchs hadn't come out of some goodness in their hearts. They'd seen the situation as an opportunity to advance their cause, and now they had "expectations." Nothing ever came free.

Kovis smiled as he patted Kett on the shoulder. "I believe you will appreciate the role I envision warriors holding during my reign." He squeezed the man's shoulder. Even though he hadn't mentioned anything to me, it seemed he'd already done much thinking about the relationship between sorcerers and warriors that needed mending.

"We look forward to hearing more," Formig agreed.

A knock came on the ornate glass of the balcony door, and Bryce bowed, then stepped forward. "This just arrived for you, princess. The message accompanying it said it was to be delivered with great urgency." Our guard handed me an envelope, then turned and left.

Kovis looked at the envelope, then up at me as I flipped the missive over. I knew in a heartbeat who'd sent it by the wax seal it bore, my brother Rankin, and my stomach twisted.

"If you'll excuse me," I said, receiving nods from the nomarchs as I stepped inside, closing the door behind me.

I read the note quickly.

Ali,

I was surprised, to put it mildly, by what you
wrote in your note, but on the off chance Father
was telling the truth we immediately dispatched
inquisitors under cover to all seven of the provinces
he did not reclaim in his campaigns. This should
come as no surprise, but we are finding that what
Father told you about those regents being corrupt
and living off the backs of their citizens, is
completely unfounded and no doubt him
attempting to manipulate you to his side.

I drew a hand over my mouth. He'd been so convincing. And to think I'd nearly fallen for it, yet again. How could I be so gullible? Sunshine and rainbows... would I ever learn?

I emphasize that this is preliminary information.
We have embarked upon more in-depth
investigations just to make certain, but that's what
we've discovered thus far. I know time is not on
your side, but I wanted to at least let you know
where things stand. I will update you as things
unfold.

Your loving brother,
Rankin

What does the letter say? Kovis asked.

I took a deep breath. *It seems my father lied about those regents.*

No surprise, Kovis replied.

I shook my head as an empty feeling filled the pit of my stomach. I'd nearly worshiped the ground Father walked on until recently. I thought I'd put it all behind me. Perhaps my head had, but apparently not my heart. How could it still hope? I knew the signs, this was definitely the despondent feeling of crushed dreams.

I rejoined Kovis and our guests after a while and forced myself to engage, even laugh at points, despite my mind being elsewhere.

The cloud that Rankin's letter had stirred up had not dissipated by the following morning. Between that and my grief over losing Rasa, I needed a break. Kovis as well as Kennan did too from what I'd seen. Understandably, grief continued to plague both of them. Thankfully, time wasn't the only remedy, at least I hoped not because I wanted to show them something that might speed healing for all of us.

I'd told my sister where I wanted to take her beau and Kovis, and she'd agreed that the three of us needed to share it together, without her. So Kennan kissed Alfreda soundly on the lips after breakfast in our rooms, making her blush, as she excused herself.

Kovis squeezed my hand and grinned, no doubt enjoying seeing his brother in love, as well as healing at last.

Clad in our leathers, we and our guards headed to the stables. I was sad to see that they had significantly fewer residents after the battle. Nothing and no one had been spared by Father's minions.

I shook off my melancholy, and at length, atop our mounts, Fiona lead the way out of the stables. I took the path to the right at the fork, up the steep mountain toward the cemetery, then glanced back. Kovis's shoulders drooped. Kennan's expression was slack, his brown eyes dull.

Kovis cocked his head when I didn't stop at the overlook to survey Veritas like we usually did, but sounds of a city getting to the tasks of the sun, still rose to meet us—pounding, sawing, shouting as construction continued, as well the general hustle and bustle of citizens going about life, in new and different ways. People would never be the same either.

We approached, then passed the ornate but rusted gate to the royal burial grounds and followed the rock wall that spanned the space until it ended.

"Where are we going?" Kovis asked, his tone rising.

I grinned, looking back over my shoulder. "I have something very special to show you." My heart picked up speed as we neared our destination.

Kennan leaned forward in his saddle when I stopped Fiona seemingly in the middle of nowhere. Kovis glanced at his twin, confused as well.

"Can you help me down, Kovis?" Turning to our guards, I called out, "Please give us privacy. We won't be far."

We dropped the reins and let our mounts graze on the newly emerging grass. They wouldn't wander off.

It was hard to believe it had been little more than three moons since Rasa had shown me her handiwork. My heart panged. I hoped nothing had happened to all of it with the warriors coming this way during battle. Worry aside, I hoped seeing it would be a comfort to these two, as well as myself.

Kovis took my hand in his, and Kennan strode beside him. I exhaled as I scanned the area. A host of boot prints marred the once muddy ground, but Rasa's creations appeared untouched.

Knee-deep snow had covered everything the last time I'd been here; the fluffy white had smoothed all the rough edges of the trees, shrubs and other vegetation that surrounded us. Everything looked different now, not quite as magical, with the arrival of Spring—green shoots were just emerging from their winter sleep below ground, and trees and bushes were pregnant with buds that would burst any sun, but I could see what had drawn Rasa to pursue her artistry here. I drew in a deep breath, savoring the clean air. It seemed a world apart from the city.

"So, what do you think?" I said, stopping. I couldn't stifle a chuckle.

Kennan glanced about, lips slightly parted, not saying a word.

I bit my lip. How I hoped they loved it like I did. "Rasa showed me this." I met Kovis's eyes. "She told me she'd never shown anyone else, not even you two."

I felt for a trace of Wood magic, but nothing immediately showed itself. I rubbed an eyebrow as I continued searching. Kovis and Kennan gave me curious looks.

I fingered my jaw after some time passed, and I still hadn't located what I sought. "I need Wood magic to make this work."

Kennan blinked. Kovis shifted.

There. I finally found Wood, all the way in the city, and I closed my eyes. I raised my hands, palms out, and directed the pair's gazes with a nod, just as Rasa had with me.

Not far away, the green buds on the branches of a bush about my height, erupted, growing to become stems with leaves.

Kovis's lips parted and Kennan brought a hand up to the back of his neck as they watched. The stems kept growing and soon tangled with the other fast-growing stalks. The form grew taller and... the beginning of two front legs appeared.

"Is it a horse?" Awe filled Kovis's words.

I shook my head. Kennan furrowed his brow.

I infused more magic and made a fin sprout from the creature's back, exactly as Rasa had.

"It's a hippocampus!" Kennan clapped, as I shaped a tail.

"That's amazing," Kovis murmured.

The corner of my mouth turned up as I put the finishing touches on the creature—a mane, ears, and flippers for its feet. "It is amazing, isn't it? Rasa was very creative."

Kovis shook his head. "I had no idea."

"She told me this was her outlet." I didn't need to say, what from. "She built a collection of figures over the annums."

Kennan's mouth dropped open. "There's more?"

"Yes! Absolutely!" I drew my hands up and brought to life from memory, a sheep, a ram with enormous horns, a sea serpent with its body arching out of the ground six separate times, giant frogs around a pond, a horse-drawn carriage, and even an entire maze.

Kovis and Kennan stood speechless as I restored more and more of Rasa's creations. With each one I breathed life into, I felt as though hope and life were being restored to me, too. Judging by the pair's grinning, hooting, and hollering, it seemed they felt similarly.

Once I finished, not that I had any idea if I'd rejuvenated everything Rasa had created, I said, "When she showed me all this, she thrilled with each exclamation I made. Joy replaced worry, lightness replaced heaviness, and she seemed younger than I ever remember."

Kovis drew his lips together. Silver welled up in the corner of Kennan's eyes.

"These have been here all this time." Kennan's voice wavered.

I nodded. "They've stayed hidden because when she cut off her Wood magic, they blended back into the foliage of the hilltop. She trained them to reform this way."

Kovis swiped at a stray tear.

"Like your mother's garden, I wanted you to have this to remember Rasa by, hopefully it will help you heal. To me, it's evidence that people can grow beyond their circumstances. It's also why I'm using the altairn, clutching a vine in its talons, as the symbol of my new women's centers.

Kovis took my hand in his, entwining our fingers. "It's perfect."

Chapter Fifty-One

Glowing torches surrounded the green-and-white-striped blanket Kovis and I lay stretched out on, the three-quarter moon gifting its ambience to the sandy, sloping bank of the large pond that stretched out before us. Two birds called to one another as they swooped low over us, then turned back toward the quaint little island in the middle that was barely visible in the darkening sky.

"It's been a busy sennight. How are you doing?" We'd been going, going, going for the last five suns, and even though we'd been together plenty, it felt like Kovis and I hadn't connected. I was glad for this snippet of time to just unwind and reconnect.

"Yes, it has been busy. Good, but busy. I suppose it's a mercy because it's distracted me." Kovis stared unwavering at the stars peeking out above, arms behind his head.

I didn't disagree. We'd both been working through our grief over the last moon, but there was nothing that was going to make Rasa's passing hurt less. In some respects, I didn't want to get past the ache. I kept hearing her voice in greeting or the sound of her shoes on the marble floors; she had a unique step about her, and my mind kept filling it in, in familiar situations—I didn't want that to fade.

I smiled as I ran a finger over the teardrop sapphire surrounded by diamonds, and the thin silver ring that now cozied up to it on my finger. "I'm glad we said our vows before my aunts."

Going back to Dream, thanks to Velma, had been... wonderful, happy, memorable... yes, all that, but more. It had been... meaningful. A warm feeling filled my heart as I pondered the love I had for my family.

Too bad Mother hadn't attended. The thought struck a sour note and I stopped myself. No sense in hoping for what would never happen. I'd learned the hard way with Father.

Kovis rolled over and rose up on his elbow. "I agree. To say my vows to you, before them, was—" He shook his head. "—very special. Goddesses who've been around since before time began..."

"Yes, and to receive their blessing..." I drew a hand to my heart.

A smile eclipsed Kovis's face, and he chuckled. "I nearly died when they offered to *show me* how I might pleasure you, eternally."

I shook my head. "That was quite embarrassing. Aunt Ta's voice carried a bit."

He snorted. "I'm not convinced but what she meant to have everyone overhear her."

"But it's nothing compared with you and Aunt Dite..."

Kovis chuckled. "She was a bit... amorous." He wagged his eyebrows.

"The two of you just fed off each other."

"She's rather amusing. She really gets into my overlarge wings."

"I've never seen Mema so flustered. My siblings were cracking up, so was Grandfather for that matter. Ta even got a rise out of Uncle Thao. I've never seen him amused, much less enjoying everyone's company."

"Perhaps it's a new beginning."

"Speaking of new beginnings, Aunt Nona told me all those spheres disappeared along with that huge one that occupied their rooms."

"Did it?"

"Yes, we talked and near as we can figure they disappeared right around the time Velma, Alfreda, and I sent those abominations into oblivion."

"That's great, well done." Kovis lay back and stargazed for several heartbeats until he asked, "I know how... confusing it felt when my father died. How is your family doing?"

"I remember parts of that time for you, weaving your dreams." Kovis turned his head and our eyes met. "I'd say there's equal parts relief and grief."

Kovis gave me a knowing nod.

"Mema understands Father met a just end. But he was her son and that will always grieve her, same for Grandfather. My siblings, I'd say they are relieved. He can't hurt anyone ever again." I let my words linger... so many atrocities. "But the significance of a god being made mortal stirs fear in them. I understand. Before coming to Wake, I'd never once contemplated mortality."

Kovis bobbed his head. "Are you afraid to die?"

"I'm reconciled to it. Coming meant gaining you." We both smiled. "The trick is wringing every measure of life out of each and every sun." I sighed contentedly. "I don't regret giving up immortality. I've lived more in the last annum than a hundred annums, in Dream."

"That's high praise for we mortals."

"It's true."

Melodic sounds rose into the night as the lake's water ebbed and flowed against the shore in gentle waves. Insects chirruped and frogs croaked. A coypu scurried across the loose stone of the path somewhere close by.

"Are you ready for the morrow?" I asked, breaking our silence.

"For which part, being crowned emperor or celebrating our vows before our citizens?"

"Either. Both."

"The marriage part..." Kovis smiled as he looked my way. "I cannot wait to declare my love and commitment to you before our people. I plan to kiss you openly, thoroughly, and brazenly."

I chortled. "What kind of example will the emperor be setting?"

"The example of a man crazy in love, unashamedly showing his affection to everyone willing to watch." He brought his chin down sharply. "They'll be jealous."

I giggled. "Scandalous. It'll rival the wedding dresses Madame Catherine initially proposed for both Velma and me."

Kovis's eyes danced. "Do tell."

"You should have seen them. Open backs all the way to our waists."

"And what's wrong with that? She knows how to work her magic in ways I'll appreciate."

I cuffed his shoulder. "I wouldn't mind if only you and I were to attend."

Kovis beamed.

"Velma didn't 'appreciate' it either."

"So what did you finally agree on?"

"I'm not saying. You'll have to wait and see in the morning." I wagged my brows.

"When did you say Jathan and Velma are marrying?"

"In a fortnight."

"Oh that's right, on the vernal equinox because it's the same sun as the festival of sandlings in Dream."

I nodded. "It's my favorite celebration because it commemorates new life, which is the promise of the future, for both realms. I hadn't realized Velma enjoyed it as much as I, but it seems she did."

Kovis ran a finger along my jaw. "New life is definitely that," he murmured.

"So what about the emperor part? How are you feeling about that?"

"I'm looking forward to naming Kennan crown prince."

I drew my lips into a line. He hadn't answered my question. "I'm looking forward to seeing that, too. It's good to see him more like himself again. He's grown so much…"

"Your sister's helped as much as anything. He's head over heels in love with her."

"I'm glad to see them both healing. I predict it won't be long until we see them wed as well."

Kovis smiled. "They're good for each other."

"But what about ruling? How are you feeling about that?"

His expression turned contemplative. "... I've seen how my father as well as Rasa ruled. While there was good in both, I think the bad outweighed it many times. I guess you could say I've seen what not to do, but I've not seen what *to* do." He ran a hand through his hair. "I want peace. I want to build a lasting empire where we all work together to strengthen each other, no matter if a citizen has magic running in their veins or not."

"I agree. I want that, too. I think most do, and I have every confidence you will make a very good emperor. You're wise and kind and fair. I know you'll establish rituals and laws that will unify and strengthen this empire. And I'll be right beside you, supporting you all the way."

Kovis shook his head. "No, you won't."

I furrowed my brow. "What do you mean?"

He smiled as he sat up. "I would like you to share power with me, equally."

"I don't understand." I rose to sitting.

"You've been a princess your entire life. You're not unfamiliar with the crown. You didn't rule, but you've been around the conversations. You understand the life of a monarch as well as a region's citizens. I don't want you to become some pretty consort on my arm. I'm asking you to help me rule, to help me figure this out, together."

My mouth fell open. Never had I anticipated what he proposed.

"We have different strengths and weaknesses," Kovis went on. "You're more compassionate than me and have a heart for our peoples' worries. Not to mention, you're the most powerful sorceress this empire has ever known." He chuckled. "I've got a head for strategy and trying new things. Our people need both of us."

"The most powerful sorcerer the empire has ever known wants my help." I pointed at my chest, smiling.

"If you're willing, I'd like you to be sworn in as empress along with me."

I leaned back and blew out a breath. "How long have you been thinking about this?"

"Ever since the weight of the crown came to rest on my head. The burden is too great for one person to bear alone so many times. It nearly crushed Rasa at points."

I drew a hand to my jaw. "I've never heard of such a thing, an emperor *and* empress?"

Kovis chuckled. "As I said, I have a head for trying new things."

"That you do, and I love you for it." I cupped his cheek with a hand. "You'll surprise everyone. Imagine the Council."

We both snickered at the thought.

Kovis took my hands in his, looked into my eyes, and with earnestness in his voice, asked, "So Ali, would you do me, as well as our people, the honor of being their empress, ruling together to make the Altairn empire great?"

I drew in a long breath and let it out slowly. "It's a tremendous weight a ruler must bear. I count it a privilege that you would ask me to share it with you. While I've never once imagined becoming an empress, honestly, the notion excites me. Kovis, the good we might do, I would be honored to become empress."

Kovis brought my hands to his lips and kissed my knuckles, as if sealing my pledge. "Thank you, my love." He exhaled. "I'm relieved. I want to do right by our people, and now, I think we can."

A grin lit up my face. "Beecham will dirty his pants knowing he has two of us to deal with," I added. "And as empress, I'll get to order you around."

Kovis guffawed, then rose and met my lips with his. "I'll love every heartbeat of it."

He laid me back on our blanket, and his hands made quick work of my dress. My hands did the same to his tunic and pants, and we basked in the fullness of each other, celebrating a new life, a new beginning that I'd never dreamed of.

Download the Epilogue and see how Ali, Kovis and their siblings' futures go at
https://lrwlee.com/get-the-twinkle-twinkle-epilogue

What's next? God of Secrets series

Everyone has secrets, so why do The Powerful live above the law? Four words, The Empire of Secrets. Where confidences can be managed... for a price.

God of Secrets is a Greek mythical retelling about Harpocrates, the god of secrets.

Sign up to the mailing list at https://lrwlee.com/never-miss-out/ so you know when the first book is coming out.

Meet Harpoc and Pellucid Rose!

You can make a huge difference by Leaving a Review

Did you, your sandman, or sand maiden enjoy this book? Share your thoughts in a quick review on Amazon. It can be as short as a sentence! Make a difference.

———————

FaceBook Fan Group

Did you have an emotional roller-coaster ride reading this book? Do you need others to talk to about it?

Join The Sand Maiden FaceBook group at

https://www.facebook.com/groups/LRWLeeStreetTeam

All the feels and fanning you can handle!

Other Books by L. R. W. Lee

Be sure to check out L. R. W. Lee's award-winning, seven book, coming-of-age, epic fantasy series

Andy Smithson

Download the first ebook free from Amazon now at smarturl.it/BoDF

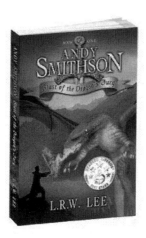

Video games can't train you to fight dragons!

Andy Smithson just found out how much the zap of a wizard's curse can sting. But after an epically bad day, he finds wizards are the least of his problems.

An otherworldly force draws him to a medieval world where fire-breathing dragons, deranged pixies, and vengeful spirits are the way of things. Trading his controller for a sword of legend, Andy embarks upon an epic quest to break a centuries-old curse oppressing the land. It isn't chance that plunges him into the adventure though, for he soon discovers ancestors his parents have kept hidden from him are behind the curse.

Blast of the Dragon's Fury is a coming-of-age, epic fantasy adventure featuring fast-paced action, sword fights, laugh-out-loud humor, with a few life lessons thrown in.

Get it now at smarturl.it/BoDF

_____

Connect with L. R. W. Lee

BookBub has a New Release Alert. Not only can you check out my latest deals, but you can also get an email when I release my next book, by following me here:
https://www.bookbub.com/profile/l-r-w-lee

http://www.LRWLee.com
https://www.facebook.com/lrwlee
https://www.instagram.com/lrwlee/
https://www.pinterest.com/lindarwlee/
https://www.twitter.com/lrwlee
https://www.goodreads.com/author/show/7047233.L_R_W_Lee

———————

Acknowledgements

This is always my most favorite section of any book because writing a book is a team sport. LOL. I mean that. If not for the input of the following folks, this book would not be what it is.

Top on the list of people I want to thank (someone who shall remain a nameless mystery, but you know who you are) is a critique partner and an aspiring author who read the roughest drafts of each and every chapter of *Twinkle, Twinkle* and gave constructive feedback. She began helping me back with *Good Night,* and her insights with this book have been no less valuable. Getting immediate feedback on a chapter by chapter basis has helped me calibrate the ebb and flow of each part and has produced a better result that I believe readers will find satisfying. Thank you for all your time reading as well as reacting to, at times, my outlandish thoughts and writing. LOL. I appreciate you and cannot thank you enough for how you've contributed to me. #IAmBlessed

I also want to thank my beta readers: Rachael Rousseau and Debbie Turk. Thanks to your comments and feedback, you helped make this book even better, and for that I am grateful, because you make every reader's experience all that much better. <3 So much love.

The other group of very special ladies that I want to thank is my merry mayhem makers (aka Dream Realm Street Team moderators): Courtney Belaire Griffith, Georgina Gallacher, Kiersten Burke, Samantha Zeman, Cabiria Aquarius, and our newest additions Brittany Gingrich and Alexandra Wilkerson. You all have made our fan group, Citizens of Wake, so much fun. Thank you for your dedication to making it an encouraging place where bookworms can come and be encouraged, and not with just books, but with life in general. You all make it a very special place to hang out, and I thank you.

Beyond the street team though, you all also make our moderator group fun. You constantly crack me up with your comments about one thing or another. I feel honored to be able to be a part of your lives—celebrating two engagements as well as two home purchases and the ensuing reno projects (lol), thrilling as one of you announced you're expecting twins, but also sharing with another of you the stress of looking for work, and another the excitement, yet angst of starting university. And for those of you who've been privileged to live a less challenging life at the moment, thank you for your stability and commitment to sharing your life with us—we can't all be crazy at the same time and you help keep us sane ☺

As a personal note, I want to thank all of you as well for your support as my hubby went through cancer diagnosis and treatment during the first five months of the year. It was a scary time, but you were there with me the whole way. <3

Made in the USA
Lexington, KY
17 November 2019

57167828R00205